INVERCLYDE LIBRARIES

MSS

INVERCLYDE LIBRARIES

This book is to be returned on or before
the last date above. It may be borrowed for
a further period if not in demand.

For enquiries and renewals Tel: (01475) 712323

D0268033

Patricia Ferguson trained in nursing and midwifery. She lives in Bristol.

THE MIDWIFE'S DAUGHTER

Violet Dimond, the Holy Terror, has delivered many of Silkhampton's children — and often *their* children — in her capacity as handywoman. But Violet's calling is dying out, as with medicine's advances, the good old ways are no longer good enough. Grace, Violet's adopted daughter, is a symbol of change herself. In the place where she has grown up and everyone knows her, she is accepted, though most of the locals never before saw a girl with skin *that* colour. For Violet and Grace the coming war will bring more upheaval into their lives: can they endure it, or will they, like so many, be swept aside by history's tide?

PATRICIA FERGUSON

THE MIDWIFE'S DAUGHTER

Complete and Unabridged

CHARNWOOD
Leicester

First published in Great Britain in 2012 by
Penguin Books Ltd.
London

First Charnwood Edition
published 2013
by arrangement with
Penguin Books Ltd.
London

A catalogue record for this book is available
from the British Library.

ISBN 978–1–4448–1624–2

Published by
F. A. Thorpe (Publishing)
Anstey, Leicestershire

Set by Words & Graphics Ltd.
Anstey, Leicestershire
Printed and bound in Great Britain by
T. J. International Ltd., Padstow, Cornwall

For Richard, Tom and Roly

The Meeting

Joe Gilder came from Yorkshire, where he had grown up just about half-starved until he was nearly fourteen, when his mother had remarried. Presently the new husband had taken Joe to one side — lifted him bodily, in fact, to one side of a long dark glass-strewn alleyway — and given him to understand that he, Joe, would without any doubt be best off making himself scarce. The husband was scrawny, but Joe was scrawnier, and so he had taken the hint.

A great deal of water had flowed under bridges since then. A great deal of blood had flowed too, some of it Joe's, at the time when he had been Corporal Gilder, and shot at by German lads, though since those days no one had ever heard him decry any nation but the French. Mr Gilder's hatred of France and French people was one of the strongest things about him. Frenchmen, when he was Corporal Gilder, had approached him in broad daylight and tried to sell him their sisters; when he was dazed with thirst one summer near the Front after days of marching in the blistering heat, French people, for whom he had been fighting all these years, and for whom his friends had died, had refused him a drink of water, from a village well, until he had paid for it. Grousing about the French seemed to keep Mr Gilder limber, and free his mind for other lighter things.

1

He told only one further story about the War.

'I were sent to get the rum ration. A nip for every man, in a tin bottle. Halfway back and a shell bursts right by me, blows me to kingdom come. I'm there in the bottom of this hole, and I know I'm hit. I'm dying. That's what I thought. And God help me I reckon: if I'm going to go, I'm going to go pissed: rum for twenty and I'm knocking it back like water, drunk as a lord I were all night till they come for me — saved me life, that rum!'

A jovial story, told to please. Every time he told it, Mr Gilder felt a faint lessening of that terrible infinity of time when he had lain in agonized confusion in the mud, waiting to stop seeing. Every second of the eleven hours and nearly forty minutes had gone by, one by one, while the chill earth gritted wet beneath his fingers, and his eyes had kept on opening, all by themselves.

Though the lessening never seemed to last very long. Every now and then, going downstairs to make his wife a cup of tea in the morning, or unlocking the back door to look out over his sunny garden, Joe would suddenly know that despite what felt like the pleasant reality of the scenes before him, that terrible night, dead and cold as ice, was still somehow *going on* somewhere, flowing slowly, like a glacier of darkness. Certainly it showed its continuing existence by way of occasional nightmares. And all he could do by way of reply was jeer at it, entice others coarsely to laugh at it with him; a puny enough response, he knew, but better than none at all.

On his lapel Mr Gilder even now was careful to wear the little badge that proclaimed him a wounded soldier. The bursting shell had untidily scooped away most of his left buttock.

'Leg wound,' said the doctor in the field hospital, and Joe had thought him a prissy old fool — a medic who couldn't say arse, for Pete's sake! and had laughed about him with those of the other men still capable of laughter. It had not occurred to him for several weeks, until the wound was well on the way to healing, that a buttock is merely where a leg leaves off. That without a buttockfull of strong elastic muscle, a leg is a poor weak prop-like article, hardly capable of forward movement, barely able to take any weight at all.

'I'm afraid it's going to be more like having a false leg than a real one,' said a different doctor, in the convalescent hospital this time. This was a big grand house Joe was at first barely aware of, with lengths of stone corridor and shining acres of parquet flooring. After a week or so he was moved to a bed beside one of several great tall windows, so that through it he could see a terrace with stone pineapples on either side of it, and one or two blokes in wheelchairs being trundled about between flower beds; but when he raised himself up on his elbows, which still in those days involved much tremulous effort, and peered right out beyond the flowers and the distant lawn, further out, further still, he saw a long unbroken haze of darker blue, where far away the sea was meeting the sky.

At first he had been afraid to look again. He

knew that beyond that apparently wide stretch of water lay the lads still fighting in the endless war. If he strained his ears he would hear them; gentlefolk hereabouts, it was said, were much put out at luncheon by the distant thud of artillery.

'Quiet today,' he had remarked to a passing nurse, that first day beside the window. 'Can't hear nowt.'

'What? What d'you mean?'

'Can't hear the guns.' He gestured towards the window, and the sea, and France.

'Where d'you think you are? Only it's next stop America out there: this is Cornwall.'

'Is it?' In truth this conveyed very little to Joe's mind, as geography was one of the many things his education had entirely neglected. 'Is that in England?'

The nurse laughed. 'Some people think so,' she said.

Presently the house grew walls, and other beds, and other men, assumed shape and then routine. Every other day nurses brought folding screens and a laden clinking trolley, and carefully tortured him, packing and repacking the raw hollow of flesh with coiled lengths of wet crêpe bandage; gnarled locals of both sexes, speaking an almost incomprehensible dialect, helped him briefly stand while his bed was made, shaved him, cut his hair, wheeled him lying on his stomach on his trolley up and down the long corridors, and eventually took him out into the stunning sunshine of the terrace.

The sea glittered and changed its colours, sometimes sporting a small white sail or a plunging fishing-boat. Several weeks went by. The torture lessened. Someone measured him up for crutches, someone else showed him how. He stood; he hopped slowly from one side of his bed to the other; he crossed the room. Every day as he stood for longer, hopped further, he grew more despondent. Pain had filled so much time, given his days such shape; trolley-dreading had almost been a full-time job. Without it he began to understand what lay ahead.

Seagulls wheeled over the terrace, eyeing the tables set out there in fine weather, where one day, at breakfast, Joe overheard one of the other men idly announce that he knew for a fact that the house was keeping a negro slave in the basement, to do the washing-up.

No one took much notice, as the man in question was a known liar and prone anyway to sudden spells of vagueness connected to his head wound. Presently however someone else chimed in from across the table, a new chap called Dexter, pale as death from pneumonia.

'Surely not a slave, old chap, that's all been done away with, hasn't it?'

There was a pause. It was a listless group sipping its tea. Joe was standing up, as usual, leaning on the wall, his good leg protesting already that it was tired working all on its own. Sometimes Joe felt quite angry with this leg. There was nothing at all the matter with it and yet it was always making such a fuss, quivering and aching and constantly threatening collapse: letting the whole show down.

Everyone else sat rather slumped in their

chairs, exhausted by the toil of dressing, washing, shaving and making it as far as the terrace breakfast table, though Dexter himself was not yet able to walk that far, and sat now in a battered heavyweight wheelchair, his skinny legs wrapped in a blanket.

'Though there is a darkie here,' Dexter added at last. 'In the kitchen.'

'A coon,' said the liar, whose name was Bowen.

Sit down, sit down, begged Joe's good leg. It seemed completely unable to remember that sitting down was a thing of the past. Lie or stand, that was the drill these days. But Joe had had enough of lying down. Besides there had been an attractive hint of playfulness in Dexter's tone.

'There's not,' he said.

Dexter looked up at him. 'Ten bob says there is.'

'Get out,' said Joe easily. 'Tanner.'

'Sixpence it is,' said Dexter.

Others round the table had quickly entered the bet, but settling it would involve risk. Men were not supposed to visit the kitchens or even hang about outside them without good reason, and it was generally agreed that settling a bet would not count as one of these. In any case the kitchen, Dexter pointed out, was effectively enemy territory, staffed as it mainly was by hoary locals of uncertain temper: 'They should be women,' said Dexter. 'And yet their beards forbid me to interpret that they are so.'

But Joe had not done anything of his own

volition for what felt like years; not since the day he'd joined up.

'I'll go,' he said, and swung his way over to Dexter's wheelchair. 'Cop hold.' He laid his crutches on Dexter's blanketed knees. 'Haven't got yer brakes on, have yer? Where am I going, round the corner, is it?'

He pushed, experimentally. The handles seemed to take his weight. He could shove the thing forward, and then catch up with it, one near-hop at a time, the bad leg taking just enough weight. Slowly they ground across the terrace, past another table, past the open glass doors of the ward, where long pale muslin curtains shifted a little in the breeze.

'I say,' said Dexter presently, in the tone of one mildly interested, 'are we taking the stairs?'

Joe stopped. He had not realized that the terrace was raised. The curving flight of stone steps at either end beside the stone pineapples led down to the wide flagged path about the house, and so he was stranded; no one had explained stairs to him yet. He had forgotten stairs existed. But then they had never been a barrier before.

Dexter spoke up: 'I think we need brawn here, Gilder. Where's that chump Bowen gone?'

Bowen was still at the table, gazing out to sea, but was at length induced to bump Dexter and his wheelchair slowly down the steps, while at the top Joe hesitated, considering. Could he lean on the broad stone banister? There were no real hand-holds. Don't make me, said his good leg, trembling beneath him. There would be swinging

7

involved, there would be a swing out into stony nothingness. The banister hard to his palm.

'Your turn, peg leg,' said Bowen, leaping up the steps again, and he picked Joe up, as easily as once the reluctant stepfather had, prior to the private word in the long dark glass-strewn alley; Joe had time for a moment's swift nostalgia, for threats so simple and so personal, before he was propped fairly gently against Dexter's wheelchair on the flagstones at the bottom of the steps.

'Good man,' said Dexter. 'Afraid we've rather cut off our retreat.'

'No-Man's-Land,' said Bowen.

Joe said nothing, but remembered the taste of rum.

'We must advance with all due caution,' said Dexter. 'Oh, are you leaving us, Bowen? Ah. Farewell, then. Bowen appears to have a prior engagement.'

'Very busy man,' said Joe, pushing the chair forward. Slowly they neared the corner, turned it.

'Through there, I think,' said Dexter, as they approached a small arched doorway. 'Kitchen garden. Watch out for Mr McGregor.'

'You what?'

Through the arched door the path abruptly turned to cinder, which was much harder work. Joe was sweating. His arms began to ache and tremble almost as much as his good leg. In slow silence they passed a plot of spinach and an onion bed. 'Alright?' said Dexter.

'Bum hurts,' said Joe.

'*Dulce et decorum est*,' said Dexter. 'You have

8

given your arse for your country, Gilder; an honour granted to few.'

'Listen!' Now they were nearing an open door in the undistinguished brickwork at the back of the house. Windows beside it also stood open. From it came unnerving kitchen sounds: the rattle of china and cutlery, saucepans clanging, taps running, and shrill voices raised over the racket. What was left of the fun of the whole expedition seemed to drain away right there and then.

'Dear Lord,' said Dexter. 'Sounds a bit lively. Don't you think?'

Joe stopped. He thought about lying down. 'Call it quits?' he said.

As if in reply Dexter abruptly had a coughing fit. His face went scarlet, his eyes streamed. He threw himself about in the chair, as if he were fighting with himself. The extra tension of seeing this made Joe's head swim, the tearing noise of it seemed to pierce right through him like spears. His good leg began to shake violently beneath him.

'Help!' he cried, or thought he did, and then became aware of someone embracing him, holding him upright, of buxom shapes and sweeping skirts, of someone stooping in front of Dexter and the terrifying cough falling suddenly silent. Someone took his arm, firmly, and helped him forward, through an open doorway into a hot bright place, fearfully crowded, full of strangers, cross old women in a row, all glaring.

'Sorry,' he squeaked, and then fell silent, for he had suddenly understood how close he was to bursting out crying. He felt almost faint with embarrassment and shame, caught trespassing; caught out anyway.

'We — we went the wrong way,' he muttered.

'Got confused,' said Dexter croakily.

The woman nearest him, the cook presumably, from her general menacing air of command, big square face and brawny forearms, did not smile back. She leant back against the table behind her, and glared down at him, and then up at Joe, who looked quickly away. She turned to the woman beside her, and spoke, in the local dialect.

'What are we to do with these here, Mrs Dimond?'

This was another old witch, even fiercer in appearance, since in fine music-hall style she was holding a large wooden rolling pin upright like a floury truncheon in one knotty red hand. There was a pause while, slowly shaking her head, she appeared to consider. Then she said:

'You reckon . . . they like cake?'

'Well now, Mrs Dimond,' said the cook slowly, deadpan, 'I believe they might. What d'you say, young man?'

'Oh . . . gosh,' said Dexter, instantly brightening, and there was suddenly something like a party atmosphere, and fussing, and laughter. For mainly the women in the kitchen, as Joe at that time could not begin to imagine, had looked at Dexter and himself and seen not marauding soldiery or trespassing young men, but something more like children; a famished child in a wheelchair, a crippled child on crutches.

10

'Here. Eat up, go on.'

'Where you from, my lovely?'

'How old are you?'

'Coffee or chocolate?'

'Have another bit, go on.'

And then Joe saw her. He saw her hand first, as she held out towards him a plate of little round honey tarts still warm from the oven. He remembered the bet, and unconsciously shook his head, disowning it; still, he couldn't help but stare, at her delicate wrist, her small fingers. He saw a blue dress open at the throat. He saw her neck, dark, very slender, and at last he dared her face, oh, just a girl, a girl's smile, eyes glistening sweet as blackberries. He saw that everything about her was normal and real; the only difference was that it was all brown. A commonplace prejudice dropped away from him before he had so much as thought to voice it.

'Thanks, Miss — '

A giggle. Oh, how pretty she was!

'Now then, Gracie,' said the old witch-one, Mrs Dimond.

'Take a bite, do,' said Gracie, in that same local-yokel accent, that he'd thought made you sound so countrified and daft; but in her mouth it was cosy, coaxing, as lovely as her name: suited her. When she slipped back to work over by the window, behind a big white enamel-topped table, he couldn't stop looking at her. He watched as she took the covering tea cloth from a large brown china mixing bowl and drew something out of it, creamy-white, elastic, clinging: bread dough?

Joe limped closer, until he could lean against the other side of the table, where he watched her scatter it with flour and knead it, busily pulling and tucking it into itself. Occasional flecks of raisin surfaced now and then, to be quickly folded back into the depths. He felt shy. But he had to speak.

'Miss? What you making?' He nodded at the dough.

' 'Tis for buns,' she said, and again the accent struck him as somehow intimate, though at the same time wonderfully exotic. Presently though he noticed that he couldn't quite make sense of her hands. Curious; something kept looking strange, as if her slender floury fingers somehow didn't bend as they should. He concentrated; and finally understood that her hands looked strange because one of them was: her left normal, but while her right hand gracefully shared the turn and tuck, turn and tuck, there — and there, again — something was terribly wrong with it. The ring and little fingers were missing, the merest stumps; the middle finger too short.

As soon as he realized this the words jumped out of him: 'What's up with your hand?'

She stopped still, though not before the right hand had slipped to hide itself behind the left.

'Accident,' she said, without looking up, then quickly unfolded the mismatched fingers and set to work again.

Joe felt stunned. Over the blood thundering in his ears he kept hearing himself asking her, *What's up with your hand?* as if there was some way he could go back and intercept himself. He had forgotten how normal people behaved, he thought. It was being here; it was one of the things you talked about, in this place: What brings you here, then?

'Sorry,' he said. 'I shouldn't have asked.'

She stopped work again, and this time gave him a straight look. He held his breath, so sudden and so strong was the personality in that glance.

'No matter,' she said. ''Twas long ago.' She took up the canister, and swiftly floured the dough again. 'What about you?'

He gave her the cheery version he had given his mother, the shell that had caught him in daylight, knocked him out, the stretcher, the field hospital, the good ship home, and here. But when he had finished she gave him another look, and it was as if she knew how much he was lying. It occurred to him that perhaps she had told such smoothed-out versions of the truth herself; that she had, in fact, just done so.

He told her his name, and asked if he could help her somehow, could he do a bit of kneading for her, perhaps? Would she show him how? Partly a joke, and to try and take away the taste of what he had asked her, mainly because it looked like a good way of standing closer to her.

'You can help with the shaping, if you like,' she said. Was her tone a little warmer? His heart thought so, and thumped excitedly in his chest. 'You got to wash your hands first, mind.' She gestured at the stone sink behind her.

'Anything you say,' said Joe, to this warmer

tone, and saw breathlessly that in reply she drew her skirts out of his way with a little half-mocking flourish.

At the sink he took the edge in his wet hands for a moment, and leant forward to lift his weight free. But he had forgotten his leg, for a little while, he realized. Had he ever once forgotten it before? He thought not.

''Ere. Dry yer 'ands.' Proffering a clean blue and white tea towel, ironed smooth. He could have laid it to his cheek.

She was very little, close up.

'Is they proper dry?'

'They proper is,' he answered, as near to her accent as he could get, and that set her off giggling, you'd think no one had ever tried to make her laugh before, he thought gloriously, it was a while before she could speak at all.

'Put yer 'ands out — no, over the table! Palms up. That's right. Stay still.' She snatched up her canister, and gave it a quick merry shake over his hands. The fall of it was so light he could barely feel it. It was like feathery down, it was like a childhood dream of warm snow. When he rubbed his fingertips together he felt no gritting at all, not even dustiness, it was like rubbing silken nothing.

'There. Now you can touch it,' she said. He saw the tip of her tongue as she laughed now, flashing him a little sideways glance. Saucy! His knees trembled, but with glad excitement.

Joe put his hands exactly where hers had been on the dough, and pushed at it with his right-hand knuckles.

14

'It's warm!' It was unlike anything he had ever handled before, at once weighty and buoyant, an impossible airy heaviness. It seemed responsive. He turned it with his left, as Grace had, and it seemed to fall naturally into his hands. Close to, he could faintly smell cinnamon in it.

'Let me cut it. Here. Now, you take 'im, and you roll 'im into a ball, see? Like this.'

She had floured the enamel table in front of her. She spun the piece of dough under her palm, and turned it at once from fragment into nicely rounded little bun-shape. She used the injured hand, and he saw the swirling scar halfway up her forearm, where once a flame had travelled.

'Should make a couple of dozen,' she said.

'There's never enough,' he told her. His bun looked nothing like hers, try as he might. 'It's all skew-whiff, look!'

'I'll make you one special,' said Grace, turning to look up at him.

★   ★   ★

Joe had held various jobs before the army had let him in, underage though he indubitably still had been; mainly running to fetch things, or cleaning, none of it skilled or even practised, and nearly all of it the sort of thing you tried not to think about afterwards, except that the smell of it stayed in your clothes. He had rarely thought of the future then, and these days he generally tried not to think about it at all. But on the way back to safety (let out of the back door into the kitchen garden, and through that into the perfect legality of the old croquet lawn) it occurred to him that people would always want bread. You took the cleanly silken fineness of flour, he thought, and added to it, and turned it into something wholesome that people would always want more of. And you could do it standing up. No: you had to.

'You owe me a tanner,' said Bowen at lunch.

'Bet's off,' said Joe.

'The committee feels,' said Dexter, 'that the case is insufficiently proved.'

'What?'

'Not a negro.'

'What? Course she is,' said Bowen. 'I seen her. Black as Newgate's knocker.'

'Ah, but there you are wrong, old love,' said Dexter. 'Newgate's knocker considerably blacker, I'd say.'

Her glance that went right into you, thought Joe, her wonderful laugh. How could a girl as beautiful as that even look at a cripple like himself? Though at the same time, and at a level too deep for thought, he wondered whether her being a darkie didn't in some way even things out a little.

'Still counts,' said Bowen.

'Sorry, mate,' said Joe, 'but you can kiss my arse. What's left of it.'

* * *

'I'll make you one special,' said Grace, turning to look up at him; and she had. To one side of the

16

heaped tray of ordinary thinly marged buns served at tea-time that afternoon was a paper bag with his name pencilled on it, holding not only an extra-large supremely sticky extra-fruited buttered beauty, a bun of buns, but a little note.

6 May, '18

Dear Corporal Gilding, it was nice to meet you, here is the bun you helped make.
   Yours sincerely, Grace Dimond, 7a Market Buildings, Silkhampton

Joe folded the note and put it into the special pocket of his wallet. He kept the paper bag, too. His recovery had begun.

1

As the century turned Mrs Dimond reached her fiftieth year. Her husband was dead, her son long since settled in Canada, with a wife and children she would never see. On the other hand Mrs Dimond herself was in excellent health, her son wrote to her now and then and sometimes sent her money, her kitchen garden and henhouse repaid her efforts, and the cakes and pies she made for sale at the market on Wednesdays and Saturdays brought in a small but useful sum.

But Mrs Dimond had a better and more satisfying source of income. She might, for instance, be sitting quietly of an evening, knitting by the fire and thinking about bed, when there would be footsteps running along the passage outside and a sharp rap at her back door: a summons. She would generally have been expecting the call, but not always.

Expected or otherwise Mrs Dimond would then in a calm pleasurable excitement rise, take up her special bag, and go out in her coat and hat and boots to wherever she was required, sometimes far afield in bitter winds and rain, arriving soaked and chilled, and not always to any degree of household comfort.

Tonight, though, on a chill blowy midnight in March, the place is clean and warm and dry, the top-floor back of one of the rundown but still respectable town houses behind the square. The oil lamp from the kitchen downstairs sits on top of the chest of drawers, an almost unprecedented coal fire burns in the tiny corner grate. Mrs Dimond has brought the special bag, and is carefully unpacking it.

Also in the room, officially, is Mrs Bertram Quick, otherwise Miss Rosetta May St George, who barely six months earlier had high-kicked in taffeta with seven other girls in a London chorus line. At present though, lying back on the bed, she is unable to remember any of these handsome names, and when Mrs Dimond asks her, kindly enough, what she is called, can only come up with 'Rosie'. Then she lapses back into hectic groans.

Mrs Dimond takes no notice of these. She is unbuttoning the front of her own dress. She takes a folded piece of flannel out of the special bag, slips it inside her bodice, and buttons up again. The door opens, and Mrs Withers, the landlady, a woman her own age, bustles in carrying a cup of tea.

'Now then, Mrs Dimond,' she breathes, handing it over, 'I hope I ain't got you out too early.'

Mrs Dimond takes the tea in a sudden silence: the groaning has stopped. Blearily Rosie looks around, dull-eyed. 'Oh my Gawd,' she says, as if in greeting, her voice husky from all the groaning, and closes her eyes again. Her cheeks and lips are flushed scarlet, her hair is damp and plastered to her head.

'She keeping anything down?' asks Mrs Dimond.

'Not so much as a *drop* of water,' says Mrs Withers, who is fairly bristling with excitement.

'Got to get her up,' says Mrs Dimond. 'If you want to save the bed.'

Mrs Withers' eyes widen. She half-laughs: 'Bless me, I'd forgotten!' She turns to her guest. 'I help you up, Mrs Quick? Come on now, my dear. Take my arm.'

Mrs Quick appears for the moment incapable of voluntary motion; perhaps too the name confuses her. But Mrs Withers is built for heavy lifting, and presently has her hauled bodily off the bed; she holds her more or less upright while Mrs Dimond whips off the bedclothes, unfolds several newspapers from the pile kept ready for her beneath the bed, and lays them in a crackling layer over the lower half of the mattress, before covering all of it with the large heavyweight rubber mackintosh from the bottom of her own special bag. More newspapers on top, quickly; and she barely has the bottom sheet back on to cover everything before Rosie begins heaving and groaning again, louder and louder, sagging in the landlady's arms. Mrs Dimond carries on unhurriedly tucking in sheets, then folds up the blanket and counterpane and piles them on to the only other free surface, the floor beneath the window.

'All set,' she says, and picks up her teacup. This time the groans sharpen into screaming; Mrs Dimond sips her tea.

'Best back on the bed, I think,' she says, when she can be heard again. 'You got a wet cloth for her head?'

With the next pain the screams are louder and wilder still and after it Mrs Dimond gives her patient the flat stick padded with clean strips of rag wound round it and sewn into place, to bite on. 'You're scaring folk,' she says, though on the whole Mrs Dimond sees no reason why folk — husbands especially — should not be given a proper scare now and then. Pity the chap's not downstairs taking notice as he should.

For Mrs Withers has already let on that Mr Bertie Quick, celebrated London tenor though he may be, has yet to make any sort of appearance here in Silkhampton, where this poor little piece, wedding ring or no, has been sat on her lonesome (rent fully paid right enough) these past three months. Nor, Mrs Withers had whispered, had there been so many letters with a London postmark; only two, in fact, and them in two different hands. Weren't it a fearful shame!

But to this Mrs Dimond had said only: 'Is there hot water ready? I needs to wash my hands.' She had spoken gently, so Mrs Withers had not felt chastened, or not exactly. And Mrs Dimond had let her watch as she had taken a tiny bottle from the special bag and carefully shaken something thrillingly purple out of it into the bowl, which had swirled the water with pink.

'Strengthens it,' said Mrs Dimond, as she washed her hands. She did not, as it happened, believe in the necessity of potassium permanganate. Carbolic had been well enough, and plain hot water good enough for her own mother. But she liked Dr Summers.

In the upper room now, she takes up the wet

cloth, turns it cool-side down, and lays it again on Rosie's white forehead.

'Take a little sip of something now,' she says, and she picks up the cup of sugared water, and holds it so that her patient may drink. She notes the soft hands that touch her own as her patient sips and sighs.

'Am I dying? I'm dying, aren't I ... ' Her voice trails away into a squeak of tearfulness.

'Course not,' says Mrs Dimond sharply, for she regards this sort of thing as impious, as well as slack-fibred. Where was the woman's pride? 'Everything's just as it should be,' she adds, but her touch is gentle still as she straightens the pillow, smoothes the ruffled sheet. 'We must all be patient, see?'

After another hour or more of patience, something changes, and Rosie flings the padded stick aside with a sudden angry energy. Her breathing is deeper, more free. Uttering a series of bracing yells she half-rises on the bed, and casts herself about on it with a new vehemence.

When this pain goes she collapses, falls back heavily, does not stir as Mrs Dimond draws aside the hem of the nightdress, and has a quick look.

Not yet; but soon.

'Get yourself on your side, my dear,' says Mrs Dimond, 'lie on your left side, and let the Lord deliver you.'

'Oh, what's happening?' asks Mrs Withers eagerly, rather bedraggled herself by this time; she has been popping downstairs, as she put it, for some time now, keeping the stove going, dozing off beside it and then popping up again,

23

as now, with more coal or a fresh pot of tea.

'Not far off,' says Mrs Dimond.

It does not occur to her to carry out any sort of examination. She's heard of them. But what goes on inside a labouring woman is God's business, not hers. Besides it's clear to her anyway that something has altered within: the inner gates have yielded. Now the pains will begin to shift the heavy curl of child downward towards the further outer doors. Though these too will not open all by themselves. Mrs Dimond stands at the bedside.

'When it starts again, you put this foot on me. Here. Like this, alright?' Mrs Dimond helps Rosie raise her trembling leg, sets her bare foot against the lightly padded hardness of her own hipbone.

Rosie sees Mrs Dimond as safety, as life itself, but very far away, as if she were on the other side of a great gorge or chasm. Agonizing effort is the only bridge back to life, and she knows some die crossing it. She is on her own. Mrs Dimond's eyes say calmly: Yes, I know.

Mrs Withers' knees crack as she kneels on the rug on the other side of the bed. Though she holds Rosie's hand, she too is far away, on the other side, in safety. The room is very quiet. When Rosie shifts a little, as the next pain starts, the bed crackles beneath her.

'Now then, now then!'

'Oh Christ help me!' cries the labouring woman, and then falls silent as within her (thinks Mrs Dimond) the womb rises and takes command.

'That's the way,' says Mrs Dimond approvingly, who has heard not swearing but prayer. She sees that the woman on the bed will obey as she should. Some don't; some for a while forget themselves and lie writhing and shrieking, as if forsooth they could escape somehow from the duty of obedience, and from their own selves. Such craven panic tends to slow the whole business down a good deal, fit retribution, some might say; but the business in any case cannot be hurried. Let them scream if they must, is Mrs Dimond's motto. Let them scream, and presently they will stop.

Now though, in dutiful obedience, the woman on the bed, her left leg braced against Mrs Dimond's steady hip, pushes down inside herself. Her right leg is firm too, against the foot of the bed. She half-rises on her left elbow, and heaves. Her whole body is rigid with effort. Here is true hard labour, thinks Mrs Dimond, strange and hidden labour, soft parts turning as if to steel.

After the pain Mrs Dimond gently lays down Rosie's leg and draws down her nightdress. The room is quiet again. The wind mutters outside, the fire burns. Mrs Withers dampens her cloth and wipes her tenant's face, which is completely relaxed now, as if she were asleep.

'Won't be long now,' says Mrs Dimond coaxingly. At least half an hour, she thinks. Perhaps more. Not for the first time she looks at the big round belly under the flannel nightdress, and thinks about the sleeping baby so tightly crammed inside. She knows gestation takes place

25

in sweet perfect sleep, and that the baby is safely woken only by the long-drawn-out process of birth.

The woman stirs, groans, and the rubber sheet and the newspapers packed beneath it murmur back.

'Again.'

Twenty minutes slowly pass. The leg is raised and braced and lowered again. Hidden from view the curled sleeping child slowly descends, while the soft parts between the labouring woman's legs, at first rounded as the child's head pressed against them from within, appear to swell, and yet then, miraculously, carry out the Lord's will by reversing the swelling, growing slowly thinner and thinner until they can draw themselves back into nothingness and let the child through. Mrs Dimond, taking another swift look between pains, speaks for the first time in several minutes.

'Now then: don't you push no more. 'Tis the littlun's turn now, he must come out by himself. Nearly there now.' She folds back the nightgown so that the private parts will be untrammelled.

On the bed Rosie is clattering up from the dressing room with the other girls for the final number, all of them tricked out in the feathered headdress, the saucy little flouncy skirts, but as the curtain parts and they step forward in line Rosie notices how strangely familiar her own skirt feels, realizes that she has somehow come onstage at the Alhambra, Leicester Square, in her landlady's old flannel nightie, but as she stands there despairing in the ferocious theatre lights Mrs Dimond cries, 'Here, now! I said don't you go pushing!'

Mrs Withers pulls Rosie close, and hides her face in her bosom.

Now a taut oval bulge of greyish membrane is peeping through the opening doors of the mother's private parts. Mrs Dimond does not touch it. She notes the intact cawl, and wonders whether it will stay that way, though she herself scorns the superstitions about such things. She can make out a flattened darkness of curls through the opaque surface.

'Next one,' she says, and as she speaks a living fountain of warm flecked water gushes on to the bed as the cawl bursts. 'Don't you go pushing now!' The woman's foot still braced against her, Mrs Dimond bends as the head keeps on coming, and when the pain stops the outer doors, now thin as cloth, have parted so well that a large oval of wet thin dark curls, the back of the baby's head, elongated by its slow passage through those tight inner places, shows through, resting there.

'Slowly now,' says Mrs Dimond, waiting. 'Let him come on his own.'

Minutes pass. 'Softly now.'

With the next pain the nape of the child's neck at last clears the narrow way, and the gates part, the mother screams once, and the whole head rises, goes on rising, and at last comes free. Now a strange compound beast lies on the bed: a panting woman, her nightdress folded up to her breasts, and down between her parted legs someone else's slick, wet, drowned little head, face-down.

27

'Now then,' says Mrs Dimond, and slides her right middle fingertip past the back of the head, making sure that during its long secret sleep the baby has not coiled its own lifeline cord about its neck: sometimes babies hang themselves alive that way, and you must loosen the loop if you can. The pointed little head makes no movement. Every feature of the face below is congested, swollen. Its cheeks have a deep blueish tint.

Mrs Dimond can see the mother's heartbeat in the fluttering skin over her ribs. Her own heart too is beating fast. With her dry and steady left hand she unbuttons the front of her blouse, so that she can reach inside more easily.

'Over soon.' A coal shifts in the fire. Two slow minutes pass. Then one more. The baby's head is bowed, meek.

Then Rosie stirs, and whimpers, and Mrs Dimond bends, her hands a net to catch the baby as the blue little face at last turns towards its mother's left. The mother gives a bursting yell as first one shoulder and then the other slip through, and then in a rush of warm fruit-smelling water, the child and its great bouncing jellified rope of twisted white cord come free.

'There now,' says Mrs Dimond joyously. 'Praise be!'

The mother lies collapsed, limp as a dead woman, her eyes closed.

Mrs Dimond takes out and shakes open the folded square of flannel warm from the front of her blouse, covers the baby's wet little body with it, and lifts it clear of the mucky gathered water between the mother's legs. In Mrs Dimond's hands the baby wakes alive, and sets up a good clear crying.

'A lovely girl!'

At once the dead woman stirs, laughing with a sort of surprise, as if she had for a moment forgotten that all her pain and labour had a cause and an outcome. Herself again, with the half-wrapped bundle of damp baby clutched to her chest, she greets her daughter, and the happiness in her voice is part of Mrs Dimond's deep reward.

'Hello!' crows Rosie to her first child, and only daughter. 'Oh, hello, you! Hello!'

As if in reply the baby forces open her swollen little eyelids, and her clear eyes glint in the lamplight. She stares up at her mother from her blood-stained wrapper, alert, astounded, fearless.

Mrs Dimond is still at work. She grasps the firm glistening rope of cord, feeling the strong pulse in it. For a moment or two more mother and child are still one; then the transmitted heartbeat fades, stops, and they are two different people, forever more.

Straight away, Mrs Dimond thinks, the cord accepts its death. Its gristle instantly loses the gloss and vigour of life. From the special bag she takes the two twists of clean twine, ties one tight ligature, ties two. In their happiness the mother and daughter barely notice her take up her big well-sharpened scissors and sever the cord right through, between the two knots. All is well, no blood seeps from either side.

'Put her to your breast, mother,' says Mrs Dimond, 'so we can all rest easy.'

All three laugh a little at the baby's instant enthusiasm. 'She knows what she likes,' says Mrs Withers, dabbing at her eyes. Mrs Dimond is tired; it's nearly five in the morning, and in any case, for private reasons of her own, she has not slept well for some time. Luckily the afterbirth doesn't linger, and she has to wait only twenty minutes more before Rosie gives a sudden gasp and the nasty thing comes sliding out, a warm solid flop between her legs, baby's side first, slithery membranes trailing after, and all of it limp as a jellyfish.

Mrs Dimond has never liked the look of afterbirth, the inner surface so threaded and embossed with thick twisted blood vessels, the outer lobes the colour and soft texture of calves' liver, flesh at its fragile fleshiest. Still she examines it, as Dr Summers has insisted she must. Quickly the thing grows clotted and cold as she spreads the membranes, the double bag that held the baby's long watery sleep. There's the hole she made leaving. No part seems missing. She tips the whole slimy nastiness into newspaper and folds it into a parcel. In the morning Mrs Withers' boy Martin can take it to the end of the garden and bury it there. Some she knows just put it straight on the fire, but Mrs Dimond can't abide the smell.

She washes out the bowl, and in Dr Summers' honour drops a little more potassium permanganate into it before giving her patient a good wash in the bed, and, with Mrs Withers' help, rolling her to and fro so that they can take away all the sodden newspaper and the mackintosh and make up the bed afresh. Mrs Withers has brushed and re-plaited her hair for her, and gone downstairs to see about a bit of breakfast. Dawn is showing through the gingham curtain, and one or two birds are already singing.

'Is there blood coming away, down below?'

Rosie, Mrs Bertram Quick again, shakes her head. It's possible to see, now, how very young she is, though of course Mrs Dimond has delivered even younger, in her time.

'Then I will take my leave. Sleep tight now.'

'Oh, Mrs Dimond, wait, take my hand, oh thank you, thank you, you were so kind. I don't know how I would have managed without you. You were like a mother to me.'

'Get away,' says Mrs Dimond rather crossly, scenting dramatic carryings-on, of which she disapproves, and ruffled at the accusation of mere kindness, when she has been doing her duty and God's will, as well as earning an honest living. 'You must pay for the soap and the fixings, and for my time. I'll wait upon you a week,' she adds.

'Don't go. Please. May I ask — what's your name? Please?'

Mrs Dimond considers this fresh attack with suspicion. 'Why?'

The girl in the bed smiles. Fresh and rosy as the dawn, thinks Mrs Dimond, surprising herself.

'I just wondered,' says Mrs Quick. 'I need a name, you see.'

31

'What about your husband then, won't he want a say?'

'Of course.' The smile fades abruptly.

At the door Mrs Dimond turns. 'I'll bid you good day,' she says austerely, but turns back before she closes it. She meets her patient's eyes again. How strange to have shared so closely, and to part so entirely! An impulse towards the girl on the bed surprises her again, by its strength and sweetness. Fresh and Rosie as the dawn. Afterwards, telling the story to her sister, she will dare to wonder aloud whether even then some part of her guessed the truth: that after her long unblemished and devoted career as the parish's best handywoman, this was to be her very last completely untroubled delivery. And a good one it had been too, neat as you like, praise be.

She smiles at Mrs Quick, Rosie, her own rare oddly playful smile. 'It's Violet,' she says, and closes the door behind her.

* * *

In her heart she was a dissenter, and never took Communion; but there was no Chapel within practical reach, and in any case St George's Silkhampton was safely Low, so on her way home Violet Dimond called in as usual for a moment of communicative quiet. The birth had been a gift, and she must show proper gratitude. And she had difficulties of her own to consider.

Nearly a month earlier, on the ninth of February, she had suffered from a terrible nightmare. The ninth of February had been a special date for Violet for the last fourteen years; though one year she had been busy at a childbirth, on all the others she had marked the anniversary by staying up until midnight, sitting at her kitchen table with a lit candle, a small china cup set beside it. The cup was of white china, with a blue bird painted on it. On the ninth of February fifteen years before, this cup had held a drop of good milk, and Violet's daughter Ruth had drunk from it, though her little hand had trembled so much with fever that she could barely raise it to her lips. It was the last thing she had held.

During her latest vigil though, when Violet had lit her candle and set the precious cup beside it, and sat quietly in prayer for a while, she had fallen asleep.

She had often dreamt of Ruth in the years since her death, but always vaguely. She would wake up knowing that she had had a blessed glimpse, never more, though that was better than nothing. This time she dreamt with what felt like ordinary daytime clarity that she had come back from market on a Wednesday afternoon and gone to put the kettle on, and instead found herself walking by Rosevear Lake, miles away; and standing on the bank alive again, her dark eyes sparkling as before, was Ruth, holding out her arms, and dancing with excitement. Wild with joy that the terrible misunderstanding about death was over at last, Violet ran towards her, aware even in her delight that the child was too close to the water, but the faster she ran the further away Ruth seemed to be; Ruth, oh come

33

away from the edge, begged Violet, running without motion, watching helplessly all the time as her daughter turned and slipped and fell into the deep grey cold of it, struggled in the water, calling out for her, choking and drowning —

Violet had awoken, with her heart bucketing like a runaway train. She had fallen asleep instead of keeping vigil; the dream was no more than she deserved, she thought. But a few nights later, in her own bed, the nightmare had come again, and then again. Not even prayer could banish that final image for long.

★　★　★

In the church, Violet sat in silence for some time, thanking the Almighty for the continuing miracle of childbirth, and thinking other less precise prayerful thoughts. It was quiet, though she could just hear the increasing sounds of early-morning traffic outside. You were so kind, so motherly, said the girl on the bed. Presently Violet's head sank on her chest, and she noticed that the aisle was strangely thronged with small children all crouching in silence, their little heads bowed, as if in prayer, but then one of them looked up, and was Ruth struggling and calling out for her, Ruth choking, drowning —

Gasping, Violet awoke.

And there of course she was, alone in the blessed peace of the church. She trembled as she pulled out her handkerchief to wipe her face. Its folds, its clean smell, soothed her. The normal traffic noises went on distantly rumbling outside.

She felt that she had heard them all the time, that she had dreamt without being fully asleep. But then she had slept so badly, these past weeks.

Why now these horrors, when she had not mentioned Ruth's name to a living soul these fifteen years? She stood up, and the movement turned something in her memory, and showed her the crouching, silent little children. At once it seemed to Violet that there was some meaning in them that she might grasp, if she tried. It was as if her mind was like a jar of muddy water. If she let it stand, would it clarify?

Painfully, for her knees were not what they were, Violet knelt right down upon the cold stone of the church floor. She set down her scarf and the special bag, and knelt in silence, her eyes closed, picturing the children bowed as if in prayer.

Several minutes passed. Then she gave a little start, and looked up. It had occurred to her suddenly that the nightmare, though so painfully of her lost treasure, might not, strictly speaking, be her own. Was it possible, after so many years, and so many spent apart?

There was only one way to find out, thought Violet, shifting to sit down on the pew behind her: she would have to go and ask.

'Lord help me,' said Violet aloud: not exactly in prayer.

2

Three days later, just past nine in the morning, Violet took two guineas from the old tobacco tin hidden beneath a loose tile in the front-room fireplace, picked up her big tin market box, and left her house. It wasn't market day, though. She crossed the quiet square and set off up Northern Road towards the railway station.

There was no one else waiting on platform three, for the coast. There was a Waiting Room, she knew, and through it a Ladies' Waiting Room, probably empty at this hour of any actual Ladies, but it was safer, she felt, to stay out on the platform, to catch the very first glimpse of the distant approaching train. Violet walked to the far end of the platform and sat down on the market box in the mild sunshine. She rarely travelled alone, and remembered that the tiny faraway stage only lasted a moment or two before the immense hurtling fury of arrival, and doors flung open, and the fearful scramble to get in or out, the shouts and the clouds of steam and whistles blowing.

But things went smoothly enough. The third-class coach stopped almost right in front of her, the door opened easily enough, the market box slid itself in with no trouble, and no one else got in or out at all. Safe for at least ten minutes, Violet looked about her. The carriage seats were wooden slats painted navy blue, with thin musty-smelling purple cushion-things to sit on, and framed pictures, screwed into the wooden walls above the seats, of lovely Cornish places to visit — a ruined castle, a meadow where some children were having a picnic, and two different sunny harbours with boats. After a few moments she recognized one of these last as a pale elongated and impossibly tidy-looking version of Bea's own village, which made you wonder at least, she thought, about the others.

Presently the train began to slow down in the first of what Violet knew to be a series of frequent short stops. She put her gloves on ready and then tore them off again to find her ticket. She allowed herself a little daydream, in which she had been somehow able to let her sister know she was coming, and Bea had been pleased, and so come to meet her, cheerily waving as the train pulled in. This made her real anxious loneliness much harder to bear, which served her right, she told herself, for drifting into such idle nonsense in the first place.

But it was as easy as before, the platform similarly quiet. It was not quite ten as she set off, not down towards the scabby old boats and fishy dereliction of the real working harbour, but in the other direction, inland along the deep hedged lanes; for it was not at home that she wanted to catch her sister, but at work. It was a pleasant enough walk, but for the market box. She had to keep stopping to shift the strap of it from hand to hand, for it was full of cakes — three dozen tiddlers and three good plate-sized, packed in many layers of newspaper

— but the walk was only a mile and presently she arrived at the great gates. These stood open; there seemed to be no one about. Before her lay a winding carriage drive, for once real gentry had lived here.

Violet sat down for a moment on the market box, to gather her strength; it would be shameful, she felt, to bother the Almighty about what mood your sister was in. Then she made her way crunchily down the gravel drive, set about on both sides with fairly tidy lawns, past the great front door, and turned right towards the back, expecting all the while to be challenged, ready to answer any sharpness with her own.

At the side of the house was a door, half-open. The corridor inside had a working look to it, bare worn floor-boards. Violet nudged the door open with a corner of the market box and went inside. Smell of cabbage. A big bare staircase to her right, dark corridor ahead.

'Hello there?'

Far away, from some other floor, she could hear a strange rhythmic noise, which resolved itself soon into the sound of children, chanting something aloud. From closer at hand came another flattened hubbub of childish voices. While she hesitated, a door opened, and a girl with big round cheeks, dressed as a kitchen maid, came bustling down the corridor with a bolt of washing in her arms, and singing under her breath, until she looked up, saw Violet, looked again, gave a little snorting scream, and leant back *thud* against the wall, clutching at her washing, face slack with fear.

For an instant Violet herself did not understand: it had been so long since she and Bea had pulled this particular stunt, though once it had been one of their dearest occupations.

'I'm her sister,' she said, and nodded her head. Don't worry, you're right, said the nod: there really are two of us.

'Oh my Lord!' said the kitchen maid, now eagerly grinning.

'I've come a-visiting,' said Violet firmly. 'She in the kitchen?'

'In her sitting room. Shall I show you?' After that the maid couldn't speak for tittering. Violet followed her hunched shaking shoulders through several dark corridors, arriving at last at a half-glazed door, the window curtained with lacy net. 'Missus! Mrs Givens!' burst out the kitchen maid, rapping on the door, her face scarlet. ''Tis a visitor for you!'

The door opened, and Bea looked out. She nodded coolly at Violet: 'Morning. Come along in,' then turned to raise an eyebrow at the kitchen maid, who instantly stopped grinning and scurried off back the way she had come. Bea closed the door.

'Vi.'

'Bea.'

In the past shared ownership of the same face had often irritated Violet and Beatrice. As little girls they had fought all the time, rolling one another ruthlessly across the cottage floor and banging one another's heads against table leg and coal box; as bigger girls they had traded stinging slaps and sudden pushes, and as young women their stand-up rows had still sometimes ended with one or other of them flinging herself wildly at her sister's head to claw at hairstyle or best blouse, once in public, so that they had been pulled apart by variously appalled and rapturous neighbours. But those days were long gone.

'Tea?'

Violet nodded. 'Brought you summat.' She indicated the market box. 'Plenty for all on 'em. And one or two left over. Look.' She opened the lid, and at once the room was full of the honeyed fragrance of fresh baking. 'Raisins *and* currants.'

'They won't go to waste,' said Bea, busy with the teapot. The kettle on the little spirit stove in the hearth had clearly just boiled.

'You ain't put out?' asked Violet. ''Cause they're best et today.'

'Knew you was coming,' said Bea complacently.

While it had always been Beatrice's habit to embrace their strange connection, Violet's to make light of it, the effrontery of pretending that, in superb acceptance of her own insight, Bea had actually been expecting three dozen fairy cakes out of the blue — this was too much, straight away.

'Know why and all, do you?' said Violet spitefully.

'Looking tired,' said Bea, in the same tone. 'Keeping well? Sleeping alright?'

Violet hesitated; sighed. Not five minutes, she thought, and it's already business as usual. She remembered the crouching children of her church-dream, and made an effort: 'Well no,' she said, more gently.

40

There was a pause. Bea set out china, pink-flowered teacups and saucers and milk jug all the same, and produced two buttered buns on matching plates.

'Me neither,' she said at last.

'Bad dreams?'

Bea nodded, eyes averted. Ah, thought Violet. But she could not bring herself to ask any further, lest Ruth be named aloud.

While Bea poured the tea, Violet looked about her. The room was a sort of large cupboard, she thought, cosy enough, if you didn't mind not being able to see out, the one window being so high, and with a proper rocking chair set beside the neat little range, though the fire was out. She sat down opposite Bea at the small square table. Anyone peeping in at us, thought Violet, would see a strange sight, the matching china and matching women; like herself Bea was in black, full-skirted.

'Remember playing Mirrors, Bea?' She was thinking of a long-ago game they had mainly played in public in the street, for the amusement of other children, the two of them pretending to be one posh lady and her reflection as she sat at her glass, pulling faces while she plucked her eyebrows or bristly chin, picked her teeth, and painted her cheeks and lips with rouge; the secret accord between them had made almost simultaneous movement easy, Beatrice following Violet, or Violet following Beatrice. And more than once, lost in a complete shared concentration, forgetting their audience, they had reached a certain mysterious point of departure, when neither of them seemed to be following the other; when for a little while they could literally act as one, without effort, without thought. There had been something wonderfully exciting and satisfying about this practice, some quality of flight about it, as if they were sharing wings. At the same time it had felt dangerous; Violet especially had suspected that they were opening themselves to some power offensive to heaven, of the kind once labelled magic, or witchcraft.

But sometimes, in different mood, they had played the game in private, and as a contest. Then whichever of them had been following would try not just to keep up but to overtake, to force the other to follow instead, both in a hostile silence moving faster and faster, in more and more jerky and unpredictable ways, until one of them — Beatrice usually — would lose her temper completely and hurl herself forward through the non-existent frame of the imaginary mirror, a girl attacking her own reflection, an image lunging out to tear at reality's hair.

'Remember playing Mirrors, Bea?'

Bea said nothing, but lifted her cup in her left hand, just as Violet was lifting her own in her right. For a moment Violet spoilt things by half-laughing; then suddenly the game was on, as if they had never stopped playing it. A bite of bun, the pause while chewing, a big swallow, back to the teacups, Violet following Bea, but remembering instantly the possibility of gaining control herself. For almost a minute, they Mirrored one another, more and more seriously as their movements gained complexity, the hand up to theatrically push back a lock of hair, the sudden lean backwards, arms folded, sitting forward again resting on one elbow, half-rising, sitting back down again, Violet all the while grimly hanging on, not a single chance to pull ahead, until at last Bea caught her out completely, smacking her hands palm down on the table just as Violet had anticipated clapping them together.

Violet felt Bea's fierce triumph: *Me!*

'You,' she agreed, aloud. She saw that for the moment they could be in accord.

'Ought to get going,' said Bea, also equably. Presently she stood up, took her apron from the hook on the door and put it back on. 'We'll take 'em some cakes,' she said, and gave Violet a big enamel plate.

'How many?'

'A dozen first off. Here, I'll take 'em.'

'Where are we going?'

'This way,' said Bea. Holding the piled plateful of little cakes in one hand she stepped smartly out of the sitting room, and Violet followed her up a flight of stairs, along another stretch of corridor, and down another staircase to a double-door, which she rapped on and opened.

'Come on in, Vi.'

It was a large room, with several small windows leaded in little square panes. Someone near the door stood up as Bea entered, a nursemaid, holding a baby. 'Morning, Mrs Givens.'

'Morning, Beth. This here's my sister, Mrs Dimond.'

Beth, naturally, goggled a little, but said no more; perhaps she had already been warned. Violet in any case took no notice of her; her heart was jumping inside her with fright, for the room was full of crouching little children.

'Come along, my lovelies,' cried Bea, 'see what I've got for you!'

At once the children, little ones, not old enough for schooling, boys and girls together, all of them clad in grey, got up in a body and tumbled towards Bea quite as if she were a favourite; leaving behind them on the oil-cloth floor the scattering of wooden bricks, the little babyish heaps of treasured special leaves and pussy-willow mice that they had been playing with, and Violet almost laughed aloud. Though it was sobering to reflect how her dream had misled her. She had allowed herself to fear a fantasy; doing Satan's own work for him, she told herself.

'Let 'em outside, will you, Beth,' said Bea to the nurse-maid. 'We don't want crumbs all over. Come on now, line up then.'

They were too little, thought Violet, to take notice of a stranger, even one that looked so familiar, and anyway the cakes held all their attention. She watched the hubbub of straight-forward delight at the unexpected treat, Bea holding the plate just out of reach while the children got themselves into a fairly orderly queue towards the open door, some of them leaping up and down with excitement, all of them craning to see what she held.

'What do you say?'

'Thank you, Mrs Givens!' in ragged piping chorus.

Violet watched the cakes distributed by a door now opened on to a small cobbled yard. The boys in dark grey shorts, of a heavy worsted, the girls in lighter grey pinafores, and all of them, thought Violet, bearing some mark of the unmothered: the plainest hairstyles, a dried-snot trace well-crusted here and there, a tang of old urine from yesterday's wetted drawers. But they were rosy and plump enough; she knew of children otherwise.

'Out you go now!'

When the nursemaid had followed them, Bea turned to Violet. 'There's one more,' she said. She held up the plate, with the last cake on it. 'Through to the sickroom.'

Their eyes met, and Violet understood that here was the source of the nightmares that had so troubled them both; that Bea had sent her. In childhood they had often dreamt in common, but very rarely since. And dreaming can be a nonsense, Violet reminded herself. There is only One we can trust in.

'Here,' said Bea, handing Violet the plate. 'You give it to her.'

They climbed a creaky wooden spiral staircase behind a door in the corner of the Infants' room to reach another corridor, where Bea at once opened a further door and held it for Violet to pass through.

At first she was a little dazzled after the dark corridor, as a watery brilliance reflected from the lake outside made the Infirmary walls almost seem to glow. It was a large square room with four iron bedsteads against one wall, smoothly made up, and opposite them four iron cots. Only one cot was occupied.

Violet looked.

'Oh,' she said.

Something resembling a human child was half-lying, half-sitting in the cot in the corner. But it was like no other child Violet had ever seen before, a terrible yellowish-grey in colour, with a thin lifeless scrabble of russet fuzz on its head, and skinny wasted arms and legs, spidery.

'Negro,' said Bea. Violet turned this word over and over in her mind, until at last she understood. She had never seen such a thing before, hadn't ever considered the matter. She had seen occasional black men: once a group of them singing in a music hall years back, once one looking none too well all by himself on the docks at Plymouth. She knew they existed, black men, knew that they lived among the lions in Africa, waving spears and sometimes eating missionaries. Of black women she had no notion at all, but pictures of the singers in their striped jackets, and the bedraggled sailor, and the fierce spear-throwers safely on the other side of the world, all flashed confusingly into and out of her mind, leaving her struck dumb with surprise, and something like awe.

A negro child! What a sight to see, what an astonishing thing!

'Dear heaven,' said Violet, using the strongest words at her disposal. 'Oh my goodness me!'

She judged that the child was between two

and three years old. She was mute in the cot, not looking up when the door opened, and very still, all but her right hand, whose fingers were playing with a stray tape from the neck of her nightdress, laboriously rolling it up, then unrolling it. Her breathing was stertorous. Violet could hear it from across the room. There was a smell too, of sweetish decay, of sickness, stale air, and old urine.

'Pneumonia,' said Bea. 'Thought it'd finish her off.'

Violet could only whisper. 'Where she come from?'

'Some place over Exeter way, left behind, don't know her name, nor nothing else.' As she spoke the child listlessly raised her head and turned towards them, and Violet for the first time looked fully into the small greyish-yellow face.

There was a silence. The baby turned again to the stray tape; Violet gave a little gasp of pain and shock.

'Yes,' said Bea.

For the child looked entirely familiar to them both. Apart from her colour and the thin dull frizz of hair, the baby in the cot could have been Violet's own lost daughter, Ruth.

'You didn't think to tell me?' whispered Violet, when she could speak again.

'Didn't think she'd live.'

'Ah,' said Violet, conceding the common sense of this.

'But she don't speak,' said Bea. 'See? Even when it looked like she'd live, I couldn't — the doctor reckons she's simple. She ain't right, Vi.

And *look* at her. What was I *supposed* to tell you?'

Violet nodded. Yes: that colour. How could a negro child look like Ruth? 'Can I take the bars down?'

'Here. I'll do it. They took a drownded woman from the harbour there a month back,' added Bea on a whisper. 'Another darkie, see: maybe the mother.'

'Can you leave me a while?'

'Well — I suppose so. You know where to find me?'

'No. I'll manage.'

'I'll be in the kitchen,' said Bea. The door closed softly behind her.

Violet put the plate down on a table near the window, and went back to the cot. For a moment she stood looking down at the baby, now looking up. She had never felt frightened of a child before. She knew black men were not as good as white ones. How could they be, when for the most part they lived in grass huts, and were cannibals and so on, still using spears when white men had rifles? They were primitive natives. This child was one of those. Was, perhaps, disgusting.

She moved a wooden chair near to the cot, sat down, swallowed and slowly put out a hand. Violet had never been one to make free with other women's children. It was years since she had even touched a little one, apart from the immediate necessary handling of birth, and then she passed the baby at once to its mother.

Would her own flesh shrink from this alien?

48

The child's thin fuzz of hair was softer than it looked, baby-fine. Violet's fingers trembled as she stroked it. Then her arms seemed to decide for themselves, and reached out and slowly took the child up and set it gently on her lap.

It made no sound or struggle, but sat stiffly upright, fingers holding fast on to the stray end of tape, but all of them still now, a little frozen claw.

Violet felt stiff too. Her heart pounded in her chest, her mouth felt dry. She held the rigid foreign creature close. 'There, there,' said Violet, and began to rock herself and the baby gently to and fro. Presently she thought of other things to say:

'I'm Mrs Dimond,' she said in a tender coaxing tone no patient of hers had ever heard, nor ever would. 'I've come to see you.' She went on rocking. The baby felt warmer in her arms now, softer. 'There, there,' said Violet, over and over again, rocking them both.

A long time went by. Very slowly, the child seemed to loosen and unfold herself. Her hand relaxed, and she let go of the tape, and leant back, curled against Violet's bosom.

'There, there.' Violet hardly dared to breathe, went on rocking and murmuring, but when the child at last turned her head, and made the faintest suggestion of snuggling, she felt an almost overpowering sense of physical happiness, a glowing and profound relief, as if long trouble or pain had suddenly ended. My daughter, said her exultant body. Here is Ruth given back to me.

49

Violet's mind fluttered, turning up more flashing pictures of half-remembered bits and pieces of information, grass huts, slaves picking cotton in America, cannibals wearing bones through their noses. Here was not Ruth, part of Violet told herself sternly. Ruth was safe with her Maker. This was someone else's child, product of unquantifiable sin. This was a child no one wanted.

'Got summat for you,' murmured Violet, slowly standing up, the baby in her arms. She carried her over to the window, where the lake reflected the blue sky and glittered in the sunshine, looking as unlike the drowning-pool of her nightmare as any body of water might; all the same she picked up the cake and turned to sit down again facing well away from the window, the child once more settled on her lap.

'This is for you, this is,' she said tenderly.

Sitting sideways now, the baby looked down at the cake, back up at Violet. Seen close at hand Violet saw how dull the eyes were, how chalky and dry the lips. The greyish khaki colour was partly one of sickness, she realized. There was Death in that face, thought Violet, and her insides at once turned over with dread, with resolution. 'You eat it,' she said, 'it's nice.' She smiled at the baby's apparent doubt, saw her fumble. ''Ere. Let me. Look, now.' Neatly she broke the cake into four. It smelt golden with egg and sugar. Violet lifted a fragment to the baby's mouth, and she ate.

'There. Ain't that nice? Want some more?'

Now she was feeding herself. She was of that

age, Violet saw with a pang, to put nearly all her fingers into her mouth as she ate. Still not eager, though. Not stuffing it in the way a child ought. No appetite, thought Violet, as the child turned listlessly away. So sickly still. Her mind raced ahead, to possets, to proper broths given little and often, to egg yolks stirred into mashed potato, and nourishing custards. *Ruth*, said her body.

Mine anyway, said her mind.

'Now then,' said Violet, putting the barely touched cake aside, 'I'm going to make you all nice and tidy. 'Cause I can tell you's a bit on the damp side, ain't that so, my lovely. Then I'm a-going to see my sister; and then we're a-going to see the Matron. And then I'm a-going to take you home. See?'

The baby made no sound. Doctor reckons she's simple, said Bea in Violet's head.

Taking you home with me anyway, thought Violet. Maybe not today, but soon as I can.

She remembered the curious sensation she herself had had in St George's Silkhampton, that all would be clear to her if she let herself alone, let her mind clarify. She felt sure now that this was a divine message she had been meant to understand. That the child looked like Ruth was not a snare, but a signal. This was what she was meant to do, her duty, her delight.

Violet smiled at the strange-coloured baby, now her own, she was certain, by God's dear grace.

The child said nothing, and did not smile back, but drowsily turned her head, and hid her face against Violet's neck.

3

The Matron was puzzled, but asked few questions. It was hardly her place to hang on to a child someone was ready to give a home to. Especially a child so deeply unpromising.

'She ain't even British — have you really thought about this, Mrs Dimond? Neighbours'll have a deal to say. There's other little girls be less trouble. No? Sure, now?'

But mere weeks after Violet's first trip to the Home, she was walking down the gravel path the other way, the baby in her arms, on her way to Bea's house in the village down by the harbour.

Bea had married a fisherman, who had done very well for himself before being carried off by a certain winter storm. He had left Bea with the leasehold of a snug cottage right against the harbour wall, and she rented it out for the winter to her nephew, also a fisherman. Every April though the nephew and his family decamped to a less tidy cottage two miles inland, and then — like many of the other houses in the village — the place was let at a very different rate to a range of people with money to burn, artists mostly, who sat yapping about the light for weeks on end, painting pictures set up on easels all over the village, along the harbour wall and at various vantage points on the lane that climbed up to the clifftop. One or two of Bea's guests had taken it upon themselves to paint their pictures on the inside of the cottage walls too, though so far there'd been nothing, said Bea, that a good bucket of whitewash couldn't put right.

This was mid April; Bea had put off her first summer tenants for a week, so that Violet and the baby might take a little healthful sea air. The lane was fairly dry and easy underfoot, and quiet, apart from the birdsong. Larks rose in almost every field as they passed.

'Hear that, Grace?'

Violet sounded calm enough, though her whole body seemed to her to be thrumming with emotion. Triumph strengthened her arms, holding the baby wrapped snugly into her own winter shawl. 'Look, Grace, primroses. There, bluebells. See?'

Within she felt a shocked alarm, almost a panic, as if she had not, after all, carefully arranged and applied, produced documents, shown references, signed her name, but simply marched into the Home and committed a terrible crime: she had kidnapped a child, this one, so heavy in her arms. She had stolen a baby! What was she doing? And yet she was exulting, wild with triumph.

It was hard work feeling all this at once, especially as at the same time she had to keep repeating the various rational explanations and reassurances some part of her seemed constantly to forget, fluttering back again and again to the notion of crime.

How could it be His will to take another's child? Not stolen, thought Violet grimly, once again. Not stolen, given away.

Given away, like a kitten! No, given away properly, with all due form, thought Violet, and in accordance with the law.

Given, taken. Lost, found. Someone lost this child, and I have found her.

Stolen her!

'See the bluebells?'

And all the time the child made no sound at all, no struggle, just went on looking in silence, one little hand grasping the lapel of Violet's jacket. That was a blessing, for Violet. She had noticed it happen, just as they reached the top of the hill, and she stopped for a moment before beginning the long winding descent towards the village and the sea. As she stood there panting, the small brown hand worked its way free of the shawl and reached out, and took hold.

'That's right, my lovely, you hang on tight!' Violet had said, but the child made no response to her encouraging smile, though she rested her head against Violet's neck, as if she were contented enough.

In this way they reached the edge of the village. The wind picked up as Violet made her way down the steep main street. There were few people about at this hour of the day, but she knew word had got out; word always did. She was barely halfway down before one or two women suddenly found reason to nip out on to the cobbles and accost her.

'Why, Mrs Dimond, ain't it? Afternoon!' But for once, this time, looking exactly like Bea Givens was only a sideshow.

'That the little dark maid? Can I see her, like?'

54

'Ain't that a marvel!'

'She that colour all over?'

'Will it get darker, she gets older?'

'Where she come from, then?'

Violet stayed where she was, not hurrying away, answering questions pleasantly enough, letting them stare a little, while the baby, unsmiling, turned her face away.

A voice inside Violet seemed to be giving her advice. Hold your head up, said this inner voice. Be bold. Do nothing hole-and-corner. Let them stare; and they will stop staring all the sooner.

All the same she was shaking a little when finally she climbed up the trio of slanting stone steps to the cottage backing right against the harbour wall.

'Here we are!' She unlocked the door, closed it behind them, and carried the child inside, across the room to the small far window. She sat down on the little painted window seat and looked out, drawing a long sigh of relief. A few small skiffs still bobbed in the harbour. Once she had sat thus with her own baby Ruth on her lap, just so, all those years ago, when Bert Givens had been alive, when her own husband had been alive, and her son in little breeches, a lifetime ago that felt like yesterday.

'I see the sea, and the sea sees *me*!' chanted Ruth, in Violet's memory.

'Look at the boats, Grace!' It seemed to Violet that the baby made no response at all, just dully saw whatever was in front of her, without a single spark of understanding.

Left behind because she was lacking, Bea had

said. Not the other way about.

A knock at the door startled her. But when Violet, sliding the child on to her hip, went to open it, there was no one there. Had someone knocked and run? What sort of silly game was that? Neighbours'll have a deal to say, Matron had said. There was other little girls be less trouble.

Then Violet looked down, and saw that whoever had knocked seemed to have left something on the doorstep, a bundle. She poked it with one foot, then slowly stooped and picked it up, worn blue cloth knotted together with something soft padded inside. She took it and closed the door again, noticing as she did so the little basket bed Bea had borrowed from a neighbour, set nicely made-up ready in a corner. Would the child consent to lie in it?

She checked her, found her dry enough, and laid her down at last. It was the first time she had let the child go, since taking her in her arms in the Home that afternoon, since kidnapping her. Violet tucked the flannel sheet well in, suddenly aware of how much her arms ached. The baby at once shut her eyes, and appeared to sleep.

There was something unnerving about this instant compliance. Ruth at a similar age would have protested, or just climbed out again, laughing.

Violet stood up, her insides all fluttering with panic once more. She had been so sure that there was nothing really wrong, that sickness and abandonment, poor mite, were enough to account for the baby's limp inertia. But suppose after all she was wrong? She thought of the child's hand reaching out to hold her lapel. Wasn't that a sign in itself?

Was it enough, though? Had she not held on to the tape of her own nightdress with just the same empty concentration?

She busied herself, putting a match to the fire, setting out her things upstairs in the bedroom, checking the larder, finding a new loaf in the bread crock, butter and milk and a basket of eggs on the stone slab in the lean-to, flour, potatoes, a jar of rice. Neighbours: they would call. Those not brass-necked enough to approach her straight away in the street would all of them arrive on the front step sooner or later, partly for the traditional amusement of seeing Bea Givens' face on someone else, but mainly for the new far-more thrilling sight of the negro child.

Coming back into the main room she saw the bundle, and knelt to open it. There was a little pile inside, of clothes. One by one Violet held them up to the light: a little knitted jacket, worked in complex local stitching, in thick creamy double-knit, two pairs of black knitted stockings, well-darned but with plenty of wear left in them, two small flannel vests that tied together with little tapes of binding, three soft well-boiled squares of flannel napkins, and a further square of the tough cambric that would hold a sodden napkin well in place overnight. A hoard of well-used but well-made well-kept items, left privately, for no payment, not even thanks.

Violet sent thanks anyway, in the right

57

direction; it was well to remember, she told herself, He who had directed her steps this far. If some neighbours had a deal to say, He was perhaps reminding her, there would be others leaving kindly gifts.

A coddled egg, now. Bread and butter. Tea for herself. She checked the fire, and set the kettle in place. A week here; a holiday, perhaps, but full of dutiful purpose. She would take the child every day to the sea, to the new tide, and they would breathe in the strengthening air. She would feed the baby three proper meals a day, she would do the sewing, all Bea's mending sure enough, but also the summer blouse of her own she meant to turn into a Sunday-best dress for the baby. If neighbours had a deal to say, Violet thought, as she slipped her apron on, they would say it all the more quietly, all the more uncertainly, if the child was neatly dressed, and properly cared for.

There was a sudden creaking movement from the basket bed on the floor. The child was awake, and turning herself about. It was a laborious process, as if sickness had returned her to infancy. Pulling on the basket's stiff handles, she managed at last to sit up, and looked dully about her. Then she saw Violet. For a moment they gazed at one another, Violet unconsciously smiling, instinctively still, the child's face registering the merest flicker, as of doubt.

'You awake now, lovely?' Violet breathed at last.

At the sound of her voice the child's lips parted, her eyes widened, and there at last, suddenly, was the first glorious transfiguring smile, her face as if lit from within. She let go of the handles, and urgently held out both her arms.

'Hello, my Grace,' said Violet, and bent at once to enfold her.

*   *   *

She began to stand at the end of their second day in the cottage, hauling herself upright by pulling on anything handy, the edge of the armchair by the fire, the coal scuttle, the tablecloth, though luckily Violet had just that moment cleared the china. She slept a great deal, in the basket bed by day, in Violet's arms at night, the bed crackling with carefully laid newspapers and the trusty special-bag mackintosh. Every night, sometimes more than once, she woke screaming. Often it was a minute or two before Violet could fully awaken her. But apart from that she barely made a sound. She ate little, quickly losing interest after the first few bites.

But by day she began to seem less languid. Every morning after their breakfast porridge they went down to the beach and sat upon the rocks there, taking the air and watching the boats.

'Morning, Mrs Dimond. How's the little maid doing then, she thriving? Hello there, Missy!' Villagers sometimes joined them; most often, thought Violet, those with nothing better to do.

On the fourth day one of Bea's less respectable acquaintances, a woman known locally as Old Bet, arrived at the cottage, as most of the village had by then, for a good look and a gossip. Old Bet smelt strongly of unwashed clothes and something even more acrid, which Violet suspected to be drink. Her hair hung in grizzled grey hanks about her face, some of her front teeth were missing, and several ancient blackheads lay deeply buried on the gnarled bridge of her nose. But she brought gifts.

'These do fer the cheel?'

From beneath her arm Old Bet drew something wrapped in newspaper, which turned out to be a pair of worn but still serviceable small brown leather boots.

'They'm from my old Missus over to the Hall,' said Old Bet. 'She give 'em to my daughter.'

'From Wooton Hall?' Violet was startled. Wooton Hall, where Old Bet's daughter worked as a kitchen maid, was on the other side of Silkhampton. But there are trains every day, Violet remembered. Word would get out, and nowadays word could travel very fast.

'Quality,' said Old Bet, fingering the leather. Violet picked one up. It was true, the boot was softer than it looked, and beautifully stitched, and laced with darker brown ribbon.

'Look, Gracie. Shall we see if they fit?'

Grace, who had been sitting as usual very still on Violet's lap, now made a strange movement, a rocking forward. Why, thought Violet with a little stroke of excitement, was the child *taking notice*?

She picked up the boot and opened it, pulling the ribbon laces apart, and held it for Grace to slide in her little stockinged foot. It seemed, by

60

chance, almost a perfect fit; perhaps a little large, thought Violet, pressing the rounded toe to feel the baby's own toes beneath. She slid the other one on, drew the laces together, and tied two large bows.

'Stand up, then!'

She slid Grace down the valley of her skirt to the floor. 'There! How do they feel? Do they hurt anywhere?'

The child made no answer, but stood gazing raptly down at the boots. They looked outsized, thought Violet, on her poor skinny little legs.

'What d'you reckon then, Gracie? Give 'em a try, eh?'

Gracie walked. She kept her eyes on the boots, carefully placing them, one by one, over to the window and then, turning, all the way right across the room towards the door.

Violet could not quite contain herself. 'But she ain't walked at all before!' Old Bet clapped her hands, pleased as Punch. At the door Gracie turned, and gave her adopted mother a huge smile of triumph.

'Why, Gracie Dimond!' Violet patted her lap, and Grace for a moment hesitated, as if gathering herself together, then half-ran stumblingly back again, throwing herself into Violet's arms with a sound that could almost have been a laugh.

'The difference those boots made to that child!' Violet told Bea afterwards. They brought all sorts of firsts: first walk, first run, first walk to the beach just holding Violet's hand, first walking on the harbour wall.

First hint of playfulness: while Violet was getting tea ready that afternoon, Grace held on to the table leg, stamping each boot in turn, and Violet had a sudden vivid memory of her son as a very little boy in St George's Silkhampton one weekday morning years ago, when it was all hers to sweep clean; he had climbed up into the gallery and raced about there, hammering his feet on the wooden floor.

She had scolded him. 'Hey, you stop that right now! Where d'you think you are?'

Ah, and Bea had been there too, on one of her rare visits, and had of course not hesitated to stick her oar in.

'Oh, leave off — there ain't no one here, unless you count the Lord, and He's got a soft spot for littluns.'

'What would you know about the Lord?' Violet had answered angrily; forgetting herself, forgetting where she was. Bea always knowing best!

Bea had shrugged. 'If he rackets about now, be easier for him come Sunday.'

'And what would *you* know about children?'

Well, thought Violet now, remembering this with a qualm, I wasn't to know, was I? No child of mine was going to riot in God's own house; why hadn't she told me straight off she'd just miscarried again?

All the same some vague impulse of contrition now made her lift Grace up, and set her on the painted wooden window seat, and give her an encouraging nod.

'Go on, then!'

The child stamped; the hollow seat sounded a

satisfying thud. Now there could be no mistake about her chuckle of delight. She drummed both feet as hard as she could.

'Gracie Dimond, what a shocking noise!'

And later still came the first normal tears, at bedtime, when Violet took the boots off, and Grace set up a healthy wailing like any other little child.

'You can't wear 'em to bed, Gracie!'

Finally Violet had to wrap the boots in a bit of clean flannel, and set them beside Grace in the basket bed, so that she could go to sleep still embracing them. When she carried the baby upstairs later on, when she went to bed herself, Violet was careful to take the boots as well, so that she would feel and see them straight away when she woke in the night.

But that was also the first night Grace had slept all through. In the morning she sat up almost as cheerful and bright-eyed as any other little girl, Violet told herself, and later, the boots back on her feet, ate all her porridge; and instead of languidly letting Violet hold the cup to her lips, she took it up herself, and drank all her milk without spilling a drop.

'Ain't you a clever girl!'

★ ★ ★

That was the morning they both walked nearly all the way up to the top of the hill, taking it slowly, stopping in the vantage points as if they were the rich folk come to do their painting, calling in at one or two shops and the houses of those of Bea's neighbours Violet was completely sure about.

In all these places Grace was stared at, of course. But they would stare at any stranger, Violet reminded herself. They had stared just so at Bea all those years ago, when she had first come as a bride, they had snubbed and ignored her for being foreign, for coming from the town. Though being Bea she had soon enough given them better reasons, thought Violet. And they had boggled all over again when she had first turned up herself, for a visit, by chance wearing a straw hat with a rosebud tucked into the ribbon, exactly the same as Bea's own.

On the way back down again though there was some proper unkindness. Or proper stupidity, more like, thought Violet. Two or three half-grown boys followed them down the street.

'You got a monkey there.'

'You got a coon!'

'Monkey in a bonnet, ha! Monkey in a bonnet!'

It had been a few minutes before Violet had understood what they were saying, and why. The face she had turned on them had been more puzzled than angry.

'What you talking about, monkeys? Ain't you seen a little girl before? Something wrong with your eyes, is there?'

'That's a black girl,' said the biggest one stoutly, though he took a step back.

'I'd noticed,' said Violet. 'This here's Grace; she's my own. And less of a monkey than you are, Billy Danfield. Judging by your ears.'

64

Afterwards Violet had been a little ashamed of this. It had been so much the sort of thing Bea would have said. Still it seemed to have worked. Though they knew who she was, she thought, as she unbuttoned Gracie's knitted jacket back at the cottage; and where she was staying. Neighbours'll have a deal to say. Stones to throw too, perhaps.

'They'll get used to you. Won't they, my lovely? Soon enough. And they'll have me to deal with first.'

That evening she gave Gracie a soft-boiled egg shelled into a cup, which she ate in its entirety, dipping into it with her bread and butter. By then she could sit up properly on the other chair drawn up to the table, Bea's sewing box taking her just high enough to reach her plate.

She must learn her manners, thought Violet anxiously, watching her, for the same reason that she must look taken-care-of. There should be no room for those who want to call her names. Not when there are those ready to call her names anyway.

'When we go home,' said Violet, 'we'll see if you can walk all the way to the railway station, shall we? Going on a train soon, Gracie! You'll like that.'

Grace put the empty cup down. Her small face was smeared with egg and butter. She looked steadily at Violet, seeming to consider her words. Then she nodded, her delicate eyebrows raised.

'Train; chuffa chuffa!' said Grace, and she smiled.

4

Violet was used to a certain amount of public attention. While she had never enjoyed the frank looks and cat-calls a certain sort of young man had given her in the old days, and hurried along avoiding all eyes (unlike her sister Beatrice, who had gone in for looking right back, and even answering, sometimes), for years now Violet had been pleasantly accustomed to respectful greetings. Wives made sure to acknowledge her in the street, and she was used to a certain cap-doffing and forelock-touching deference from their husbands, often labouring men otherwise very rough in their manners.

For she was Mrs Dimond, the parish's best handy-woman. There were several others, of course, in a place the size of Silkhampton, but everyone knew that Ma Higden, though competent, was sometimes the worse for drink, and that Mrs Trewith's legs were so bad that she could manage only her closer neighbours.

But by now anyone in Silkhampton of the poorer class, aged thirty-five or under, stood a fair chance of having been seen into the world by Violet Dimond. On any street at any one time there might be two or three people she had once wrapped in flannel warmed at her bosom; most often these days she attended the childbeds of women she had herself delivered. Sometimes all the children gathered together for a summer's evening play out on the street were Violet's, though most local children tended to fall silent at the sight of her.

She was Mrs Dimond, urgently sent for in the middle of the night, ready to practise the arcane behind closed doors, in possession of the grisliest secrets of the hidden adult world; sent for, sometimes, in resignation, in grief; for apart from the unspoken horrors of birth, Mrs Dimond was also the woman you went to after a death. Everyone knew she made no charge for laying-out. So far there had been several whose first and last human touch had been from Violet Dimond's practised hands.

In short Violet had status in Silkhampton, even a mystique, so the first journey back from the station carrying Grace in her arms was an unpleasant surprise. Though it was the time of day when honest folk were working, a large number of idlers seemed to throng the meaner streets about the railway yard, hanging about on corners and leaning out of windows the better to stare at her as she passed. The sudden smack of these hard glances reminded her uncomfortably of the long-ago ribald young men; one or two were clearly minded to break off whatever they had been doing and follow after her for another look. A set of shrill and dirty little boys who should have been at school set off after her as well, two of them racing ahead to get in front of her, and bobbing along backwards in the road. She was spoken to without ceremony, even rudely:

'What you got there, Missus?'

'That a darkie? That's a darkie, ain't it? Where d'you get'un?'

'Hey, Mrs Dimond!'

Violet made no reply, though she treated one particularly noisy and importunate urchin to a brief pale-grey basilisk stare of her own, after which he slunk away. Don't hurry, said the inner voice she had heard before, when first arriving at Bea's village. Don't hurry, and don't look down.

It was hard to say what sort of luck it was that Gracie chose this moment to awake. The long walk up the hill to the station had exhausted her, and she had fallen deeply asleep as soon as the train was fairly started. Now she wriggled in Violet's arms, pulled herself upright and peeped over Violet's shoulder at the dirty little boys, at the dozen or so folk ambling along in the mud of the street behind her.

There was an immediate response, a quick increase in crowd-noise, a leap of satisfaction, as if by looking back at them Grace had somehow performed. Violet held her all the tighter, and walked on without looking back. The temper of the crowd, she told herself, was not necessarily malevolent; they had just been seizing on something new to look at. Though of course such neutrality might change on an instant. It would be her task, she thought, to work out beforehand why such an instant might arise.

The gathering fell back as Violet left the rougher streets behind. Now there were just passers-by startling, taking second glances, and elbowing one another.

'Missus,' said someone, touching his hat. He

68

stopped, and so did Violet. Mr Crowhurst, who worked in Fuller's shoe shop. Cobbler, and father of two, one very recent; both Mrs Dimond's.

Violet nodded, a little taken aback. He would never normally stop her in the street. 'Morning, Mr Crowhurst. Mrs Crowhurst well?'

Mr Crowhurst was quite a young man, his face pale and greasy beneath his hard round hat. He made her no answer, but cried, 'Well I never! What you got there?' his tone jocose, familiar.

Violet paused, to let him know what she thought of him.

'This here's Gracie, from the orphanage,' she said coolly, 'come to stay with me for a bit.' The last few words gave her a slight pang, for she knew they were a lie. But it had occurred to her that a certain vagueness, where Grace was concerned, might be all to the good. If folk assumed she was here only temporarily, they would be less inclined to fuss, and by the time they knew she was here to stay, why, they might not bother to at all. The lie was giving them time to behave themselves.

'Well well,' said Mr Crowhurst now, abashed, and stumbling a little over his words, 'I'll bid you good day then, Missus.' He made off, but Violet was almost immediately stopped again.

'Good morning, Mrs Dimond, and oh my goodness me, what's this?'

'This here is Grace, as I'm taking in for a little while. Say hello, Gracie, to Mrs Thornby.'

Eleanor Thornby was not local, but had come from the next county as a girl, and married Ned

69

Thornby in the days when Thornby's on the square had been a perfectly serviceable draper's. Now Thornby & Son had expanded next door, and on to upper floors, and begun calling itself a department store. Over the years Mrs Thornby too had acquired a certain double-fronted splendour. She was active on several local Ladies' Committees, with the likes of Mrs Caterham, or Mrs Grant-Fellowes; was known to have taken tea at Wooton Hall. Her children, of course, were not Mrs Dimond's, but had been delivered in the nursing home, by Dr Summers himself.

'D'you talk?' said Mrs Thornby now, to Grace, who made no reply, except to look soberly back at her. 'What big eyes!' said Mrs Thornby, 'though I suppose they always *do* look big, don't they! Contrast, you know,' she told Violet. She turned back to the baby, leant closer: 'Shy, are we? Eh?'

But the child's attention was caught, Violet saw too late, by the big curling feather on Mrs Thornby's great hat, and before Violet could stop her she had reached up and made as if to grab at it. Mrs Thornby stepped back smartly with a little cry.

'Oh — isn't it quick!'

Instantly Grace set up a furious wailing, frightened at Violet's sudden movement, deprived too of the beautiful softness of the feather, which had so called to her hand, begging to be stroked. Violet mouthed her apologies and escaped over the noise. She felt panicky; something in Mrs Thornby's tone had undone her. There had been nothing tentative about Mrs Thornby; her interest had been so straightforward, so guileless: a

70

good-humoured woman at the zoo, tempted to take a stick and give the exotic creature behind the bars a gentle ladylike prod.

They will get used to her, Violet told herself, as she carried the still-sobbing Grace through the narrow alley, to the safety of her own back door at last.

I will get used to this.

★　★　★

Inside Grace fell silent, and put one finger in her mouth, looking about her. Violet set her down, arms aching.

'There! This is home, Gracie.' For a minute or so Violet watched her, standing still in the middle of the room. She thought piercingly of her daughter Ruth, the last little girl to stand just so. There seemed no likeness at all today; strange how fleeting it was, coming and going day by day. Violet remembered Him who had led her this far, and sent up a quick prayer for strength.

'This here's the fire, which I must light right off, if we're to get any dinner. What d'you say to fire, now, Gracie?'

'Hot!'

'That's right. Very hot. You stand right away there, then. That's a good girl. Just a minute . . . '

Violet set going the fire she had left ready-laid in the range, realizing as she did so that for the moment there could be no more popping out to the shops on minor errands. Not on her own, anyway. She would have to take Grace too, even to childbeds, and wherever they went — well, it would be non-stop, she thought, for a while.

'Not that I'm anyone to talk,' she said to Grace, as she went to find her shopping basket. For hadn't it taken her a little while herself, to stop seeing the child's strangeness?

'Now then, what am I after?' Violet asked herself aloud, as usual when she was getting ready to go out; but this time she heard herself, and understood for the first time that she was no longer alone in the house, that from now on there was someone to talk to, someone who would hear and answer. It seemed to her then that despite making an honest living, despite letters from her dear son Bobby, despite church and the bible-reading group and the sewing circle, despite the market and friends and acquaintances in the street, despite all these riches, that without ever knowing it she had been drowning in loneliness for the last fifteen years.

In the front room Grace had clambered on to a chair so that she could look out of the window. 'Not much to see that way,' Violet told her. 'We got the garden t'other side.' She saw herself taking Grace's hand and showing her all the different beds and the henhouse and the apple and cherry trees Mr Dimond had so neatly espaliered along the sunniest wall, saw herself teaching her new daughter all she had missed teaching Ruth, and her heart filled with painful happiness.

Grace meanwhile had slid down to turn her attention to the basket, which was a handsome one, fairly new and trimmed with fancy plaiting all around the edge. She bent to put one arm through its long leather handles, but she was so little that when she stood up the basket was still resting on the floor.

Violet laughed, and Grace at once took her arm out of the handles, bent to carefully put it back again, and, with a quick check to make sure Violet was still watching, straightened up again. Once again the basket stayed put. The face she turned to Violet now was all mock bafflement: why, the child was joking with her, Violet saw, trying to make her laugh again; and her near death not four weeks past! She could hardly speak for smiling.

'Come market day, we'll see if we can't find you a basket all for your own, shall we?'

'Littlun?' said Grace. 'Little basket?'

It was her first sentence, first question.

'That's right, my lady,' said Violet, sweeping her up, basket and all. 'Little basket for a little madam.' She kissed Grace's cheek, and they went outside.

5

Over the next few weeks Violet grew very tired indeed of making the same replies to the same questions, put to her over and over again by what seemed to be an infinite number of people, some of them downright strangers. Never you mind, she was sometimes tempted to reply rudely, to some further shameless piece of nosey-parkering. But the inner voice warned her to treat all curiosity as benign.

'This is Grace. Say How Do to Mrs Gundry . . . '

To Mrs Warne, to Mr Pender, to Rose Whitely, to deaf old Marjorie Skewes from upstairs.

To the Reverend Mr Godolphin. Who actually came calling, simply opened the back garden gate one morning, and stood there turning his hat in his hands.

'Why, vicar!' exclaimed Violet, in surprise. She had been sowing runner beans, much impeded by Grace, to whom she had finally given the smallest trowel, and who was now haphazardly applying it over by last year's potato patch, where she could do least harm.

Violet stood up, aware of her muddy hands and rough sacking apron, and then of Gracie's earth-flecked hair and stained pinafore.

Perhaps she made some gesture indicating this; at any rate Mr Godolphin at once spoke, all smiles: 'Quite alright, quite alright, just passing, thought I'd call upon the young lady I've been hearing so much about, and there *is* the young person, good morning, there!'

Mr Godolphin prided himself on his ability to put his lowlier parishioners at their ease. However, like many local men, gentry or otherwise, he was, though not fully aware of it, a little afraid of Mrs Dimond, afraid and embarrassed: constantly aware at some level of how she earned her living, that she had seen things best left unwitnessed, and that she was actively involved in all kinds of grotesque and dangerous female activities. There was about her too a certain quality of watchfulness, that made him uneasy; and she was less inclined to smile at him than other women.

She was more clearly suspect too, for her Methodistical leanings, the Bible group, the refusal to take Communion; on the other hand she came to church twice every single Sunday, and her unusual authority in the area surely encouraged other less determined souls, thought Mr Godolphin, to keep up their own attendance.

'Come and say good morning to Mr Godolphin, Gracie! No, not in your mouth, not till we wash your hands! Sorry, Vicar.'

'Not at all, not at all, charming! Yes . . . yes.'

His tone, though, held a certain speculative edge.

There was a pause. Had he been an equal, Violet would have spoken: What? What's the matter? As it was she stood in silence, and waited.

'Though there have, ah, been comments.

75

Comments made. To me. About the, ah, about our young friend here.'

'Oh yes?' Violet's heart gave a zestful thud of anticipatory anger, though outwardly she went on calmly watching Grace back at work on the hole in last year's potato patch.

'Some feel,' said Mr Godolphin carefully, 'that Grace is perhaps a little young for St George's.'

This was nonsense, and they both knew it. Small children came to church and when they yelled were taken out and hushed in the porch, or taken home if there was no help for it; when they were old enough they might attend the Sunday school; but Grace, after sitting in puzzled silence through the first half of her first Sunday morning service, had fallen asleep during the sermon, and made no sound when awoken for the final hymn, a pattern she had luckily repeated the following week.

It was simply a way out; one Violet was not at all ready to take. The words jumped into her mouth: 'A little young?' she asked. 'Or d'you mean a little dark?'

Mr Godolphin bit his lip. 'I'm afraid there are some who feel,' he said slowly, 'that your, ah, charge has no place in St George's.'

'Why's that then?' said Violet, determined to make him say it, determined that he say the words, so that he himself would hear them on the air, and know how he shamed his cloth.

He was silent. For himself, he had thought Grace utterly delightful. Like many he had never seen a negro person before, not in the flesh. Grace, introduced to him after the first service, had smiled at him, and hidden her face in Mrs Dimond's skirts, as shy and pretty as any little child he'd seen; but Samuel Pearce, his own verger, and Mrs Restarick, who was so active in church matters and who had personally funded the installation of the radiators, had each separately come to see him in order to explain their misgivings as to the continued presence in St George's of the 'unfortunate creature' (said Mr Pearce) so inexplicably being carted about by that hitherto perfectly worthy Mrs Dimond, who had ('kindest way of looking at it', said Mrs Restarick) just gone completely off her head. One or two other rougher parishioners had been more forthright, and asked him indignantly why he was allowing an animal in church, and told him that if he went on doing it they would find a church more fit for clean respectable Christian Englishmen. And women.

'Well, now,' said Violet, watching him. It was perhaps a question of numbers, she thought. If he's had complaints, how many? Is he counting all the ones that stayed silent? Which way would the silent ones go?

'I thought perhaps we might compromise,' said Mr Godolphin at last. 'I wondered if you might consider coming to the earlier service.'

'Won't there be folk at the early one, then, who reckon Gracie's *too young*?'

The true answer to this was, that there well might be. But it was a small enough congregation at nine in the morning. And all of them happened to be the sort of people Mr Godolphin felt pretty sure of being able to talk round, or even firmly squash, should need arise.

'And what about Evensong?' said Violet, before he could come up with a presentable version of this. 'Are we allowed at Evensong?'

'My dear Mrs Dimond, please, it's not a question of allowing, or not allowing — '

Violet's face said: isn't it?

'It's simply a matter of trying to do our best in a, in a far from perfect world. I myself welcome your, your charitable act. Applaud it. But — ' and he gave a little entreating shrug, palms spread — 'we must make allowances — in our hearts, Mrs Dimond — for those as yet unready to do so.'

Why's that, then?

'It's my duty to welcome all to God's house, to His own house here at St George's. How can I allow the arrival of one new parishioner to dishearten and displace others?'

Violet folded her arms. They said: coward.

'And I shall continue to pray, Mrs Dimond, for Grace to receive a proper loving Christian welcome from all our parishioners; I feel sure that time is all that is required; which is why I have come to ask you to consider this — I agree — unusual proposal of mine.'

Inwardly he was running through the usual (again rather thinly sprinkled) Evensong crowd: Mr Pearce once in a blue moon, the Restaricks hardly ever, except at Christmas, of course. The rougher sort never.

'I think Evensong will be alright,' he added, and at last fell silent.

Violet raised her eyebrows. They said: think?

'I should very much like,' said Mr Godolphin, 'to see you and Grace at Evensong. Every week.'

Violet nodded. Presently he took his leave, and as he closed the gate behind him she saw that he felt he'd managed the little difficulty rather well. In her heart she marked him down. He was no Good Samaritan; if he'd seen the wounded traveller in the parable, he would have passed on by, oh, regretfully, no doubt, with just that little heave of his shoulders, those spreading helpless palms. Oh, if only I could help you, dear me, what a pity!

Whited sepulchre, thought Violet with pleasurable scorn, for she had never had much time for vicars in the first place.

Dr Summers was a different matter. Would he busy himself bending to the mean silliness of others? Would he ask her the usual nosey-parkering questions? It was painful to think that he might. He was more important to her than Mr Godolphin; for one thing, he was her bread and butter. They had (as Violet put it) been working together now for upwards of thirty years.

Dr Summers took on the ladies, or at least, any woman who could meet his full private obstetrical fee. For the less well-off but provident there were trades unions and savings clubs and local insurance schemes, backed up by the Council, while the poorest of all, the improvident, the destitute, who hadn't so much as a spare ha'penny to pay anyone anything at all, let alone any savings, relied on his charity, and on that of the hospital he visited.

79

The fact was that Dr Summers attended only the childbeds of those who directly paid him his full fee. He generally stayed away completely from all the others, who were then charged a much lower fee in order to keep him and his expensive qualifications safe in bed at night, though if anything seemed to be going wrong, of course, Mrs Dimond was free to call him; that was their arrangement.

Dr Summers did the paperwork, and collected the much lower fees; Mrs Dimond did the deliveries, and was paid whatever the household could manage, a sum that varied from several shillings to nothing at all, or goods in lieu, some useful bit of carpentry or boot-repair or basketful of plums. None of this seemed at all unfair to Violet: Dr Summers was the one with all the learning, and though she had called him rarely over the years he had always come promptly. More than once he had taken a woman into the cottage hospital, and delivered a living child when Violet had thought all was lost; she had watched him insert his forceps, and knew that he had a gentle hand, that matched his gentle manner.

★ ★ ★

'Well, now, what have we here?' Dr Summers got up from behind his desk, and walked round it to meet them. 'We meet at last, hello, young lady. I've heard all about you!'

'This is her; this is Grace. Doing well, sir, thank you; but I was thinking maybe you'd take

80

a quick look at her, sir, if you'd be so good.'

He was a faded man, once gingery, now a rusted brown.

'Do sit down then, Mrs Dimond, will you, and take her on your lap, that's it, now then, Miss Grace, if I might have a quick listen to your lungs, young lady, if you please, just pull the blouse up a little, will you, Mrs Dimond, good, deep breath now . . . thank you . . . good. Cough pretty well settled now? Yes?'

When he had finished examining Grace he leant back against his desk.

'I did write to my colleague, you remember, Dr Jefferson, who saw her in Exeter. But I'm afraid there are no further details to give you. I gather the lodging house was down by the docks there, and that the woman involved — the, ah, you know the one I mean — was in employment, you know, fish-packing, that sort of thing. There doesn't seem to have been any husband on the scene. No papers of any kind, I'm afraid. Nothing to go on at all.'

'She ain't got no certificates,' said Violet, who was in fact unsure how much certificates mattered. She had few herself; but then she wasn't just starting out in life.

'Well — how old do you think she is?'

'I'm seven,' said Grace suddenly, and the grown-ups laughed.

'That's our door number, Gracie! What do you think, Doctor?'

'How many teeth have we got, Mrs Dimond? Open up, please, Miss Gracie, that's it, wide as wide, show me your breakfast . . . ah . . . let's say, two and three-quarters, and it's what, June, so that's, well, that's somewhere in September, 1900. The turn of the century, no less. She can have my birthday if you like — that's the ninth. What d'you say, Miss Gracie, shall we share birthdays?'

It occurred to Violet when she was home again that he had not mentioned Grace's colour at all; nor had he refrained from mentioning it, as if out of politeness, as some so clearly did, which was often just as awkward. He had behaved as if there had been nothing unusual to notice or pretend not to notice; just seen another little girl.

Violet marked him up.

6

Bea arrived, uninvited, for a visit. She brought with her a pillowcase stuffed with old skirt lengths, and was weighed down on the other side by her sewing-machine.

'You needn't a bothered,' said Violet stiffly, seeing it. 'I run her up a coupla dresses.'

'So I see,' said Bea.

It was typical of Bea, thought Violet, that the only thing she had always taken seriously was *frocks*.

'I ain't run up a dress in my life,' said Bea, 'and I ain't starting now.' She had a proper tape measure, and real French chalk, and cut out a paper pattern from newspaper, and held it up against Grace's back, and made no end of fuss, thought Violet. Neglects her own mending, but if there's ever a chance of something *showy* —

'She'll grow into this, come winter,' said Bea. The coat was to be of a soft dark blue plaid, with a matching muff on a length of silken cord, to go about her neck.

'Look at this, for the lining! Sky blue!'

'I'd a thought you'd have enough a sewing,' said Violet, 'all them poor tykes.'

'Nice change get away from grey flannel,' said Bea, sucking thread. 'Make something proper, like. Here,' she said to Grace, 'you have a look at these!' and she took up her button-tin, gave it a rattle, and held it out for her.

Violet felt all her most ancient fears rise within her: sitting there at her own table by her own window, enticing her own child, was another, who was still, somehow, herself. The familiar suspicion that she was outside her own body looking at herself came back to her, unnerving as ever, and with it the old anxiety that her sister was not only another version of her self, but a better, more successful one. Why, folk had always liked Beatrice more than they had liked Violet, straight off, from when they were the size Grace was now, even their mother had favoured her! Bea always laughing and shouting and carrying on, blowing her own trumpet, making sure she always came first, you could be sure of that!

'I ain't stopping long,' said Bea, sidelong from the sewing machine.

As if wearing her face wasn't bad enough, Bea must listen in to her thoughts as well! For a moment Violet was tempted to rush over and commit the old strange act of slapping her own cheek; at which Bea let go the little wheel, and sat back, and looked straight up at her.

Violet heard the thought as if it had been spoken: We're past all that. She nodded slightly, to show that she had understood. Then Bea turned back to her sewing, and Violet, ashamed, went out to her onion bed to dig herself into a better frame of mind.

The truth was that Bea had seen the world, and Violet had not. Violet had stayed in the town where she was born and worked hard, and tried to live a sober Godfearing life; and yet these solid virtues always seemed diminished in the presence of Beatrice.

Bea had never really been interested in learning their mother's skills. At first, growing up, they had fought to accompany her, taking it in strict turns to carry the special bag, sit up all night with some labouring woman's older children, go in at last to help with the delivery, to watch and remember.

But: 'You go,' said Bea one night, when it was certainly her turn. She'd rather finish trimming her new petticoat, she said; and that was that. They were thirteen. 'I ain't cut out for it,' she said later. 'I ain't got the patience, all that blessed waiting about. And I'd as soon touch a toad as another dead Christian.'

And yet their mother had not reproached her, had helped instead to find her other work, first in kitchen service at the vicarage, where she had complained a great deal about having to get up at five, and then as an under-housemaid over at Wooton Hall, where her skilled refurbishment of an outworn dress given to her by the housekeeper attracted first the attention of one of the growing daughters of the house, and then of the lady; a year or two later, installed as the daughters' own maid, Bea went with the family to London for the winter, and lived there, and saw London town, and helped the young ladies get ready for all sorts of parties and balls, and sat up at nights sewing and tearing apart and re-sewing and cutting and basting.

Nearly three years of this adventure; she was carried abroad, even, visiting Paris, and staying with Miss Daphne and her cousin at Nice. She had been there when their mother died suddenly, of heart disease.

Then there had been some falling-out with the young ladies, the nature of which Violet had never discovered, but Bea had come back to England too late for the funeral, announced that she had had more than enough of service and fancied a bit of a change, and taken a job Violet hated to remember even now, serving *drink* to all sorts of *men*, in a public *bar*, of all places, a haunt of low sin and wickedness, though she had, naturally, soon had the luck to encounter handsome Bert Givens there, and he had turned out steady enough, for all his blue eyes.

Of course it was a shame that none of their babies had lived beyond a few days. But Bea had turned her hand elsewhere, taken on the old four-ale Red Lion just up from the harbour, and by slow degrees extended the licence, modernized the kitchen, made a new separate entrance for the refurbished saloon bar, turned upper storerooms one by one into bedrooms, all (thought Violet) pretty enough in their slapdash finery, and finally advertised the Red Lion Hotel — Sea Views, Every Modern Convenience — in several London newspapers. Then the place was full, from May to November, while less-well-heeled locals were made welcome all year round in the tap, and Bea by some accounts had made a fortune, which accounted for the lease on the cottage by the harbour wall.

But it had accounted too, some said, for the fine and, as it turned out, under-insured new boat that had drowned Bert Givens along with his three-man crew, so (almost-thought Violet, for such ideas were too mean and self-serving to be fully aware of) much of the pain of Bea's worldly success had been pretty well cancelled out.

A lifetime of balancing, thought Violet now, almost consciously, as she hauled up the shovel, first Bea wins, then I do, then she does, and all the time I'm working out who has won, and who has lost, and her thought was right that she sent me, we are past all that, she is past all that, and I must try to be past all that too, for Grace's sake, and for my own soul's sake, Amen.

Here her thoughts surfaced, and presently Violet prayed aloud under her breath as she turned the crumbly earth, begging for forgiveness and for the strength to rise above her own smallnesses and jealousy.

When she went in again though, to see about some dinner, Bea had Grace on her lap, letting her turn the handle of the sewing machine. It gave Violet a fearful pang; it was instantly obvious to her that she could never hope to compete, that Grace would remember Bea now, and ask when she was coming again, and talk longingly about her, and miss her. It was a second or two before Violet could see the sewing machine as a divine test she was already in danger of failing.

Help me, Lord, thought Violet, and went to put the kettle on without another word.

* * *

The following week Violet took Grace to the market, Gracie wearing one of the dresses Bea had made for her, a dark blue cotton with a little red and white gingham at the collar and cuffs, and looking, Violet thought, as pretty as a picture, though she had not of course said so, for fear of making the child vain; especially as Gracie was clearly tremendously proud of herself in this dress, and looked about her with a conscious turn of the head, all ready to be admired, it seemed to Violet.

Many in Silkhampton had met Grace now, and no longer started at the sight of her. Some petted her in a sort of luxurious sorrow, as if saddened by the thought that there was nothing to be done about so much unwonted darkness; some merely petted her; others crossed the street to avoid her. There were several, Violet had noticed, who were always somehow on the other side of the street. A few, waiting to be served in a shop, suddenly remembered something, and dashed away should Violet and Grace arrive to stand behind them; some remembered the something when they had just arrived themselves, and saw Violet already in the queue, her foster daughter at her side.

It is not all malice, Violet told herself, it is mainly unease at novelty, and this she went on firmly believing, until such times as malice was made unmistakeable.

'Some folk don't know how to behave,' she told Gracie, when she thought there was at least a chance that the child had understood some fresh slight shown her. 'Some folk ain't got no more sense than they was born with, and more shame to them.'

Mrs Warburton, for example. Passing the stone pillars of the George and Dragon's portico, they had come upon a group of mothers talking with their little ones, and as they squeezed by Violet had seen one of the women tug at her own daughter's skirt, to move her well away from Grace, lest even their clothes touch. The tug was deliberate, showy; for Violet to see, as much as for the little girl herself. Here, Violet was forced to admit, was malice proper. She made it her business to look into that mother's face, and was not surprised to find that it was that poor drab Jessie Warburton, whose children she had delivered, and whose husband drank his wages.

'Something bothering you, Mrs Warburton?'

A hesitation; taken aback. But Mrs Warburton clearly felt that right was on her side.

'Why yes, there is. What's that dirty thing doing here, you answer me that!' She grinned a little as she spoke, as if she took a nervous pleasure in her own daring.

'What dirty thing is this?' Violet kept her voice low and cool and steady, her delivery-voice, deep with authority. With all her power she willed Mrs Warburton to fear her.

'That, that dirty black,' muttered Mrs Warburton.

Violet left a pause. She felt others around her in the little crowd waiting for her to speak. They were waiting, she thought, to decide which side to be on.

'My daughter's clean as any little girl here,'

89

said Violet mildly. 'This is just another child, Mrs Warburton, and of such is the kingdom of heaven.'

Mrs Warburton's pale lips folded in at this. What could anyone say, against the Word itself?

'And thou shalt love thy neighbour as thyself, Mrs Warburton; that's a very hard one, for some.' At this Violet looked up, and caught the eye of Mrs Warburton's actual next-door neighbour Maryann Harvey, one of those standing by, and slightly raised her eyebrows. This drew a laugh, for everyone knew the Warburtons were a noisy lot, what with all the drunken shouting and carryings-on.

'Morning, Mrs Harvey. That your young Phoebe?' Now Violet simply ignored Mrs Warburton, turned aside from her. She had delivered Phoebe, of course, and a tricky feat it had been, for the baby had been a full month early, and not ready to suck. Violet had shown her how to feed the child drop by drop from a spoon. There was Phoebe, dear little thing, clearly the apple of her mother's eye. Would Phoebe's grateful mother stand by while the Warburton talked of dirtiness?

'That's my girl,' said Mrs Harvey, and turned too, shutting Mrs Warburton out. 'Say hello to Mrs Dimond, Phoebe, as saved your life! And who's this, what a pretty dress, is this Grace?'

Yes; this was grace indeed, thought Violet. If it was a little shameful to drag Him into a street argument, to indulge in religiose theatricals, how the crowd all about had heard her words, and swung towards the light! This was heaven's grace, thought Violet, that had once again swiftly lent her Bea's own wit, to banish sin where it stood.

They took their shopping home in equable silence. Grace adored her new little basket, a miniature version of Violet's; she had insisted Violet put some shopping in it, and with tremendous ceremony was carrying home a reel of cotton, two needles, and a pink sugar mouse in a paper bag. Violet carried everything else, but with a light heart. Every now and then she smiled down at the child's proud delight.

It had never before occurred to her that Divine grace might be playful.

7

The visitor came on a Tuesday afternoon, just as she had settled Grace for a nap, as the child was fretful and a little feverish; Violet was waiting for the last set of pies and meanwhile taking her mop to the kitchen floor, where she had spilt flour, when she heard the rap on her front door.

No one usually knocked there or waited for the door to be opened, so the visitor had been kept standing on the pavement for a while, since she had taken no notice of Violet calling 'twas open, but just gone on knocking until Violet had at length set the mop down and gone to open the door.

It was Mrs Thornby, the lady whose great feathered hat had so fascinated Gracie.

'Mrs Dimond, good afternoon. May I come in, please?'

Violet was too surprised to speak. She had seen Mrs Thornby often, of course, glimpsed in passing many times over the years, carrying a smart little shopping basket about in the High Street or the market, in the pew the family always used at church, with other grand ladies in the old tithe barn at Christmas time, and at fetes in summer; but hardly to speak to, yet here she was, asking to come in! Still speechless Violet stood back, so that there was room for her visitor to enter.

'Thank you,' said Mrs Thornby. *Thenk you.*

Her hat today was less splendid, though it was still large, and trimmed with much intricately folded netting. It sat very neatly on her hair, which was teased out in some way as if to accommodate its breadth. She also wore a tightly fitting blue cotton jacket trimmed with darker blue velvet ribbon, and a dark green skirt with a flounce on it, trimmed with the same velvet. To Violet she was all perfumed magnificence, which would have surprised Mrs Thornby, as that lady was on purpose for this visit wearing her oldest clothes, and had been feeling quite self-conscious standing on the pavement outside in case anyone she knew saw her there in such shabbiness.

'May I sit down?'

Violet had absolutely no turn of phrase to deal with this unprecedented situation. By and large few crossed her threshold. Callers stood upon the doorstep, and conversed there if need be. She met her own friends and family connections at church, at the Bible group, or at the market; she chatted in the street sometimes. But her circle did not practise any sort of casual dropping-in. They saw virtue in keeping themselves to themselves. Despite her own unrivalled access to other people's households — over the years there were few of the poorer streets she had not entered — Violet kept so unthinkingly to this code of privacy that she had never once revealed to anyone any detail of her patients' domestic arrangements, no matter how inadequate these might be. This was not exactly discretion; more that it had not even occurred to her that there was anything to be discreet about.

Mrs Thornby's smile went on smiling. Again she prompted: 'May I?'

Of course, do forgive me were the words she was expecting, the sort of phrase that, as people said, went without saying. On the other hand when it actually *did* go without saying, how uncomfortable was the silence while it went on not being said!

But Violet had never in her life heard anyone gracefully beg forgiveness for some slight social error. She was not even sure what it was that Mrs Thornby was asking; the possibility that she had really meant *Can I sit down* made a sensible reply even harder to formulate.

'So that we can have a little chat,' said Mrs Thornby helpfully.

All the self-possession and restraint with which Violet Dimond usually met the world, dealt with life, with death, deserted her at these sinister words. She became frightened and flustered. The pies were in the hot oven, waiting. The floor was half-wet, there was washing-up to be done, a sick child asleep in the bedroom. It did not occur to her to ask Mrs Thornby to leave, to come back if she must at some better more convenient time; she could not conceive of questioning gentry.

'Please,' she said, and Mrs Thornby, taking this as permission, first turned to take in the Tuesday afternoon disorder — the flour bag gaping open, scraps of pastry rolled into an unpromising ball in a flour-scummed bowl, dirty saucepans still sitting stacked inside each other rimmed with gravy, the flecked wet floor and carelessly set-aside bucket — then selected one of the two wooden chairs, turned it so that it backed the window, and with a certain ceremony, with the merest hint of a gentlewoman at last treated properly, subsided her skirts upon it, and sat down.

Violet waited.

For a moment more Mrs Thornby waited too, hoping that Violet would also sit down, so that the little chat would feel less like an interview. Should she, could she, ask the woman to be seated, in her own home? She decided that in all conscience she could not.

'Mrs Dimond, I am here, in my own small way, to represent His Majesty's Government,' she began, words she had been happily, if a little nervously, practising in her head for some time. At the sound of them finally in the air, being spoken, being true, she took heart.

'As I expect you know, there have recently been many changes to the law in respect to the practice of midwifery. I refer of course to the Act of 1902. I take it that you are familiar with these provisions?'

'I'm on the Roll,' said Violet, beginning to tremble. 'Bona fide.' She pronounced this *boney-fidey*, as Mrs Thornby had been warned that she might.

Mrs Thornby managed not to smile. 'Yes,' she said. 'We know. That is, partly, the problem, d'you see?'

'Dr Summers put me on the Roll. You ask him. He'll tell you,' said Violet. 'I got the letter.'

'Mrs Dimond, I have no doubt that you are at present admitted to the Roll, and therefore legally entitled to attend deliveries and to charge for your services. However, as I am sure you are aware, as an entirely unqualified person your admittance must be seen as a purely temporary measure. I feel quite sure that Dr Summers will have made these terms perfectly clear to you.'

'Yes, ma'am,' said Violet.

For to be permanent there had been a special training you had to go in for, so that you would understand the Latin that the doctors all used, and then you had to take a written examination, all of this costing, forsooth, upwards of forty pounds. Straight away Dr Summers had told Violet that he would personally advance her the money, not understanding, of course, that she would borrow from no one. Then a day or so later he had come back again and said that, having discussed the matter with Mrs Summers, who fully shared, he was pleased to say, his own very high opinion, Mrs Dimond, of her traditional experience and native skills, rather, he should be glad, indeed he should be honoured, ma'am, to pay for this training himself, if she would be kind enough to consider such an offer; what did she say to that, Mrs Dimond, hmm?

Of course it was partly that he was worried in the first place he would be called out all hours to deal with her cases, and not have so much time for the ones that paid full whack; and then any properly certified midwife would soon set herself up to rival him, and take not a fraction of his fee, as Violet did, but all of it. But it was like him, Violet thought afterwards, to ask her so gentle, as if she were a lady. To say he would be honoured.

Still, there had been nothing for it but to admit what she had thus far managed to keep entirely from him and from anyone else like him who did not absolutely need to know, which was that while she knew her numbers, and could read print well enough and sign her own name, she could write only slowly, having learnt so late in life.

'We was taught so's we could read the Book,' she had explained to Dr Summers, hoping to ease his evident discomfiture. 'We didn't *need* the writing, see?'

So she might know the answer to every question in the examination, but writing them down legibly, and in time, and in public, would be entirely beyond her. She had had to be content with temporary admission to the Roll, on Dr Summers' say-so; when the letter confirming this had arrived she had felt all the shame of it, had barely been able to bring herself to read it, but stuffed it back into its envelope and hidden it, badge of wholly inferior status, in the suitcase beneath her bed.

'Yes, ma'am,' said Violet now.

'However,' said Mrs Thornby with relish, 'I am empowered by the plenary system of the Central Midwives' Board, on the local committee of which I have the honour to serve, to visit and assess you and your standards of practice and your personal circumstances, and to make a report to that body on these matters. D'you see?'

Violet did not see at all. In a fog of bewilderment and distress she watched Mrs Thornby deftly remove her gloves fingertip by fingertip, then open the small embroidered bag on a strap round her wrist and extract from it a tiny elegant leather-bound notebook with a propelling pencil tucked into its spine in a special slender pocket. After she had opened it at the right page and smoothed it and written something down in it, she looked up with what was perhaps intended to be a reassuring smile.

'Well, now. Shall we begin? I should like first to see your record book, please.'

'You can't do that, not rightly,' said Violet.

'And what do you mean by that?' Mrs Thornby was brisk. Allow no nonsense, that was the advice she had been given. She had arrived expecting some: and here it was.

'You can't see my book,' said Violet, 'because I ain't got one.' She had no idea of being impertinent. But as she spoke she realized in baffled dismay that anyone happening to catch this exchange might well have sniggered.

Oh, sorry, that sounded rude, but it's simply the truth!

It was no more possible for Violet to say this sort of thing, or even think of saying it to gentry, than it was for her to produce a detailed written record book. She was left in wretched silence, while Mrs Thornby absorbed the unintended snub, took it to heart. Noted it down, indeed, with her nice little propelling pencil.

★ ★ ★

98

Nor had Mrs Thornby liked the special bag. When Violet had fetched it, at her request, she had shrunk back from it with a little start of horror. Nor would she take it in her hand, but Violet must describe its contents, which Mrs Thornby then checked against a list she had ready in the back of her little leather book. She had also asked who did the rough work, and how often Violet changed her bed-clothes, and whether her windows opened, and whether she considered her drains effective, and how much she drank.

It was at this stage that a strange high-pitched mewing sound came from the other room, whose door stood ajar.

Mrs Thornby looked up. 'What was that? Was that a cat?'

More curious noises followed. Violet, appalled, thought that she recognized them all too well. 'No, that's . . . that's my — '

Wailing incoherently, Grace suddenly appeared in the doorway, her face all blubbered with tears, and bringing with her as she stumbled towards them a powerful smell of vomit. Clearly she had been very sick in her sleep, for the thin yellow sourness seemed to be everywhere, in her hair, her neck and all down the front of her petticoat.

Violet, almost giddy with embarrassment, jumped up to catch hold of her, trying to steer her away from the visitor, who rose smartly, but still spoke pleasantly enough over Grace's whimpering: 'I see I have kept you from your duties long enough, Mrs Dimond. Forgive me.

No, don't trouble, please, I shall see myself out. Good day to you.'

And she was gone.

* * *

When she had finished tidying Grace, and changed the bed, and put everything in to soak, Violet remembered the pies. Eighteen steak and mushroom still in the oven! There was nothing for it but to throw the whole smoking trayful out of the back kitchen window, where they lay in a pile of sooty ruination until the birds found them next day.

'Nine shillings down the drain,' Violet told Grace. She was still in the dark about the whole visit. Why had the lady come in the first place? Mrs Thornby! Why had she taken so many notes?

'We ain't a charity case,' said Violet, puzzled. Over the next few weeks the thought of Mrs Thornby and her little propelling pencil kept coming back to her. She couldn't think why the picture made her so uneasy.

8

The months passed, slowly, quickly: Grace grew out of her beloved boots, and into the coat Bea had made her. She could still wear it the following spring, when she started Sunday school.

Violet had checked first, with Mr Godolphin.

'Oh, now, I'm not at all in charge of that. That's our admirable Miss Pyncheon's concern,' he had said at once.

'I know that, sir,' said Violet mildly. 'I was hoping maybe you'd speak to her for me. Make sure she reckons Grace ain't too young.'

She saw him hesitate, and almost felt for him. Because she knew by then that there was just no way of knowing beforehand, no matter how sensible someone usually was. Sometimes educated folk asked questions made you want to clock them one; sometimes even gentry forgot themselves, and passed by staring; then, say a few minutes later, some work-worn tough in hob-nailed boots would stop to smile down at Grace, and tell her what a pretty little maid she was.

Perhaps the tough would have spoken just so had Grace been white; on the whole Violet thought not. Would frank admiration make up for unkindness elsewhere, cancel it out in some way? Maybe, thought Violet. But lately she had begun to wonder whether the admiration and the unkindness were not after all just two sides of the same coin.

Well, there was nothing to be done about that, except take precautions where you could.

'I'll speak to her,' said Mr Godolphin, and he had done so, and Miss Pyncheon, he reported later, had graciously indicated that all were welcome to the St George's Sunday school.

(' . . . even niggers, I suppose,' Miss Pyncheon had added doubtfully, but there was really no reason, thought Mr Godolphin, to quote his young supervisor word for word.)

The Sunday school met in the old tithe barn. Mr Godolphin had been trying to raise funds to build a proper church hall for years now, one with proper plumbing and other modern conveniences, but in the meantime the tithe barn just about served. The children Grace's age were kept safely penned into a corner by painted screens, with someone's big sister (one of mine, noted Violet) keeping an eye on them.

'This here's Grace!' That first time, the children already there looked up, staring with the absolute but vague curiosity of the very young. Violet felt a little clip of triumph: it was clear that none of them saw Grace as different. It did not occur to her that for the moment Grace herself would see no difference either.

She let go of the child's hand, and watched her hesitate at the opening, then move towards another little girl sitting on the rug with a family of peg dolls in knitted skirts; watched her wait until the little girl looked up at her; watched Gracie's tentative smile, which was surely irresistible, thought Violet, and yes, there, the other little girl (one of those Houghtons, wasn't it? Lily, perhaps? One of hers, she had delivered them all) was already smiling back, so that was alright, Violet told herself.

Then back to the anteroom, to give Miss Pyncheon, beaky and bespectacled behind her desk, nearly all of the usual rigmarole, for all she was a young lady: Yes, Grace was staying with her for a while; yes, an orphan; yes *of course* baptized (possibly re-baptized, the Reverend Godolphin had maintained, but since this was impossible to confirm, it wouldn't hurt, Mrs Dimond, to make absolutely certain, would very early next Thursday morning suit?) and no, regular English same as anyone else, why, getting her to *stop* talking was the difficulty these days! No, she ate ordinary food. Yes, knife and fork. No, not India, Dr Summers thought, Africa probably, but no one knew for sure; yes: a little girl, just the same as any other.

★   ★   ★

More time slipped by. Grace began to go out by herself, to join the other children playing in the street or in the nearby market square, where the uneven set of the cobbles made a rubber ball bounce at satisfying random, where boys might play football, but where girls might unfurl great lengths of washing-line skipping rope.

Once one of the big girls brought a rope twenty feet long, so heavy that it took two at either end to turn it effectively, and for a while the fashion for skipping through it was so powerful that even the boys joined in; it was hazardous play, for the heavyweight rope could catch anyone mistiming their leap a sharp crack on head or shoulder, and often did.

Oh, the glamour of those endless summer evenings, watching the big boys and girls haul the rope high into a great turning almost-shape, the smack as it struck the cobbles, and the queue of heroes and heroines each waiting in turn to hurl themselves fearlessly through it and out again! Grace sitting on the kerbside with Lily Houghton, admiring, sometimes allowed to join in some smaller game where extras were needed, often begging in vain.

'No, buzz off you two: ain't for littluns.'

Games played across the street, using both pavements as refuges, games of pretending to creep up on someone whose back was turned, of ritual exchanges: British Bulldog; Cat and Mouse; England, Ireland, Scotland, Wales on the paving stones; games played by street lamplight.

These were out-of-school children, with different groupings and alliances, differing ages, and often boys and girls together; those blithely tagging one another across the market square one evening might well coolly ignore each another at school the next day. There was an after-hours loosening of the usual social school rules; it was perhaps partly due to this loosening that Grace at nearly five was able to slide so easily into the shifting crowd. One day all the children were white, the next day there was a brown one; at first several noticed her colour, and made comments, and argued over who had first heard tell of the darkie Mrs Dimond had brought home, and when; but there was a furiously competitive game of Chiggy-Backs going on at the time, and presently Grace's strangeness had somehow ceased to be remarkable without going through any preliminary stage of being news.

'That a darkie out there playing with you?'

'What? Oh no, that's just Gracie Dimond.'

★ ★ ★

'Mamma, when I grows up, will I look like you?'

'How d'you mean, my lovely?' Alert at once, Violet went on busily rubbing suet into flour.

'Will I look like you? Will I be white, when I grows up?'

A pause. How to answer this? 'Why? Do you *want* to?'

'Well, everyone else is. Lily is. Same as what you are. And I'm not, I'm not right, am I?'

'What you talking about?' said Violet crossly. She had not imagined this; had thought only about the reactions of others, their unkind nonsensical ideas; had never for one moment imagined that the child might take on such ideas herself. 'The good Lord made you as you are,' said Violet, with less heat. 'You're His doing, so how can that be wrong? There ain't nothing wrong with you.'

'But I'm not the *same*. I'm not the same as what everyone else is.'

'No, my lamb, you ain't. And nothing we can

do about it.' She turned back to the flour bowl.

'So I won't — change?'

'There's lizards change their colour,' said Violet, 'so I've heard. And lobsters, when you boil 'em. But not people. We don't change. You're stuck the way you are, and I'm stuck the way I am. 'Cause d'you know what,' said Violet, changing tack, 'if I could change to be the same as what you are, I'd do it straight off.'

'Would you?' Smiling now: picturing it, no doubt.

'I would.'

'Why? Why would you?'

So's you wouldn't be the only one, thought Violet, but she could see that this might be the wrong answer.

''Cause I like your colour better than anyone else's in the whole wide world,' said Violet. 'So there.'

'Do you? 'S' at why you chose me?'

'I didn't choose you. The Lord led me to you.'

A pause. Did the child seem a little easier? At any rate she seemed ready to change the subject: 'What you making?'

'Leek pud — want to help?'

★   ★   ★

Lily Houghton was the youngest of ten, and soon Grace began going to play with her and one or other of the family in the big grassy meadow outside their battered cottage. Grace liked Lily's garden, its forecourt full of broken bits and pieces of things Mr Houghton hoped might one day come in handy. Mr Houghton had gypsy blood, which was held by many to explain his fecklessness and idle disposition, and was in some way, Grace gathered, also connected with the fact of the nine brothers and sisters.

She liked the house too, the way it was so full of beds. She never went inside, for there was no etiquette for such intimate visiting, but Lily had told her that upstairs there was a room for all the boys, and another for all the girls, while Lily's mother and father slept in the big bed downstairs.

'You playing with that Houghton girl again?'

'She's my best friend, Mammy!'

Violet thought the Houghtons were a disgrace, ungodly (for the parents rarely came to church themselves), idle, and shameless. She had delivered all ten children, including Lily herself, and so had some idea of the domestic disorder obtained beneath their roof.

'Bad enough when she just had the five of 'em!'

If it had been her daughter Ruth hanging about with Lily Houghton, Violet would have been more forceful. But this was not Ruth. This was Grace. It had uncomfortably occurred to Violet that Grace might in some way need someone to look down on.

Officially Violet was egalitarian, for she knew that all were equal in God's sight. But in her heart, in her unexamined feelings, she accepted worldly social ranking so completely that she hardly understood that it was there. Without thinking about it she constantly applied her own

107

social level's respectability-formula, to do with relative degrees of cleanliness, diligence and self-respect. Those far above her, like Dr Summers or Mrs Thornby, were automatically assigned absolute levels of cleanliness, diligence and self-respect, and were thus beyond all judgement; but everyone else might be seen to rise or fall. They generally rose slowly, due to quiet steadiness of purpose, a well-deserved promotion, a night-school certificate gained over the years, but dropped fast, when someone essential died or took to drink or lost their way in some other fashion.

Lily Houghton's mother had been a Trewortha; she had once been a tidy local girl anyone might buy a packet of seeds from, as she stood behind the counter in her father's general hardware shop off the square; but she had gone and taken up with Percy Houghton, and slowly slipped down with him to Silkhampton's lower social depths, and did not appear to care about the broken perambulator in the front garden, or the rusting buckets, or the pile of woodwormy fence posts growing their own tall camouflage of nettles.

No one inside that house seemed to look at Grace Dimond with anything but pleased appreciation. Weren't Lily's friend a clever pretty little slip! Hadn't her sainted Ma delivered them all!

The social formula working there, just as it should.

But then, thought Violet, Gracie's eyes were as dark, or darker, than Mr Houghton's own, or those of most of the children, all of them so gypsified. Mr Houghton was alien, in his way; but Grace was more so. Sometimes it even occurred to Violet, though it pained her, that the Houghtons might all of them take comfort from the presence of her own dear Gracie. There was surely no one else in the county who made Perce Houghton look like a local. So Gracie's colour could turn the social formula upside down.

'You playing with that Houghton girl again?' Spoken in mere disapproval; never quite the full-blooded scolding and forbidding Violet would have preferred.

* * *

'I don't want to go to Sunday school no more.'

Violet at first took no notice. 'Everyone goes to Sunday school.'

'I ain't,' said Grace.

First defiance. Violet was shocked. 'Who you talking to, young miss? You talking to me like that?'

'I'm not going, I *hate* it . . . '

'You can't hate Sunday school, don't talk so wicked!'

Grace burst out crying, and presently Violet thought to ask a few questions.

'Someone hurt you? Someone hit you?'

Sniffing, Grace shook her head.

'You quarrelled with Lily? She not your friend no more?'

'No. I mean, she is my friend.'

Violet sighed. She was inclined to shrug and

leave well alone. As she hesitated, Grace said, 'Miss Pyncheon — ' and stopped.

'Miss Pyncheon what?' asked Violet, and at once there was a different quality to the silence in the room.

'She — ' said Grace, looking down, as if she were ashamed. 'She — '

'What, you made her cross? What did you do? You do summat wrong?'

'No!' wailed Grace. 'I didn't do *nothing*, she just comes and she rubs all on my head like, and she laughs, and she says I'm like a — ' Grace's voice failed her.

Violet took the child on to her lap. 'Like what, lovely? Come on, you tell me.'

'And they all laughed,' cried Grace wildly, all on one high note, 'and then Tommy Dando brung one in, the next Sunday he brung one, and then today Sal did, and they jumps 'em about, they got arms like *this* and they do gurn like *this*. And they say 'That's you, that is, that's *you*!''

'No no, wait, I'm lost here. Who's bringing *what* in?'

'They are. Golliwogs. She said as I was like one, and they all laughed.'

'Miss Pyncheon said you was like a golliwog?'

And 'Bright little girl here, Mrs Dimond!' this same long-nosed four-eyed Pyncheon piece had said smarmy as you please, just the week before!

Grace nodding.

'Well, that's what's I call proper silly!'

Long practice at hiding her feelings soon enabled Violet to appear calm. 'And daft of you

110

too to take notice!' she said. 'Don't you let them see you mind — you have to make out you don't care, see? That's the only way they'll stop.'

Violet slid Grace down from her lap and got up, to look out of the window into the wet garden.

'But do I have to go to Sunday school again, Mamma? Please, don't make me!'

'We'll see,' said Violet. 'After dinner we must see to those sprouts,' she added.

But as she dug she was thinking. It would clearly be no use to give Miss Pyncheon a row, though that had been her first hot intention. That might get Gracie banned, or spoken to unkindly. And perhaps after all the woman had meant no harm; many didn't, for all their foolish questions about whether Grace could manage her own buttons like a Christian, or speak English.

So, what to do?

She remembered the mothers gathered by the George and Dragon's portico, and how she had somehow found her sister Bea's own keener wit. What would Bea do about the Pyncheon woman? It occurred to her, slowly, that she could simply find out, that she could write to Bea, and ask for advice.

It was rather a desperate thought. For one thing it was giving up something. The Dame School they had intermittently attended as children had taught Reading, so that all might come to the Good Book, but left out Writing altogether. Bea of course with her superior quickness had soon mastered it anyway, and besides had had years of practice writing to the people who had come to stay at the Red Lion, or at her harbourside cottage. But Violet had learnt so late in life that even now there were letters she was not completely certain about. To write to Bea would give her sister live ammunition.

Or would have; she remembered Bea looking up from the sewing machine, thinking *We're past all that* at her. Could it be true? Over the years there had been several other occasions when she had decided to trust Beatrice, and those had never gone well. But this is for Grace, thought Violet. Perhaps it must take two of us to raise her. Perhaps that was why there are two of us in the first place, for who could guess at heaven's wider plan?

The next day Violet went to the tobacconist and newsagent round the corner, and bought the smallest bottle of ink, several sheets of notepaper and two envelopes in case of mistakes, and began her first-ever letter to her sister. It took her all morning, as well as all the paper. Grace was busy too; Violet had found an old envelope, opened it out, and set the child to drawing a picture on it for her, of what these blessed golliwog-things looked like, for she was actually none too sure, toys having played so little a part in her own life.

'Blue trousers, see. And the jacket's got stripes and they big buttons. And black all woolly hair standing up. My hair ain't like that, is it? Is it, Ma?' She seemed recovered.

'Nothing like,' said Violet, sitting back. She felt exhausted, and her fingers were covered in ink, it seemed to get everywhere, and there was an unfortunate blot on the last envelope, but the thing was finished. Before she posted it she had another inspiration, and sent Bea Grace's picture folded into it as well.

Then there was nothing to do but wait, and hope that when it came Bea's reply was not in that small slanting joined-up loopiness so many liked to go in for; Violet sometimes couldn't read that sort of thing at all.

She would be quick, Violet was sure of that. So it was a surprise and a disappointment when the days went on sliding past, and no answering letter came.

Nearly a whole week went by, until late on Saturday afternoon, when the postman Joss Haine banged on the back kitchen window. He had no letter though, but a brown paper parcel, shoe-box size, and it was addressed, in Bea's fine hand, not to Violet but to Grace.

Here was a quandary. All Violet's instincts as a sister were to open the parcel herself, in case Bea had sent something she disapproved of. But the writing, no matter how she held it up to the window, went on saying 'Miss G. Dimond' plain enough, and to open someone else's mail, Violet understood, was actually against the law of the land, since unopened all of it belonged in some way to the King himself.

But Grace wasn't yet five years old, if you used the doctor's birthday. And the King was in London: he could mind his own business. Violet snipped through the string, her heart beating fast with guilt. Beneath the lid, folds of material, fine check gingham; beneath those, lying full-length, a soft little figure, a rag-doll; pinned to its front a note, in small but clear print.

Violet was not much of a one for presents. By and large, Christmas and birthdays she gave decent blouse or skirt lengths, items undone and re-knitted from something else, pincushions, or handkerchiefs, so Grace took the re-wrapped parcel with some surprise.

'What is it?'

'Look and see,' said Violet lightly, and with an effort added, 'It's a present from Aunt Bea.'

'Oh, Ma!'

'Some might say as it's a rag doll,' said Violet, as Grace shook the doll free once more from its gingham wraps. 'We know it's a golliwog, that's white.'

Grace looked up. 'Can you *get* white golliwogs?'

'You got one right there,' said Violet. She held up Bea's note, and read it aloud: *'Hello, I am a white golliwog.'*

Apart from his colour the golliwog clearly looked as much like Grace's picture as Bea could manage, further embellished with boots of brown felt laced with green wool, button-fly trousers, a tight jacket with smart lapels — 'Oh, it comes off!' cried Grace, in delight — a ribbon tied in a bow round his neck and a big flat blue-eyed smiling face of embroidered creamy-pink flannel, surrounded by a halo of wild yellow woollen hair. Sticking neatly from the perfect miniature pocket of his jacket was a starched lace-trimmed handkerchief, embroidered in one corner.

'Look, Mammy, oh look at the hanky, it's so fine!'

It was a minuscule bee, Violet saw, when she had her spectacles on, a bee in flight, above a tiny purple flower. A violet, she realized, after a moment.

'What d'you reckon then?' she said.

'Should I take him to Sunday school?'

'If you want to. He's yourn.'

'Won't they be — well, angry?'

'Might be,' said Violet, smiling. The bee, and the violet! She hardly knew what to think herself. 'Tell you what,' she went on, 'don't you take him in tomorrow; but just talk about him, let 'em all get up an interest, like. Then maybe let them talk you into taking him in next week, see what I mean?'

'I do like him though. He's lovely! What shall I call him?' Grace bent the doll's legs, and made him sit upon her knee.

Violet pretended to give the matter thought.

'Ooh, I don't know. How about, let me see — how about Tommy?'

And was rewarded with giggles.

The doll was too precious, it turned out, to be taken to Sunday school at all. Its sheer existence helped; the other golliwogs seemed to pain less. At any rate, Grace no longer mentioned them.

But in fact, said Grace, her own white version was really a little girl-doll, whose name was Miss May. Miss May was unhappy in her button-fly trousers, and presently, told of this, Bea made her petticoats, and a little ruffled frock, helped Gracie make her a pinafore to go over it, with a special patch pocket for her fine handkerchief, and changed the hair for flowing yellow wool tresses. On the back of the head Bea embroidered another face, one with eyes closed, and smile more dreamy, to be hidden by day by Miss May's new mob cap, so that at bedtime the doll could go to sleep too.

'Mammy, can we make Miss May a proper little nightdress?'

Violet was puzzled. If Bea had made Miss May brown, in Gracie's own real colour, would it still have been an insult? It seemed to Violet that it would. But why was Grace so delighted with a dolly of creamy-pink? But then Violet herself was a different colour from her foster child — was that the connection Gracie saw, just the other way round?

It was strange, watching Grace look after Miss May, talking to her, making her cosy in bed, or scolding her for idleness. Violet had thought the dolly would be a sort of weapon, even an instrument of revenge, as Bea had surely intended. But Grace had turned it into a well-loved toy, a source of innocent pleasure and contentment; a mystery Violet could only take to church with her.

*　*　*

Violet had given the idea of schooling some thought, and in the last week of the summer term steeled herself, and made an appointment to see Mr Vowles the Headmaster. It was an awkward interview, for Violet was very frightened

116

indeed of this august and learned personage, a gentleman in his place of work; she had no idea that Mr Vowles felt rather the same way, uneasy in her presence; without giving the matter any clear thought, he knew her to be mistress of physical events he himself had only sketchy and fearful knowledge of. At the same time she was only a poor local woman, with the accent he still found mildly comical, despite several years in the county.

'I don't want the child picked on,' said Violet, sitting stiff with anxiety on the other side of the desk, her shopping basket clutched on her lap. 'She'll need looking out for.'

'I must say, I think you're rather looking on the black side!' Mr Vowles said jovially, and then blushed, in case Mrs Dimond thought the double meaning intentional, though in fact it had taken him entirely by surprise. He was disappointed she had not brought the little dark child with her, since he had never yet met a negro. He pulled himself together.

'Especially for the Infant classes,' he went on. 'And they have a very nice, safe, separate playground.' On the whole he was pleased; he felt that admitting this exotic would make his school seem a wider more interesting concern; something he could perhaps lightly mention to old friends whose careers for the moment sparkled more brightly than his own.

'I look forward to meeting Miss Dimond,' he said, with perfect truth. And it would be so interesting, he thought, to consider those things one heard: whether, for instance, the child would be gifted in terms of musicality and rhythm — certainly the only black people he had seen himself so far had been singers — and whether as she grew up she would evince other signs of the so-called typical negroid character, such as light-heartedness, and irresponsibility, and of course an exaggerated sensuality.

In fact Mr Vowles prided himself on suspecting that racial characteristics overall were a piece of modern nonsense, one seized upon, moreover, by a self-serving establishment; for Mr Vowles was liberal in outlook, and despised the Empire, though he was careful about saying so.

'Be frightfully jolly,' he said to his wife that evening, 'if the kid turns out to be a tone-deaf intellectual,' and they both laughed.

★　★　★

She had been knitting so long that it was hard for Violet to explain how it was done; her hands knew what to do so effortlessly that describing their movements was almost beyond her. She had to keep taking the tight knots of Grace's earliest efforts away from her, to let her hands talk for her, at the same time trying to slow them down enough for Grace to follow, though this often meant that she somehow lost track herself.

I'm getting old, thought Violet, for the first time. But still Grace learnt quickly.

'In . . . round . . . through . . . off. In, round, through, off.'

'That's the way!'

Presently Grace sat every evening on her little

stool on the other side of the fire, the strip of blue between her needles slowly lengthening, growing more even. Violet had forgotten the pleasant cosiness of childish talk, the delight in daily minutiae. She heard about Lily Houghton's brothers and sisters, and games they had all played together in the orchard where Mr Houghton had bestirred himself to put up a swing, and where Sidney Houghton had run after Gracie and Lily with a grass snake as was dead; Sidney liked animals, said Lily, but they did go a-dying on him; and once picking blackberries he had stood on a wasps' nest and got all wasps crawling up his legs, and run about roaring and leaping and trying to pull his britches down all at once, the funniest thing you ever saw, Lily's older sister said, as had seen it with her own two eyes.

Violet herself said little. Without noticing it she had fallen into her own oldest role, that of receptive audience, for once long ago her sister Beatrice had sat just so, turning the world for their private entertainment.

'Can I do a different colour, Mamma? Can I do patterns?'

'In a little while. Give me your hand a minute ... good ... ' Violet was knitting Grace matching mittens, a matter of some urgency, as every other little girl at Sunday school was currently sporting them. Couple more rows, she thought.

'Won't Aunt Bea be surprised, when I shows her my own scarf! Can Aunt Bea knit? Can she knit as good as what you can?'

Knitting ain't fine or fast enough for her, thought Violet, but out loud she only mentioned her husband's mother, who had made real lace for ladies.

'That my granma?' How did you make lace then, Grace went on blithely. Could Mamma make it? Was it knitting only with string, like?

Violet could not answer. She had felt a most curious sensation wash over her, when she understood that Grace thought herself to be her own child. Not insulted, exactly: but the ghost of that feeling, mixed with simple surprise. How could she — ? How could I possibly — ?

But what are you doing, Violet asked herself, finally catching on to her own responses. Of course the child will think she's mine; won't remember any other by now. I'm her mother, no matter how widowed or old I am; or how white.

If she were white, I would have foreseen it, expected it: well, more fool me. It's her innocence sees no difference, finds no puzzle.

The innocence made Violet's heart ache, though at the same time it seemed to her almost divine, and beautiful. But soon enough Grace would be starting school; it would not do then, to let her talk of her mother Mrs Dimond, or her grandmother the Silkhampton lace-maker. Folk would sneer, and those who would rather leave the shop than queue behind her would enjoy that sneering all too well.

For a moment it occurred to Violet that Grace's future, every tiny eventuality, was all of it set with possible snares. She'd noticed this one just in time, she could stop Grace stepping into it; but surely there would be others no one could foresee, a cruel multitude of them.

'Look now,' she said, her voice sterner than she had intended, 'her with the lace, she weren't your granma at all — you know that, Gracie, surely; we two ain't related by blood. You're an orphan, by rights; that means your own poor mother, she died. That's why you was in Aunt Bea's Home for a while.'

There was a silence. Grace stopped knitting. She looked up once, a quick stricken glance at Violet's face; then away.

'Don't you remember?' asked Violet, more gently. 'Gracie?'

Grace shook her head. It seemed to Violet that she had grown smaller. She sat so still.

'You was only a baby then,' said Violet, over her own rising sense of panic. If only she could take it all back! If only she could take it back, and think about it, and come up with — but with what? There was no easy way to tell a child she was an orphan, surely?

Grace's fingers found a loose loop of wool in her lap, and twisted it about. 'So — you ain't really my mamma, then? Aunt Bea ain't really my auntie?' Her voice broke.

The truth was always best, Violet reminded herself. 'No,' she said. 'Not really.'

'Who was, then?'

'Don't rightly know,' said Violet. There was another pause.

Grace went on pulling at the loop of wool, and Violet was piercingly reminded of the dying baby in the Home.

Help me, Lord. Oh, help me, Bea. What am I to say?

She cleared her throat, and the words came sweetly into her mouth: 'But you're my own little girl now though,' she said. 'You're as much my little girl as ever my Ruth was.'

For the truth was always best.

'Gracie? And no one ain't ever going to take you away from me,' Violet went on. 'Not ever. That's a promise.'

Then at last Grace let the knitting fall. Violet took her daughter on to her lap, and held her tight.

* * *

Grace didn't really take to knitting, it turned out; gave up altogether soon afterwards. Violet made the scarf herself, finished with a fringe of woollen tassels, but it was the mittens Grace loved best. In her usual way she refused to take them off at first, even indoors, despite the obvious drawbacks.

'They're beautiful,' she said. She held them up. 'I'm like everyone else now!'

Violet only smiled.

9

Word soon got about, and some of it turned ugly. Many were sorry, or professed themselves to be. Mrs Harvey, little Phoebe's mother, spoke to Violet with genuine tears in her eyes; she was expecting again, and had hoped to have the blessing of Mrs Dimond's attentions this time too. But for some the news was more in the nature of a lark: Mrs Dimond, the Holy Terror, was deposed. Served her right, mean old besom, carrying on like the Old Testament, and messing about with darkies!

And others who had been grateful for Violet's services for years suddenly felt alarmed, and counted themselves lucky to have survived her ignorant ministrations. At least now there was a proper trained midwife, who knew what she was doing!

For Violet Dimond had with immediate effect been removed from the Roll of bona fide midwives; Dr Summers had come to break the news in person.

'I did my best, it's — to be honest, it simply isn't up to me any more.'

'So . . . that means I can't work no more? Is that it?'

'Not delivering. No. I'm so sorry, Mrs Dimond.'

'What about Ma Higden — Joanie Trewith?'

'Oh — well, neither of them were on the Roll

in the first place. So they weren't subject to any sort of report. But they weren't practising legally, and they still aren't.'

'Are they going to be stopped, then?'

'Certainly. Unless they want to be arrested,' said Dr Summers.

Ma Higden, Mrs Trewith, behind bars for helping out!

Violet herself barely noticed her own precipitate loss of status, though several children — one she had delivered too — followed her about the streets for a day or two, suddenly unafraid, shouting things, jeering. She was too busy.

For even before she had shown Dr Summers out, she was calculating. There were the contents of the tobacco tin in the front room. There was a little in the Christmas club at the greengrocer's in the High Street, and a small sum in the Post Office. There was money put by for her own funeral, saved over many years with the Co-operative in Exeter. There was almost nothing she could sell. She had earned enough to live on, and no more. She had savings to last for two, maybe three months, if she was careful; and no more.

She knew of some nursing work, but had to turn down nights, while Gracie was so small. She charged for a laying-out, since she had discovered that the new professional lady midwife was not allowed to touch the dead at all, for fear of infection; the dead man's family were in desperate straits though, so she could not ask for much. There was some cleaning work, rough work; but the pay was not enough to live on. She wrote laboriously to a service register in Exeter, thinking to live-in somewhere, as widow with orphaned grandchild, and sub-let her home. But the difficulty would always be the added complication of Grace's colour. Who would take on an elderly woman with a stray negro child? Some would, she had no doubt, but how was she to frame the application?

There were one or two local charities, set up to keep folk out of the workhouse; Violet did not try them. Mrs Caterham, Mrs Grant-Fellowes and Mrs Thornby were on the boards of both; she could not bring herself to ask for charity from those who in the first place had plunged her into want. Not yet. Reluctantly Violet accepted a pound from Dr Summers, when he came round again to let her know that despite his initial hopes there was no question of a Council pension. She began to sell off her hens, and killed the weakest layer, making it last more than a week. To lose the final two meant no more eggs; but keeping the birds meant feeding them, and this would soon be impossible if she wanted to manage the initial outlay to make her pies, and pay the quarterly rent.

She wrote to Bobby, and considered writing to her sister Bea. But she knew that whatever she might have managed in the past, in the Red Lion Hotel days, Bea was now essentially in service herself, without a penny to spare. And her husband's nephew and his children would have first call if she did. No; Bea must be last resort.

'Old folk don't need so much,' she said, when Grace noticed that there was more on her own plate than on Violet's. But every mouthful the child ate soothed Violet, satisfied more than mere hunger.

Slowly the weeks went by, but the savings shrank fast. Bobby sent a postal order for ten shillings, with his apologies. Things had not been going well for him. They were moving again, south to America, to another mining place somewhere; it was true what they said, any deep hole the wide world over, you'd find a Cornish lad with a shovel at the bottom of it. He would write again with more money when he could, and when he had an address. What else could he do, but go where the work was?

But I can't do that, thought Violet. Wherever I go the work is forbid me. She spent some of the money on new boots for Grace, who would soon be starting school.

She found herself thinking continually of the terrible time long ago, when her own father had been away looking for work. There had at first been not enough to eat, and then even less, and finally for an indeterminate length of time nothing at all, and then her mother had gone somewhere, perhaps to look for him, and she and Bea had stopped talking, stopped arguing, stopped even whining, stopped doing anything but lie in one another's arms in their bed — for it was cold, wintertime — as if waiting, in a silence full of pain, that took slow stealthy charge of every bit of you. How your twisting empty innards panged, how your cold legs cramped, how the light hurt your eyes!

Bea had known all the time that their mother

would come back. But Violet had allowed herself doubt, and it seemed to her now that this doubt had gone right into her, stayed there and stained her all the way through. We were six years old. How good we were, the two of us, me and Bea, how quiet and meek we were, waiting for death!

Sometimes twisting in a brief doze Violet awoke unable to remember for a moment where she was, and whether she was hungry in childhood or in old age. By day she spent as much time as she could in St George's, praying and trying to think straight.

If only she could have the inspection again, knowing what it was for! Mrs Thornby's face, when she showed her the special bag; hadn't been able to so much as touch it. She had thought it *unclean.* Violet knew the contents of the bag were as clean as she could make them, quite as clean, in fact, as they needed to be, but all the same whenever she remembered the scene her empty insides dissolved with shame. A lady had considered her unclean. For some part of Violet, this was enough.

And Dr Summers must have known what was to happen for nearly a whole year, she realized. The clever ladies on the committee had read Mrs Thornby's report and decided together that Violet Dimond was unworthy; and ever since then all sorts of wheels had been quietly turning, advertisements written and placed, interviews arranged and conducted, and the appointment finally made; and all the while Violet had been going about almost as usual, tending to the child, working in garden and kitchen, without the least suspicion — apart from the curious shiver that had troubled her so at each childbed lately, at the memory of the propelling pencil — that her livelihood was to be taken from her, and that she was to be shamed and cast out in the name of the public good.

Was it because of Grace?

If an ordinary pale little English girl had stumbled in sickness out of the bedroom, would Mrs Thornby have written a different report?

Violet thought back. Perhaps; perhaps not. But surely Grace had sealed her fate; made sure of it, poor little innocent. For the first time Violet understood what she had done in taking Grace on, realized fully that those ready to despise Grace for being brown would include herself in their hatred. She had thought to protect Grace; but from, as it were, the enemy's own side of the fence. Well, it seemed that she and Grace must be dark together — and she had already, so early, been exposed as helpless!

Violet remembered again the time that she and Bea had waited quietly for death to take them, and of the fear that had ever since possessed her. It had always seemed to Violet that to be alive, and especially to be a woman, was mainly to do with fear. But for Grace, surely, this would be more so: she would be dependent on others, but more so. She would be judged for her looks, but more so, subject to the whims of men, but more so, vulnerable, but more so.

And her mother all the while powerless, and on the same losing side. She was ruined. And Grace with her.

On the way back she decided: she would give up her home and the garden, her own so usefully these thirty years, and she would write, this very afternoon, to Bea, offering — no, asking — whether they might not come to the Home, she and Gracie, so that she might work there in exchange for board and lodging. She wouldn't need a wage, she would tell Bea. But they must have a roof overhead, she and Grace together.

At home she got down on her knees by the cold hearth, and prayed aloud for strength.

She was aware as she spoke of the thought that often made itself apparent in her mind as a sort of low grumble, suggesting that all this disaster had happened to her because she had adopted Grace. For a while she attempted not to let the thought surface. But it occurred too often for that.

It was certainly true, she thought, giving up on prayer for a moment. But if she had the chance, if she could go back and change things, would she do anything differently?

I'd listen out for that Mrs Thornby, thought Violet, answering herself, and when she did her knocking I'd creep up all quiet-like, and turn the key against her.

I could not have done anything else differently, she decided. Not from the first time I see her little face.

Slowly, rather shakily, Violet arose. She must think out exactly what to write, she told herself, before she put pen to paper, think out all the spelling. She would have to buy a sheet of paper and an envelope and a stamp, but she had just enough for that, thank heaven. As she brushed off her skirt there was a rattle at the door. Violet started, and for a dreadful moment thought again of Mrs Thornby. She crept to the door, all quiet-like, she thought, dizzily, and stood behind it.

'Who's there?'

There was no reply, and presently Violet noticed the envelope poking halfway through the letterbox. Bobby again, so soon! She pulled the letter clear and hurried back to the kitchen with it. But as soon as she had her glasses on she saw that the handwriting was different. Someone else had written to her. A stranger: this was a hand she had never seen before. She sat down, in case it was something nasty, and tore the envelope open. There was no letter at all; nothing but a single sheet of paper, which she recognized after some scrutiny as a postal order, made out to herself, and for ten shillings. She was still trying to understand when she noticed the tiny slip of paper still in the envelope. This had such small writing on it that she had to stand up and hold it directly to the window. Another unknown hand. It read: *To be paid weekly.*

Her first thought was of Dr Summers. Had he not offered to pay for her to do the special course? Had he not told her barely a fortnight since how much he felt he *owed* her? And no one else she knew could afford to lose more than twenty pounds a year. But this was not his handwriting. His wife's perhaps, the occasionally glimpsed Mrs Summers?

Whoever had sent it, it was charity.

Violet's eyes filled with tears. All my life not a farthing have I taken that I didn't earn, by the honest sweat of my brow! I will not take it, I cannot. And not even knowing who it's from! Suppose it was the Committee, suppose it was Eleanor Thornby herself!

Violet sank down again into her chair, and tried to think. It came to her that her prayers had simply been answered; and that the Lord was also testing her. She must now decide whether to accept the help He had prompted, or refuse it.

I would rather starve than take charity if I were on my own. But if I were I wouldn't need it in the first place.

I'm not on my own though. And by my own choice. No one made me take her. Would I rather starve Gracie than take charity? When she asks me for bread, shall I give her a stone?

Violet put her hat on, went to the Post Office, cashed the postal order, and bought bread and cheese and a ham hock and some dried peas, and ordered in coal.

'Ooh, Mammy!' Grace cried that evening on the doorstep, as she came in. 'Oh, what's that lovely smell?' All ready for bread and marge again, poor mite, thought Violet, or another bowl of thin porridge.

'Wash your hands,' she said soberly. 'The Lord has provided.'

★   ★   ★

131

Silkhampton Council School was in Bishop's Road, on the eastern edge of the town, a walk of half a mile from home. It was a red-brick building, with separate entrances for boys and girls, and to one side, reached by footpath, a big stretch of green beside the railway line, so that in summer all the children could play on the grass and wave at passing trains. There were two rows of flushing toilets out on the far corners of the yard, there was a central hall with parquet flooring, and four large classrooms, one for Infants, one for Juniors, two for Seniors, all equipped with paired solid wooden desks with fixed seats and inkwells and lids that lifted sideways through a natty little finger-sized hole. All of these things were still rather new, and only just acquiring the overall school smell, that long-term patina of chalk, floor polish, and clothes and footwear worn too long.

Violet was extra-careful with Grace's appearance that first day, and drew some comfort, on the way there, from considering how well the child was dressed, from her summer flannel vest to her lightly-starched pinafore. Her new boots shone, her hair was neatly pulled back into a little round ponytail, ministrations which had made her go very quiet, though for days now she had been hopping about demanding to know when she was to start.

To start in the lion's den, thought Violet, but had done her best to hide her own fears. She timed their arrival in the playground for just before the bell rang; there would still be many there, she thought, who had no idea of Grace's living in their midst.

'Look, there's Lily!' Grace let go of Violet's hand to wave.

'You be a good girl now,' said Violet, and watched her race away across the playground, without a backward glance. She thought suddenly of a boat ride she had once taken with her young man, a lifetime ago, on a fine summer afternoon: of the blithe and beautiful butterfly that had flown across their bows, and gone on fluttering past them, lightly heading out to sea.

I must go home via St George's, she thought.

★　★　★

But at school Grace was a spectacular and immediate success.

Whatever some parents might say, for the older children she was instantly a thrilling novelty, a source of giddy excitement. She was all the rage. How different she was, and yet how the same, a cute little native girl, as sounded just like you did! And her so sweet in the face, pretty as a picture! And tooken up by that holy terror Mrs Dimond, as your own Da still took his hat off to!

All that first term Grace was sought out, pampered, even squabbled over, especially by the great girls of nine or ten, pretty Sally Killigrew, Linda Coachman, and strange to say Mrs Thornby's own Norah (not at all pretty, Violet noted, with some satisfaction), who vied with one another to pick her up should she chance to fall over while playing in the schoolyard, who coaxed her to sit on their laps, and took it in turns to cuddle her. An admiring gaggle of them tenderly accompanied her home each day at dinner-time and after school was over.

'Goodbye, Gracie, see you tomorrow!'

And young Susan Warburton turned out to have a rolling squint in one eye, and very damp hands. For a while it became the fashion to chase Susie about the Infants' playground at break time, calling her names.

Grace, playing hopscotch with Lily or Annie Mercer, would look up now and then, as Susan Warburton, her face set with misery, fled another troop of jeering boys and girls. *Rat tails!* That was what they were calling after her.

Why? It made no sense at all to Grace. Unless it was a reference to Susan's thin, mousey hair. Sometimes Lily and Annie joined in. 'Rat tails! Rat tails!'

Grace hung back. She ignored Susan and tried not to sit near her and avoided speaking to her, same as everyone else, and she was very glad it was Susan being chased and not herself. But something stopped her jeering with the others. She hid at the edges of the playground and pretended not to see.

★　★　★

After school, after tea, the drifting neighbour-hood crowd of children, mixed in size and age and sex, played street games together in the long sunny evenings, and Violet, watching them sometimes from a chair set in her open front doorway, felt that Grace had ceased to be different; that familiarity had made her local. There was a lot to be thankful for, thought Violet.

Sometimes in hot weather she took her chair right out on to the pavement before her front door, exchanging a word now and then with other mothers also taking their ease in the golden evening sunshine, knitting, or shelling peas. Now and then she might remember with some pain her old work, her lost expertise; but there was sweetness in this late motherhood, in waiting for her darling aged seven, or eight, or nine, to come in for her supper before bedtime.

The children played, thought Violet, just as once she and her sister had played, with the others who were children in those far-off days. Children like birds, flocking or calling, you would notice them from time to time, as every spring you saw the primroses; strange, holy, to remember that they only seemed the same, that every year they were different birds, different flowers.

By then she had also found herself decent work, helping out at a local bakery, not just with the pastries but behind the counter in the afternoons. The mystery postal order still came, as regularly as the note had said it would; Violet had opened an account for it in Grace's name, in the Post Office, and let Mrs Bold suppose the money came from Bobby, and so far no one had dropped any hint they knew anything different.

Now and then, in an emergency, she answered a call to a childbirth, as so many of the poorer sort went on urgently knocking on her door. Was

135

it still illegal if she worked without payment?

Yes it was, said Sister Goodrich, the lady midwife herself, coming round to remonstrate one afternoon, and to threaten Violet with the law. She was a fair fat young woman, with pale eyelashes and a hard-to-follow London accent, perhaps not such a lady after all.

'The head was right there, I had no choice!'

'That's what you said last time, Mrs Dimond.'

'That's what *happened* last time. Am I to stand by, and let some poor creature deliver on her own, like a horse in a field?'

'You are not qualified to attend a delivery; if it happens again I shall report you to the police,' said Sister Goodrich. She was young enough to have been one of Violet's own; as she strode off down the street Violet wondered, indeed, who had delivered her. Someone like me, I don't doubt, she thought.

After that she was more careful, and when next she was called out let the poor wretch of a mother pretend that she had arrived just too late, and that the baby had come before she had; a shameful lie, but how could Violet Dimond risk a fine, or even gaol, with such a small child to care for?

Sister Goodrich was unimpressed. But she was gaining ground in any case. Presently Joanie Trewith, so long a martyr to her legs, was carried off by them altogether and died, and Ma Higden found work at the rope factory; and soon in that country the time of the handywoman, of the local wise woman, the experienced amateur hand, for good or for ill, was over. For a little while Violet Dimond was the very last of a tradition older than any profession, older than history, older than writing and houses, perhaps older than weapons, older than fire. Then that tradition ended, and no one, not even Violet herself, remarked its passing.

10

Like most parents Violet failed for a long time to notice that her child's inner life was beyond her understanding. The baby's feelings had been clear enough, transparent as a glass of water, and Violet had gone on assuming the same simplicity.

'What did you do today?' she might ask, on the way home from Sunday school, never suspecting for a moment that the account Grace gave her was in any way censored. But Grace had seen her mother's face, when she had told her about the golliwogs, and tried to be careful ever afterwards. There were certain things Violet should be shielded from; she must be kept happy — that was Grace's aim.

'We did about Noah and the animals, we played a animal game, I was a elephant,' she might reply, leaving out what Tommy Dando had said on the subject of animals, first privately into her ear, and then publicly, so that his nearest friends all laughed. It was best to keep such stuff from Violet; and easier, somehow. By the time you were home it might almost not have happened at all, if you didn't mention it to anyone.

So Grace really had thought of the secret prayer all by herself.

First of course she would kneel beside the bed in her nightie, to say aloud the prayer Violet had taught her:

'Now I lay me down to sleep
I pray the Lord my soul to keep.
If I should die before I wake
I pray the Lord my soul to take.
God, help me be a good girl please, Amen.'

Then Violet would turn down the bedclothes, and say 'In you get then, my lovely,' and help Grace climb in, for the bed was chest-high, had to be pushed right up against the wall on one side to stop her falling out.

'Warm enough?' Violet usually asked, while she tucked in the bedclothes. Then she would blow out the candle, and kiss Grace's cheek. 'Straight to sleep now. And I'll be popping in and out.'

Grace would wait until Violet had closed the door behind her before preparing for the secret prayer. She couldn't kneel again at the bedside, even though that was the right way to pray, for while she could slide out of bed by herself, she knew she would never be able to get back in again on her own. Instead she lay still and flat on her back with her palms pressed together, like the stone knight in St George's.

'Dear Lord, hear my prayer,
Let me be like everyone else.
Let me wake up white in the morning.
Let me look like everyone else.
God, help me be a good girl please, Amen.'

Sometimes Grace felt sure that the strength of her longing would be enough. God couldn't go on ignoring her, not when she could feel the secret prayer powering up into the sky like a rocket all the way through the night to where He was sitting with the angels in heaven, where appeals so pure, so absolute, must surely always be heard. Soon enough God would take notice and turn His eyes on her and simply do what she asked because it wasn't so much, it wasn't parting the Red Sea or being raised from the dead or walking on water. It was just being the same as everyone else, so little to Him, though it would be so much to her.

Often Grace lay in bed afterwards picturing how surprised everyone would be when God answered her and she woke up just like everyone else. How Lily would stare, how they both would laugh! And as for Tommy Dando, wouldn't he feel silly then!

She would pretend nothing had happened. Ha! 'What you staring at?' she would ask, very snootily. No; she would just shrug her shoulders and ignore him, her nose in the air, but laughing all the time inside.

The secret prayer only faded when she started school, and slowly realized that if she wanted everything to be safe, if she wanted the house not to burn down, if she wanted Violet to be happy, if she wanted everything to stay as it was, orderly and secure, there were more important tasks that must be performed, in the right sequence, and at the right time.

She must, when going through to bed, pause in the doorway and note the shadow of her own left foot, held up behind her at a particular angle. She must fold her clothes in the right order, pile them on the chair so that their folded edges faced the wall and not the bed. After Violet had heard her bedtime prayer and gone away, there were the songs. They were 'Bobby Shaftoe', 'The Harp That Once On Tara's Walls', and 'Greensleeves'. They must be sung aloud, but quietly so that Violet would not hear, all the way through and word-perfect; any mistake meant starting again from the beginning, and they must all be done before Violet Popped In for the first time. That was the most worrying part, from Grace's point of view. Some nights Violet Popped In sooner than others.

Usually though Grace was able to get through all the songs before Violet softly opened the door again and stood on the threshold in a rush of lamplight. Grace could just make out the reddish glow of it through her closed lids. For it was essential then to pretend to be asleep. Sometimes instead of going away again back to the mending or knitting, Violet stole closer so quietly that Grace could hardly hear her, and stood for a moment beside the bed, presumably looking down at her sleeping child, though of course Grace could not open her eyes to make sure.

On rare best-of-all nights, Violet bent and gave Grace a careful kiss on her forehead, and Grace would thrill all over with happiness. A kiss from someone who thought you were asleep was special. She liked the idea of it, the loving picture of it in her mind, the sleeping child, the watchful mother, the formal blessing of the kiss. And if it happened after all the songs had gone well and

141

everything else had been properly attended to, the house was completely protected, and all night long nothing bad could happen, and even tomorrow was partly taken care of, or at least influenced in the right way, though of course you could never be quite sure.

For she was aware that to some at school her colour was a species of affliction. Not as bad as that of Fat Maggie Barnes, or of Clifford Petty, who had to wear a giant-sized boot on his clubbed left foot just to stay upright, or of Judith Laws, who wasn't all there, and whose ears were on sideways. They were set low on her head, too, and her little mouth was squashed right up beneath her nose.

All these oddities were too familiar to be remarkable, but anyone who felt like it could make use of them, sneer at Fat Maggie, brush against Cliff in the playground and knock him over, playfully remind Judith about her ears. Or you could theatrically shun them. Or even feel a sort of affection for all three, for being so obviously inferior. This was the afflicted group that some in Grace's class sought to place her in; while the struggle was all the harder for not being fully conscious, it was her business not to let them.

Though now and then schoolwork itself made Grace stand out. History, geography: black people were subject, unable to govern themselves; always ending up murdering each other, selling one another into slavery, cruelly burning widows alive and, of course, eating one another. It was all stark truth: the map of the world on the wall showed just how hard the British had had to work, all the pink bits showing where they were keeping black people from hurting one another.

'Slaves, your lot,' said Clara Collier, preening in the playground; Clara Collier, who owned one dress, whose neck and throat were dark with grime so old it had a gloss to it.

'Cannibals,' muttered Tommy Dando in the classroom, leaning dramatically away from Grace across the aisle, as if she might forget herself and take a bite out of him. On a sudden inspiration she pretended back, slightly widening her eyes, making a greedy yearning face at him: yes, tempted. As if it were impossible not to he instantly responded, holding out one tentative arm in mock-daring invitation; she bared her pretty teeth and briefly snapped them at him, and he grinned outright. All this neatly furtive, while Miss Foster's back was turned; generally only the class's lower beings got caught. Tommy was too magnificent for lines or the strap. Too canny.

But Grace Dimond had made him laugh, and everyone in the class had noticed.

*   *   *

The following year there was a Coronation Garden Party at Wooton Hall. This great house stood on the clifftop within sight of the sea, three miles outside Silkhampton, so the children of Silkhampton Council School were collected by several charabancs at mid-day and shepherded into the extensive grounds, where various delights awaited them; everyone knew that the Redwoods had more money than sense. A real steam roundabout with horses rising and falling in time to the piping organ music, as well as swingboats! And there were long white lines painted in the grass, so that the children could run races, and everyone who won was given a red ribbon on a safety pin, or blue for those who came second.

Grace was fast. Grace won the girls' flat race for the Junior Girls, and the egg-and-spoon, and tied to Lily Houghton and brilliantly in step when all about them were falling over in struggling heaps, the three-legged race. Only Tommy Dando won more, and beat her in the final Race of Junior Champions at the end, though not by much.

'Cheating, legs that long,' murmured Grace to him, sidelong, as they went to collect their prizes, 'Spindle-shanks.'

'Duck-arse,' he whispered back, in the same teasing tone.

'Come and have some lemonade, my hearties,' said Mr Billy Redwood, when his mother had finished pinning on Grace's blue rosette. He was a jolly pink-cheeked young man, who had fired the starting gun and jumped up and down yelling on the sidelines, just as if he had gone to the Council School himself, instead of far away somewhere else with his brother. Grace thought he was very good-looking, and gave him a particular smile she had secretly been practising in front of the small square of mirror by the kitchen door.

What did the Honourable William Philip Fane Redwood make of Grace Dimond? He knew about her, of course, vaguely, as he knew about most things in the town that was in many ways his property, or would be, one day.

'What's your name again, little girl?'

What gave him the idea? What kind of impulse? Perhaps he could not have said himself. Though it was something to do with his least-favourite aunt, Dora, who from the drawing-room window had earlier remarked loudly on the general shocking plainness of the children of the poor; and especially singled out the coloured child, who, she thought, rather spoilt what simple bucolic charm the scene might otherwise have had, the romping villagers so enjoying the typical summer loveliness of an English country garden.

'I mean to say, this is a traditional garden party in a fine traditional place,' said Aunt Dora. 'And then you get this ghastly negro running about ruining everything. I think it's a real shame.'

'Come along, you two,' said Billy Redwood now. 'Got something to show you.' And Grace and Tommy Dando — by now swapping glances, by now altogether comradely in shared merriment — followed this baffling toff into the cool dark enormity of the Hall, down several stone-flagged corridors, to a room bigger than any Grace or Tommy had ever seen before in their lives, bigger than the school hall, bigger even than St George's Silkhampton, with acres of slightly springy floor to clump across, a high ceiling painted with clouds and swirling human figures trailing yards of material, and several huge windows looking out on to a terrace edged with stone pineapples, and beyond that the long silvery line of distant blue sea.

'Look here! Jolly, don't you think?'

Mr Billy Redwood was standing now by a picture in one of the room's far corners, a large painting of a beautiful lady in a shining light-blue dress, a young lady, though her hair was white, and all piled up on top of her head like an ice-cream cone.

Grace and Tommy exchanged more glances; they were both on the edge of uncontrollable giggles. 'Thank you, sir,' squeaked Tommy, while Grace had to look at her feet, the better to hold herself in.

'No, no, look — look here. See him?'

Mr Billy was pointing now into the corner of the picture. Grace looked, and saw for the first time in her life a picture of someone very like herself. A dark brown boy, no older than she was, younger, perhaps, was standing beside the glowing voluminous skirts of the white-haired lady. He was wearing what looked like a sort of turban, yellow and shiny, and a long green coat and breeches.

'His name was Barty Small; see him? What d'you think of him?' said Mr Billy, very pleased with himself.

Grace said nothing. Barty Small's dark eyes seemed to be looking right into her own. Why, he must be the white-haired lady's foster child, as she herself was Violet Dimond's! She was not the

146

only brown child to have lived here so!

'Brought over from St Kitt's,' said Mr Billy, as if this explained something.

'What happened to him? When he grew up, like?' Grace asked at last. But Mr Billy did not know.

'Oh, far too long ago. A hundred and fifty years ago at least. He grew up, I suppose. Yes, I think he definitely lived to grow up.'

This was alarming; Grace asked no further questions. Though she asked them of herself, later on, for a long time afterwards.

Had Barty Small sat on the white-haired lady's lap while she stroked his hair and took her pleasure in his strangeness, his similarity? Grace thought of the older girls so friendly to her when she had just started school, walking her home and kissing her goodbye, those prim young ladies, Linda Coachman, Norah Thornby, Sally Killigrew with her golden hair, big girls of nine and ten taking it in turns to hold her strange brown hand.

Barty Small had definitely lived to grow up, in England, in the time of the King Georges. What then? There was a Lizzie Small, same colour as everyone else, in the Junior girls; there were other Smalls in the churchyard of St George's; were they some other family with the same name or — had Barty Small stayed, and married? Were there folk walking about Silkhampton now, whose great-great-great-something he was? Now there was a thought. If it was so — where had the darkness gone? And if somehow Barty Small could know that his colour had vanished over the

147

years, would he mind? Or would he be pleased?

Perhaps Barty hadn't stayed at all; perhaps when he had grown too big for the white-haired lady's lap he had fled to the city to find others like himself, in the ports, in the dockyards. Aunt Bea's nephew the fisherman had told Grace that he had himself more than once seen men her colour, sailormen, some in uniform, over Falmouth way, or down to Plymouth Harbour. Perhaps Barty Small had run away to join the navy. A man could do that sort of thing. A man could always escape, couldn't he?

★ ★ ★

Also in the Coronation Year there was a school photograph, taken at the beginning of the summer term, the whole philanthropic enterprise down to Pyncheon's Photographic Studios in the square. Young Mr Frederick Pyncheon himself spent an entire afternoon arranging all sixty-four children pyramid-style at the edge of the meadow, the smallest cross-legged on the ground, the second row sitting on school chairs brought outside for the purpose, the third standing behind them, and the last most-favoured row standing at the back, raised on benches from the assembly hall. Then Mr Pyncheon had disappeared beneath his cloaked apparatus and effected some species of minor explosion.

Violet knew about the school photograph, and took an interest. She was herself already the proud owner of a photograph, which stood on the top of the cupboard beside the fireplace. It was in an oval tin frame, and was very small, and seemed to show the young Mrs Dimond in her wedding clothes, wasp-waisted, deeply buxom, her pretty face tilted invitingly, a teasing look in her eyes and a rather saucy hat to one side of her head.

Few saw this photograph, but it was a great source of satisfaction to Violet Dimond. Every time she dusted it she was pleasantly reminded, now that the danger of personal vanity was safely past, of how very good-looking she once had been, and at the same time had the consolation of remembering how firmly she had avoided making use of her good looks to ensnare herself or others in sin. There was the further happiness, now all this time had passed, of knowing that her sister Beatrice, whose photograph it actually was, had despite her own best efforts rather failed as a sinner as well, having suffered no worse fate than to marry (just in time, it was true) the author of her downfall, who, while he couldn't hold a candle to Ned Dimond, of course, had not turned out too badly either, all things considered.

So Violet very much looked forward to seeing the school photograph, which was to be publicly displayed for the first time at the school's annual summer fete in July, at the very end of term. This was an even greater occasion than usual, in view of the Coronation, with stalls set up in the playground, folk-dancing exhibitions, a poetry recital, and Scenes from Shakespeare acted by the boys.

When the Scenes had reached their fine

dramatic end the stalls started up again, and Violet made her way to the table just outside the Boys' entrance, where the new school photograph was on display beneath a painted banner reading PYNCHEON'S PHOTOGRAPHIC STUDIOS. There was a little gathering already there, jostling for a closer look. Violet waited her turn, then put on her spectacles.

There was the carefully arranged pyramid of children, boys and girls together, the boys in their dark trousers and jumpers and big white collars, the girls all in white pinafores, their hair loose on their shoulders, with ribbons here and there, oldest at the back. She had delivered many of them, Art Coachman, and Sally Killigrew, pretty as her mother. Not that pudding-faced Thornby girl, of course. But little Bertie Flowerdew, cross-legged in the middle holding the slate with *Silkhampton Council School 1911* chalked on it. There was that Tommy Dando, as had upset Gracie all those years ago; and Lily, of course; and there, beside her on the end of the second row, was her own dear girl, all smiles. Violet thrilled all over with delight; and nearly laughed out loud. She looked again to find poor boss-eyed Susie Warburton.

'Ma? I've spent all my money. Can I have another penny, please, please — there's the china stall, I ain't gone on it yet, I dint see it in time, oh do.'

Violet tore her eyes away from the photograph. 'What?' She looked down at her daughter's eager face. 'China stall?'

'You pays a penny,' said Grace urgently, 'and

150

they gives you three balls, and you throws 'em at the ol' plates all laid out on shelves, and smash 'em all to bits!'

'Shocking waste of china,' said Violet, but she paid up, and watched Grace run off. She turned back to the picture for one last look. It was something about the light, presumably. Something about the black-and-whiteness; but oh, thought Violet, what a joke to see the Warburton child on that photograph, or the Thornby girl, ha! better than any china-smashing: for all the children in the photograph seemed to be the same odd colour.

Look at it whatever angle you pleased, by some accident of placing or light (and how annoyed Mr Freddie must be!) it was a picture of sixty-four grey-faced children, in clothes of black and various shades of grey, beneath the dark-flecked leaves of a black oak tree; Gracie merely slightly greyer than the others. It was a similar joke, thought Violet, to the picture of Bea at home, the one that looked so much as if it might be of herself. Why, how shockingly the camera could lie, after all! It didn't know what it was seeing, thought Violet. How could it, a mere machine? It was held up and shown things, and manoeuvred about, and what it gave out after that might just be downright wrong.

Like people, I suppose, thought Violet, and she went to find the china stall, to watch the fun of breaking plates, and admire her Gracie's throwing arm.

11

Usually Violet and Grace visited Bea every Easter, staying in the cottage on the harbour for a week of sea air and dress-making and alterations. One year though, with only a day's notice, Bea wrote to put them off. She had been offered a paid booking instead; would Violet send her Grace's latest measurements, for a nice bit of cotton lawn she had put by?

'And not a word of apology!' Violet was disappointed, for Grace's sake, she told herself. Poor mite, she had been so looking forward to the seaside!

In fact Grace could hardly believe her luck, and offered Bea a silent prayer of gratitude. She loved her aunt, and her aunt's sewing machine, and her clever fingers. But Porthkerris was not Silkhampton. There were visitors there, always new and unfamiliar faces, stares, second glances, and now and then a level of non-friendly attention that Grace could feel on the air. Sometimes it was all she could do to walk up the hill and down again, for the curious eyes she felt on her from so many windows, from so many idling passers-by. It was hard to carry on chatting to Violet or Bea, feeling so looked-at. It was hard to frame words, her mouth would feel stiff.

Once when she was on an errand on her own she had felt something soft hit her skirt just below her knee, and looked down to see what looked like a handful of prawns all scattered at her feet, flaccid old ones, the dirty juice of them running down to drip on to her boot. She had not dared to look around to see who might have thrown them, but turned and ran home again, and pretended that she had fallen.

The woman in the bakery would sell her a loaf, it was true, but she was careful to lay the change down on the counter.

These were small things, hardly worth seeing, certainly not worth talking about. If she had told her mother, what would Violet have said? Take no notice. Just foolish unkindness — and prawns, not a stone! How could a few prawns hurt you?

No one threw them at *you*; it is not *your* touch that is despised. As yet Grace did not quite think these things clearly. For the moment she had only the feeling that she was making a weak fuss about nothing much, and at the same time being crushed almost to death by the combined weight of an army of men and women like the baker, like whoever had thrown stinking fish at her, an army she had no defence against, whose movements she could not predict.

'I don't mind really,' she said now, watching Violet crossly feed Bea's letter to the fire. 'I prefer it here.' Where the army was at any rate of known quantity. Silkhampton was divided for Grace into possible and impossible areas. There were tracks through the forest, places where she blended like anyone else into the ordinariness she longed for more and more as she grew older.

School was largely safe, especially while Tommy Dando did not look unkindly upon her. Mr Vowles the headmaster tended to boom down at her, and jovially call her his dusky or nut-brown maiden, but she could see he meant to be friendly. The church was fairly safe; since she was nine she had sung in the choir, and if anyone objected after all these years they had not done so to Mr Godolphin. Though sometimes Grace wondered if that had anything to do with the rood screen, ornately carved with trumpeting angels, that so effectively hid the choir from the congregation. And the choir left the church via the back door, through the vestry; no need for any of Silkhampton's church-goers to notice Grace Dimond in their midst.

Every Sunday Grace had that thought, and every time tried to repress it, as making the sort of vain self-centred fuss Violet so disapproved of.

'Course they're not staring at you! They got better things to do!'

That was another of Violet's mantras. And it might be true for any other young girl, it seemed to Grace. Any other young girl who felt stared at and judged. The girl Ruth would have been, had she lived. But not true for me.

And she had the strange feeling too that Violet knew it, that she was being wilfully blind to something real, in a way that old folk, grown-ups, so often were. The blindness must be important, then; serve a purpose. Be the only way.

★　★　★

The fact was that now she had turned thirteen Grace knew, some of the time, that she was repulsive. When she looked in the mirror, it was her colour that she saw, and her colour was wrong.

She no longer prayed to be changed, but now and then she daydreamed about it. Suppose she were the same as everyone else! Everything would be different then. Everything would be better. She would learn to be a real dressmaker in London, she would make Ma silk dresses and warm winter coats, and take her for drives in her own car, she would get married, of course, but not straight away, and she would buy Ma and Aunt Bea adjoining fine houses exactly the same.

Sometimes at night, getting ready for bed, Grace looked straight at her reflection in the small mirror beside the sink and studied her own extreme otherness. No boy would give her a second glance, she thought. No one would want to marry her any more than anyone would take on squashed-up Judith Laws. And like her, in some deep ways Grace hardly existed at all. There were no pictures anywhere of anyone like Grace Dimond.

There were schoolbooks, of course, with pictures of natives wearing absurd and shamefully scanty clothes, and carrying silly babyish weapons, spears and so on. There were novels: there was the hideous embarrassment of *Uncle Tom's Cabin*, with the people like her talking like children, and being generally downtrodden, there was the beautiful Foulata in *King Solomon's Mines*, who loved Captain Good, even though 'the sun cannot mate with the darkness,' as she pointed out to him while neatly dying in his arms; there were girl-cannibals with nasty habits in *The Coral Island* — but nowhere were there any girls like Grace, being normal in proper clothes, being ordinary, talking English. No illustrations, no postcards, no magazine. No comic. No cheap novelette or girls' paper. No newspaper picture, nothing.

No illustration featured Judith Laws either, of course. She didn't exist, other than in her own odd self. No heroine squinted; Susie Warburton didn't exist either.

I just don't count, thought Grace sometimes as she pulled on her nightgown. There is no one else like me in the whole wide world. The desolation of these thoughts came to her sometimes in the street, when someone spoke civilly to her, or tried to be friendly, even, and made her hang her head and blush, made her hands clasp one another in front of her and writhe together, as if they were anxious all by themselves.

★   ★   ★

So the safest place of all was the Silkhampton Picture Palace, which opened without much fanfare (but to gathered crowds, so many that the police had to come to keep order for four nights running, so fevered was the queue for tickets) in the spring of Grace's last full year at school.

Rumours had begun weeks earlier, when

156

workmen had moved into the old tithe barn, unused now since the opening of the new church hall at the time of the coronation. There was wild talk at first of an opera house, or petrol pumps, but soon it became clear that the company in charge was Pyncheon Photographic Studios, and that Mr Freddie Pyncheon intended nothing less than Silkhampton's first cinema.

Grace went with Lily, the second week after the opening. The first thing to be surprised about was the anteroom of the tithe barn, freshly painted pale green, and with a wooden kiosk newly built into one corner. The next thing was Miss Pyncheon herself, beaming inside the kiosk.

'Gracie, dear, how nice to see you! Hello again, Lily, enjoying it all?' This was a very different Miss Pyncheon: her narrow face almost glowing, transfigured with excitement. 'Two fourpennies?'

So grown-ups, even the pitiable ones, could still be subject to powerful emotions! It was an unsettling thought. Grace and Lily could not help meeting one another's eyes, and grinning with embarrassment as they turned away with their tickets. Various framed photographs had been hung about the anteroom walls, above the ancient panelling. Grace would have liked to examine them, for Mr Pyncheon was known to take his photographic trips all over England, but Lily was anxious to show her the new cinema, and to establish once more that she herself was an old hand at Picture-going.

'Come on, we need to get good seats!'

They gave their tickets to Ted Hall from school, another surprise, standing in his Sunday best beside the velvet curtains now hanging over the great arched doorway. He tore both tickets in two with practised nonchalance, at the same time giving Lily a special soft look, which she enjoyably ignored.

'This way!'

They parted the heavy velvet, and went inside. Transformed! The tithe barn was all dark now, from the shutters built over the windows. Here and there electric lights burnt with unusual dimness, and straight away they were approached by a figure waiting ready with a lantern, Ted's big brother Geoff.

'Fourpennies, is it?'

They were directed towards the back of the hall, but not as far as the raised platform where the dearer seats were. The seats were real theatre seats, whispered Lily, whipped-out numbers and all from a music hall gone bust over Plymouth way. She sat down almost at the end of a row, and Grace sat beside her in the aisle seat. This sort of behaviour was typical of Lily. Giving Grace the aisle seat meant that there could be no other person sitting right next to Grace, or rather, no chance of anyone making clear their disinclination to do so. Did Lily know what she was doing, when she acted this way? It was impossible for Grace to know, since it was also impossible to ask. There was a chance, she felt, that if she did, something fragile would be broken. It was best not to speak sometimes. None of this was fully conscious: just glimpsed,

158

and turned away from.

They had been almost first in the queue, but the place soon filled up about them, until it seemed half the town was crammed inside, and people were standing at the back, and huddled about the doorway, everyone talking and shouting as if they were at a party, until at last the lights dimmed further, all by themselves, like magic, and someone started playing the piano in front of the old stage at the front of the hall. Suddenly an enormous light flared into being on the closed stage curtains, its edges wavery with the old velvet. Ted and Joe appeared onstage to pull the curtains aside, disclosing a great white screen set up on wooden struts, huge, almost filling the stage, and now brilliantly lit. Looking up and behind her Grace saw that the light came from what looked like a tiny slot of window let into another new wooden kiosk, this one built up in the high old gallery at the back of the barn. The light started out very small and too fierce to look at, but spread out as it beamed, so that when it reached the stage it all but filled the waiting screen.

Meanwhile the pianist went on playing, something sombre, but with a clear beat to it, exciting.

'It's ol' Freddie himself, he's proper brilliant! Plays every time!'

Another surprise. Sometimes Mr Freddie Pyncheon stood in for the usual organist at St George's, when Mr Bundy was absent. Once or twice Miss Pyncheon, too, had stepped into the breach, especially at choir practice. But this was piano-playing like nothing Grace had ever heard him play before. This was suddenly jaunty, a dance, a light piece of prettiness.

'Makes it all up as he goes along, see!'

The show began with a newsreel. The King opened parliament. He rode in a coach like Cinderella's, through city streets few watching in the tithe barn had ever really seen. Grace, for a few seconds more, was aware of herself, Grace Dimond sitting in the dark in Silkhampton, and at the same time watching the King himself walking about in London, talking to real people, being real himself. Grace Dimond seeing the King!

Then the film cut to a garden party and for a little while Grace ceased to exist at all. She had gone to the party, where ladies in clothes as delicate and beautiful as flowers walked about the grass in silken high heels, carrying parasols made of petals, or of something else as light, as faery; wondrous beings attended by gentlemen in masculine versions of the same unimaginable finery, in top hats that gleamed in the sunshine. Real ladies and gentlemen, of London, the King's own friends, taking their ease among the rosebeds, and on view, on display, like splendid creatures in a zoo!

All the while Mr Pyncheon played the piano, butterfly light and waltzing for the garden party, swiftly military when soldiers appeared, and so cleverly that the soldiers seemed to march in time. Then the screen went black, for a moment, and words appeared:

'Cowes Week!' whispered Lily, and giggled,

amidst other mutterings from elsewhere in the audience. 'Come again?'

Grace shrugged, hardly bothering to register her own puzzlement, but the film soon turned out to be nothing to do with cows at all, but with boats, and people in white hopping in and out of them, with other splendid views of the seaside, and not all pebbles and rock like the stretch beyond the harbour at Porthkerris at low tide, but a huge clean beach of bright sand, with ladies almost as lovely as the King's friends sitting upon it beneath enormous umbrellas, their children jumping in and out of the shallow foamy water. There were little beach huts, and flags blowing in the breeze, and donkeys, and all the while the music sang blow the man down sea shanties, and Grace was there, at this seaside place she had never even imagined, almost able to smell the sea and hear the waves turning.

Then there was another film, a little story about a man whose wife insisted he helped with the spring cleaning instead of going out to play tennis, and who messed everything up so much, knocking over buckets and breaking windows, that at last his wife begged him to go and play tennis after all. The music was very bouncy so you could tell the story was meant to be funny, though somehow it was not: hardly anyone laughed at all.

Lily was vexed. 'Much better last time,' she said loudly, when the lights came up. 'That was daft, that was.' But Grace could hardly speak at all for wonder. She had visited the royal garden, she had floated there, seeing but unseen, and

161

outside, in the ordinary daylight at once dull and glaring, she still felt some of that glorious abstraction.

You sat in the dark, and then became part of whatever was on the screen: it was a double invisibility, both real and make-believe. In the Picture Palace you could disappear twice over. It was the safest place of all.

'When can we come again?' said Grace.

★   ★   ★

Violet put up a bit of a struggle. News from London was one thing, stories might well be some licentious or immoral other. Especially if they came from America.

'But it's Miss Pyncheon, Ma, in the tithe barn! She ain't going to show nothing dirty, is she? Honest — where's the harm?'

'In idleness,' said Violet, 'sat there in the dark.' But she could remember broadly similar arguments with her son Bobby years ago, about beer money and football. She'd had more energy in those days. And then her dear boy had turned into a man and disappeared almost as if he had never been. Looking back now it seemed to Violet as if those years had passed in days.

'Waste a money,' she said, but her heart wasn't in it.

Grace was old enough to know that it was best not to bring up the subject of her Aunt Bea. But it was hard not to, when she thought how much Bea would enjoy the Picture Palace. How she would love to see the ladies' dresses, as fine, or finer, than those of the Redwood ladies long ago, when Bea had been their own maid! She risked it:

'I write and tell Aunt Bea about it? The cinema, I mean — maybe she'll come and visit, we could all go!'

Violet folded her lips in a way that meant trouble. 'She ain't replied to my last.'

Grace was allowed neither to defend nor criticize her aunt, which had made for some tricky moments over the years. 'Ain't seen her for ages,' she said at last, her voice and manner entirely neutral. Grace was good at neutral: practised.

'You and me both,' sniffed Violet, and the conversation was at an end.

★ ★ ★

The newsreel had been a disappointment, as usual — since that first time there had hardly been any beautiful dresses at all — but the story afterwards had been thrilling. There had been a terrible moment when she thought the little boy was going to drown right in front of her, and Grace had to hide her eyes. But the faithful dog, despite being so ill-treated, had leapt to the rescue just in time. It was a wonderful relief to join in the applause when the lights came back on, and Mr Pyncheon stood up at the piano, and bowed.

And it was odd, Grace said as they trailed out of the barn, when you came to think about it, because she couldn't actually remember him playing anything at all.

'He was though, at it hammer and tongs,' said Lily, laughing at the violent picture her own words suggested.

'Well, I know. But you know what I mean. You sort of — don't really listen to him, do you?'

'Funny job. Getting ignored all day.'

'Sounds alright to me,' said Grace.

They both sobered. Lily's mother had arranged work for her, starting the following month, in service at one of the big new-built houses where the perry orchard used to be. Sometimes Lily talked about the electricity and the bathrooms with hot-water taps, and sleeping in a bed all by herself for once. But Grace knew she was afraid.

'At least you ain't going far,' she said. Three of Lily's older sisters were long in service already, and hardly ever had time to visit.

Grace herself was staying at home. For the present, was how she put it, when anyone asked. For ever, was how she sometimes put it to herself. She could work in a shop perhaps. In Silkhampton. There would be occasional new-comers coming in and staring and asking her the usual stupid questions, and looking taken aback or amused or excited when she sounded local; but mainly everyone hereabouts knew her, knew Violet, and saw her or didn't, but either way would not *startle*. Grace hated startling people. Or better still she could work in the back of a shop, hidden altogether, busily doing — something useful, away from all eyes. Factory work no: too many strangers, perhaps rough people.

Rough people tended to be open. They Said Things. Service no: same possibilities, smaller scale perhaps, but harder to get away from.

'When I start up my dress shop,' said Grace, 'you can come and show the latest.' She knew this was what the ladies did; Aunt Bea had several times accompanied the young Redwood ladies to places in London where pretty young girls had come in and out wearing all sorts of lovely new dresses, showing the ladies styles of daywear, and tea-gowns, and dinner dresses, and ballgowns, once even nightdresses and underwear!

'I ain't doing knickers,' said Lily.

'You'll have to. I'm the boss. I'll say, Put them drawers on, Houghton, or you're sacked.'

'Can't I do the ballgowns?'

'Maybe. If I'm in the mood. It's going to be on the square, or just off the north side. Dark green paint, my name in all swirly gold writing.'

'A lovely dress in the window!'

'No no no, that ain't class: just velvet drapes and a vase of flowers. String of beads maybe.'

'How will folk know it's a dress shop then?'

'Word a mouth,' said Grace. 'Ooh, Lady Snotface, what a charming costume! Makes you look less like a baboon than normal — where'd you get it?'

'Why, Mrs Ratbag, ain't you heard?' said Lily. 'All us Snotfaces goes to Gracie Dimond.'

'Ain't there a waiting list?'

'Only ten years,' said Lily.

Round the corner they ran into trouble. Tommy Dando, Art Coachman and Ted Hall, three abreast on the pavement.

Grace only saw Tommy.

'You bin to the pictures.' That was Ted Hall.

'You should know,' said Lily to him sweetly.

'I seen that dog one sixteen times,' Ted admitted.

'But he still cries at the end,' said Tommy.

'No, I don't!'

'Every time!'

'I do not!'

'Where you off to, girls?' That was Art Coachman: Linda's brother, buck teeth.

'Never you mind,' said Lily, linking arms with Grace. The sun was warm, the day was lazy, late afternoon. The light on the pavement was golden. Grace stood in the shade of the striped canvas outside Fuller's Shoes, Lily beside her, in the sun.

'Come on a picnic,' said Tommy Dando. 'We're going to the river.'

The other boys glanced at him, very quickly, but Grace saw. An instant plan, then.

'Not likely,' said Lily. 'All muck and cowpats anyway.'

'Not the place I know,' said Tommy. 'Is it lads? Place you can paddle. Show us your ankles,' he added encouragingly.

Lily did not reply; she gave a little squeak as of outrage, grabbed Grace's hand, gave her a tug. Together they dodged round the boys and ran.

'Ladies! Perfectly civil invitation!' Tommy bellowed after them, as they tore along the pavement, breathless with joyful indignation. Ankles indeed!

'He's got his eye on you,' said Lily later, when they had calmed down. They were sitting on one of the low walls around the strawberry field, where the lines of white-green berries lay neatly on their thick straw beds.

'Oh no,' said Grace vehemently.

What did Grace know about Tommy? She thought she knew a great deal. His full name, his parents, where he lived. His easy place at the top of the class, his handwriting, his husky voice reading the lesson sometimes in Assembly. More, closer, his particular smell, snuffed many times over the years, the shape of his hands, his straight eyebrows, so dark despite the fairness of his hair, his bright blue eyes. The way his shirt fell over his chest, the hardness of his wrists, the down on his forearm. His smooth cheek, pink as any pretty girl's. The casual swagger of his long legs.

Grace had not actually spoken to Tommy directly for years; not since the day Mr Billy had taken them both to the ballroom at Wooton, and showed them Barty Small and the Lady. They had been in the same room often since then, the same halls, the same Picture Palace, the same church, and for some time Grace had often been flamingly aware of him, careful to note his whereabouts, marking him out, so that she safely could turn away and pretend not to have seen him at all.

Nor had Tommy tried to speak to her; even today he had turned to Lily.

'Why d'you say that?' Grace asked now, to get Lily to say more.

But Lily only shrugged.

'Reckon it's you he likes,' said Grace, still trying.

'Don't talk daft,' said Lily.

Grace instantly began to worry that what she had said almost in jest — that Tommy liked Lily — was actually true. This was somehow rather enjoyable, a manufactured anxiety, as unlikely in its yearning unsettling way as the dress shop with *Grace Dimond* over the door in gold lettering: both dreams of a future full of drama, and wild success, and love, and loss.

Life's not like that, said Violet's voice in Grace's head, Life is duty.

But then there was always Aunt Bea in Grace's head too, muttering something a little different. More on the lines of: What's duty but scouring and cookery! Stay away from all that, Gracie my love!

'Got any money?' said Lily. 'We could go home past the chip shop.'

'Got sixpence,' said Grace; so they did.

* * *

Sometimes she thought vividly of escape. Not of her own, but of Barty Small's, the brown boy in the picture at Wooton Hall.

When he was this age . . . I bet when he was my age . . . when he was rising fourteen . . .

At night, sleepless beside Violet, Grace pictured Barty Small grown up, Barty not-Small enough now for the white-haired lady's caresses. Barty Small rising as a distant clock struck one, getting out of his bed fully dressed and ready, his buckled olden-times shoes wrapped in a cloth beneath his arm as he crept in his socks down all the back flights of stairs from the attic where the servants slept, perhaps to the kitchen to take a bit of bread, something set out ready for the servants' breakfast ... everything dark and quiet, the house dogs there raising their heads, standing up hopefully, stretching as Barty softly draws the bolts on the kitchen door, and trying to nose their way outside to go with him, but No, home, stay home, he tells them, giving their silken heads one last stroke, and closes the door silently on their whines, knowing he will never see them again. Never see anyone here again!

Grace in her bed walks him down the long gravelled drive in the moonlight, a few coins in his pocket, bread and bacon wrapped in the cloth that had held his shoes. He is running away to join the navy, he is running away to sea. He tramps along the starlit summery lane the three miles to Silkhampton, and the whole town is dark and asleep, not even gas light then, not so much as a candle lighting the square, but he passes right along past Market Buildings, outside this very window, and Grace sees him so vividly, she feels sure that what she is imagining must simply be the truth, that it really happened just like that, because of the connection only she and Barty share. She knows that for a moment he paused outside her window, just feet away, standing quite still in the moonlight, as if aware of her, the girl in the future, the one like him.

Then he turns, and walks on into the darkness

towards the coast road.

That's what you can do if you're a man, thought Grace. You can run away. You can take a chance. Did Barty find his own people again? Did he know their names? If he found them, how could he bear it that he had become so foreign to them, and they to him?

And the fact is, thought Grace, everyone who looks like me is a stranger to me. Even if I wanted to take a chance, leave everyone and everything I know, even if I were brave enough to run away, there is nowhere on this earth that I could run to. I would only ever find strangers. Only ever be one.

Grace turning her face into her pillow, and allowing herself for the moment to despair. Violet all the while breathing softly, fast asleep beside her.

12

The following year he sent her a valentine. Well, someone did.

'Who's that from?' said Violet at breakfast.

Grace handed the card over.

'Well?'

'I don't know, it ain't signed.'

'No need for that tone,' said Violet, holding the card at arm's length. Grace thought that there was every need: Violet was often so vexing these days. Sometimes just the sound of her breathing was enough to make Grace long to leave the room, to flounce off, but there was nowhere to flounce to, unless she went to bed. There was no getting away from Violet for long.

'What tone? I dint ask for it — how come it's my fault?'

'I dint say anything was your fault. I just asked who it was from, that's all.'

'It's a *valentine* card!' Grace cried. 'How should I know?'

Violet looked at her daughter, and sighed.

'Have it back please,' said Grace, quiet with fury, and she reached across the table and almost snatched it; she was suddenly certain that the card had come from someone insulting, someone whose merest glance was insupportable — sly Timothy Bineham, or Cliff Petty clumping along on his giant boot, dim dreadful boys who would class themselves with her, with smart clever comely Grace Dimond, and all because —

'You ain't finished your porridge.'

'Don't want it,' cried Grace, and banged the door behind her, her coat unbuttoned, her hat on anyhow, her gloves still in her hand. She ran through the garden, out into the back lane, and along it to the street behind the square, where she had played so often as a child. Her own quick footsteps, her neat little iron-clipped heels on the pavement, calmed her, they sounded so grown-up.

She reminded herself soothingly that she was going to work.

* * *

The wool-shop job was Violet's doing. Years before, she had attended Mrs Ticknell, delivered her of a healthy male child, and then to the surprise of all present sent urgently for Dr Summers, and stayed calm, even unsurprised, when three minutes later instead of the afterbirth a small pair of feet had suddenly descended between the new mother's parted legs: he was a *footling breech,* as Dr Summers had explained afterwards.

Well before the doctor arrived though Violet had turned Mrs Ticknell about, sitting her on the edge of the bed, and sat herself down facing her as the second twin — another boy — descended slowly over the side of the mattress, his legs, little bum, his back, one bent arm, the other, each shoulder, gently holding him, carefully freeing up the cord with one quick hand, until the baby hung there by his neck, nape showing. Then she

172

let go; her hands hovered, but she let him hang, while Mrs Ticknell screamed, and her mother hid her eyes.

'He's got to come slowly,' cried Violet, and then she took the baby firmly by his two heels, and swung him upwards, his back to his mother's front, and held him there upside down, some of his little face now showing — chin, nose, puffy closed lids — until by degrees the whole of his head at last slipped free, and he took his first breath, gave one long wail just as Dr Summers arrived downstairs, pinked, and opened his eyes: Gerry Ticknell, Jim's younger brother, the two of them as dear a pair of cheerful boys, said Mrs Ticknell, as ever warmed their mother's heart.

'I hear you got a place for a girl,' said Violet over the wool-shop counter two decades later, and Mrs Ticknell, what with one thing and another, could only agree, that yes, she had, and that yes, she'd heard young Grace was that clever with her needle; so yes, why not, a trial, perhaps; six months, maybe; see if it suits — both ways, mind, Mrs Dimond, both ways?

Ticknell's Wool Shop suited Grace very well.

Besides wool the shop dealt in every possible embroidery and fine-sewing requisite; its clientele were thus not only local and on the whole well-heeled, but feminine. Men were rare, strangers more so. The atmosphere, the smell of cleanly new wool, was busy but tranquil. Here was a place, anyone opening the shop door might feel, where the quiet purpose of everyday making and mending had its true importance recognized. The darning or knitting or sewing in your lap was part of the business of being a woman; it had the ordinary dignity of work.

Grace was general assistant. She swept the floor every morning, opened the blinds, propped open the front door to air the place, took a bucket and hard broom to the pavement just outside. Sparkling cleanliness was Mrs Ticknell's aim.

'Gotta be just so, if you want ladies,' said Mrs Ticknell.

The ladies spent the most, on embroidery silks and canvases, gloves and hat-trimmings.

'See here, Gracie, look!'

And Grace would be summoned to admire Mrs Ticknell's latest acquisition from the mysterious sweatshops and alleyways of manu-facture, the box of pale yellow silk rosebuds, the fat china cherries complete with stiff paper leaves, the wreath of forget-me-nots as delicate and airy as the real thing, all packed in tissue paper, all to be carefully itemized and laid away in the right labelled drawer in the stockroom at the back, or in one of the numbered drawers in the shop itself.

'Put the fire on, Gracie, let's be cosy!'

Mrs Ticknell, altogether forward-looking and ambitious, had gone for gas, and the shop was warmed by a metal square of greyish grids hang-ing face-down from the high ceiling. To light it Grace had to catch and pull down its dangling chain, using the special wooden pole-with-a-hook, a faintly fairground pleasure; the gas would catch with a sudden liquid curl of racing blue flame, and the grids begin at once to glow deep scarlet.

Warm and comfortable: there was a row of upright wooden chairs beside the counter, in case of queues, and along the far wall a sofa with claw feet, upholstered in grey velveteen, and much set about with cushions. The sofa and the little table in front of it were for the use of customers, but both were also lures: the cushion covers, changed frequently, matched or contrasted, exhibited Mrs Ticknell's own virtuoso cross-stitch tapestry, or trapunto, or quilting, and the table was covered with a newly starched lacy cloth every week, and one or two of the latest magazines for ladies, and vases of flowers, sometimes artificial, and scattered artfully with charming lavender bags, delicate place mats or babies' dresses, all of them for sale, but also suggestive in themselves of things a passing customer might decide she simply must make now, for herself — all the essentials so readily to hand, for a price, of course.

Just before nine every morning, Grace turned round the sign in the door to read OPEN and went to stand behind the high oaken counter, proud before the wall of shallow square shelves full of wool in great twisted hanks, and below them the bank of fifty little drawers, each with its number on an ivory plaque, all of them neatly crammed with the multitudinous items of haberdashery: the different types of needles, the extended families of pins, cards of bias binding, hooks and eyes, French chalk, ribbon, cords, tassels, elastic and hundreds and hundreds of buttons, every colour and size and shape sewn on to cards by the dozen, with *Best British Make* written across the top in brown printed scrolly letters. All of which, in less time than Mrs Ticknell had at her most hopeful imagined, Grace had off by heart, down to the last buttonhook — what a clever little thing she was, what a memory!

And Grace's manner, too, was just right, thought Mrs Ticknell; always gentle and polite, always ready to help but also quick to withdraw, to let well alone while someone wrestled with difficult choices. That was rare, thought Mrs Ticknell, increasingly proud of her own foresight and general acumen in taking Grace on in the first place, and soon quite forgetting that Mrs Dimond had ever leant meaningfully upon her counter, or that she herself had ever had doubts.

Because the drawback — well, that was hardly her fault, poor girl (thought Mrs Ticknell). Hardly her fault that she was what she was.

* * *

It had certainly given Mrs Ticknell pause at first. Would custom be put off? Would the ladies, the essential high-spending ladies, decide to shop elsewhere?

There were one or two other shopkeepers that might, she realized, during the increasingly fraught and sleepless week of Grace's initial evening training sessions, see her hiring of Grace Dimond as an advantage of their own. One or two smaller, dingier and hitherto altogether less classy traders might tweak their stock, lay themselves out to please a little more, and coax away her livelihood. She was about to ruin her own business, just through being too obliging!

But as she went to open the door to old Mrs Wrightson on Grace's first Monday morning Mrs Ticknell, to her own surprise, knew a sudden moment of strange inner resolve. Various religious tracts, bits of old sermons, other more political speechifyings, half-heard, barely remembered over the years, leapt into her head as if of their own accord, all muddled together, but still with a sort of grandeur to them. They spoke to her firmly: *Grace Dimond is a nice bright girl — are we not all men and brothers — let Mrs Wrightson get used to it — let her go hang if she won't!*

Meanwhile the rest of Mrs Ticknell, the part that considered bills, quaked with unease, for Mrs Wrightson spent all day every day at her embroidery frame.

Give her a chance to get used to it, said the inner grandeur. *Let all seem normal!*

Mrs Ticknell drew herself up straight, and as she ushered her customer in said as lightly, as casually, as she could:

'Good morning, Mrs Wrightson — have you met my new girl here, Gracie, helping me out, for now?'

Grace, schooled beforehand, bobbed Mrs Wrightson a curtsey; and old Mrs Wrightson, after a single tiny start of surprise, had smiled back, and kindly said how nice for Mrs Ticknell, and could she trouble them for a little more of the pale ochre, or order some, and the high grand feeling inside Mrs Ticknell went pop and vanished, though she remembered it afterwards, and was powerfully pleased with herself for being on the side of Good.

Mrs Wrightson had a certain local cachet; her approval, or benign indifference, made others more likely to approve, or at least not mind one way or the other, thought Mrs Ticknell. But here she was wrong. Once word got about, there were considerably more casual visitors to the shop than before. Most locals had heard tell of Mrs Dimond's act of adoption, widely considered at once baffling and sanctimonious, and had at least glimpsed the strange exotic kid herself, over the years. Now there was an easy chance to have a good look at her, and talk to her face to face. If one or two customers were lost, rather more took their place. Grace Dimond was not off-putting, Mrs Ticknell finally realized; she was if anything more of a draw.

And then she so quickly grew practised and knowledgeable, and ready to help with the interminable stock-taking, bane of Mrs Ticknell's life, and stay late on ordering nights, and finally at quiet times take over altogether, so that Mrs Ticknell could nip out to the shops or visit the market, or have a peaceful cup of tea uninterrupted at the back! Those were fine times for Mrs Ticknell.

On the whole fine for Grace too. Sometimes she stood with her palms spread on the counter, inhaling the quietness and the rich cleanly smells of new material, glorying in the jolly fact that she was playing at shops with an actual shop. A real heavyweight mechanical till, and real money! It was easy, that was the thing that struck her most; easy to remember the stock, to keep the accounts straight, to check the orders. She had not been fully aware of the constant effort she had put into being unnoticeably average at school, but now she felt all the pleasure of turning the effort the other way round, and letting herself shine.

At first she had herself feared being something of a spectacle, had envisaged goggling crowds, and hadn't slept much during that initial training week either.

There was never exactly a crowd, but often there was goggling.

'Where are you from then?' she was asked, often. The tone was generally kindly enough, she thought, but who ever asked that of Mrs Ticknell, or leant, say, across the counter in the chemist's shop next door to enquire about the origins of the assistants there, and then pursed their lips or popped their eyes in disbelief on being told, no matter how demurely? Or smiled outright, as if she had said something funny? Amused, she supposed, at the endless joke of what so many persisted in seeing as an exotic-native appearance instantly contradicted by her accent. Some never seemed to tire of it.

All the same: 'It ain't that bad,' she told Lily Houghton, trying to be kind, for compared to Lily's place the woolshop job was hardly work at all, though the days were long and her feet often ached with the standing, for Mrs Ticknell allowed no sitting at all behind the counter.

And she was learning so much, not just about dress-making. Mrs Ticknell, once she relaxed in

Grace's company, was a revelation in herself. She knew everyone Grace knew, often in far more scurrilous depth, and was rarely silent for more than two minutes together.

How was Mrs Dimond, as had saved her dear boy Gerry's life, no, never would she forget that! Of course Mrs Dimond was a twin herself, fancy! How was Mrs Givens, out at the Home, wasn't it? A gifted needlewoman, Bea Givens. Did Gracie know that the two of them had once been famous for their tricks and games, long since?

'The Kitto Twins, that was their maiden name right enough, Beatrice and Violet Kitto. Bea pretending to be Violet, Violet pretending to be Beatrice, they'd take anyone in, their own mother sometimes; everyone knew now and then your poor Ma'd end up getting no dinner, because Bea would come in and eat up, and nip out, come back in again saying she was Violet, see?' Mrs Ticknell laughed.

'And they used to do this act where they made out they was one person — you ever see that? Well, no, I dare say they don't do it no more. Years back, this was. I only seen it the once, I was maybe four or five, so they must have been what, sixteen, seventeen, great grown-up girls they seemed to me. Out on the old common — where the bus depot is now — they had a little table set up, and stools to sit on, either side. And then they acted, being the one girl, see? Like in a looking-glass. They each had a hairbrush, and us-all stood about watching, and wherever you stood they looked like one girl sat in front of her glass, see, a-brushing her hair, and parting it, plaiting it! Plait one side then the other, never seen anything like it, tying on ribbons — blue they were — good as a circus, except I remember — it made you feel all funny inside, bit like Alice if you see what I mean, going through the looking-glass, you know that book?'

More bewildering than any Lewis Carroll, for Grace, was the idea of Violet playing with Aunt Bea, of them being giddy girls — embarrassing really, even slightly horrifying. Surely Violet had always been as she was now, reserved, affectionate, dignified, and above all, old?

'Mr Dimond? Ned Dimond, ooh he was a looker, tell you that for nothing, all the girls were after him, Ned Dimond! Had a way with him and all. Everyone thought,' (here Mrs Ticknell lowered her voice, for all they were dusting the back room well after closing time) 'that he had an understanding with your auntie, with Beatrice; but she went away to London; that was when all of a sudden he's engaged to Violet, married inside the month! Some said, getting her own back for all them dinners . . . you see a flat box up there, Gracie, labelled 'Lewin'?'

Mrs Ticknell sounded a little self-conscious, aware perhaps that she had overstepped a mark.

'All so long ago now, and I dare say there was nothing in it anyway,' she added piously, as Grace passed the flat box down to her. 'That's the one. Look — ordered and paid for, and never collected these thirty years!'

The box held a pair of beautiful gloves

wrapped in tissue, of fine slippery knitted silk, in cream and palest pink, with ivory buttons and wrists edged with filmy lace.

'Whose are they?'

'Well, they're Miss Lewin's,' said Mrs Ticknell. 'Shocking thing — you heard a Miss Peony Lewin? No? Strangers, her folks owned a brewery, well, more than one probably, took on the old manor house out on the coast road — where your auntie works now, don't she, this was before it was a Home, of course, the Lewinses takes it, has it all done up very fine, you know it, surely?'

'Yes,' said Grace, her heart beating fast, longing to ask if Mrs Ticknell, fount of all local knowledge that she seemed to be, knew that she herself, Grace Dimond, had once been a nameless and abandoned infant at that very Home. Presumably she did; but the habit of careful quietness held Grace's tongue. 'I know it well,' she said.

'Course you do, a-visiting your auntie,' said Mrs Ticknell comfortably, 'and this was before I took over here, 'twas still Miller's then, but Miss Peony Lewin comes in, the daughter — her own carriage outside, you'd think she was royalty — comes in all by herself, orders these here gloves, and takes a single cambric nightgown, very plain; and the very next day ups and drowns herself in the lake there, Rosevear Lake, in nothing but that very same nightgown — bought her own winding sheet!'

'Oh, but why?'

'No one knows,' said Mrs Ticknell. 'I dare say

she had her reasons, poor girl, just put the box back where it was, will you, dear? Miller's wouldn't sell 'em on, and nor shall I; but lots of folk — you really not heard this? — have *seen* her, they do say.' She lowered her voice. 'At the Home, of a summer evening, she comes to watch the children play, a-standing in the reeds with her two arms folded, like this! My cousin's girl as works there, her friend, saw her there come sunset, with her ankles in the water, nearly died!'

Mrs Ticknell knew all Silkhampton's misfortunes. Carriages that had overturned fifty years before, spilling their occupants out on to the road at high speeds, horses that had bolted in the market square, swinging heavyweight carts sideways into the screaming crowds, badly built scaffolding, thatch struck by lightning, robberies, riots, rick-burnings, murders and shipwrecks; she knew the names of all the men lost when Bert Givens' boat went down (one of them a relative of hers, by marriage) though not the name of the local woman who had left her baby lying as she thought safe in a corner of the field one harvest time ('Pigs eat *anything*') and every date and detail of the entire county's mining disasters, collapses, explosions and floods.

Sometimes Grace came home from work feeling a bit like Violet after a day in the kitchen garden, needing a long sit-down and a cup of tea. At the same time it was somehow rather exhilarating: there seemed to be so much more to Silkhampton than Grace had ever suspected. It was as if Mrs Ticknell was letting Grace in on the grown-up world, the one that had to be kept secret from children.

And all the while, as she talked, Mrs Ticknell sewed. If there was no one in the shop her hands were never still. Some of the time she used a small sewing machine bolted on to one end of the counter; sometimes Grace turned the handle for her, when she needed both hands for something tricky. Often though no machine could stitch fine enough.

'Want to do this? I show you how? Here, take it, go on. No; smaller than that. That's right. Littlest bite you can.'

And then the doorbell would go and a customer come in, and Mrs Ticknell would instantly put her work aside and jump up, full of gleeful energy.

'Morning, Mrs Withers! What can I do for you?'

★   ★   ★

On St Valentine's Day, leaving home so fast, Grace arrived early; the shop was still locked, the blind down inside. She did up her coat in the mirror of the dark window, and adjusted her hat. The street was fairly quiet; she stepped back on the pavement, and studied her own full-length reflection.

She had made the plain wool coat herself, copying the narrow close fit from a picture on the front cover of one of Mrs Ticknell's magazines for ladies. Her hat was of toning velveteen, its angled brim threaded with malleable boning wire, trimmed with one slanting feather and a gathered length of dark gauze tied in a bow at the back, with trailing ends that were lifting a little in the light chill breeze.

In the darkened glass Grace examined the coat and the hat, and the pretty line of her cheek, and the slight womanly curve of her breast, and was struck with something like awe: it seemed to her that, standing just so, in the same pose as the lady in the magazine, her reflection was actually perfect. An intense happiness gripped her, a lightness inside that seemed to her to have nothing to do with the sin of vanity; it felt more like honesty. Look, see? Perfect!

And there was the card in her pocket, she remembered. Why not from Tommy Dando?

Just as she thought this there was a sudden grit of footsteps beside her, too close, so that she looked round startled, and it was him, taking a hurried step back as if he was startled too, one gloved hand rising automatically to his hat.

He coughed a little. 'Morning, Miss,' he said.

Grace did not speak. He was hardly a stranger, but he had accosted her in the street. She looked away, her lips parting.

'Miss Dimond. Sorry, I — ' He stopped. He took the hat off, and for a moment held it to his chest. Then he clapped it on again, and was gone.

For a minute or two more Grace stayed where she was on the pavement, lost in almost unendurable excitement. She was looking her best, and knew now that her best was spectacularly elegant and pretty; and he had been there to see. He could not have missed her beauty.

She remembered the time she and Lily had bumped into him after the pictures, and how he had not looked at her, any more than she had looked at him. Not straight, just tiny glances. Because a quick glance was all you could bear. How wonderful it would be to take a proper long look at him! That's all I want, Grace told herself. Her lips went on smiling all by themselves.

She drew a deep shaky breath, and then the black holland blind in the half-glazed shop door went up, and Mrs Ticknell appeared, her front hair still in curling rags.

'Hello, my lovely,' she cried, as she unlocked the door, 'ain't that hat turned out well!'

'Oh, thank you!'

'Just like a fashion plate, apart from, well, you know — '

Grace laughed from sheer good humour. Apart from that, of course. A shrug to that, today.

' — still, a real young lady!'

'A young lady what's handy with a mop and bucket,' said Grace, unbuttoning the coat.

'That's the kind for me,' said Mrs Ticknell. 'Light the fire first, though.'

They were very busy for a while. In a coarse sacking apron Grace swept and swabbed the pavement outside, then took a different broom and mop to the wooden floor within. All the wooden surfaces and shelves and glass-fronted cupboards had to be dusted and polished, and a great many lengths of material and other folded items needed to be taken up, shaken and re-folded, in the constant war against moths. The windows needed almost daily attention, inside and out, the rugs had to be beaten, the dried flowers shaken and rearranged, the allurements of sofa and table neatened and re-styled, the embossed metal sides of the cash register given a quick polish; it was often a race to get everything freshly dried and dusted before opening time.

'Have you done the window stuff?'

Ostrich feathers today, set in one of Mrs Ticknell's enormous vases, the velvet beneath them scattered with other accoutrements essential to headwear, one or two big velvet roses, a little basket of assorted silk ribbons.

'Yes, ma'am.'

'Good girl. Fly cuppa tea?'

Mrs Ticknell needed tea as much as she needed talk. There was no tea-drinking in the shop, of course; that was unthinkable. But behind the shop, through the stock-room, was Mrs Ticknell's own kitchen, with a smart enamel gas stove where you could boil a kettle just like that, in two minutes flat, without needing a fire at all.

Today as she filled the kettle Grace thought to herself, as usual, When I have my own home I will have a gas stove just like this one, but this time quickly felt almost dizzy at the sheer effrontery of the idea that came with it, that this vague future gas-stoved house would not just be her own, but also Tommy Dando's.

Oh, my Lord, what a thought!

Half-laughing aloud at herself she made the tea and ran back to the shop to relieve Mrs Ticknell.

But he sent me the card!

While Mrs Ticknell was in the kitchen she took the valentine out of her skirt pocket and unfolded it. She wished she hadn't done that now, the crease all wonky like that. How could she have ever thought it was Tim Bineham or poor old Cliff? It occurred to her for the first time that Tommy had been there early outside the shop in order to see her, that he had come on purpose, and that if so, he might well be there another day too.

The card trembled in her hands. Another day he would be prepared, he would speak. He would say something. How would she reply?

The shop doorbell rang and someone came in. Grace scrabbled the card back into her pocket.

'Good morning, Miss Thornby, what can I do for you?'

Grace usually felt very awkward with Norah Thornby. Several times over the years, she had seen her mother Violet, on catching sight of Mrs Thornby, draw herself up in a manner that in anyone else might have seemed a bit theatrical, and then turn on her heel, or cross the road. It was no use asking how, of course, but Grace knew that Miss Thornby's mother had once badly wronged her own.

And Norah was Guy Thornby's sister.

One summer when they were ten, Grace and Lily had played a game of teasing Guy Thornby. He was only in Silkhampton in the school holidays, and was very easy to spot, so neatly dressed, so hilariously posh and weedy, and generally carrying his mother's parcels for her, or

188

her shopping basket. It had been wonderfully funny to keep him in view, making faces at his back, laughing, darting behind street corners or into shops whenever he looked round, then falling into step behind him as soon as he turned back.

The following summer they had played it again, in fits of scornful giggles; but the year after that things had changed. Guy Thornby was different, or they were; at any rate, as he left the playing field where they had watched him idly tossing a cricket ball from hand to hand all by himself, he had stopped near the place where Grace and Lily lay hidden, as they thought, in the long grass beside the railway embankment, and given them a friendly little wave.

After that the game had swiftly altered. He stopped being the object, and joined in, spotting them back. All unspoken, all without any direct contact whatever, new rules developed: you only won if you were first to point your forefinger. Then only if you pointed both at once.

They spied on him at the church fete, popping out from behind the different stalls, hah! winning three times in a row. He dropped behind his parents on the way home from church, crouched to re-tie his shoelaces, jumped up quickly, hah! He cheated, suddenly leaning out of his father's motor car as it shot by, hah! Lily hid behind the sandwich board outside the tobacconist's, jumped out, hah! Grace at dusk outside the tall house in the square, ready to jump out, hah! from behind the lamp post, but spotted instead, and by Mrs Thornby herself, smartly tapping down the stairs towards a waiting taxi, taking Guy's arm, and saying, casually but still loudly enough for Grace to hear, 'What's that grisly creature doing here?'

Guy not looking round that time.

Even now Lily still dug Grace in the ribs with her elbow from time to time: Guy Thornby, two rows ahead at the Picture Palace, Guy Thornby on a push bike, look! But Grace remembered his mother's words, and that if he had deeply blushed he had not looked round, and that she herself was grisly, and a creature, and somehow though the words were hardly the worst she had ever heard they hurt more than she might have expected, and sometimes still did.

'Good morning, Miss Thornby, what can I do for you?'

Miss Norah Thornby, of course, was a real young lady, of the kind quite unfamiliar with mop or bucket. Though she had for a time attended the Silkhampton Council School (considered perfectly adequate for a daughter, though not of course for the boy), she had left early, in the year of the coronation, sent to a private boarding school for young ladies outside Plymouth.

Even so, Miss Thornby too had her own reasons for feeling uneasy.

She had known from an early age that her mother, Mrs Thornby, indefatigable in her charity work, had done all that she could to save the local poor from the revoltingly dirty and untaught likes of Violet Dimond, which made talking to Grace Dimond awkward enough; but further, while Grace had forgotten her earliest school days, Norah remembered everything, had in fact a painful nostalgia for her time at the Council School, for those simple days when she had not known, not even suspected, that she was that unlucky and hopeless thing, a plain girl. And she remembered clearly one especially happy summer dinner hour in the meadow, when the infant Grace had consented to nestle on her own lap, on the bench beneath the damson tree, while they made daisy chains together. Miss Thornby remembered adoring Grace Dimond.

And now grown-up Grace was so stylish, so very pretty, so composed. So different, of course, from Norah Thornby, who had turned out unfortunately tall and stolid, as Mrs Thornby herself so often sighingly remarked, in private and otherwise.

Miss Thornby knew that she was meant to look down on Grace, representative of the lower orders, member of an inferior race. But somehow she just couldn't manage it. Not being able to correctly look down on Grace Dimond was just one of the many things Norah Thornby felt inadequate about.

I envy her, thought Norah, and was ashamed of herself, not so much for the sin as for committing it about someone so far beneath her; circumstances of such potent and complicated social unease that she could hardly stand up straight, let alone speak normally.

'Good morning, Miss Thornby, what can I do for you?'

'Oh, ah, um — ' said Miss Thornby, and blushed. She was a blusher just like her brother,

191

her freckles frequently disappearing in a blotchy tide of crimson.

Normally this sort of thing was enough to make Grace stumble a little too, shyness being so infectious. But not today. She had glory within this morning, enough to deal with a dozen Norah Thornbys.

'I think your order come in this morning,' she said warmly, and she opened the deliveries drawer, flipped through it, brought out the right little packet. 'Here 'tis — was there anything else, Miss?'

'Um — no, thank you,' said Miss Thornby.

'Two and six then, please.' Grace loved Ticknell's cash register. It had round metal keys, white inlaid with black, like tiny versions of the organ stops in St George's, spelling out all the possible numbers and coins, some in combination. You firmly pressed the right ones down and in return little ivory tickets popped up in the glass top, spelling out the bill you'd just keyed in, while at the same time the tray below burst itself forcefully open with a great rattle of loose coin. When Grace had first started work she had often forgotten the till tray and it had caught her hard in the stomach, but now she tended to play a little game with it, standing just out of its reach, or neatly stepping sideways at the last moment. Missed me!

Miss Thornby took her change. 'Ah, Grace — ' she began, then stopped. Grace, she had half-imagined saying, Gracie, my dear, do you remember, not so long ago, that last school fete, and the folk dancing in the playground, and the Scenes from

192

Shakespeare, Teddy Hall was Henry V, he stood on top of the bicycle sheds, do you remember that? I was there, I was there then!

'Yes, Miss?'

'Nothing, sorry,' said Miss Thornby, smiling effortfully.

'Who was that?' said Mrs Ticknell, entering a few minutes later, her hair in proper order and a clean apron on. 'Oh, her. Brother got all the looks there — he's joined up, that Guy, did you hear? Off to France.'

'Is he?' Grace kept forgetting the war. It was so boring. And it had seemed to promise such excitement at first, so many young men standing about shouting on street corners, and people putting flags up, and the old Silkhampton Colliery Band playing military marches on Sunday afternoons. But then it all just fizzled out. Though newsreels at the Picture Palace now tended to feature young recruits practising at rifle ranges, singing round campfires, or lining up for breakfast.

'Only eighteen,' said Mrs Ticknell.

This seemed a fair soldierly age to Grace, but she could see she was meant to look serious, and did her best. Poor Lily would be sad; it was clear she still had rather a crush on him, thought Grace, pityingly. As if a gent like Guy Thornby would look at a girl like her! At an under-housemaid! He was a right old sissy anyway, thought Grace, compared to Tommy Dando, who'd make two of him. And Tommy not sixteen yet.

'You go and have your tea now. Just five minutes, mind!'

13

It was more than a week before she saw him again. He was coming out of the baker's just as she went in. He started, she made no sign at all. Still when she came out again she knew he was there. Yes: idling in front of the tobacconist's, pretending to look at the pipes in the window. She walked towards him, unhurriedly, making it clear she had not seen him, until just as she reached him he turned, touched his hat, and fell into step a little behind her.

'Miss Gracie?'

She went on walking, and so did he. Her heart hammered. She kept her face averted.

'I've got a letter for you. Can I give it to you?'

Grace hesitated, then briefly turned her eyes to his and felt the warm shock of his returning gaze.

'Alright,' she said, to the distance.

He gave her not the envelope she had instantly pictured, but a small folded note, passed quickly from his right hand to her left; then he tipped his hat, turned, and casually made off back in the direction they had come from. The whole thing was over in seconds.

Grace too walked away as if untroubled. But he must have had the note ready in his pocket. Perhaps he had carried it for days, waiting for the chance to speak to her privately! Oh, what on earth did it say?

Suppose it wasn't from him!

The horrid thought that Tommy was somehow acting as a go-between for someone else — Art Coachman, perhaps, or someone else's older brother — made it hard to carry on walking home normally, instead of instantly finding out there and then. But an open note in the hand would be so visible. As it was despite all his care there was still a chance someone had seen. That someone might tip Violet the wink. Saw your Gracie this morning, talking to young Tommy Dando, on the street bold as brass! Thought you ought to know, Mrs Dimond. Thought it best to tell.

She waited until she was home, and sure that Violet was still out at the market, then unfolded it.

His handwriting. One line of it:

Dear Grace, I think about you all the time. Tom

She gave a great gasp, then rushed to the mirror, to see her reflection's response; it looked back, glittering with joyful amazement. He thinks about me all the time! About me. He thinks about me: all the time.

Grace had to sit down for trembling, and covered her eyes with her hand. She could hardly breathe for happiness. What a thing to write to her, to trust to her, what a thing to hand over in the street — the openness, the daring!

Though of course he was handsome Tommy Dando, who never got caught at school, who never got the strap, who could charm his way out of, into, anything. A thought that sounded rather like Violet at her driest; but Grace did not heed it for long.

There was supper to get started, and various other daily tasks waiting, but for now Grace could do nothing but sit in the armchair by the dying untended fire and give herself up to a delicious inner swooning, that felt somehow constructive, as if it was an achievement in itself: active dreaming.

So when Violet came in half an hour later Grace was for a moment simply puzzled by her scolding.

'What's this — you ain't done nothing at all, you lazy girl!'

★　★　★

Violet had begun the afternoon with a fairly heated exchange with Rose Whitely, who for years had kept the pie stall in the market, and for whom she was a regular supplier. Mrs Whitely had agreed, out of the kindness of her heart (she at first implied), to move the stall from its usual prime spot to one altogether less favourable, in order to accommodate a friend's new cheese-selling venture. Violet had quickly discovered that the friend was in fact the woman who ran the dairy in North Street, known to be ruthless in all business matters, and who had simply paid Mrs Whitely to change her pitch.

Mrs Whitely tried to keep the sum involved a secret, but she was no match for Violet, who was disgusted.

'If you're going to take a bribe,' she said, 'you should at least take a big'un. What was you thinking of? You're going to lose that much in the first month!'

Mrs Whitely wrung her knobbly hands. 'Oh, Mrs Dimond, d'you think so?'

'I do; and what's more I'm going to lose it too.'

'But I've took the money now!'

'You spent it?'

'No.'

'Give it back to her then. Say you've changed your mind.'

'I can't do that!'

'Why not?'

'I just can't!'

'D'you want me to, then?'

'Oh, Mrs Dimond, would you?'

'Well, if you won't,' said Violet. She sounded merely resigned, though within she was alight with pleasurable fury and ready for battle. Spoil my business, would you? Prey on the weak-minded, and then with a mean, no, a cheese-paring bribe?

So Violet had exchanged a few plain words with the woman in the North Street dairy, set the money down on the counter, and coolly walked out leaving it there, which was all nicely enlivening enough, but as she passed St George's she was hailed, diffidently, by a woman she knew she ought to know.

'Mrs Dimond, ain't it?'

Not one of her own, surely? Violet hesitated; she had never yet forgotten a woman she had delivered. 'Yes?'

'It's May Givens, ma'am,' said the woman

anxiously. She was younger than Violet, though it was hard to tell by how much, her figure youthful, her face all wrinkles. 'My husband, he's your sister's nephew, Bert Givens' nephew.'

'Oh,' said Violet. Not one of her own then, so that was alright. Wife of the fisherman, who had the cottage by the harbour every winter. 'George, is it?' she said.

'That's right, ma'am. I was hoping to speak to you, hoping you'd put in a kind word.'

'Who with?'

'With Mrs Givens. Your sister, I mean. On account of — see, we've always had the field cottage for the summer no question, but she's still so angry — we can't stay where we are, you see, ma'am, we have to get out come the end of March, and if we can't go to the cottage, I don't know where we can go, not with the four of 'em and all, and George, he's tried talking to her, say he's sorry, but she won't see him, so I says to him, to George, I says, what about a-going to see you, Mrs Dimond, see if you can maybe have a word with her, and he says no no, 'cause it's all on account of your young Gracie in the first place, but I — '

'What about her? What about Grace?' said Violet, sharply breaking in.

Mrs Givens took a small grimy handkerchief from her sleeve, and dabbed at her eyes. 'She ain't told you? He dint mean nothing by it, Mrs Dimond, I swear, he's that fond of her, we all are — '

'Let's go and sit in the church porch,' said Violet, since May Givens' voice was rising and

198

falling altogether too loudly for someone naming
Grace Dimond. They passed through the lych-
gate and the churchyard, where the daffodils
were rising. There seemed no one about. Violet
sat down on one of the stone benches beside the
great church door, and after a moment's hesitation May Givens sat down beside her, though not
too close, and folded her hands submissively in
her lap.

'So. Your husband — he insulted my
daughter?'

'No, no! Mrs Dimond, please, he dint, not on
purpose! He just called her by his own little
name for her. He dint know it were wrong. He's
done it years — the maid herself, bless her, she
don't mind.'

Oh doesn't she, thought Violet, and her heart
hardened.

'And what is his own little name?' she asked.

May Givens looked as if she might cry with
embarrassment.

'Come along,' said Violet unkindly, 'I ain't got
all day.'

'It's just Half and Half,' muttered May Givens
finally.

'What? What did you say?'

'Half and Half. He dint know it was wrong.
How's young Miss Half and Half, he asks her,
only out of fondness, but your sister, ma'am, she
flared up proper! She laid right into him, ma'am,
she ain't let him near her since!'

'He called my daughter Half and Half?'

Mrs Givens nodded, the dirty handkerchief at
her eyes again.

'Why would he call her that?'

'It ain't that bad though, is it? He dint mean nothing by it, he — '

'Yes yes yes,' said Violet. 'How did he come up with it, this name? What does it mean?'

'Well, I don't know, ma'am, not rightly,' quivered Mrs Givens, who was clearly not used to lying, her eyes all over the place.

'Tell me what it means,' said Violet, in her old implacable child-bed voice. Mrs Givens actually gave a little squeak of fear.

'Oh, if you please, ma'am, I'm so sorry — it's about a drink!'

'What sort of drink?' said Violet icily; her views on alcohol were widely known.

' 'Tis one they take more in the north, ma'am,' said Mrs Givens. 'Two types of beer mixed together in a glass, mild and bitter. Chap wants one those, he says, 'Give us a pint of Half and Half.' See?' she finished timidly.

'And George called her that?' What nonsense was this?

Mrs Givens nodded. 'We're that sorry, Mrs Dimond, honest we are! Will you talk to her, please, to your sister? Only I got my children to think of, and we always do go to the field cottage at the end of March, regular as clockwork, will you, Mrs Dimond, please?'

Violet thought. 'I will talk to my sister,' she said at last, then interrupted Mrs Givens' instant clamour of gratitude: 'I'm not promising it'll come to anything, mind.' There seemed to be nothing else to add that would not imply criticism of Bea, so she said briskly, 'I'll bid you good day then,' gathered up her belongings, and left. She still had several purchases to make, and crowds to struggle through, and then it rained; and the constant questioning in her own mind seemed to get so in the way, was a roughly jostling crowd of itself.

Don't think about it, she told herself. Wait until you get home. Wait until you've seen Gracie. Perhaps like last week she'd have the supper on, good girl that she was, lovely smell to greet you, spuds all done and waiting, kettle singing. Get these leaky boots off, have a warm by the fire!

So it was extra hard to open her own front door and find Grace sitting idle in the dark with her coat on.

'What's this — you ain't done nothing at all, you lazy girl!'

★ ★ ★

If he hadn't put the letter in her hands himself — if she hadn't, of course, known his handwriting — she might have wondered, in the days that followed, whether the note was actually genuine. Once he passed her in the street, and just touched his hat, as if to some general acquaintance. Once he was standing on the other side as Mrs Ticknell locked the door behind her at closing time, but as soon as she looked across at him he turned and sauntered away in the opposite direction, as if he hadn't seen her at all.

Had he changed his mind? Had putting himself in her hands somehow been too much for him? It seemed to Grace that perhaps just admitting you thought about someone all the time might in itself be enough to stop you doing it, a sort of cure. If so Tommy Dando had cured himself at her expense, and passed on his affliction.

Dear Tom, I think about you all the time, too. There isn't a single moment when you're not there on my mind.

She sang about her work all day; despite the constant longing for him to make another move, contact her, arrange somehow even to meet, she had never been so happy in her life before, she thought. She hardly needed to eat, and often couldn't, but luckily Violet, usually so prone to maternal nagging about three square meals, seemed not to notice, or at least made no comment, thank heaven, but then perhaps she had finally, finally! noticed that Grace was a grown woman, who could decide for herself when she wanted breakfast, or that she didn't feel like supper.

Strangely enough, she could sleep very well, climbing happily into bed early most nights, often an hour or two before Violet, lying there in a blissful state of easy dreaming, drifting off sweetly picturing his face. Often she had pleasant dreams that made her laugh when she awoke, for while most of them seemed to hark back to the school playground, or to the classroom the year she had sat next to him, she was still her grown-up self in them, and so was Tom Dando and all the other ex-children, grown up but leaping just as they used to in and out of the great heavy washing-line skipping rope that took two at each end to turn; often a dreamland steam roundabout faintly played fairground music, and once Mr Billy Redwood had clearly said over it, 'Look here, jolly, don't you think?'

Grace at work the next day remembering on and off all the time that she and Tom Dando had once been comrades, just the two of them following Mr Billy across the enormous room with the windows; Barty Small looked out at her again, once or twice, but he had lost his power to move her. It was herself and Tommy Dando that she kept seeing, standing close together, meeting one another's eyes, and trying not to laugh.

They would laugh together again soon, thought Grace, letting the inner swooning take hold once more as she waited for Mrs Ticknell's kettle to boil, or shook the dust from the window-dressing velvet, they would laugh together soon as adults. As sweethearts.

Oh, when, when would he speak to her again?

* * *

Violet too was preoccupied. Before she had even reached home on that market day, she had understood that there were two parts to the conundrum Mrs George Givens had presented her with. There was the silly name itself, the nickname, hardly the worst she'd heard, and certainly not the worst Grace would have come across herself, poor girl; its meaning though seemed clear. George Givens must surely have the idea that Grace herself was, well, half and half.

Only half black; half white.

Was that what he thought?

Violet could not dismiss this, mainly because it had occurred to her once or twice over the years that Grace was — surely — paler than the only other black people Violet had seen, the sick-looking sailor propped against the harbour wall at Plymouth, and the music-hall singers. She had inwardly shrugged, telling herself that if white people varied so — no one would mistake a Greek for a Norwegian — why shouldn't all black folk have their own differing shades?

But the idea had always been there in the back of her mind, she realized. So perhaps George Givens, who had certainly travelled more than most, who had for a while, now she came to think of it, served for several years in the merchant navy before he married, perhaps he had merely noticed something true; noticed something he must have thought we all knew already, thought Violet, or how else would he have so carelessly let slip his foolish name?

And maybe he was none too bright, but he certainly seemed fond of his adoptive cousin, and Grace had often spent whole afternoons at Porthkerris, volunteering to help with the four little ones, his children. The name was not meant unkindly, thought Violet.

So why had Bea, who must surely know her own nephew perfectly well, flown into such a passion about it? Was it the name she minded? But it was merely feebly insulting compared to so many others. She must surely know that too.

Was it perhaps not the name at all, but the

assumption behind it?

Why would that bother you so, Beatrice?

Even asking this question, putting it in so many words, made Violet's heart beat so fast that she would have to sit down to ease it. Because as soon as she asked it, other ideas and questions formed themselves, dizzying questions, ideas that made her hold her breath.

She thought of the dying baby in the cot at the Home, lying back rolling and unrolling the stray end of the night-dress tape. She thought of the greyish face looking up, and being so like Ruth's. She saw the turn of the little girl's head, proud in her new dress at the market. She thought of Grace this morning smiling into the mirror as she adjusted her hat to the perfect stylish angle; just as once the young Bea Kitto had, vain and pretty in her sweet-faced teens. She thought of Grace's clever fingers turning a seam so lightly you could hardly see the stitches, or working out from looking at a picture what the separate pieces of a fitted coat should look like, and drawing them out on paper, and making first a careful try-out version from old sheeting before she cut the fine wool.

Bea would have done things like that. If she'd stayed at home.

But she did not. She went away, and stayed away, missed our mother's funeral, and — dear God! Oh dear God — said she'd parted brass rags with the Redwoods, and wouldn't be a lady's maid no more for all the tea in China; and went instead to the old Red Lion in its dirty four-ale days.

Bea who had given Grace a fine new blouse for Christmas, but sent by post; Bea who had kept Grace and Violet at a distance, more than this past year, making up paying guests for the cottage by the harbour wall. Bea who had not answered two letters. Bea who had told lies.

Violet, leaning on her spade in anguished thought for several minutes, straightened now, set the spade gently down against the wall, and without even washing her hands left her garden and went straight to St George's to pray for strength, for the surely almost supernatural strength that she would need, to get by herself on the train to the coast, and visit her sister at home.

14

The following Saturday, Grace's half-day nicely timed to chime with Lily's own monthly afternoon out, he was suddenly there beside her in the slowly moving crowd leaving the Picture Palace.

'Afternoon,' he said.

Grace immediately began to tremble all over, her knees shook. She peeped sideways up at his face, turned quickly away. But she had managed a smile.

On her other side Lily took her arm. 'Hello, Tommy,' she said.

'Like the show?'

Grace hesitated; both films were nothing to her now.

'Very much, thank you,' said Lily archly.

Tommy smiled down at Grace. I wasn't asking her, said his smile. I was asking you.

They reached the anteroom of the old tithe barn and the door propped open to the street. Lily tugged a little. 'We're off to the market now,' she told Tommy Dando. 'Aren't we, Grace.'

Tommy Dando appeared surprised. 'Why, so am I!'

Lily giggled, exactly as if, thought Grace anxiously, she really thought Tommy was speaking to her. Together they moved off towards the square, the two girls arm-in-arm, Tommy Dando on the edge of the pavement, gentlemanly. It was a bright blustery afternoon.

Outside the George and Dragon a red-faced tall fat man in an overcoat stood yelling on a soapbox, with Union Jack flags flapping on either side, held by a couple of bored-looking soldiers.

' — any young man, any young man with a heart, with a soul, must come at last to his country's aid!' the red-faced man was shouting, as they squeezed their way past the small listening crowd.

'When you going?' Lily asked Tommy Dando.

'Tomorrow, if they'd let me,' he said seriously, and for the first time Grace felt a pang of fear. Stupid war, what was it supposed to be about, anyway?

They reached the square. It was past four, and some of the stalls were already being tidied for dismantling.

'It's later than we thought,' Grace said.

'It's tea-time,' said Tommy Dando. 'Would you like some? Ladies?'

'How d'you mean?' Like Grace, Lily had never set foot inside any of Silkhampton's various public establishments. The rough ones were only for working men, and altogether too rough; the others only for gentry, and much too posh.

'We could try the Little Owl,' said Tommy. 'On me,' he added.

Lily and Grace met one another's eyes. The Little Owl Tearooms! Did they dare?

'Thank you,' said Grace, in her best polite shop-assistant manner, which was instantly too much for Lily, who giggled, her hand to her mouth.

'Come on then,' said Tommy Dando, and he

208

offered Lily his arm. She took it and they walked all the way down North Street and into the Rope Walk, and there were the tearooms, the windows all steamed up. They were a fairly new venture, a place where ladies might meet and drink tea and rest during shopping expeditions; run by the two Misses Lawrence, the daughters of the General. On the far side of the road Grace suddenly stopped. It had occurred to her that she had forgotten for the moment who she was.

'We can't,' she told Tommy.

'Can't what?'

'Go in there. I can't.'

'What d'you mean? Why not? It's only a shop.'

Miss Lawrence, Miss Jane Lawrence. Ladies both; not wool-shop regulars. What were they like? Whatever they were like, they were at home. They had opened their own home up as a tearoom when the old gentleman had died. Grace swallowed.

'I don't mind,' said Lily, with her usual unexamined tact. 'Let's go somewhere else.'

'This is best,' said Tommy. Grace looked at him. Did he have a clue? But he was Tommy Dando, of course: the charmer for whom everything was possible. Perhaps boldness too could be infectious.

'Alright then,' she said. They crossed the road and he opened the steamy door, Lily in first, then Grace, then Tommy. He closed the door behind them, the bell tinging.

Grace's heart beat very fast. It was a long time since she had knowingly risked such public insult. All of them, she knew, were too young and too poor for the likes of the Misses Lawrence, even Tommy Dando, whose father managed one of the dye works out past the railway station, where Tommy himself was currently working. The ladies and gentlemen who usually took tea at the Little Owl would hardly appreciate sharing their pleasures with an office clerk and a housemaid. And with the addition of Grace Dimond there was every chance, Grace knew, that there would suddenly be no room, no table free, no matter how many chairs stood empty.

Once long ago she had gone with Aunt Bea on a picnic in the country with a troop of other children from the Home, a great wagonful of them, climbing down in a meadow at the other end, where several ladies were waiting, and the ladies had handed every child a paper bag with a pasty and an apple in it, and there had been games, and races, and a man with a thing like a wide wooden barrel, with seats inside, and a handle; it held four children at once, and the man turned the handle, and spun the barrel round and round, like a tiny roundabout, and the children sitting in it screamed with joy, whizzing round in tight circles, laughing and giddily collapsing on the grass afterwards. They had all queued up for a go, but when Grace reached the roundabout the man had turned her away. At first he had pretended not to see her, then he had given her a little push, in the small of her back, to get her to go away. He had not spoken to her, not one word.

Grace had gone to her aunt and wept, for she had only been four or five, and not able to grasp yet what the problem might be. Aunt Bea had gone and talked to the man, and presently called Grace over, and picked her up and set her down in the barrel with the three other children waiting there, except that they were all sitting directly on the seats, and Grace was sitting on her Aunt Bea's shawl, spread out there, though it was her best paisley.

'Don't want you getting splinters in your bum,' she said to Grace, and though her words were jocose her tone had not quite matched it, so that Grace was still uneasy, and hadn't really liked being spun round anyway, glad when it was all over and she could jump out with the rest and lie on the grass pretending to laugh with the others.

'Can I help you?' One of the Miss Lawrences, the younger one, Miss Jane. The place was nearly empty, someone turning round briefly to stare. It was lovely, Grace thought; like Ticknell's wool shop, only a tearoom, all clean and cosy and designed to allure, clean white tablecloths, pictures on the wall with little gas lamps, and such fine china, flowered and delicate, and silvery teapots.

'Tea for three, please,' said Tommy Dando cheerfully. He was taller than Miss Lawrence. His smile, Grace saw, was ravishing. Miss Lawrence, Jane, was a woman after all, despite her poor scrawny frame, her frizz of greying hair and white bony nose. She was ravished.

'Well, ah, yes — it is quite near closing time, but ah — '

'We'll be ever so quick,' said Tommy, and Miss

Lawrence swung her poor old head almost coquettishly, and with a girlish simper pulled out a nearby chair. It was at a table half in the alcove at one side. Lily let Grace take the most hidden alcove seat and Tommy pulled out the chair opposite for Lily, so that he himself must sit between them. He shifted the chair just a little, so that he was closer to Grace. He hid her, too, from the doorway, Grace noted.

'Well, Miss Houghton, well, Miss Dimond,' he said, mock-grave, and suddenly it was all any of them could do not to giggle, the three of them sitting in the Little Owl Tearooms, as if they were gentry!

'How you gonna pay for this?' whispered Lily; shared daring had made them all suddenly intimate.

'I got money,' said Tommy, with a shrug. 'What would you like, Gracie?' He gave her a direct look and for a long, dizzying moment she looked back. He had to swallow, she saw, before he could say anything else. 'Cake?' It came out slightly squeaky and they all laughed again.

'Tea,' said a voice, flatly. It was Miss Lawrence, the fatter, older one that the place was named after, Tommy said, when the tray was unloaded and she had made her grim way back to the kitchen.

It had been an uncomfortable moment, sitting still and quiet while Miss Lawrence set out the tea things. Grace had looked down at the tablecloth, careful not to risk meeting her eyes. It seemed to Grace that looking up would indicate that she, Grace Dimond, was enjoyably, even

212

sneeringly, aware that she was being served tea by the daughter of a general.

I'm such a come-down for her, she had thought, as a side plate was set in front of her. It was not the first time Grace had felt a confused pity for someone clearly unhappy in her presence, dismayed by her own existence. They've been taught something wrong, Violet used to say: they know no better than to mind what colour another good Christian is. But while that might be ignorant, cruel, ungodly even, almost-thought Grace, it was still minding. The pain was still real, the dismay still genuine, and if hardly intended still all down to Grace: her fault. Poor Miss Lawrence!

Grace was barely aware of this complexity of muddled guilt. She only knew that while Miss Lawrence unloaded the tray she felt dreadfully uncomfortable, a common enough feeling for her, and that it was better, safer all round somehow, to keep her eyes down. She did not notice that Lily too was keeping her own head down, and hiding her work-thickened servant's hands.

'Cheer up,' said Tommy to them both, when Miss Lawrence had gone, and he had pointed out her Owlish qualities. 'Don't mind her — ol' ratbag.' It was like a gust of fresh air, his irreverence. And so male. What is this nonsense, his frank tone said.

'Got any scones left, please?' he asked the thin one, Miss Jane, as she scurried past to another table, and presently she brought them a plateful, with a pot of cream and some home-made

213

strawberry jam in a little crystal bowl.

Then they talked and ate and laughed, not too loudly, and there was no one near enough to notice if they held the knives in the wrong way, or that Lily finished up the milk jug by swigging directly out of it. They talked about the Picture Palace, and the best films, and Miss Pyncheon's new hairstyle, which was as short as a man's, and Lily's oldest sister's place over in Plymouth, where the husband and wife sat at opposite ends of a gloomy great table as long as a cricket pitch, and never spoke to one another from one week's end to the next. Tommy talked about his own sudden if temporary rise through the office ranks, with so many older chaps out at the Front. He only hoped the whole thing wouldn't be over by the time he was old enough to go to France himself, he said. Two of Lily's brothers were there already, said Lily, and her mother was that pleased, the money coming in so regular.

'Any more tea in that pot, Gracie?'

When they were ready to leave Miss Lawrence brought the bill, and Tommy counted out the money a little showily, perhaps.

'Do keep the change,' he said drawlingly, as he put away his wallet. Punishing her, Grace saw, for all that she had so silently conveyed to them, even to him, in the set of her shoulders. Lily sniggered, but Miss Lawrence merely thanked him, and put the sixpence in the pocket of her apron.

'You didn't have to do that,' said Grace, when they were back outside. From the corner of her eye she saw the sign in the Little Owl Tearooms

214

door turned swiftly about, to read CLOSED.

'Oh, it's quite the usual thing,' he said, pretending to misunderstand her, and after a second's hesitation she pretended to be reassured.

'I got to be getting back,' said Lily, 'or they'll have my guts for garters. Thanks for the tea.'

'Pleasure,' said Tommy, grinning. 'Dear ladies!' and he gave them each a separate wildly exaggerated bow, bade them good night, and walked quickly away into the gathering darkness: not seeing either of them home. Well, perhaps it was for the best, thought Grace, though she had been hopeful, even let herself picture the two of them walking back towards Market Buildings together, slowly, in the lamplight.

But in any case this had been a sort of public declaration. She and Tommy and Lily; the gossip would be all over Silkhampton by this time tomorrow, that he was, in all likelihood, courting one of them. It was just that Silk-hampton could not yet be sure which one. There was safety in that, she saw. For them all.

★ ★ ★

Violet decided to try cunning first. She wrote inviting Bea to visit, not a word of reproach, going into some detail about a film she herself had lately seen with Grace at the Picture Palace.

It was a special camera, Grace had told her. They set it up beside the rosebuds or whatever else they wanted, filmed the buds opening, and then speeded the film up later so that what really

215

took hours seemed to take no time at all. This sounded convincingly mechanical enough. But somehow the sight of the young roses seeming to exhale as they held out their petals to the light gave Violet a tremendous lurch at her heart. The movement of the flowers like a turning dance, the fresh unfolding petals so eager, so unaware of their own fragility! Violet, sitting in rapt forgetfulness beside Grace in the fourpennies, had been startled back into herself by the sudden realization that she was near tears.

It was not until they were on their way home that she made the connection between the busily innocent flowers and her own past. She thought of all the babies she had seen into the world. How lucky she had been, how privileged! Over and over again she had witnessed the moment. She had never thought of birth as beautiful, only as profound. Now she found herself on the edge of a thought that seemed almost blasphemous in its presumption: that the pleasure she had taken in the dance of the quickened flowers, their speedy passage from bud to full-blown rose, might be some faint echo of the divine pleasure of the Creator Himself, as He saw His frail children make their strange cascading entry into His world, then stretch and unfold themselves, turn towards the light, in a span of time only He could properly encompass.

'I sit down a minute,' said Violet, for luckily they were passing a low wall at the time.

'You alright?' Grace was alarmed. She had never known Violet to have a single day's illness before, not so much as a headache.

216

'Just felt a bit dizzy. There. Alright now.' She rose, steady as usual. 'It was them flowers,' she said quite crossly, to Grace's surprise, 'I can't be doing with them.'

All the same she was sure Bea would enjoy them, their near-magic. She wrote too about how much Grace longed to take her aunt to the cinema — had Bea even seen a proper moving picture yet? The way Mr Pyncheon played the piano too, it was as good as a concert! And the weather still so cold and so wild — why not spend a few days in your own home town, Bea? Perhaps next week? Please to write back and say. She was Bea's only and loving sister, Violet Dimond.

She would wait a week, she thought. A week was long enough. If Bea made no reply, or wrote with some further excuse, she would take action. She would no longer allow Bea to pretend that things were simply back the way they were, the distant crosspatch way they generally had been, before Grace. We're past all that, Bea had said then, plain as day. That was still true, thought Violet.

And yet she doesn't know how much I know. She won't know May Givens talked to me. She doesn't know I know about Half and Half.

Half of what, Bea? Half of whom?

A week, Beatrice Givens. And then I come to you.

15

Tommy Dando walking towards Market Buildings one March evening after dark, pausing not
outside Grace's window, so near the lamp post,
but a little further on, where he can slip into the
shadows of the alley, and disappear from view.

Tommy Dando so tall and healthy-looking,
his lively face so often full of laughter. Perhaps
only his mother has any suspicions about him.
Lately, since she caught him going through
her handbag, she's been keeping her purse in her
pocket. But then, she's never liked him much.
Her heart belonged to his elder brother, who
died of diphtheria when he was eight. Tommy
aged five was ill too, but before he could get out
of bed again knew that in his mother's eyes the
wrong brother had lived.

He sleeps badly, always has.

Once, just after his own eighth birthday, he
took Sam's cap from its peg where still it hung,
and slipped out of the house with it, coming in
only at dusk, and making sure his mother was
there in the doorway to see him approach,
wearing the cap just the same way Sam had,
and trying as best as he could to capture Sam's
distinctive quick-paced walk.

He did not know why he did this, only that it
had seemed like a good idea: his mother would
see Sam again, even if for just a little while, and
be glad — that was the general hazy notion.

Afterwards he could not remember why he had been content with so much haziness. It had seemed to him at the time that the haziness had a sort of authority to it.

Sometimes even now Tommy Dando looks in the mirror in the new lean-to bathroom and tries to see Sam looking back. There's not much resemblance; Tommy favours his father, broad and fair and strapping. Sammy was dark and delicate; his eyebrows had a particular slant to them, flyaway, witty.

He prefers the mirror best after a bath, when the steam has fully blurred his image, and the water darkened his hair; you can certainly see the likeness then, Tommy thinks.

Other times it's just lumpish Tommy Dando looking back, the one with nothing inside him, nothing at all.

★　★　★

He doesn't really know why he's here, in the alley beside Market Buildings. Hadn't planned it. Was on his way home, just turned left instead of right, and somehow here he is. He's curious, he tells himself: what's it like, her place? He can't imagine, he has so little to go on. There's his own home, much bigger, on both floors at any rate, and there's his uncle's farmhouse; these are the only private houses Tommy has entered, apart from the brief astonishments of Wooton, all those years ago.

He reaches the end of the alley, turns left, and slides up the catch to the garden door. It opens without a sound. Henhouse, silent. The cinder path leads straight between the dark leafy beds to the door at the back of the house. Of course the old hag upstairs, Mrs Skewes, may well be vigilant at the back, though all seems in darkness up there. Lucky she's stone deaf though, the cinder path so noisy underfoot. He crunches unhurriedly up the path in the manner of one expected, just in case the hag is watching anyway, and knocks softly on the downstairs window. A few moments' wait, then the blind is cautiously pulled to one side, and he catches quick sight of Grace's startled eye, her eyebrow. He pulls off his hat.

Will she let him in?

She shouldn't, of course. He knows that Violet Dimond is out, for this is Tuesday, her Bible-group meeting; she won't be back for over an hour. But he is not visible to anyone, standing here. If Grace refuses him, he won't lose any public face, at any rate. If she lets him in, well, who knows what might happen, how far he might get?

The door opens.

'What you doing here!' she whispers joyfully.

'Just visiting,' he whispers back, trying for casual, then looks away before adding: 'I had to see you.'

'Why?' Breathless.

'It's been so long!'

Three days. She smiles up at him. He smiles back, in some confusion. A familiar confusion. When they're apart he thinks about her all the time. He longs for her. He can't help wanting to

220

see the line of her cheek again, to check it, as if it might suddenly have changed and not be as precious as he dreams it is. He needs to check too on the curve of her lips, and the delicious little crescents that appear on either side of them when she smiles.

These things always turn out to be as wonderfully enticing as ever, and yet each time he sees her, her colour takes him by surprise. She isn't white in his daydreams; but in the flesh she's so dark that every time he first sets eyes on her again he hears Ma say what she said the first time he mentioned, in passing, what a pretty girl Grace Dimond was growing up to be: 'You bring that creature here, my boy, you don't call this place home no more. Nor me your mother.'

Not raising her voice, not even looking up from her sewing; though said with relish.

No point pretending not to understand her, no point asking why. Though it soon occurred to him that he had rarely heard such talk from her before. He knew that plenty of locals didn't mind Grace Dimond, took no notice of her difference, hardly saw it any more, even downright liked it; though plenty felt otherwise, of course.

He saw his mother being careful which of her cronies she spoke to, relaying her speech, enjoying the stern drama of it. *I told him straight, you don't call this place home no more!* The chosen gossips all gravely nodding, backing her up, helping her feel certain. When all the time, Tommy suspects, she is merely seizing on Grace Dimond as a reason to be angry with him, to get rid of him. She yearns to be implacable. She longs with all her heart to unmother him.

Hardly a new idea to him, but not one he has ever looked at closely. Every time he feels it approaching he shies back from it, and turns his attention to something else. It's quite easy to do, for now. Especially when all he has to do is relax his guard for the tiniest half-second and he's dreaming about Grace Dimond again, about her narrow waist and cloud of strange exotic hair, that he has not touched since they were children.

He has forgotten how hard he pulled it in those far-off days.

'What you doing?' he asks now.

'Peeling spuds, if you must know.'

'Miss Pert. I have a cuppa tea?'

'No!'

'Go on. Ask your Ma, bet she won't mind,' he adds, with conscious cunning.

'She ain't here,' says Grace, as he knew she would.

'Well then, where's the harm? Only stay a minute. Eh? Gracie?'

She thinks about it for a few seconds more, then opens the door a little wider, and lets him in.

★   ★   ★

It wasn't that there was no answer at all. That would almost have been preferable, Violet thought. But her sister had sent her a postcard, a trade one, the sort she used to stock in the saloon at the Red Lion, views of the harbour at Porthkerris, with all the general mess of fish crates and rags and surly dirty-faced old fishermen entirely tidied away, and on the back she had written in her loopy handwriting, which still took Violet some effort to translate, that she did not herself care for the moving pictures, and that there was sickness at the Home, they were that short-handed, she had hardly any time to herself at the moment. She would be sure to let Violet know when that changed, she was, affectionately, Beatrice Givens.

It was the strange slackness of the lie that most dismayed Violet. Where did Bea think she was living, Paris again, perhaps, or the far side of the moon?

It was simple, spotting Effie Hook in the market — Effie, parlourmaid now at Wooton, whose old mother Bet had once passed on a special pair of little outgrown boots from the Hall.

'Morning, Miss Hook. How's your mother getting on these days, alright?'

No stopping her: Old Bet always had been rather a handful, of course, but she had grown childish with the passing years, and had lately taken to leaning out of the upstairs window of her cottage, cracking her knuckles and making familiar remarks to passers-by.

Old folk were often such a worry, agreed Violet. And was it true, now, what she'd heard about the new harbour wall?

There was, it turned out, a great deal of other local news, and Effie Hook was pleased to relay it all, with never so much as a mention of sickness; and all the Home staff came from Porthkerris, apart from Bea herself. Most lived out, too; and walked home together every evening, as garrulous and gossipy a bunch, thought Violet, as any other, if not more so.

So it had been an easy lie, easily disproved. Bea had always gone to such trouble before, at least in the wrong-doing Violet actually knew about, constructing deceptions at least as convincing as the truth and often more interesting: the hairy-faced tramp who had hobbled in, transfixed her with his one glaring eye, and swiped all the cheese right off the kitchen table; the enormous spotted dog belonging to some snooty traveller that had run barking out of the George and Dragon and jumped up and knocked her right over on to the grass, thus staining the back of her Sunday skirt; the letter —

— the letter from my young man Ned Dimond all those years ago, addressed plain enough to *Miss Kitto* that she said was for her, when all the time it was for me, oh, the vixen, thought Violet, and for a moment forgot what it was she was supposed to be feeling, the essential questions that had to be answered, Beatrice Kitto, my trial, my constant burden, my curse!

She would go on the train again, and visit in person, Violet decided, when she was herself again. She would not go empty-handed; she would take gifts. She would take a few other things with her, so that if necessary she might stay the night. Heaven only knew what she would find, what story or stories, indeed, Bea might favour her with. The truth might take time.

But I will discover it, thought Violet, and called in at St George's on her way home, for a little contemplative quiet, and to ask for strength

224

in resisting her own feelings. It was hard though to maintain her usual respectful formality. She tried her best to offer more regular prayers, but the thought that kept forming seemed to have come straight out of her childhood, the shared twinned childhood she and her sister had both been so glad to leave behind:

Oh Lord, don't let me thump her. Please don't let me thump her too hard.

* * *

He entered warily into a tremendous smell of baking, for this was a Tuesday, and the market box stowed beneath the table was full of the afternoon's pies, only lately cool enough for Grace to stack into place. It was a largish room, lit with oil lamps, the fire burning low in the range. A tap dripped in the sink in one corner, a newspaper sheet covered with potato peelings beside it on the wooden draining board.

He felt instantly a little checked; the room was so clearly respectable, home of people with standards. It was not so different from his own home, he thought, though of course they had gas, and a proper scullery.

Grace standing looking at him, one eyebrow raised. Everything about her was neat and perfect, he thought. How calm and poised she looked! A little weak quiver of bashful fear ran all over him, as if he were some drip, he told himself scornfully, as if he were Art Coachman or Ted Hall. Stand aside, gentlemen: let me show you how. To deal with a woman.

'You look nice,' he said.

'I *am* nice.'

'I know.'

There was a pause.

Inspiration. 'You going to the dance Saturday?'

'The Church Hall?'

'That's the one. I'll be there. Come with me?'

She gave him a straight look, made his insides melt quite away. 'No. We're too young to be walking out. You know that.'

'We ain't children,' he said.

'We ain't grown up.'

'What you scared of? You scared of me, Gracie?'

I'm scared of the world. I'm scared of everything. Of course I am scared of you. 'I'm scared of my mother,' said Grace lightly.

'Who ain't?' said Tommy Dando, and they laughed, though it was not until later that Grace felt a little ashamed, though it was hard to tell whether they had really been laughing at Violet, or just somehow laughing at everything and nothing in particular, because they were alone together, and so in love with one another's full exchanging gaze.

While they laughed though he was able to step forward, to get closer to her. He said, 'I must go,' very softly, almost into her hair.

'Yes. You should.'

He bent, and kissed her cheek. 'Goodbye, Grace.'

'Goodbye,' she said, and then he was able to put his arms round her. Of course his Uncle John came calling straight away, no stopping that dirty old dog. But he felt safe enough, his coat on, and in any case they weren't pressed right up, just standing together, warmly embraced. A long moment passed. He felt love, felt loved. It was like a dream of happiness, smooth within, untroubled, a deep enfolding.

Then she pulled away, she opened the door, and the cold damp air flowed in harshly, emblem of the outside world, always waiting.

'You gotta go,' she said, and she wouldn't look at him. He gave the hand on the doorknob the barest touch with his own, as he went. The door closed behind him.

And there he was, outside in the dark, awash with feelings he had — he quickly told himself — not much use for. Pete's sake. This wouldn't do at all. Grow up, he told himself as unkindly as he could. What was he playing at, what was he getting into? He didn't want this. He wanted out, out of Silkhampton, out of England, out of all dull backwatery hopelessness; what was she up to, talking about *walking out?* Catch him walking out with anyone!

And yet, and yet . . . he remembered that long sweet embrace. He remembered that he had not wanted it to change, had not wanted to take it further.

Why, taking it further hadn't even occurred to him! What a cowardly fool, what a waste! What might have happened if he'd only chanced his arm!

Oh, but it had felt complete in itself, that long enfolding.

Girls' talk, that was. Soppy girls' talk. Just standing there *cuddling!*

He walked home feverish with argument, unable to agree with himself about anything.

16

The following Saturday afternoon, as the market was packing up, Violet made the journey to the station, the old special bag in her hand, co-opted as suitcase, and caught the train to the coast. The special bag held her toothbrush and one or two other personal items, a large rabbit pie in an old biscuit tin, and a fruitcake wrapped in waxed paper, for Bea to keep or cut as she chose.

She boarded the train with a heavy heart. Bea had done her best to avoid her, to avoid Gracie. So Violet was doing something she had always tried to avoid her whole life long, pushing herself in where she knew she wasn't wanted.

But what else can I do, Bea? It's driving me mad, not knowing. Half and Half. And I told May Givens I'd talk to you.

Violet looked out of the window at the late spring fields. There had been several soldiers on the opposite platform, boys in uniform, being seen off, some she recognized; one or two her own. Gerry Ticknell had followed his older brother, she had lately heard, and joined up; getting ready to leave a perfectly good job at the solicitor's office.

She remembered the day she had held Gerry Ticknell's whole body in her left hand, the tiny chest fitted into her palm, turning him so gently from side to side to free each little shoulder, drawing down so carefully each little arm, freeing the face and holding him there in stillness, refusing to let him rush, so that he would hurt neither himself nor his mother in his final entry into the world.

She rose stiffly as the train drew into the right stop. The last time she had done this journey alone, she realized, had been the time she came to collect the sick baby, nameless then, from the Home; just a few weeks after visiting Bea that time, because of the horrible dream of drowning that had come to them both. Bea's dream, somehow sent to her. A lot had happened because of that dream, she thought, as she climbed down on to the empty platform. Her legs felt heavy, the bag almost too much to carry.

She set off grimly, turning as before away from the village and along the stretch of winding lane that led to the Home. Few now, she thought, would remember as she did the days when the Home had been Rosevear Manor, and a fine house for the gentry. She herself could remember the carriage the old family had used, the crest painted on the side of it. She remembered a wedding that had taken place at St George's, the crested carriage then all tied about with hoops of flowers and white ribbon, and the ancient gentleman, father of the bride, or maybe grandfather, who had stood on top of the portico of the George and Dragon afterwards, flinging down money to the local children waiting below, she and Bea among them, scrabbling in the dirt, and hopping and crying out, for the coins had been heated almost red-hot before he threw them. And for the first time it occurred to Violet that this trick, this heating of the money the old gentleman threw, was actually a mean and nasty thing to do, and all for his own pleasure, him in his thick gloves.

He must have had a spirit stove up there with him, Violet thought. Burning on the portico, going to all that trouble, the old beast. And yet we thought nothing of it at the time. We burnt our fingers, but we kept the pennies.

At last she reached the gateposts, where once before she had sat down on the market box and decided not to bother the Almighty about what mood her sister might be in. There it stood, the Home, the old Rosevear Manor. She thought of that silly goose Mrs Ticknell filling Grace's head with nonsense, stories best forgotten, then remembered abruptly that Aggie Ticknell had more serious things to worry about now. Sorry, Aggie. I know you've been good to my girl.

Oh, how reluctant she was, to go any further! The closer she got the more peculiar she felt, so weighted down all over. Were these Bea's own feelings? Was she sitting in the housekeeper's little cupboard-room sending out waves of dejection?

Give over, thought Violet, and made herself quicken her pace. It was getting on for four, but dry and bright still; there were grey-clad children playing in the meadow about the great house, and one or two enormous perambulators parked in the sunshine. Violet waved austerely to the nursemaid sitting by with her knitting, and walked round the side of the house as she had all those years before, the day she first saw Grace.

She made her way to the housekeeper's room along the stone-flagged corridor, through the same smells of laundry overlaid with cabbage. Was Bea in, after all? Suppose there was no answer to her knock?

Violet felt herself tremble a little, standing in front of the half-glazed door, the same net curtain. She was not expected. She was not wanted either, she knew that much.

She rapped on the door, and after a little pause, Bea opened it.

For a long moment neither spoke. Bea stared out, startled, frankly horrified; Violet stared in, startled, frankly horrified. *We are playing Mirrors*, came the thought both shared.

'You bin ill — Bea, what's wrong!'

Me, she heard Bea's thought, grim, amused.

'Alright, you,' said Violet, forgetting in her distress that usually she refused to countenance the very idea of transferred thought, between twins or anyone else. 'Am I coming in or what?'

Bea eyed her briefly, then stood aside. Violet entered. The place was certainly not as it had been, she saw straight away. It had a smudged look, cluttered; the tablecloth was surely last week's, or even older, there was a tumble of inelegant bits and pieces on the dusty mantelpiece, a broken plate, a lamp covered in black, a saucerful of old bread crusts. Bea took a couple of newspapers off the second chair, looked round idly, and dropped them on the floor, where they slewed sideways.

'Sit yourself down. Cuppa tea?'

She moved all the time with a strange heavy

231

slowness, as if just standing upright was an effort, and one she could hardly bring herself to make.

'Bea? I make it, shall I?'

And instead of casting her a sharp look, instead of instantly giving out something hot and strong about whose place it was and whose kettle and so on, this strange new Bea gave a weak little shrug and sat down at the table, without so much as a word.

Violet checked the kettle — heavy enough — and lit the spirit beneath it.

'Bea, you ain't — you ain't lost your place, have you?'

For clearly Bea was not doing much housekeeping, for all her title. But she shook her head, with a sigh that was something like a laugh.

'Oh, they'd never sack me here,' she said, and for a moment Violet thought she was going to say more, but she just looked away. In silence, trying to collect herself, Violet rinsed the thick old brew out of the teapot, and found the tea caddy sitting on the dresser shelf with its lid not put on properly.

'I dint hear you was ill. Or I'd a come sooner. Got any sugar?'

There was a sugar basin on the dresser, but when Violet took off its cracked lid there was nothing inside it but a few crusted tea-stained old smears.

''Ave a look in the cupboard,' said Bea, leaning her head on her hand, and didn't so much as stir when Violet opened the middle cupboard, and things piled there rolled out on to the floor — several wrinkled nearly empty paper bags, a packet of tea. One of the bags held sugar. Violet tidied everything back and used a teaspoon in the sugar bag.

Tentatively she set the dirty sugar basin beside the sink, a declaration of war on any other day. She even waited a second, for the first explosion. But nothing came; Bea seemed not to have noticed anything at all.

It seemed to Violet that she had come across something like this before, more than once, in the old days; but Bea was far too old for the strange languid melancholy that now and then afflicted women after childbirth.

More than melancholy sometimes. Violet sat down, resisting the impulse to brush the stained tablecloth free of crumbs, and gave the teapot a stir. She remembered Hetty Whitgift, who had trembled all over on first holding her baby, as if he were made of petals ready to bruise at her touch, who had taken all day (said her mother-in-law, disgustedly) just to get the baby dressed; who grew more and more quiet until you could hardly get a word out of her, and who went running down the street in her night-dress early one morning (the nightdress not fit to be seen, either, for various reasons) crying that the Devil himself, pink and bristly as a full-grown pig, was sitting stark naked on the stable-roof, playing with himself, and scraping his sharp little hoofs on the tiling.

But it had not been childbirth that prompted this particular melancholia of Bea's. Or only, perhaps, in a manner of speaking, thought Violet, with an inner qualm. What was it May Givens had said?

'How's young Miss Half and Half, he asks her, only out of fondness, but your sister, ma'am, she flared up proper! She laid right into him, ma'am, she ain't let him near her since!'

Bea hardly looked capable of flaring now. She had flared up too much, thought Violet, and burnt herself out like a firework.

'I get a coupla plates out?' She spoke almost to herself, expecting no answer, getting none. She opened cupboards until she found the china, took out plates, found a cake stand made of crinkled glass. She took the cake out of the special bag and unwrapped it, instantly releasing its warm toasted smell. It looked very well, too, she thought; she had studded the top with almonds, and glazed it with a glistening wash of apricot jelly. She found the knife drawer, selected the sharpest-looking, gave it a quick furtive wipe with the waxed paper she had wrapped the cake in, and plunged it in. The caramel smell intensified, irresistibly. She set a slice in front of Bea, and was ready.

'You ain't yourself, Bea,' she said. She slid a full teacup over, well-sugared.

Bea took a sip, set the cup down again. Her hands trembled, Violet saw, with a constant fine tremor.

'I *am* myself,' said Bea, with a sigh. 'That's the trouble.'

Violet felt a little flash of the usual scorn; Bea striking one of her poses, even now. The sarcastic words rose to her lips: What's that supposed to mean? She managed to keep them in though, said nothing at all, but broke off a small corner of fruit cake, and put it in her mouth. It felt inedible there. She swallowed it with some difficulty.

'Left Gracie at her work,' she said at last. 'Aggie Ticknell's got her doing all sorts these days, alterations, she brought home a jacket from Wooton last week, going to put in a whole new lining all by herself. What colour then, she asks the maid, and she says, Oh, you choose, just like that! So Gracie's doing the sleeves in sky blue, and the rest in bottle green. Won't you drink your tea, Bea?' she added, in a different voice. 'The sugar'll do you good.'

Bea said nothing. Her head was bowed, so it was some time before Violet could be sure that she was crying. Finally a tear dripped down on to the tablecloth.

'Bea? I know you don't want to see me. But I couldn't keep away no more. See?'

Bea took her hand away, and raised her head. She looked so much older, thought Violet (noting her own lack of pleasure), that their days of playing Mirrors properly were surely over for good. Her skin had a horrible puffy gloss to it, her jaw had sagged.

'May Givens come to see me,' Violet said. 'Because you won't let them the summer place, or talk to her George, on account of something he said, about Grace.'

How silly it sounded! Like a children's argument. She said you said he said —

'Don't care about that,' muttered Bea. It was as if she could hardly be bothered to move her lips.

'What is it then? I know what he called her, Bea. I know, see.'

That made her look up. 'Oh yes? And what do you know? What do you know about anything?' This said in spiteful anger. Violet put her hands together in her lap, folded them together as she did sometimes in church. The touch of her own trembling fingers reminded her of Him who was always there to comfort and direct her, if she was only wise enough to ask.

'Please — ent I your sister?'

Bea sneered. 'You're my sister alright.'

'What have *I* done?'

'Been born. Been there all the time. Been there all my life. That's all.'

'What are you talking about?'

Bea leant her head on her hand again, as if her sudden burst of fury had worn her out. 'You,' she said sullenly. 'Miss Butter-wouldn't-melt. Miss Righteous and Sober. It ain't fair!'

'What isn't?'

'Everything I do is wrong, it all goes wrong! And all the time I got you, being right all the time. How d'you think that feels, eh? Being me but getting it right! It ain't fair! Others go wrong, don't have to look at themselves getting it right! See?'

'So — ' Violet began and stopped. It seemed clear enough what Bea meant: that the likeness between them, the mirror image, was an added burden; but she was surely getting things the wrong way round, thought Violet. It was she, Bea, who had always done best, been most loved, liveliest, done so well; had adventures and travel and a good husband, and a fine business all her own, and how many women in this world could say that? Say as much as half of it? Not Violet Dimond; all she had done was copy their mother, and stay at home.

'But I ain't done anything,' she said, and then without a moment's thought added the truth she had kept hidden all her adult life: 'I always thought it was me, had to look at *you* being better all the time.' Her heart was pounding away though, as if in a panic all by itself, at seeing how lightly she had given up the secret.

Bea gave a tired little snuffle of laughter.

'I always could fool you.'

'Could you?'

'Easy. Tell me: you ever ask yourself why you took up with Gracie? Why you took her in that time?'

'Well, 'twas my duty — '

'Oh that stuff,' Bea broke in. 'Why her, I mean.'

'You know why — she looked so, she looked so like my Ruth. You know that.'

'But *why?*'

'How d'you mean?'

'Why'd she look like your Ruth, eh? Why did she?'

Ah. Now we come to it. Violet felt her lips stiffen: 'I thought coincidence. That's all. That's what I thought then.'

'Funny, ain't it,' said Bea. 'That's what I

237

thought too. And you know why. On account of her being black. See — ' she leant forward, 'suppose she weren't. Suppose she was the same colour as you and me, little girl lying there, spit a your Ruth. What would you have thought then, eh?'

'I don't know,' said Violet faintly.

'Yes, you do,' said Bea. 'If she was white you'd a put two and two together same as anyone else. You'd say to yourself, well, I knows my Bobby, he's over to Canada, so this ain't no by-blow of his. What's going on here then? Could this here baby be anything to do with my *sister*, ooh, is there something I don't know about my own dear *twin* sister Bea?'

'But she ain't white, is she!' said Violet pleadingly. 'So what are we talking about?'

'She ain't white,' said Bea viciously. 'But she ain't black either.'

Violet half-rose in her seat and now her own voice shook with rage. 'You know something, you better tell me — this is my daughter!'

Bea rose too, and shouted back: 'No she *ain't*, you grabby bitch!'

With one push of her strong right arm Violet swept all the china in front of her, loaded cake stand and all, sideways off the table with a terrific crash, and then with her other hand seized her sister's nose between finger and thumb, and yanked it hard downwards.

'Ow!'

Bea tore herself free and snatched wildly at Violet's blouse front, grabbing and twisting it, her other hand raking back for the furious blow.

But she did not deliver it. Her hand stayed where it was for a second, then fell. She let go of Violet's blouse; it gaped where a button dangled. Bea's reddened nose was bleeding, and both were breathing hard. For a second there was a curious crackle in the air, as of laughter.

Then Violet sank down trembling on her chair, and hid her face in her hands. She barely heard the noises, the scrape of a stool, a cupboard opening, a chink of glass.

'Here,' said Bea hoarsely.

'What is it?'

'Brandy.'

'I'm teetotal.'

'Just drink it, Godsake,' said Bea, and her tone was too tired for further offence. They sat for a moment, sipping and coughing. Violet's made her shudder with disgust, it was like drinking paraffin, she thought, but still she could feel the strength coming back to her with every burning drop.

'What George said, my nephew George, daft as a brush he is,' said Bea, her voice sounding stronger too, her eye a little more lively, 'I saw red because I'd already thought it, see. I'd already thought it. That she was maybe not full African, or wherever it is her folks are from. I'd thought it, and tried not to, if you see what I mean. But he calls her that — that name — '

'Yes?'

'And we has a bit of an argument, as you might say. And he's going, What, don't you know? All surprised. And he says, You can tell just by looking at her: she ain't black enough, she's half and half. So I says, Oh no she ain't, she's proper black! And he says no, too pale. And I says, well, I dare say there's all sorts of black folk, same as whites, why not! Look at Spaniards, I says, look at Turks. They ain't the same colour as you and me, are they? Still white though! And he says, George says, He's seen plenty, he's been all over the world, and he says, there ain't nothing wrong with her, and he don't mean nothing by it, only she's got a fair bit of white in there somewhere, and I got to face facts. Tells me! I got to face facts! So I says, Well, he can get out of my sight and stay out, and if he thinks he's taking any cottage of mine from now on he can think again. And *that's* a fact,' she finished, her voice a furious sneer, as if the hapless George stood before her still.

'But I thought that, too,' said Violet pleadingly, dismissing George altogether, 'about the other black folk, I mean. Being like us, different sorts — Greeks and Norwegians!'

'Not that different,' said Bea, after a pause.

'You're sure then?'

Bea nodded.

'So is it — that she's yours?'

A pause.

'Not now,' said Bea. 'Never mine now.'

Violet could only whisper. 'How, then?'

'Don't you know? Can't you work it out? You just need to think back a bit. About me.'

'When you was in France?'

'When I was too busy swanning about the Continent to go to my own mother's funeral. When I give up being a lady's maid, and Paris, and London, decided I'd much rather work in a dirty old four-ale bar in the back a beyond. Yes, then.'

This sounded more like the normal Bea.

'But you told me — '

'A pack a lies. Anyone who wanted to would a seen right through it. But you didn't want to, that's all.'

'I just believed you! Are you angry with me now, because of that? What sort of sense is that?'

'None,' said Bea sadly.

There was a silence. Violet sipped her drink, feeling its fiery nastiness all down her throat. 'So you — you had a child, then, Bea? Did you?'

'Didn't have a name. Didn't even do that for him.'

A boy! She had had a son! 'But you — you couldn't have children,' Violet whispered.

'No. As it turned out, I could only have the one,' said Bea. 'And he was it.'

'Oh, Bea.'

'This chap. He was a Frenchie, one a their gardeners over there, the Redwoods' gardener, I got the sack, caught seeing him. I dint care, we was going to be married. But soon as I tell him I'm expecting he does a bunk, turns out he's married already.'

'When was this, you were, we were what, nineteen — '

'Twenty. Old enough to know better.'

'What did you do, then?'

Bea sighed. 'I come back on my own, down Exeter way. Had a bit of money owed me. Stayed in a place, don't know where. He was born.

Thought of you then, Vi! And our mother. It was bad. Normal. I don't know. He was healthy-looking afterwards. I couldn't look at him, I couldn't bear him, I thought. All his coming had done to me. I blamed him, can you imagine that! I was a fool. I was the most foolest girl in Christendom, and I gave my baby away, my only one, I dumped him, I wrapped him up in my good shawl and I took him to Exeter and I walked to the workhouse there and I waited until dark and I left him on the doorstep. I saw them take him, he weren't outside in the cold for long. I saw them take him.'

'But — couldn't you — why didn't you bring him here, bring him home? Mother was dead. I'd a given you a place. My own sister!'

'Would you indeed. Maybe now you would. Not then, Vi. Don't you kid yourself.'

It was true, Violet thought. Beatrice at twenty; would I have let her, a wanton version of myself, and already ruined, would I have let her and her bastard child stay in my own home, with my own young husband? And with that old misunderstanding already, and not so old in those days, about whose property Ned Dimond first had been! Mine, thought Violet, surprising herself a little with the vehemence with which this thought occurred to her, even now. He was mine first and mine thereafter, whatever people said.

'Bert Givens and me,' said Bea, 'we only had the one, you know, my daughter, as lived a week. And the next one stillborn. Never carried another full term. So there was my punishment, I thought, right enough. I sinned and I was

242

punished for it. And before you start — '

' — I wasn't going to — '

'I meant giving him away. That was the sin, not the other thing.'

'Yes. I know that's what you meant. But you think your, your son — '

'My son, yes. Grew up and had to do with a black woman.'

There was another long pause. Violet felt weak, trembling all over sitting there, one hand still clamped round her glass full of poison. There was no sorting her emotions. There were so many of them and all at once.

There was an overwhelming sense of disconcertion. All these years she had thought she had adopted a strange little outcast, and from Christian charity; that the likeness to Ruth was a signal from the Divine.

But anyone, any heathen, would surely take in her own kin.

Grace was *kin*.

And then a great shiver of some feeling completely unidentifiable, a slew of it, ran all through her, she went hot and shivery; she was going to faint, she realized. She got herself sideways out of the chair and dropped on all fours on to the greasy crumb-strewn flags of the floor, all splashed now with cold tea, and scattered with broken china and fruitcake, though most of that mess lay dashed right up against the wall. There were the newspapers Bea had dropped, what felt like hours before. Violet crouched beside them for a moment or two, making herself breathe slowly, then got up on to her knees and asked for help.

Had she preened herself, all these years, for carrying out an especially hard duty without faltering? Had she prided herself on the superiority of her faith? And delighted in thus showing it off before the world?

Dear Lord, forgive me! I have been blind, foolish, prideful.

But the pride was essential, some other part of her mind replied. It was a necessary strength. After all, it has been a hard row to furrow; the pride helped, for all its sinfulness.

Violet felt the voice of divine reason in this, and dried her eyes, and presently was able to get up again and slide back into the chair opposite and look at her sister's face.

'So your son — '

'Fine son,' broke in Bea, her mouth a hard line. 'Fathers a child and buggers off. Like his dad, hah!'

'You don't know any of this. Not really.'

'I see her,' said Bea, 'your Gracie, sat a-sewing, and I thought, why, she looks just like *me*. I felt the needle in her hand. As if it were my own. And the shape of her cheek. I saw you in her — how many times have I sat beside you when we were girls — and I saw her, and that she was you. All these years I been blind to it. And you know why. We both know why, don't we!'

Violet shook her head, but Bea went on, with a jeering tear-ridden gusto —

'All on account of her colour! And ain't that such a good joke! God's own joke. He says, This is what it's like being All-Powerful. I can make jokes like these. I can make you give up your only child, and then just for fun I'll make you give up your grandchild too. What a good joke that is, on me now! Don't you think?'

Violet's eyes filled with tears. Bea's blasphemy seemed so full of pathos; she knew the Lord in His kindness would overlook it. She herself brushed it aside: 'You don't know any of this for sure,' she said as firmly as she could.

But as she spoke she saw again the little greyish face turned towards her in the Infirmary, and Ruth looking up at her. Ruth, Grace's cousin. Gracie, her own niece; no — great-niece. She remembered too the joy of taking the sickly baby into her arms, when her whole body seemed to recognize the child. And all the time the truth had never once crossed her mind. Nor Bea's.

'See, it was you I thought of, on account of Ruth, her looking so like,' said Bea. 'When they brought her in. They thought she would die, her lungs were that bad. And,' she added, her voice suddenly almost a whine, 'they told me she was a darkie. They *said* she was.'

'So that's what you saw,' said Violet, thinking to comfort her.

'Yes, that's what I saw. That was *all* I saw. So I missed her. I let you take her, I give her to you, when she was mine all along, my own granddaughter.' Bea laid her head down on her arms on the table, and hid her face.

Violet sat still. This aspect of things had not occurred to her at all. She tried to imagine the span of Bea's feelings.

She tried to face her own. Had there been a quiver of *dismay* in the thought that Grace was actual kin of her own, blood-related? Was she really no better than the foolish locals who crossed the road when they saw Grace coming? She examined herself, and decided that on the whole and in this case she was. It had been simply a shock, after all, she thought, the shock of things being otherwise from what you'd always thought they were. Why, she was used to it already. But was Bea?

Had to do with a black woman, Bea had said of her son: sounded indecent, Violet thought. Might there not have been a perfectly legal marriage? What was Bea assuming, about her son, about Grace's real mother? She must ask. 'Bea,' she said urgently, and the wet face tilted up. 'You ain't ashamed of her, are you?'

Bea rubbed at her wet face with one hand. 'Course not. Why should I be? No,' she added, and her voice, its plain sadness, went straight to her sister's heart. 'It's me I'm ashamed of.'

Violet thought piercingly of Grace herself; all that she too had missed, unknowingly. Surely it was all true, the likeness so clear? She thought of herself while they sat knitting that evening, little Gracie struggling with the scarf, herself with the mittens, and being cruel to be kind but cruel all the same: telling the child outright that the Silkhampton lacemaker was no relation of hers! Her aunt no aunt, that she herself, Violet Dimond, was no relation either, that no one was, in the whole wide world, poor little thing! What were they to tell her now? But that must be for

246

another day, she decided. They would talk about that some other time, not today.

Violet got up, and knelt at Bea's side to stroke her arm. 'Come on now,' she said. 'I'm so sorry, Bea. I'm sorry I hurt you. I wish I hadn't broke your things. I make some more tea now? Bea? Say something, my own dear, do.' She kissed Bea's cheek; the first time she had kissed her sister for — why, I don't know how long, she thought.

'Not ashamed of Gracie,' said Bea, turning her face to look back, so close. How ill she seemed, Violet thought, her unwashed hair coming down, her drawn sallow face all blubbered with tears. 'But I might have a son alive, a fine son, as'll desert a woman with a baby. That's what he did, that boy I left behind, I left him on the doorstep, and so he left her. And I've been thinking, I keep thinking: How am I to live, with all of this! I can't! I can't live with it, Vi, I can't!'

'Don't you talk blasphemy now,' said Violet, getting swiftly to her feet. 'Don't you dare! And you know nothing about your son.'

'No,' said Bea quickly. 'Nothing at all.'

'I meant — nothing about what he wanted or what happened to him. Look at your Bert!'

She swept a bit of broken china out of her path with the side of her boot, and began pacing up and down the small room. 'Your Bert and all his crew — heaven knows men die every day, they go out to hard work like your Bert, like my own Ned, and they don't come back alive!'

She turned about again, full of energy, full of truth, she felt, as if an obvious reality were being

247

revealed to her, and she had only to voice it.

'And I'll tell you this: I'm sorry, Bea, but I think your son is dead; I think he died. That's why the mother was on her own with her baby, trying to work for her bread, poor soul. And her — well, we don't know nothing about her neither.'

'They took her from the water. You know they did, they took her from the water, drowned in the harbour-side — '

'They took *someone* from the water. We don't even know it was her! She weren't the only black woman in the country, there's whole streets of 'em over to Cardiff, so I've heard. There, see — maybe you ain't heard the worst. Maybe Grace's mother weren't just black. Maybe she was all out *Welsh!'*

A joke; of all things, and at such a time, a joke had leapt into her mouth as if she had planned it out beforehand.

Blank; then Bea's tiny shocked breathy smile. Soon it faded into more tears, but they had less edge to them already, Violet thought. She could tell some of Bea's dreadful burden had lifted, from sharing it.

She herself was still full of strange feelings.

It had occurred to her early on that if George Givens had seen that Grace was *Half and Half,* so too might others have noticed; anyone the least bit travelled. So perhaps, unbeknownst to her, it had always been rumoured all through Silkhampton that Grace was really family, an illicit connection of her own. Had it been? Would such talk have got back to her, if it had?

On the whole she thought it would; someone like Aggie Ticknell would not have been able to keep mum, not with Gracie herself in front of her day after day. She would have dropped hints, until at last Grace began to understand her. And so far, nothing; so perhaps most of Silkhampton had no such suspicion; most of Silkhampton, after all, had hardly gone as far as the next village.

And George had maybe only given the matter any thought because Grace was, as he saw it, adopted kin of his own.

Not that I should care either way, Violet reminded herself.

And then she arrived at her own truth. It seemed to her that the long battle with her sister was now over, and for good, and that she herself had unquestionably won the field. Nothing in her own life could compare for sheer disaster with Bea's. She remembered how she had felt leaving the Home with the baby in her arms, that she was kidnapping someone else's child, stealing her. And all the time it had been poor Bea she had robbed. Nothing else could possibly count now. No further skirmish could change this final outcome. There was somehow little savour in it though.

She must be generous in victory. 'She calls me Ma,' said Violet carefully, 'but she loves you dearly. She was talking about you only this morning. How you'd love the jacket she was lining, how you'd like to choose the colours for it same as her.'

'She's clever with her needle same as me,' said

Bea, sitting up, and wiping her face with her hand.

'That's so,' said Violet. 'She proper takes after you there.'

★ ★ ★

Violet stayed the night. She had left Grace a note, implying that Bea had some minor indisposition, that she would be back the following morning, that there was a little pie all ready for her in the larder, and that she was on no account to forget to bolt the back door before she went to bed. She would perhaps enjoy, Violet thought, having the place all to herself for an evening, the bed all her own for a night.

She herself had never liked sleeping alone. Bea had showed her an empty room — heaven knew there were plenty, and more in the unused wing all locked up — but she had found herself a little uneasy about taking it. There were stories about the place, after all. Stories about the lake, especially, the sort you could scoff at perfectly easily in daylight, but which wouldn't be so much fun to think about come nightfall, when you were all alone with just a candle for company.

'Couldn't I bunk in with you, Bea?'

Of course Bea's room was in a similar state to the housekeeper's sitting room, full of dust and general disorder. They had done a little preliminary tidying there, changed the bed — there were any number of sheets, said Bea, burrowing into the great linen cupboard on the third floor, wearing a bit thin these days maybe after all these years, but look, see, the crest embroidered on every corner, just like on the old carriage one. Soft as silk to sleep in.

When the bed was done, the mattress turned and given a good bashing, the clean sheets all pulled tight, they had gone out for a breath of air, first to the front of the House, talking to one or two of the children still playing out near the carriage drive after their tea, then crunching over the weed-littered gravel round the locked-up side wing to the back, where the great stretch of water, the Rosevear Lake, lay still and mirror-golden in the evening sunshine. But no, thought Violet, she herself would never be able to look on that shining surface with any real pleasure.

'Ain't it a danger,' she asked, 'for the little ones?'

'Oh, they won't none of them go near it,' said Bea. 'Ghosts got their uses.'

When they got back refreshed Violet suggested they tackle the sitting room a little more thoroughly before supper, but there were still limits, she saw, to sisterly togetherness, and the gleam in Bea's eye as she said she'd manage it all perfectly well later, thank you, warned her that she had now fully reached them.

All the same the rabbit pie went down very well. They talked the whole time, about all sorts of things, not only Gracie and her difficulties and her virtues, her prettiness and cleverness, but about their own past, about their mother and father, how he had killed himself with work or been killed, at any rate, never paid a living wage,

251

poor soul, let him strain his sinews all day; they remembered the time of starvation.

''Twas barely a morning!' said Bea, in surprise. 'She was only away an hour or two, what are you saying?'

Violet was checked. She was convinced that she was right, and that their mother had journeyed a long way, over several days, and that she and her sister had neared death from privation in her absence. They had lain together in a bed, just as they were now.

'We remember it differently,' she said, and they agreed that this was so, and she changed the subject, for it was a painful one, even for Bea, who had thought so little of it, something that had haunted Violet's own dreams for years.

'D'you think you can sleep?' she asked, as Bea prepared to blow out the candle.

'Ain't slept properly for weeks,' said Bea gloomily, 'not for months. Not since I realized.' It was sad to see her face fall, take on the dreary lineaments it had worn earlier. Violet put her arms about her.

'Well, you can now,' she said. 'Off you go.' Bea had turned in her arms, and gone straight to sleep, as if Violet had made her do it. Violet lay and listened to her breathing for a while. She would surely never sleep herself tonight, she thought, what with all there was to think about and after a day of such emotion and talk and weeping, more in one afternoon than for ten years at least, a regular bit of melodrama, she'd never sleep tonight, that was for sure!

Her eyes closed. She slept.

In the morning Bea seemed rather inclined to be her old self again, up and bustling well before Violet awoke. She brought her a cup of tea.

'You want to go to chapel? There's a place in the village.'

Violet sat up groggily. She felt exhausted, as if she really had lain awake all night, and shook her head. She would manage Evensong tonight, she thought, back home in Silkhampton.

'I dint look up the trains. They run on a Sunday?'

'Course they do. You'll take a bit of breakfast though?'

As she dressed, Violet could hear the children playing outside. She drew the curtain back; the whole lot of them, it seemed, were out there in the sunshine at the front of the Home, running and playing and shouting together on the grass, a couple of nursemaids overseeing them and the usual row of big perambulators, each of them holding two or three, from the number of flailing arms and legs, and flapping bonnet frills.

They need a good airing, Bea said, before the service; the curate would insist on it, though frankly she wouldn't herself care if none of them heard so much as a single word of the gospel from one year's end to the next. Another rasher?

Part of this speech rang a bell with Violet. She thought back, and remembered her own little Bobby running noisily about the gallery in St George's, and Bea wanting to let him.

'If he rackets about now, be easier for him

come Sunday,' she had said, and she, Violet, had scornfully replied, to her sister, to a woman who had given up her only living child and just had another miscarriage, and in God's own house, 'And what would *you* know about children?'

'No, thank you,' she said gently, 'you have it, Bea.'

She thought some more, sipping a final cup of tea before she left to catch her train. She remembered how the little children had clustered about Bea, that visit long ago when there were cakes to give out, how fond and unafraid they seemed, running to her, clutching at her skirts. She thought of all the children Bea had helped look after all these years, how she had given up the pleasures and company of the old Red Lion, successful hotel though she had made it, to bury herself out here in the wilds, working for next to nothing, working for love. She might have missed out on children of her own, overlooked her own grandchild, but she had hardly missed out on motherhood, Violet thought.

No, indeed, Bea's way of mothering was perhaps merely just like her: carried out with grandeur, and on a wildly lavish scale. And still going on, too; still hectic.

Still paying for the moments when she watched the door of the workhouse in Exeter swing open, thought Violet, trying to imagine what that might have felt like. When she had stayed out of sight while someone bent and picked up her baby. When the someone took a good look round, saw no one, took the baby inside. Closed the door again.

How many times over the years must she have thought of those moments?

'You remember the bee and the violet? On the dolly's little handkerchief?' said Violet now. 'Loved that, Gracie did. I did too. Where'd it come from?'

Bea shook her head, smiling.

'You know Gracie's bin doing it on to ladies' handkerchiefs? Does it lovely. Sold quite a few.'

'Ladies wiping their snotty noses on you and me,' said Bea, but before Violet could reply there was a sudden sharp knock on the door, and one of the nursemaids pushed it open.

'Just come, Mrs Givens.' She held out a telegram.

'Has the boy gone?'

'Yes please, mum.'

'Alright then, Betty.'

Bea closed the door again. 'Funny,' she said, and opened the envelope. Read the slip, sat down suddenly, the thin paper in her hand.

'Here,' she said. She gasped as she spoke. With instantly shaking hands Violet found her glasses, and put them on. The telegram had been sent by Dr Summers from the Silkhampton Post Office, and read:

URGENT STOP WHERE MRS DIMOND STOP PLEASE TELL HER COME HOME STOP GRACE IN HOSPITAL STOP

17

Like a fool he'd gone to see Ted's older brother off; hadn't a notion how that was going to feel beforehand. God, it was shaming. All the men in uniform! Even Ted's brother had almost looked a man. Leaving the kids behind with the women. How was he going to stand it? Two years — it would all be over before he could get anywhere near it! It was so unfair, he thought, when he was ready now. Letting that streak of weak piss Geoff Hall go, and not him, it was ridiculous, what did your age matter, compared to your height and your strength and your manly British fighting spirit!

Ted's Ma all over him. Dozens of other old dears all snivelling into their hankies. Dads shaking hands.

Would his own mother come to see him off? Mrs Dando trying not to cry as the train drew in, Oh, Tommy, my darling, come back safe to me, Tommy, my dear!

Tom Dando not at all aware of the picture he was conjuring up, but feeling its heady influence nevertheless.

He would simply die if they didn't let him go soon, he thought. The old Silkhampton Colliery Band playing 'The British Grenadiers', it should all be for him, he should be the one in uniform, casually swinging the kitbag over one shoulder, saluting his churlish stay-at-home mates farewell, kissing his old mum goodbye, goodbye, good-bye . . .

He wanted to kick something. Looked across the platform, and saw, Oh — her mother. The Holy Terror herself, Violet Dimond. Carrying a sort of Gladstone bag and looking up the track, clearly waiting for the coast train.

What did that Gladstone mean?

Was it possible that the old hag was going to be out of the way for a while? Out of the picture? It jolly well was, he told himself: possible.

⋆   ⋆   ⋆

Grace came home tired. The shop had been busy, and Mrs Ticknell very fretful all morning, and unable to talk about anything other than her two boys, Jim off to join his regiment later that very day, Gerry still in training. She had been away two whole hours in the afternoon, coming back from seeing Jim off at the station just as Grace was shutting up shop. She slumped on to the velvet sofa, her eyes all swollen.

'Though I kept it all back, Gracie, not like some I could mention, not a tear did I shed till the train pulled out, I wasn't going to shame my boy — ' She broke off, weeping again.

Grace was frightened and embarrassed. She had never seen Mrs Ticknell, or in fact any other grown-up, cry before, not like that, not out loud. She understood that Mrs Ticknell was worried for her sons, of course, but all the same, she wished she wouldn't carry on so, you'd almost think they were both dead already.

257

'They'll be alright,' said Grace, sitting down beside her and putting her arm round Mrs Ticknell's plump shoulders.

'Oh, Gracie, do you really think so?' gasped Mrs Ticknell, and then flung herself into Grace's arms, squeezing her tight and hiding her wet face in Grace's shoulder.

Crumbs, thought Grace. Self-consciously she patted Mrs Ticknell's back. Mrs Ticknell felt very hot, the tough cotton of her dress very tightly drawn over her shoulders. She's packed right into this gown, Grace thought, and then was instantly ashamed, catching herself making unkind inward remarks in the face of grief.

'Course they will,' she said. 'They're big tough men, they'll be fine.' She sought about and came up with something else she had heard: 'You should be proud of them, fighting for their country and all.'

'I am proud,' said Mrs Ticknell, freeing herself and wiping her eyes. 'I am proud, Gracie. I just want them both back again safe and sound. That's all.'

'They'll be home before you know it,' said Grace. 'You wait and see.' Presently she escaped to put the kettle on.

★   ★   ★

So when Grace got home she was startled and rather put out at first to find the note from her mother. Especially as Violet had clearly not banked the fire up properly and it had died right down and the place was chilly. Grace doubted

258

the note as well. There was absolutely nothing wrong with Aunt Bea at all, she felt certain; her mother had clearly just gone to have it out with Aunt Bea, whatever it actually was. She'd been spoiling for a fight for months.

Honestly, what a pair! Worse than a couple of kids, thought Grace enjoyably, as she took off her good dress and put the housework one on instead. With an apron over it she poked the embers and set about coaxing the fire back to life.

Catch me and Lily having endless rows and refusing to speak to one another for weeks on end, she thought. What was it about Bea that so got on Ma's nerves? She was never as touchy with anyone else. And it was always about something really small; all that fuss, Bea's last visit, when Ma had used Bea's hairbrush, or was it the other way round? Bea flouncing off home in a bate two days early! And once a few years back they had disagreed about a recipe their own mother had used, for a particular stew, or something equally uninteresting, and neither of them had seemed able to let the matter rest.

'How can she *think* parsnips?' shouted Violet once, furiously crumpling Bea's letter, and Grace had had to jump to her feet and run up the garden to the outhouse, for it did not do to laugh at Violet at the best of times, and certainly not when she was in a temper.

The line had become something of a catch-phrase with Grace and Lily that year, an easy laugh, delightfully baffling to everyone else, to be theatrically declaimed beside all playground dissent, from the mildest squabble to fist-fights.

259

'How can she *think* parsnips?' Lily had demanded despairingly, the back of one hand pressed to her brow, when tough Joey Killigrew was rolling up his sleeves and Tim Reynolds shrugging off his jacket and all the other senior boys were gathering about them in a circle for the deadly masculine business to begin.

'How can she *think* parsnips?' The memory even now made Grace giggle.

Still smiling she got up from the hearth, where the little flames were taking nicely, washed her hands, and then lit the lamps as it was getting so dark outside. Her reflection looked briefly back at her in the darkened windows as she drew down the blinds — very taking; and she altogether lost a minute or two, in sweet formless thought of Tommy Dando.

Surfacing again: supper. The pie looked a bit small and lonely, she thought. Were there any spuds? She checked the wooden box beside the front door: yes, plenty. And would you like a few greens, Miss Dimond, after your hard day? Why yes please, Gracie, I think I would. Especially if you've got a bit of best butter, ooh good, yes . . .

What happened next was in some ways clear, in others foggy. She had run the water into the sink, and tipped the potatoes in; decided to do enough for three, for Violet and herself to use up tomorrow, rather than go to all the trouble and washing-up of spuds for one. She had put a plate to warm in the special flat warming drawer at the bottom of the range and taken the greens from the basket to give them a rinse.

Definitely got that far.

What had she been thinking about, while she did all those things?

Something light, surely, something careless. But she never could remember what it had been. She was interrupted by a light rap on the back door.

She dried her hands on the apron and went to open it; sure, afterwards, that she had been expecting someone else, someone who would never make her heart beat faster, someone ordinary, but who could it have been? Whoever she was perhaps half-expecting, opening the door so casually, it was not Tommy Dando himself. He stood on the cinder path, smiling in the light from behind her.

'Hello, my darling Gracie!'

She remembered joy.

'I come in? Just for a minute.'

'Well — not for long: Mother's — back in a minute, she's just — gone to church,' said Grace. She knew she lied. She could remember the guilt of it. She remembered wishing she had not put on the old house-dress, and that she had taken off the sacking apron.

He stepped inside and at once she was aware that something was different about him. There seemed something heavy and massy about his whole body, as if he was standing in her way, and wouldn't easily get out of it. There was a strange smell coming from him too, which she did not recognize, as the only alcohol she knew about was the whiff of stale beer that flowed out of pub doorways as she passed them on the way to work in the morning, when they stood wide open for cleaning.

'Had to see you,' he said. His cheeks were pink and his eyes very bright. He opened his arms, and gladly she walked into them. It was a different embrace though. It started off like last time, and then changed; he drew back from her and held her away for a moment, then bent and kissed her on her lips.

Just for a little while it was the most glorious thing. It was the most glorious thing that had ever happened to Grace Dimond, a shock of delight all over. His mouth was very soft, his breath full of the strange fiery smell, but still sweet, his own. Her palms were pressed against his chest, against his shirt, as his jacket was unbuttoned; her fingertips felt the thin further layer, cotton, beneath his shirt and beneath that the just-discernible resilience of his smooth warm skin. He kissed her cheek and her neck, and she slid her right hand a little further inside his jacket, and felt the steady fast thrum of his heartbeat beneath her palm. She moved the hand very gently, caressingly.

She remembered that. She led him on, that was the main thing. No use saying you hadn't realized, that you just hadn't had any idea that you were leading someone on, that you would never have done it if you'd known that's what it was.

'No — stop, don't do that.'

'Don't you like it?' He had only done what she had done, moved a hand, put it over her heart. But the hand was pressing at her breast. It felt all wrong. It was far too much.

'No, no, stop.' Right over her breast now, squashing it, as if he were angry.

'No — Tommy, please!' He dug the fingers in, hard, really hurting her, and then at last she twisted her whole body and pulled herself free, not frightened yet, but hurt, and bewildered.

'What are you *doing?*' she cried, the tears starting to her eyes.

'What are you doing?' he repeated, parodying her shrillness. 'What d'you think I'm doing, you silly bitch?'

Shock dazed her. It stopped her doing anything. It made her legs go weak, it made her arms turn to empty sleeves that swung helplessly while he pulled her about, pulled at her apron, he was so angry, he was angry with her, and why, what had she done?

'No,' she said, but instead of the scream just the merest whimper came out, and as she turned away to run he took her by the shoulder and gave her a violent shove, so that she fell over hard, without even staggering, with hardly time to put out a hand to save herself, hitting her chin and cheekbone hard on the stone flags of the floor. Before she could take a breath he was pulling at her again, trying to turn her over.

No.

A small voice inside her saying No.

No I won't. She drew up her knees and wrapped her arms round them, lying curled up on her side. She turned herself into a ball, all thickly skirted and hidden in her petticoats, let him scrabble and fumble all he chose.

'Gracie!' he cried, as if she were being unreasonable. 'Gracie, come on!'

She wouldn't move, no. He threw himself

down beside her, and grabbed at her, trying to force her on to her back, his arms were like iron, impossible iron bars, his leg casting itself over hers, trying to push hers apart, trying to force itself between them, his breath coming fast; he put his hand into her hair and pulled hard until she cried out, but no, no, no, she would not let go, she would not uncurl, she held on to her own arms, her good thick shielding skirts and petticoats caught tight, tight, between her crossed ankles, between her pressed-together knees. 'Dirty black bitch!' he hissed, into her ear, and then he shuddered all over and groaned as if he were in pain, and everything stopped.

Stopped, all of it.

Grace still curled up thinking — she remembered thinking — had all that really happened? Surely none of it had happened, not really. It was all too unbelievable, it was nonsense. None of it had really happened.

He was getting up. 'You shouldn't have led me on!' he said hoarsely. He was still angry. 'Why'd you do it, why'd you lead me on, eh?' There was a grating crash as he kicked a chair over. Her whole body winced as if it were her that he kicked. A silence, apart from noisy breathing, footsteps. Was he going?

She kept her eyes closed, with a vague notion of pretending to be dead. Playing dead, that was it, Grace told herself. Go away now, I'm dead.

His footsteps came back again, he stood over her. 'Gracie?'

Normal voice. Normal Tommy Dando, charming Tommy Dando, who could talk his way into or out of anything! 'Gracie!' he said again, and now he was everyday Tommy just raising his voice a little, for someone who clearly hadn't heard him. Should she answer? Could she?

She could open an eye. But when she opened her mouth only panting breath came out. He was holding the kettle, she saw.

'Want some tea?' he said. 'Gracie?' Slightly impatient now, as if he knew she'd heard him perfectly well all along, and was teasing him. 'Come on, get up, stop larking about. Where's the cups?'

And now, when he was no longer trying to touch her, when he sounded so everyday, she began at last to be terrified. It had all been shock before, at the stunning speed with which everything had changed, and shock had drained all her strength away, so that she had hardly fought back, hardly done anything at all, except curl up into a ball, a human hedgehog. Now she lay quiet, trying to think, her stomach turning over and over with dread. Who was he, *what* was he, that she had let into the house?

He was feeling just as she did, she thought, that what had just happened had been so unbelievable that it seemed unlikely to have happened at all; but taking it further, grasping at it, deciding that yes, in spite of all appearances and evidence and of course the actual facts concerned, on the whole it would be best, certainly best for him, Tommy Dando, if the entire incident was not just unlikely, but really impossible. Nope: none of it had really happened.

'This milk alright?'

Was it him, though, or were all men like this? Various fragments of confidential information came back to her. Men couldn't actually stop all that once they'd started, whispered Lily. That was why you had to be careful. The only way to stop them was to kick them you know where; if you kicked them good and hard they just fell over and lay there groaning all helpless!

Could that be true? Could that really be all it took?

I just didn't think to kick him, Lily.

Cautiously Grace managed to straighten herself out, and slowly sit up on the floor. She felt unprecedented: all sorts of things. Her chin hurt, and she put up a trembling hand, feeling the big swelling already arising there. Her cheekbone too; she explored it with her fingertips, and found a great tender bulge. It was all going to show, she realized, and at the thought of her mother, of Violet, a sob began working its way up and out, and to try and choke it off she stood up, as quickly as she could, holding on to the table for support.

He was standing beside the door, with something in his hand. 'Couldn't find the cups,' he said. His tone was slightly indignant. 'I could only find this one. Bit small!' It was Ruth's little blue and white cup, Grace saw, swinging by its painted handle from his big forefinger.

'I'll get them,' she said, and her voice, she heard, sounded wonderfully normal. At once she felt calmer. Her upstairs may be deaf as a post, she told herself, but Next Door aren't. If he comes near me I scream the place down and I scream *his name*. And I break the window. What have I got to break the window with, quick, quick think, what have I got? It *must not* be anything he thinks is a weapon I want to use on him. It must be something small. Ah. Yes. A potato. That one. Just right. Grab it — and smash that pane there.

All this fierce thought and detailed planning took no time at all, it arrived in a silvery flash as she heard her own normal voice saying 'I'll get them.' She kept her head down, don't meet the eyes, more of Lily's whispered advice, though surely that's bad dogs, isn't it, suggested another part of her mind, which was labouring away in clear thudding words rather than in flashes, as she opened the cupboard beside the fireplace and took out two everyday cups and saucers. From the corner of her eye she saw him set Ruth's cup down on the edge of the dresser, and felt a tiny gain, the smallest triumph, because she had managed to hide from him how important it was.

But the trouble was, she realized, as she put the tea tray together, the trouble was there seemed to be nothing else to do now but carry on and make a pot of tea. He was still standing between her and the back door. She would never get past him quick enough to the front one, and in any case that was kept locked, the key on a string beside the letterbox, so that you could in theory let yourself in with it if you were locked out at the back. But as a way out, an escape route, it was useless.

She had laid a good fire; already the kettle he had put on was singing. A kettleful of boiling water: not at all nice to have about the place when you were dealing with this sort of thing, the thuddingly verbal bit of Grace's mind pointed out. Don't want anyone flinging it, do we now? Can't you get him away from that door? How about getting him to sit down? If he sat in Violet's chair he'd be on the other side of the table from the door. Did you put up the catch when you closed it?

I didn't close it, Grace answered herself, and her stomach seemed to give way inside her. I didn't close it, he did, and I don't know how: perhaps he turned the key.

She made a good show of scalding out the teapot, and put the kettle back on the hob while she spooned in the tea. Thud thud thud: when you've filled the pot, empty the kettle down the sink. If he looks, say that we always do. Because the drain blocks.

'Starving,' said Tommy Dando, and he tried one of his smiles, but she could see it wasn't working, his face wasn't working properly, the smile looked utterly wretched. For the first time she understood that there really was something wrong with him, that he hadn't just catastrophically misunderstood her or acted out of character or (finally it occurred to her) drunk too much, that he hadn't just overdone being manly and forceful as perhaps any boy might who wasn't quite used to being one yet, no, really, no: there was something very wrong with him inside, all wrong and mad and horrible.

Cake. Biscuits in the tin. All of it near him in the cupboard beside his head. Too close. Grabbing close. Could she give him the pie?

'Come and sit down,' she said. If he sat down she could go to the cupboard and as she passed it check on the door. Could she? No, oh no, she couldn't, the blind was down too far; she couldn't see the lock at all. Not without lifting up the blind.

'No,' he said. 'Thanks,' he added. Then an attempt to be casual: 'Actually. Think I'll be getting along now. If you don't mind. Sorry about the tea.'

'Oh. Oh, alright then.'

'We're still friends though, ain't we, Gracie?'

Beginning to sound that way again, the conversational part of Grace's mind remarked. Don't you think? Sounding that way again?

'Course,' she said, sounding not too bad, almost realistically warm, even.

'And you did let me in, all lovey-dovey, didn't you? Eh?'

'Yes.'

'You would, wouldn't you, your sort.' He added softly, as if he were paying her a compliment, as if he were pleased with her: 'You dirty bitch.'

Nothing useful to say to that; better keep quiet, Grace advised herself. Right you are, then, I will.

'Ain't you, eh? Right. Bye then.' He backed, his eyes still on her, his beautiful blue eyes, one hand reaching out for the door. Not looking where he was going; and his foot caught on the

269

doormat by the threshold, and he stumbled, fell backwards, and knocked his head on the doorjamb with a strangely loud and roundly wooden *thud*.

His face looked so shocked, so outraged, and above all the noise was so funny, that even in her state of terrified half-stunned awareness, or because of it, Grace gave a little gasp. It was hardly laughter. Just a breath, really, and the corners of her mouth very briefly very slightly turned up.

But she knew instantly that she had made a terrible mistake.

'Oh, Tommy, I'm sorry, are you — '

'Alright,' she was going to finish, but she didn't get that far. The word just stopped where it was. He was too quick, his rage too much for them both. He did not move, but cast around for a weapon, snatched up the little oil lamp standing nearby on the lower part of the dresser, and threw it as hard as he could at her face.

It wasn't far. His aim was good, his arm was strong. But Grace was quicker. She flung up her hand; the lamp struck her forearm, the glass shattered, the base drenched her with hot oil, and at once she wore a sleeve of bursting flames.

Without volition or thought she took a step towards him. He backed, grabbed something as if to ward her off, threw it at her, missed, something shattering behind her; he vanished, he was of no account, had never been, Grace was alone for a heartbeat, flailing wildly at the fire with her other hand, spreading it to her other sleeve then think, *think*, not water not water

270

lamp oil lamp oil not water, coat *rug* yes, hearth rug, quick, roll quick stifle —

A silence, then banging and crying, voices outside.

'Mrs Dimond, Violet — is that you? What's going on, are you alright?'

Next door. Next-door people, knocking at the front.

She staggers to her feet. The pain is almost blinding but her mind silvery quick one last time: police no thanks no thanks, accident — all my own fault — no one here but me, I fell off the table, knocked into the lamp, why was I on the table, come up with something later, look at this blood, my hand all bloody, where's this blood coming from?

The passage, so dark, the box of potatoes where it stood all those months ago when she last looked, the string, the damn string so hard to pick up, swinging, key, I do wish you'd stop that shouting, I'm being as fast as I can, key won't go in, won't go in, goes in, turns, door-knob — slippery . . .

Grace and lots of people outside. She falls into someone's arms, and is held there.

18

She had wanted to come home after dark. And when Violet explained that the carrier had to fit them in when he could, round about three or four in the afternoon probably, she had huddled into herself and turned away, as if she could hardly bear the news.

'Can I have a veil, then?'

'A what? What for, my lamb? What d'you want one of them things for?'

Finally Bea had gone out and borrowed one, pinned it to her hat for her. Oh, what a sad thing she was then for her mother to see, so frail, a stick-like creature swathed in black netting, a ghost of herself, just able to climb shakily from the bath-chair outside the hospital into the carrier's cart, and out of it again at the other end! They had had to hold her up on either side, one step at a time, into the front door and through the living room to the bedroom all ready for her.

'Draw the curtains, please!'

That was all she said. And sunk down upon the bed, poor thing, breathing hard from the effort of walking from one room to another.

Violet had told herself then that she would soon mend, now she was home. She had thought of the sick baby in the cottage in Porthkerris, and the busy happiness of wholesome cookery.

But the new Grace seemed uninterested in

food, no matter how tempting. She seemed to have no interest in anything at all. She wanted only to sleep, or to quietly lie awake in the darkened room.

'But it's Aggie Ticknell! Really wants to say hello — I won't let her stay long — do say she can pop in, Gracie!'

'No. Tell her I'm asleep. Please, Ma.'

'It's Lily Houghton. I can't send her away again, Gracie. Won't you see her, just a few minutes?'

No.

In all the world, it seems to Grace, there is only this bed where she is safe and can be herself in peace. Everywhere else there are eyes upon her and people all thinking variations of the same thing. Everywhere she is marked out. She has always been marked out. But now she is doubly so. The monstrous truncated hand marks her out. As if there were a banner over her head, reading LOOK HERE NOT ONCE BUT TWICE and now all eyes will see not only her difference but also her horrid maiming, which was all her own fault for letting . . .

For letting . . .

And there's something else: she has discovered that she must not think his name. She feels sick just at the idea of it. She has to keep not-thinking about him, and this is very tiring, as some other part of her mind seems to want to bring him up all the time. So she has to be careful, and not let herself drift off into any apparently safe byways of daydream, because that's where he always turns out to be waiting for her.

What d'you think I'm doing, you silly bitch?

His hand digging so painfully into her breast. Sometimes she can almost feel his fingers there still, as if he's left some permanent mark.

'Mr Godolphin called again, Gracie. Left you one or two little things to read. I leave 'em here?'

'Leave them wherever you like, Mammy.'

There's a lot of this kind of thing, practically a pile of books waiting to be read. All sorts of feminine consolation sit beside them on the chest of drawers: cut flowers, miniature roses in a painted earthenware pot, a little haberdashery kit to fit in a handbag, with a hundred different-coloured threads all beautifully plaited together for every imaginable sewing emergency, new hair-ribbons, an expensive bunch of black grapes heavy with bloom, a small basket of ripe peaches, letters — a surprising number of letters of kindly concern, of sympathy, of earnest hopes for a speedy recovery.

Leave them wherever you like. Grace is too busy keeping her thoughts safe to look at any of it. Besides, it all carries some taint of the outside world, and this in itself is risky.

Sometimes she tries to imagine walking about Silkhampton, the square, the High Street, St George's, the Picture Palace. As once she walked Barty Small along the lane to the town, now she walks herself, making sure the place is in darkness, herself the only person there, no one to stare or judge or scorn.

There she is in front of Ticknell's blind-drawn window, turning for home. Night-time; she wills herself there, in the cool spring darkness. But the

274

more clearly she envisages herself the more she understands that even if she could make it true, even if she were well enough to walk all by herself to Ticknell's and back, her memory would still be working, and it would be showing her Tommy Dando across the street, laughing, touching his hat, smiling, begging her to accept the little note. Tommy Dando being his real self then; or his pretend one.

That they were both real selves, and at the same time both pretend, was for Grace the hardest thought to keep away from, though it seemed a perfect flare of danger and impossibility. People were steady, usually, she told herself. There might be him. There might be Lily Houghton. But there was also Ma. There was Aunt Bea. Mrs Ticknell, daft Georgie Givens and poor May, Mr Vowles, Mr Godolphin — none of them were pretending, were they? None of them would suddenly in an instant turn into someone else, would they?

It seemed often to Grace that they might. That she might herself. That there was nothing and no one solid to hold on to in this world.

'It's Miss Thornby, Grace.'

'Who?'

'Miss Thornby — says you were at school together.'

Grace makes a small sound, of doubt and indifference.

'Were you? At school together?'

'*I* don't know,' murmurs Grace. Faint irritation now. She closes her eyes. 'Tell her to go away. Please, Auntie.'

Along with keeping Tommy Dando out, Grace had further trouble with Lily Houghton. It was important not to think about Lily, or remember her, and this also was a real strain, a constant effort of will. But it had to be done.

Lily had visited the hospital, of course, very early on, as soon as she could beg an extra hour off.

'I said you was my sister! Dunno what they'll do when they find out it's you. Sack me prob'ly, but I don't care. How you doing, Gracie?'

How kind and nice she was then, and what a comfort it had been to see her looking so like normal life, like everyday reality! Grace had very nearly told her everything; couldn't think afterwards what had held her back, primed with laudanum as she was. Of course she knew she was never going to tell Ma, or Bea; but in one or two of her pain-free intervals she had half-pictured herself confiding in Lily. Only when she had the chance she couldn't face it somehow. Saying all that out loud, hearing it all on the air: just the idea of talking about it made her heart pound rather sickeningly. It wouldn't be just telling Lily, she realized; it would be telling herself as well. And could she really expect Lily to keep it all a secret? Surely that would be too much to ask of anyone.

Nearly a week later Lily had come again, this time on her afternoon out, so she had more time. Grace had known there was something wrong almost straight away, Lily was so elaborately

276

casual as she asked: 'Don't suppose you've heard from Tommy at all?'

Grace felt herself go very still, as if even her breathing had to stop at the sound of his name, and time seemed to slow down. Good job I didn't tell her, she thought clearly. Less clearly, she already seemed to know what Lily was going to say next. She shook her head a little against the pillow: no.

'He's proper shaken up, of course,' said Lily. 'Well, we all are. Said to say how sorry he was about the — you know, the operation.'

For by then Mr Hargreaves, the surgeon from the city hospital, had come in person, to give his more experienced opinion. But he had only confirmed Dr Summers' own. The lamp glass had sliced into three of the fingers, severing the flexor tendon of the little finger and cutting deeply into those of the next two, and the burns on that part of the hand were also full thickness. There could be no residual function, Mr Hargreaves agreed. And with any healing there would of course be considerable contraction. There really was only one way to proceed, as he feared Dr Summers already knew; the surgery itself should be straightforward; aftercare slightly complicated perhaps by the broken arm. From a table, indeed? Unusual — a cracked radial head so commonly associated with falling flat, rather than from a height, wouldn't you say? And what might the young lady have been doing up on a table in the first place? Ah. A trapped bird. These young ladies, so tender-hearted.

'Said if there was anything he could do, you

only have to ask,' said Lily now.

Grace considered her options. There seemed no way out but the obvious. 'You been seeing him, then?'

Lily wriggled, blushed. 'Oh, well, you know.' She tried to shrug her shoulders, but her face was alight with eager happiness. 'Not serious, like. Well — who knows, maybe one day!'

In the bed Grace was all heartbeat. She was one big pulse all over, and felt quite dizzy, but not unpleasantly so. Nothing mattered so very much, she thought cosily, for her most recent dose of opiate had been a large one. 'Didn't you used to say it was me he had his eye on?' she asked. Her voice sounded almost lazy, she was very pleased to hear.

'Oh come on, Grace,' said Lily, not at all lazily. 'You know he'd never — '

'Never what?'

'You know.' Lily raised a hand, and waved it a little towards Grace's face. 'He just — *wouldn't*, that's all.' Her eyes briefly met Grace's, to make sure she had understood.

'Oh,' said Grace, and there was a pause.

'I mean, of course he likes you and everything,' said Lily. 'Course he does. But, you know.'

You know: socially Tommy was well above Lily herself, said Lily's eminently reasonable tone, so what on earth could Grace have been thinking of, to imagine for one moment that he had ever seriously turned his thoughts to such a one as she?

Look at us, implied Lily's voice: we may be friends, but come now — we're hardly equals, are we?

278

Then the big pulse seemed to hammer all the harder, and Grace finally became aware that the curious discomfort she was feeling all over was actually pain, and that some of it arose from her ruined hand. She was glad when the nurse rang the end-of-visiting bell.

'I fear there may be some underlying weakness of the lungs,' said Dr Summers later that evening, as Grace grew increasingly feverish. 'Given the history. There is certainly some degree of congestion — keep a close eye on her, Nurse, will you?'

Grace was to remember him saying that for the rest of her life, the strangely vivid detail of his face looking down at her from the end of the bed, the faint rime of white stubble on his chin, the wrinkles round his eyes, his straggle of grey hair. She felt as if she had never seen anyone so clearly before. I'm keeping a close eye on you, she thought, but after that thoughts in general became more muddled, and seemed to take on a life of their own, sometimes carrying on like something at the Picture Palace, showing her things she'd rather not see, making people up, and making them disappear.

Apart from *him*, of course. She'd open her eyes and he'd be there again.

'What d'you think I'm doing, you silly bitch?' He said that often.

Strangely the memory seemed rather muffled, as if it had happened a long time ago. Though if she thought back, if she tried, she could remember joy.

'I come in? Just for a minute.'

279

There. That was what she had done. She had let him in, the horrible stranger who had looked like Tommy Dando, and then she had led him on. It was all her own fault.

Her right arm was too heavy, so she bent her left instead, and blotted her eyes with her sleeve. Though she understood then that the gown was entirely unfamiliar. Strange. Why was she wearing someone else's nightie?

Was it a cambric nightgown, very plain?

'How are you, my own dear?'

Ma?

Often Grace opened her eyes and found no one there. And she was so hot, she was boiling! A kettleful of boiling water: not at all nice to have about the place when you were dealing with this sort of thing. That's why it hurts so, Grace thought. Did I scald myself?

'Put the fire on, Gracie, do,' said Mrs Ticknell, but instead Grace reached up for the flat box with 'Lewin' written on it. The pretty pink and white gloves were just as she remembered them, and as she had always suspected — though of course she had never before dared to try them on, nor wanted to — a perfect fit. She held out her hands in admiring triumph, but then the right one began to hurt. The glove was much too tight after all. She tried to pull it off but it was so tight its hard lacy edge dug right into her wrist, and she couldn't grasp it, though it hurt her more and more, and feverishly she picked and picked at it with the other hand until at last she managed to work her fingertips under the edge and grasp it and tear at it with all her strength and it ripped away taking all the flesh of her right hand with it, a soft gloveful inside-out, bloodily contained.

'Steady now, there's a brave girl. Nearly done. Nearly there.'

Who was that? It wasn't Lily, was it?

'I'm sorry,' cried Grace, 'I didn't know what he was like, I thought he was nice!'

Where have I heard that before, said Aunt Bea, and she was sitting on the one side of the bed, and Ma on the other, both of them facing one another over the coverlet. They acted being the one girl, see? Like in a looking-glass, said Mrs Ticknell, and Grace opened her eyes again and laughed, seeing them like that, her mother and Aunt Bea, being one woman and her reflection, herself of course the dark glass between them.

How serious they looked, she thought, Ma and Bea, how serious and sad! Well, hadn't she broken all the rules of sensible conduct, and got herself hurt, and nearly set the house on fire, oh the songs that she had sung all those years ago, the special songs to stop the house burning down, that had to be sung before her mammy Popped In, 'Bobby Shafto', 'Greensleeves', and what was the other one? She worried herself for some time, trying to remember, but her hand was hurting again, and when she looked at it she saw to her astonishment that she was holding someone else's: a white slender hand, that was grasping her own too tightly, painfully, and she looked along the other's wrist and all along the plain cambric sleeve and up the shoulder and at last into the wet white face of Peony Lewin herself. She was standing in the reeds with her ankles in the water, her thin hair dank about her ears.

You wore my gloves, said Peony Lewin.

I didn't mean to, cried Grace, I'm sorry.

But Peony Lewin held her hand all the tighter, and pulled.

It's lonely in the water, said Peony Lewin, *I want to watch the children but the weeds hold me down.*

Let me go, please, I want to go home, help me, Ma, Mammy, please!

'Hello, my lovely. How you feeling?'

Ma?

Grace opened her eyes cautiously. She saw the end of the bed. No, no one sitting on it. Certainly not the Reverend Mr Godolphin, who had earlier so puzzled her by lying across her legs eating cherries out of a paper bag. She turned her head, aware suddenly of how much the light seemed to hurt her eyes.

'Hello, Ma,' she said at last. Croaky voice!

Violet seemed put out about something. Face all odd. She was so angry, thought Grace with a pang, and then to her horror realized that in fact her mother was crying, her poor face wet with tears.

'Oh I'm so sorry, Mammy, please, forgive me!'

'No, no — I'm that happy, oh, thank the Lord! Oh my Gracie, we thought we'd lost you!'

'What?' For a moment Grace had a confused idea of the sea. Had she nearly been lost in a storm, like Aunt Bea's Bert and his three-man crew? One of them Mrs Ticknell's sister-in-law's cousin's boy, Davey Bartlett, aged seventeen!

'Can you take a sip of water now, Gracie? Just a little sip now, my lovely.' Why was her mother talking like this, as if she were a sick child? She remembered that special tender tone.

She made to sit up in bed and pain riddled all through her, for she had tried to put weight on her right hand.

Then she knew. She remembered. Carefully she drew up her arm and inspected the big bandage. Not big enough, she saw. No normal glove would ever fit her again, let alone a fine one. Let alone Peony Lewin's.

'I didn't want them in the first place,' she told Violet, but her mother took no notice, just went on knitting string into lace on the other side of the fire.

★ ★ ★

All these were very hard times for Violet. She could find no peace of mind, even in the garden. She slept very badly and often felt so tired that she could hardly force herself even to do the chores she usually enjoyed, picking black-currants, making raspberry jam. The terrible wound to her child was like a steady drumbeat in the background of all her days and nights.

Oh, how dreadful the house had been to come back to from the hospital that first day! The smell alone had made them both feel sick, the scorched-meat tang, the remains of the fatal oil lamp still spread about the floor, the overturned

283

chair, the blackened rug where their poor darling had so bravely, so cleverly, saved herself from even worse horrors! In the sink the potatoes sitting still in cold water, the peeler set down beside them on the draining board, the pie untouched in the larder, one plate in the bottom oven, cold now, the range long since burnt out.

Hearing them come in, Next Door, late though it was, had knocked almost straight away, with a pot of strong tea and much exclamatory talk. How they had realized Something Was Up, how they had hesitated, who had said what to whom while they thought about it, how they had actually left their plates on the table, how their eldest had run like a hare for the doctor! and how Dr Summers himself had driven Gracie off in the dog-cart, her looking as pale as — well, as pale as she might do, in a manner of speaking, Mrs Dimond.

Deaf old Mrs Skewes too had hobbled down from above, offering her condolences while trying to see over Bea's shoulder.

'To think I were upstairs all the time!' she piped in her cracked voice, several times, until she could at last be induced to hobble back upstairs again. Missed all the excitement, muttered Bea.

Only trying to be kind, said Violet. Bea seeing the worst in folk as usual, she thought. Still it was a profound comfort to know there was someone else in the world who felt about her child as she did herself. Bea was with her as often as she could manage that first week, more than once catching the train to visit the Home in the morning and back again in the afternoon.

'I can't stay away,' she said. 'You know I can't.'

Every now and then, in those early days, Violet remembered the strong possibility that her own parents' blood flowed in Grace's veins, and felt something she still found indecipherable, a lurching inside her too complex to name. She was aware sometimes of a sense of loss; all those nights she had slept beside her darling, or held the little girl in her arms, and never known that this was her own kin! Every memory needed re-visiting, to see how it looked from behind these disconcerting new spectacles.

And would she have done anything differently, if she had known?

But there was no time to ponder these questions. There were so many others, more pressing and far more terrible: the grim interview with Mr Hargreaves from the city hospital, and then the operation to get through, over an hour helpless in a corridor, Violet sitting on the wooden bench, Bea pacing the marble floor, both of them aware all the while that in a room upstairs something permanent and terrible was being done to their child. And afterwards, not the expected and promised quick recovery, but instead a daily increasing fear, while Dr Summers talked of congestion and the possibility of constitutional weakness. Soon they moved Grace from the open ward to a room all by herself near the nurses' desk, with one high window through which the tops of trees were just visible.

The walls were pale green, the floor linoleum,

the bed high and narrow, its iron legs ending in small hard wheels. Voices and footsteps outside were muffled. The nurses came in and out quietly, often, looking like nuns in their starched headgear; early one morning, waiting outside the ward for news, at the final end of one of those near-interminable nights, Violet had peeped through the wired round window on the ward door and seen all four of the day staff, Sister and all, kneeling in prayer about the nurses' desk, and taken some consolation in the sight.

They set up a sort of tent about the bed, with a softly clanking mechanical contraption piping gas into it, so that the air Grace breathed so fast would be strengthened in some way. Now Violet and Bea took it in turns to sit beside the bed, allowed, by kind permission of Dr Summers himself, to stay all they pleased, despite the prevailing strictness about visiting time; because, as both suspected but neither said aloud, Grace by that time was not expected to live.

Mr Godolphin came many times, to pray with Violet. Once she spoke of Ruth, and told him that she did not know how she was to bear this added burden. But Grace survived that day, and the next, despite her temperature, despite her ragged panting breath. Another day passed, and another. The breathing slowed, her pulse steadied; she slept as if peacefully, and at last she opened her eyes.

'Hello, Ma!' Her own self awake, after so many days and nights of delirium! Violet could not remember what she said herself, at this wonderful heart-stopping moment, but she thought often afterwards of how Grace had answered her.

'Oh I'm so sorry, Mammy, please, forgive me!' It seemed to Violet at the time that Grace had slipped back almost straight away into her fever-dream. But later she remembered that cry for forgiveness. It came back to her more and more as the illness receded, and Grace grew almost well again, well enough at last to come home.

Because it was at home that Grace had become such a mystery, a face turned steadily away. Violet had expected sorrow, of course; who wouldn't grieve for their own friendly fingers? Especially a pretty young maid like Gracie, so careful all the time to look her best. She had expected tears, anger, bitterness; but never once foreseen this resolute withdrawal. What had she to be sorry about, poor girl?

'She say anything?'

Bea coming out with the supper tray almost untouched, shaking her head.

Grace had developed a sort of cunning.

Wouldn't she enjoy a little sit in the garden, get a bit of air? *Soon, maybe.*

How about sitting here by the window, watch folk going by? *Not yet.*

Say hello to Lily tomorrow? *Maybe.*

Never saying No until the last minute, when she would close her eyes, and end the discussion.

'She can't go on like this!' said Violet, and she would try again to get Gracie to see a bit of sense.

'Don't you *want* to get better?' She had thought the question was rhetorical, so the look

Grace had turned upon her in answer was chilling indeed.

'Oh, nonsense,' said Dr Summers, when she secretly consulted him. 'She's had a terrible shock, a serious injury; she needs time to get used to what has happened to her. And of course she has been very ill, Mrs Dimond.'

At which Violet breathed in hard through her nose; she was inclined to blame him and his nasty anaesthetic gases. He had certainly done his best to save her since, though his tonics were having no effect at all.

The worst of it was that they had thought themselves out of the woods; had counted the days until she was allowed out of hospital and home safe. But she had just gone on getting worse and worse.

When had it started, the turning-away? Was it the day, still in the hospital, that she saw her hand for the first time? She'd managed all those weeks not to see it, turning her head away whenever it was re-dressed. The young probationer usually held her other hand, Grace said, and talked to her of this and that, helping her keep still for Staff while the bandages were untied and unrolled and soaked off, the wounds examined, cleaned. But of course she had not been able to avoid seeing everything at last; and she had not shed a tear, just gone very quiet. No, she was alright, she said, when pressed. It was good she knew what it looked like. She was fine, really.

Had her voice already been flatter, less her own? Now it was as if she were under an evil enchantment, like a girl in a fairy story.

'Won't you tell me what's wrong, Gracie?'

'What? Don't you know?'

'No, I mean — what else.'

'Ain't this enough, then?' The fingers still lightly bandaged. Half a hand.

It occurred to Violet that Grace was somehow using her injury. That it was an excuse. It has all been too much for her, went this terrifying line of reasoning. Her life as the only one, the one that was always noticed and remarked on and stared at and commented on, that life has been too much for her, and this is her excuse to give up at last, and she has seized it. She is dying because of her difference. And there seemed to be nothing Violet could do about it.

Whenever she could she visited St George's, trying to let the glass of her mind settle, clarify, so that the Word might be supplied to her. But the mud of her human clay just went on swirling. Why had the Lord spared her daughter, why had He led her to help herself so cleverly, so bravely, stifling the flames when any other girl would have run about in a panic and been engulfed entirely? Months of pain so patiently endured, and had He spared her only for this, for more suffering and decline — for a slower death?

Violet's attempts at prayer in those days sometimes ended with her getting up, brushing off her skirts, and hurrying out of the church altogether, lest she reproach God outright in His own house.

⋆   ⋆   ⋆

Finally she came to a decision, and was ready.

'I'm tired, Ma.'

'I dare say you are. But it's time you spoke out.' She was sitting by the bed in the darkened room. It was four months since the accident. Grace had not got out of bed for nearly a week; there was doubt now whether she could even stand.

'What?'

'I want to know what happened. That night. And I don't see why you ain't telling.'

Grace closed her eyes.

'Don't pretend you're asleep, I won't have it. I've thought about it and thought about it and I've decided: I ain't going to let you just take yourself off. I said to myself, No! I've spent all these years doing my best for you, and perhaps that weren't good enough, I don't know. But I ain't going to stand by and let you do this, no I ain't.'

'Leave me alone, do, Ma. I'm alright. I'm just tired.'

'I should think you are, lying there day after day feeling sorry for yourself!'

No reply.

'What happened, Gracie? And don't you give me any nonsense about blackbirds.'

No reply.

'Alright then. See here then, Gracie my dear. Tell me this, then: why did you break my Ruth's cup? Why did you take Ruth's cup out of the cupboard, and smash it hard as you could on the floor? Eh, Gracie?'

A quiver all along the shut face.

'What was it, were you angry with me, was

that it? Angry with her? Jealous of a little girl, as died before you were born, is that it?'

'No!'

'Ah, so you can speak, can you! Why then? Why did you handle it? So careless! Smashed into a hundred pieces! Twenty-seven years I've kept it, as was the last thing my own child held in her hand, and I leave you alone for *one night* and you take it, and you handle it, and you throw it down, you *throw* it, the cup I swore I'd take with me to my grave, you cruel *wicked* girl!'

'No, I never! I never touched it!'

'Who did then?'

No reply.

'No, you don't get out of it that quick. If it weren't you — who done it? Who broke that cup? Gracie — tell me, you tell me now!'

Oh, she was crying; Gracie, who had not shed a tear when they showed her the terrible stumps of her fingers. 'It weren't me, I swear it, Mammy.'

Suddenly tender: 'I know. I know it weren't you all along, course it weren't. And I'll tell you something else. I don't care about it. Not really. What's a bit of old china? Honest, a bit of old china, that's all it was. You tell me what happened, and I promise no one will chide you, not me, not no one. Who was it hurt you, eh? Who hurt you, my Gracie?'

The lips quivering so, the effort. As if it was too hard to speak.

'Don't you cry, my lamb. You just tell me, you whisper, alright?'

Grace swallows. Makes the tremendous effort, and shakily whispers his name.

Pause. She is held, rocked, caressed. 'It was all my fault,' she adds aloud.

'What was?'

'I let him in.'

'What? How's that your fault? Why shouldn't you let him in, weren't he a friend of yourn?'

'But he — '

'He what? He was unkind, was he?'

'Oh, Ma,' sobbed Grace, 'he tried to *make* me. He tried to make me, all of a sudden.' The last few words made her cry aloud like a child.

'There, there, my lamb.' Rocking her. 'Don't you fret. Don't you take on so.'

'I told him no, but he wouldn't listen! He wouldn't take no notice!'

'My dear.'

'He pushed me over, he said things, he tried to — he tried, but he couldn't, I didn't let him, and then he was all funny! He says afterwards, he says, 'Want a cup of tea?' As if nothing had happened! And I didn't know what to do, I was so frightened, I was so scared, I couldn't move, I couldn't breathe, I didn't know what to do!'

'Course you didn't, no one would have — '

'And he hurts his head, see! He was going, and then he takes and he trips like, and he bangs his head, and he thought I laughed, but I dint! And he was that angry. He threw the lamp at me, he just picked it up, he was so quick!'

'My lamb. My poor girl.'

'He found the cup earlier, see, Ruth's cup, when he was still saying, 'Let's have a cup of tea,' and I pretended! I pretended it was nothing, so's he'd put it down! And he did, he *did* put it down, I dint know it was broken, I'm so sorry, I'm so sorry!'

'It don't matter. Don't you fret now. It's alright.'

'But you ain't said! All this time you ain't said it was broken, I dint know, I dint see him, I thought it was safe, I swear!'

A long silence. Grace held and kissed.

'There there. It's alright now. Don't you mind. Now then, sit up, Gracie, do, and dry your eyes. Let me get us both some tea, and there's a cherry cake yonder just a-sitting up begging to be et. Here, take this hankie. Look, it's one of your own, from Ticknell's, see the bee and the violet? Blow your nose. And you sit up now, I won't be long.'

Nor was she. Barely five minutes had passed before the door opened again.

'I'll just set this down, and I'm going to draw the curtains, alright? So's I can see what I'm doing. Lovely evening it is too, there!'

Grace blinked in the sudden shaft of sunlight; looked; saw. Stared blankly for a moment, and finally understood.

'Yes,' said Bea, smiling handsomely. She drew off Violet's lace neckerchief with rather a theatrical flourish; even Grace, stunned, speechless as she was, could see that her aunt was rather enjoying herself. 'You keep a darkened room,' said Bea, 'you can expect a few surprises now and then.' She folded the kerchief, and tucked it back into the chest of drawers. 'Ain't done that so well for years! Now then. Two sugars, I think, for you. Get your strength up.'

'You — ' Grace began, but then she saw what else was on the tray Bea had just carried in. Sitting with the cake in its toasted lining of grease-proof paper, the two cups and the everyday saucers, the matching basin, the glass milk jug, and not so much as chipped, was the small blue and white cup, Ruth's cup, that Grace had last seen set down so heedlessly on the dresser by Tommy Dando.

'You said it was broken!'

'Now don't get all airiated,' said Bea, taking off the tea cosy. 'The real one was broke right enough. That's another one just like it, that's all.' She smirked. 'Its twin — see?'

'What? *What?*'

'No, don't try to think yet, you have a bite to eat. You can't think on an empty stomach. And drink your tea, that'll put a bit of heart into you.'

'Can I have it?'

'Have what? Oh — yes, alright then, here.' Bea picked up the cup, and set it carefully in Grace's outstretched good hand.

It was almost too small for a grown-up, Grace thought, turning it slowly in her fingers, and made of the thinnest bone china, the painted bird clearly visible from the milky inside. He was just in the act of spreading his delicate wings; his plume of tail hung down behind him, echoing in shape the feathered coronet upon his head.

'Ain't hardly touched it before,' said Grace, and she gave it back.

'Makes me nervous too,' said Bea, and presently she got up and went to put it back in the kitchen cupboard. As she poured out she said: 'I just thank my lucky stars it was me found it, all the bits, I mean. Under the side table. And your Ma just in here! I never crawled about so fast. Like a scared beetle, I was.' She laughed a little.

Grace remembering: 'I think he threw it at me, afterwards. I was — he threw it at me.'

'Eat up, go on.'

'He's seeing Lily Houghton now.'

'I thought she was your friend. Ain't she?'

'She was.'

'Well, you were wrong about him, weren't you? 'Spect she is too.'

'D'you think I should — warn her?'

'Maybe. D'you think she'd listen?'

'I don't know. I don't know anything any more.'

Bea looked stricken. 'I'm sorry I pretended to be my sister; I dint do it to make a fool of you, Gracie. I dint know what else to do. See, soon as I found that cup all smashed I knew things weren't right. I never thought you broke it. Only I couldn't let her see it, Gracie. So I hid it, and then I dint know what to do!'

'So — where did the other cup come from?'

'Same place as the first.'

Grace smiled; she had no idea, of course, how this struck her aunt, who had to look away for a moment before she said, 'From the Home. You know, where I work. Well, live, really.'

'You mean, you just took it?'

'That's about it.'

'So, you — you stole it?'

'No, indeed, Missy, I did not. Plenty of other

sins I've committed but not that one, not yet. How could I steal something that belonged to me?'

'But you said it come from the Home.'

'That's right. Used to be Rosevear Manor, along of the lake, sold on a long lease. Ain't so much longer to go on it now, only about another fifteen years, still, it was cheap at the price at the time.'

'You — bought it? You *bought* the Home?'

'I bought the lease, which ain't exactly the same thing.'

'But — '

'A lease is money lost, in the long run,' said Bea. 'But I got enough to be going on with. I got other places as are mine. This ain't for your mother to know, Gracie, by the way. What I own is my business, and none of hers. And come to think of it — might be best for her not to know anything about who come in here that night, see? Maybe best she goes on thinking you fell off of the table, some things she got very particular ideas about. If you know what I mean. Besides, one thing might lead to another, and believe you me I'd just as soon she never finds out about that blessed cup!'

'So I shouldn't tell her? About — Tommy and all?' Said it! Said his name out loud! And the skies had not fallen.

'That's up to you. I wouldn't, if I were you. But you're not to talk about my business, if you please; not to her, not to no one else.'

'I promise.'

'That's alright then.'

'Aunt Bea — you won't — do anything, will you? You won't go to the police?'

'My lamb. As if I would. Now then. Another little sliver? There. Where was I? Oh yes — see, Rosevear, the family took all they wanted, left the old stuff they dint want behind, piles of it, curtains, rugs, books, pictures, junk mainly, some of it not so bad. But that cup of your mother's: it's a coffee cup really, there was a set of 'em, but the pot was broke, and a lot of it cracked — too fine to use really, daft; but I give one to your mother, 'cause her Ruth saw it on a visit, and she liked that blue bird, poor little dab. I got two more; but I wouldn't want to smuggle another of 'em past your mother, Gracie, my love. Practically give me a heart attack as it was.'

★   ★   ★

Violet, coming in much later from her Bible group, where she had made a wretched showing, hardly able to manage a word, found Bea dozing in the chair beside the range, and Grace sitting up tidily in the bed, the lamp lit beside her, reading.

'Hello, my lovely! You feeling better?'

Grace drew a long sighing breath, and laid the book down on the coverlet. 'You know — I think I am, a bit.'

Normal face! Looking her mother in the eye!

'You hungry? Bit a supper, scrambled egg maybe? Toast?'

'Ooh yes please, Ma,' said Grace. 'And can I have a bit more a that cake? Please?'

297

19

Mr Godolphin had left tracts and a list of suggested Bible readings, but he had also given her *The Time Machine* and *The Invisible Man*. His wife had contributed *Around the World in Eighty Days*, which had been lying on top of the pile, and which Grace had thus picked up first. To begin with she read it as she had read books at school: slowly, occasionally dropping two lines instead of one and getting confused, or forgetting, in the toil of reaching the end of a lengthy sentence, how the thing had begun. She skipped hard words, left out anything that looked as if it might be about scenery, and in general tired very quickly.

But now she was too weak to jump up to take a turn with the weeding, or nip out to the shops, or see what was showing at the Picture Palace. Nor of course could she pick up her sewing or mending. Perhaps one day she would recover some of her old dexterity; she still had fingers enough for that, she thought. But not yet, not for a while. There was nothing for it, unless she wanted to go back to not-thinking about Tommy Dando or Lily, or longing versions of what should have happened that night ('No you can't. Night, Tommy.') Nothing for it but to pick the book up again, find her place, and read on.

Propped up on pillows, she sat beside the open kitchen door while Violet worked in the garden.

The days that passed had a dreamy full quality to them. Grace's only household duty for a long while was eating; her employment was reading, her leisure she spent asleep. She seemed to have missed an entire season, she found; spring had passed by while she lay oblivious. Now it was almost the end of summer. Soon she could walk about the garden, even as far (thank heaven) as the outhouse; she could get up to help with the washing-up, she could, most wonderfully, have a real bath in front of the fire instead of the shallow zinc bowl beside the bed, and what Bea called 'a lick and a promise'.

Meanwhile she read all the books in the pile, and when the vicar came round asked him, with a proper shyness, whether Mr Wells had written any more.

'You liked him better than Jules Verne?'

Grace was startled. The Bishop's Road Council School had taught her to read, to write a clear fine copperplate hand, to add up in her head and quickly work out the price per dozen or gross of items costing, say, a penny ha'penny, or thruppence-three-farthings, but the notion of reading for pleasure had never come up at all. She did not really understand him, for to her a book was a book, and it was hardly her place to like one of them more than another.

'Quite right too,' said Mr Godolphin, while she hesitated. 'I mean, it's not bad for a translation, is it, but Wells is — well, he's just so readable, isn't he?'

A translation? Readable? What could he mean?

'I'll have a quick look at home, but in the

meantime I've brought you one or two others — look here, see how you get on with this — don't whatever you do mind about the first chapter, it's awful stuff, it only gets going in chapter two!'

The book was *The Pickwick Papers*, which Grace knew to be a serious gloomy grown-up book, by Charles Dickens. Grace had heard of him because the headmaster had often reverently mentioned him; in the last year at school her class had waded very slowly through the opening chapters of *A Christmas Carol*, taking it in turns to read all round the class, though Mr Vowles always made the worst readers do the most, for the practice. Clara Collier and Tim Bineham especially had been required to drone and mumble on for page after page, stumbling over even quite simple words, while Mr Vowles twitched or sighed or made sarcastic remarks at particularly inept bits of guess-work; it was dangerously easy to lose track and get caught staring out of the window, to be roused by a sudden bark of 'Carry on — Grace Dimond!'

Charles Dickens was crawling tense boredom; oh dear, thought Grace, trying to look pleased — 'Thank you, sir.'

'And this one — well, my wife enjoyed it. Thought it was pretty hard going myself. See what you think!' said Mr Godolphin, without any idea of the profound meaning, for Grace, behind these careless friendly words.

The book Mr and Mrs Godolphin had disagreed about wasn't by Charles Dickens, so she tried *Ben-Hur* first. It was the usual battle for concentration, but with a difference: now Grace had some idea that her difficulties might not lie only with herself. Perhaps she wasn't such a dunce, such a poor reader after all. Perhaps sometimes a book was just *hard going*.

But some parts of *Ben-Hur* enchanted her. Over and over again she read the glorious moment when the Nazarene stopped as He rode into Jerusalem, and blessed Ben-Hur's gruesomely leprous Ma and sister with a cure that went on for nearly half a page.

> There was first in the hearts of the lepers a freshening of the blood; then it flowed faster and stronger, thrilling their wasted bodies with an infinitely sweet sense of painless healing.

Grace read that part over and over again.

★ ★ ★

Mr Vowles himself came to call, with Mrs Vowles. They too brought gifts, one or two more books, several copies of a magazine called *The New Age* and a basket of late plums from their own garden.

'How are you, my dusky maiden, my nut-brown maid!' boomed Mr Vowles, as he always had at school.

'Delightful!' said Mrs Vowles, looking about her as she sat herself down. Violet was frightened, and hung back, so that Grace was forced to do the talking. 'Will you have some tea, Mrs Vowles, Mr Vowles, sir?'

He was a surprise; he looked so much older, his beard well-streaked with white. It soon became apparent that he could talk of nothing but the war. What, he asked Grace angrily, as she stirred his tea, was supposed to be the point of it all — was Germany to become part of the Empire? No! Was Belgium? No! And as for the conduct of the various generals in charge —

Mrs Vowles at length gently interrupted him: 'Perhaps you've heard, Mrs Dimond, Miss Dimond, that our son Hector was wounded at Amiens? We are very proud of him, aren't we, John?'

'His wound bad?' Violet asked.

'He has lost his right leg, I am afraid,' said the mother. 'But he will be home very soon, I think — we heard, possibly next week. So of course we are looking forward to seeing him very much.'

Hector Vowles; not someone Grace had ever met, as he was so much older than she was, some eight or nine years, she knew, which would make him twenty-four.

After a short pause Mr Vowles took up one of the books he had brought. 'This one here, Grace,' he said heavily, 'is for you to write in, d'you see? I always suspected there was more in that fuzzy little head of yours than you were ever prepared to let out. Know that?' He showed her the blank pages.

Grace took it from him, into her good hand. It was a beautiful book, she thought, covered in soft dark green leather, with a broad band of brown ribbon at its spine, and a silky green bookmark sewn in. It was far too beautiful to write in, she thought immediately. But it was a very nice thing in itself. Meant kindly.

'Thank you, sir.'

'It's to write your thoughts in,' said Mrs Vowles, smiling. 'A journal, perhaps, of your continuing recovery.'

'Thank you, ma'am,' said Grace.

★ ★ ★

Mrs Ticknell came to visit. How was Grace doing now? What a treat it was to see her up and dressed, like, and nearly her dear old self again! No, Gerry was doing well, thank you, she'd had a postcard only the day before, and Jim was still supply-side, thank the Lord.

She brought with her several fashion magazines. Shapes had *entirely* altered since last year, she said. And ostrich feathers were Out, just like that! It was the war, of course; sweeping about in a big hat all feathered just felt wrong — no, lines were simpler these days.

'Look at that hemline! Look at the hat!'

Business had altered so, Gracie! Embroidery giving way to knitting, especially army socks, women who didn't know one end of a needle from the other at it day and night — as if they didn't have enough to put up with as it was, poor lads limping about in blisters all over France!

'But what I really wanted, my dear, was to give you these. It's just a first try, like — I hope you take 'em kindly, as they are meant, Gracie.' Her smile was uneasy, and for a second Grace glimpsed the strain beneath Mrs Ticknell's bright almost-normal manner.

She took the wrapped parcel, and slipped off the Ticknell's pale blue ribbon. Beneath it she found a flat familiar box, and started back, dropping the box on to the table with a little gasp of horror. Peony Lewin's pink and white gloves!

'No no no,' said Mrs Ticknell immediately, 'it ain't them, Gracie! Not hers! Dear Lord, no, I wouldn't give you them blessed things! It's just the same sort of box, see?'

Grace had to sit still for a moment, while her breathing and heartbeat slowed back down, and Violet, who had been rolling pastry, turned round and spoke quite sharply: 'What's wrong?'

'It's nothing, Ma, honest, I'm fine, sorry, Mrs Ticknell.'

'I'll open it for you, shall I? Here.' Mrs Ticknell's own hands trembled a little, Grace saw. Beneath the usual tissue paper lay a pair of plain black gloves, in a fine jersey with plenty of give.

'See I had to guess, like, some a the measurements. Your size, though.'

Violet stepped over, her hands floury. 'What's this, Gracie? Oh.'

'Very kind of you,' said Grace mechanically. 'Thank you, Mrs Ticknell.'

'No, no look, dear — try them on, won't you?' She picked one up, and held it out: the right one.

There was such a strong aura of nightmare about it that Grace had to force herself to take the limp black thing from Mrs Ticknell's coaxing hand. It swung with a curious weight; it already had fingers in it, she realized: three severed fingers.

'Kapok,' said Mrs Ticknell. 'And a bit of fine corset wire. Well-covered — I don't know how it'll last, of course. And I had to guess a few things — if you could see your way to letting me take a proper measure, Gracie, I could do 'em much better, see?'

Grace put the glove on. Mrs Ticknell had slightly overestimated the stuffing, so the glove did not sit perfectly on her hand. But she had been close.

'The wire's to give 'em a bit a bend, see? I didn't want 'em looking, you know, all stiff, like sausages or summat, the wires got curves in, like, like fingers. I thought it'd look more natural, see?' She fell silent, her own hands clasped in front of her.

Grace picked up the other glove, and put it on. Watching her (her own floury hands to her mouth), Violet remembered the little girl she had told was no relation, who had lost the heart for knitting, who had held up her mittened hands afterwards, and said, 'Look, Mammy, I'm the same as everyone else now!'

Looking down at her gloved hands, palms upturned, Grace flexed her fingers. The wired kapok, of course, did not curl in; but as Mrs Ticknell had said, the false fingers had their own jointed curves. They looked almost normal; merely relaxed. In movement, thought Violet, they would hardly show at all.

Grace turned her hands over, held them palm to palm, let the fingers interlace.

'I could do 'em better,' said Mrs Ticknell quickly into Grace's continuing silence, 'and what I thought was, I could make 'em interchangeable, sort of thing, so's you'd only need say one or two really good pairs of 'em, pop 'em in and out, fit 'em into any pair a gloves you like, maybe sew 'em in extra safe, matching, lacy white in summer maybe, see what I mean?'

Grace leant forward, put her arms round Mrs Ticknell's neck, and held her close.

★ ★ ★

Miss Thornby came to call. She brought with her a small box of chocolates and the two most recent copies of a magazine called *The Film Lover's Weekly*. She seemed a young woman transformed.

'No, I shan't stop, thank you. I just came to say goodbye, Grace — well, to tell you how jolly pleased I am to see you looking so well, of course, but I'm leaving home next week, as I'm going to do some nursing, some training in London. Maybe off to France — I do hope so!'

'Well, may I wish you the best of luck, Miss?' asked Violet stiffly, one hand still on the doorknob. She could not quite smile at this child of Mrs Thornby, but she could be polite, she told herself; and Grace just behind her said, 'Won't you come in for just a while, oh do!' very nicely. But Miss Thornby only smiled back, her freckles disappearing in her fine red blush, and waved herself goodbye.

Linda Coachman came to visit, with one or two roses from her mother's garden. Her eldest brother had been killed; the army had sent back a parcel of his things, she said, all mouldy and smelling like death itself, his trousers covered in dirt, and his jacket marked with his blood, with no more concern, said Linda Coachman, than if he'd been a dog of theirs that had died. Their mother had turned sick and faint at the sight.

'Who'd a thought it would all go on so long?' said Violet.

Had they heard about Tommy Dando? asked Linda presently.

Heard what?

Gone; left a note for his mother, saying he'd heard tell he could get into the army in Plymouth, city recruitment dint ask so many questions, or want certificates. Gone for a soldier, and only sixteen!

'Surely they won't take him,' said Violet. But Bea, who was also visiting that afternoon, spoke up from the other side of the fire, said that she thought they probably would; that she had heard from one or two recruiting agents she knew, as had stayed now and then in the old Red Lion. If you're big enough, you're old enough, was their motto: some of these city places were shameless. Grace looked at her, but Bea kept her head down, as if intent on her sewing.

'Well,' said Linda, 'it was a fortnight ago he went, and he ain't come back. So I reckon he's in, don't you?'

''Spect so,' said Bea. 'How's his poor little sweetheart taking it?'

'Didn't know he had one,' said Linda, brightening a little. 'Oh — you don't mean Lily, do you, Lily Houghton?'

'Weren't she the one?'

'Something and nothing, that were,' said Linda, sniffing. 'All in Lily's head if you ask me.'

'Poor Lily,' said Grace.

⋆　⋆　⋆

The following day she decided to go out, to visit the market with Violet; ate a good breakfast, tidied her hair, put her hat and coat on, Mrs Ticknell's special gloves ready in her hand; got all the way to the front door before she realized.

'Oh — I can't!'

'What? What d'you mean?'

Grace felt faint; she staggered as she went back to the kitchen, sank down on the chair beside the range. She bent her head down, and tried to take slow breaths.

'Gracie, what's wrong?'

Presently her heartbeat went back to near-normal, and she was able to answer, 'I don't know. I just felt — dizzy.'

Which was not the whole truth. But the whole truth was so hard to understand. It seemed to Grace that she had felt frightened. Terrified! Her legs all weak, her heart walloping in her chest, her head swimming, as if it had not been Violet waiting for her beside the front door but a blood-streaked tiger. Where was the sense in that?

'I just felt — dizzy. I think I'd better stay here. You go without me, Ma. Honest. I don't feel up to it. Sorry.'

'Bit much, going on market day,' said Bea, later. 'You ain't been out for months, Gracie — you want to go out when it's quiet-like.'

But Grace knew she did not want to go out at all. She wanted to stay inside, in the bedroom where she could see out on to the street. She wanted to stay at home reading *The Pickwick Papers*.

Once Violet, sitting across from her at the fireplace, had tartly interrupted her: 'Is it *meant* to be funny?'

Grace had had some difficulty coming back into reality. 'What? You say something?'

'Yes, you keep tittering — what you laughing at?'

'Am I?' That was a pleasant new wonder; the idea that you could disappear from yourself so completely that you didn't even hear yourself laughing. That you could laugh without leaving the strange otherworldliness of the story.

Once or twice, after that, she tried reading various bits of notable hilarity aloud to Violet, so that she could share the joke, but that never worked. It wasn't, after all, a joke; it was something in the way the words lay on the page; she found that even reading them aloud to herself drained some of the comedy away. No, it only worked when you read it in private. Which was odd, because usually things were only funny when other people found them funny too.

'You got to go outside, Gracie — you can't just stop in here.'

'No, I know. I will, course I will. Presently.' When I've finished this, thought Grace, though the idea by now filled her with dismay. What would happen to her when she had finished *The Pickwick Papers?* How would she manage the thoughts that Mr Pickwick at present kept so totally at bay?

Often she lay awake and found herself thinking of her past. It had been one long struggle, an endless fight to feel normal, ordinary, the same as everyone else, and all the struggle had brought her to was a further marking-out, another outward difference to add to the first. She thought of her reflection in Ticknell's blinded window that Valentine's Day morning, and how perfect it had looked. But that had been a trick of the light, she thought; the darkened glass had simply hidden her difference, made nothing of something that was absolutely fundamental.

He would not have tried to touch me like that, if I had been white.

If she was aware, if she accepted that the colour of her face would always change everything, but in unpredictable ways, was that any kind of armour?

It was recognizing this thought that made her remember how she had felt, weeks ago now, beside the front door that market day, faint with terror, unable to so much as put her hand to the front-door handle.

It was not armour at all. On the contrary, it was simply a formless burden, and since her accident it had become too heavy to carry outside. She could only stay at home, and read, and read, the books she had already, the books she begged Violet to borrow for her from the library, Violet taking volumes from the shelves almost at random, so ill-at-ease was she in that atmosphere of silence and overt learning. Sometimes she struck gold, sometimes dross. The gold took you away from yourself altogether, gave you blessed hours of being someone else. The dross simply worked less well.

Books tell us so many comforting lies, thought Grace, rigidly awake beside Violet in the bed they had shared for so many years, accidental lies, and some that are meant. They give us endings that are not death, they give us a *now* that is never over, and — biggest lie of all — they give us men and women who understand themselves.

All my life, thought Grace, I have not understood myself at all. I have carried my weight of difference unawares, and never noticed how much it weighed me down. Well, now I do. Now I feel it. But there is still nothing to be done about it. I've always known there are no people for me to go to, no country where I will fit in.

They were right, at school, putting me in the same set as Maggie Barnes and Clifford Petty or Judith Laws; this is what they feel like, after all. They carry their burdens too, Maggie Barnes at the mirror, seeing that sweaty moon-face looking back at her, Clifford lacing up his great boot like

311

a blacksmith's anvil at the end of his leg, Judith Laws not right in the head, it was true, but did that mean she didn't catch what was said to her, or said behind her back, in those strange low-set ears?

And all this time I have longed to be the same as everyone else — well, suppose, inside me, I *am* the same, after all? The same in the important secret ways. Suppose everyone else is afraid, thinks others know better all the time, feels in the wrong?

Sometimes Grace thought of talking about these ideas with someone, but there was no one to tell. She understood that Violet had convinced herself that her daughter's difference had been more or less cancelled out by her loving care; it would be too unkind to disabuse her, especially when Grace knew some of the conviction was due to her own silence, or outright deception.

There was Aunt Bea, of course, far more worldly. But Bea already knew too many secrets. To tell her more would again betray Violet. And Aunt Bea has secrets of her own, thought Grace. How had she let Tommy Dando know which recruiting station would ask him no questions? I don't want to know, thought Grace. I don't want to risk her telling me.

Once she could have said anything to Lily. That clever tact of hers: it was as if she understood. But Lily was lost to her, and in more ways than one. She had left service, and gone to Plymouth with her two oldest sisters, who had also given up their places to work in a munitions factory, making guns or bullets or bombs, Violet had said, where once the factory had made agricultural machinery; all three beating swords out of ploughshares.

The money was very good, Aunt Bea had said straight back, and the hours were nothing compared to service, beck and call all day and half the bloody night, no need to be so sniffy about it, said Bea, and for a moment it had looked as if those two old warhorses were about to gallop into battle again as they had so many times in the past.

But then they had met one another's eyes, remembered Grace. She had intercepted that glance, and read it easily, with the new acuity her long confinement seemed to have given her. Not in front of Grace, said the glance. Let nothing upsetting be said in front of Grace.

She knew from her reading that sometimes people talked to vicars or doctors. But the very idea of trying to explain herself to Mr Godolphin made her smile. Dr Summers was a nice old thing, it was true, but he was still a man, no, a gentleman — hopeless.

Mrs Ticknell might understand. She took me on, thought Grace, at some risk. I hadn't understood that at the time. I thought only of myself, and how I was going to stand being stared at over the counter, and asked silly questions; but she took risks of her own.

I miss her, thought Grace. I miss the shop. I would love to see it again. But you didn't tell Mrs Ticknell anything, unless you wanted it spread all about the town.

I could tell Peony Lewin.

That was an odd thought to catch herself out in. Imagining talking to a ghost from a nightmare!

Until she saw the connection.

Something bad had happened to Miss Peony Lewin. At any rate, she had been so unhappy that she had taken a complete way out. There was, for everyone, a complete way out: there was that.

I have that, thought Grace, and was comforted.

20

The weeks, months passed. One day settling down after breakfast she found that there was nothing new left to read. She even picked up the film magazines Norah Thornby had left her, and flipped idly through their grainy pictures, the actors rather an ill-favoured middle-aged lot, she thought, compared to the actresses, all as young and as pretty as Sally Killigrew, or even prettier. She would have liked to visit the Picture Palace again; Aunt Bea had mooted it more than once.

'Just you and me, eh, Gracie? There's a Charlie Chaplin film. You like him, don't you? Supposed to be a really good one too. Tomorrow, maybe?'

But of course it was out of the question. She couldn't go outside without taking up her impossible burden.

'Maybe.'

There was nothing to read in the magazine though. The articles were nonsense; thin flowery stuff about the actors' plans to learn French or play Hamlet. She thought of Norah Thornby, being a nurse in London, doing something useful, important, and felt a faint stirring of something like envy. Miss Thornby useful and important, whose mother had wronged her own, whose brother Guy she and Lily had played their pointing-finger game with, so long ago it seemed. He was doing well, according to Mrs

Ticknell, he was Captain Thornby already. He was being useful and important too.

Grace was restless. It was days since anyone had called in to see her. Everyone thinks I'm all alright now, she thought. Since Aunt Bea had gone more fully back to work, and Violet had accepted more shifts at the bakery, she was alone nearly all day. Usually she worked a great deal in the garden, but today it was raining hard. There were always chores, mending, extra washing, ironing. She could use a needle fairly well, was almost used to the extra stretch required of her shortened middle finger. But all these chores left the mind free to wander, and hers often wandered into places that made her groan with despair.

She walked from bedroom to front room and back again: her country now. If only it would stop raining! Working in the vegetable garden was somehow soothing to the mind, perhaps, she thought, because it was strenuous. Could she go out and dig in the rain?

Walking back into the bedroom she had another look through her small collection of books. No, none of them ready yet to read again. Then she noticed one that had no title at all. What was this? But when she opened it there were no words either, it was blank, and she remembered Mr Vowles coming with his wife, Mr Vowles who had always boomed at her so, and called her his nut-brown maiden. Poor man, his son had died of his wounds after all, though they had got him home just beforehand.

Hector, thought Grace. It was painful to think of Mr Vowles, Mrs Vowles; they had been so

316

alight when they'd come calling, when they knew he would be home soon.

She took the book back into the kitchen and sat down with it at the table. How lovely it was, how soft its leather cover! She opened it again and held it close to her nose, and sniffed in its sweetish flowery smell of new paper. It seemed somehow full of promise, this small book.

'It's to write your thoughts in,' said Mrs Vowles, smiling in her memory. But I don't want to write them down, I want to stop them altogether, thought Grace. Anyway, the book was too beautiful to write in. She would keep it always, she thought, and if she ever thought anything really good, noble, she would write it down with a special pen, in her best handwriting.

But there was nothing else to do. It was like the early days of her illness, when she couldn't do anything but read no matter how hard the book seemed. Suppose she wrote lightly, with a pencil? Then she could rub things out as well, leave no trace behind.

Finding a pencil took some time. She had been sure there was one in the kitchen table drawer, then almost certain she had seen one in a teacup on the dresser. Eventually she found a small stub, its point broken, in her own drawer in the bedroom, and had to sharpen the kitchen knife before she could use it on the pencil, and altogether quite a satisfactory amount of time had gone by before she sat down again at the table, the book open before her, the pencil (its too-sharp point softened against one of the flags on the kitchen floor, so that it would not indent

317

the paper) all ready to use. She picked it up.

Ah. The whole weight of her hand was altered. It was the first time she had tried to write anything, she realized. Could she still do it? She went and fetched one of Miss Thornby's magazines, and made use of the margins, to practise.

She wrote her name. The edge of her hand was alright, of course, but there had been a way of holding the pen, of resting the hand against the paper, that used all the fingers, even the little one, curled in support. As it was she must hold the pencil almost like a needle, in forefinger and thumb; it was slow, but not so difficult. It felt odd, but she would get used to it; and it was still recognizably her handwriting. Her own hand, she thought.

She turned at last to the little book, its clean first page all waiting. Hesitated. Then she turned it, so that the first page would always stay unspoilt, and on the second leaf wrote her name, quite small:

Grace Dimond

She turned the page, and wrote her first sentence:

I am the Silkhampton darkie.

Somehow writing this made her heart beat fast, as if she had broken some rule. At the same time it seemed to release something in her memory. She held her breath, thinking hard.

At the Council School the top class, or at least

its strongest pupils, had sometimes been required to write essays. These were to a title given out by Miss Broughton or by Mr Vowles, *A Day in the Life of a Penny* or *The Ruined Mill* or *A Woodland Pond*. Grace thought of Mr Vowles telling them all in his booming voice to begin with the morning and work their way through the day to the evening and nightfall; this would give their thoughts structure.

Grace began with the morning, going to call for Lily after breakfast, finding her out already sitting on the wall outside her house, swinging her skinny little legs in their unlaced boots.

Grace hesitated; should she say how old they had been? She thought of the stories she had read in the magazines Mr and Mrs Vowles had brought her, *The New Age*, strange scrappy little pieces that often seemed to start in the middle and then not go anywhere very much, but just show you very keenly a bit of someone else's life.

No. I don't need to. It will be clear from what we do how old we are.

She wrote on, remembering how excited they both had been because there was a fair on the ground outside the old common, where the bus depot was now. How they had passed the morning planning their visit, until it was finally time to go to the common. She wrote about its shaggy grasses and the trees dotted about all draped with tangles of flowering blackberry. She wrote about the tents and the caravans, the skulking strangers glimpsed here and there, the stalls just opening, the coconut stall, the Aunt Sally, the firing range with rows of little tin ducks, the greasy pole, the test-your-strength stall with a hammer neither Grace nor Lily could actually lift off the ground, swing boats, and best of all a glorious thing like a roundabout, except that instead of horses to ride there were a series of small iron chairs hanging from an upper circuit, and when the whole was in full motion the chairs swung out on their chains, higher and higher, at a wider and wider angle, while their occupants, also tipped sideways and high above everyone's heads, hung on for dear life.

Lily had said she wouldn't go on it if they paid her; not that she had thruppence anyway. And Ted Hall was there in the little crowd saying it was only for boys. At that Grace had instantly marched forward, though her insides quivered with fright, paid up and chosen her chair, a chipped bright blue one. She could hardly get on, it was so high off the floor, clearly meant for grown-ups, and there were few other takers, this early in the day. Worst of all there was a thin iron bar that came down across her lap, with a hook, to hold her in. She needed holding in! And suppose the chain broke, suppose its bolts just gave? She would be hurled in her hard metal chair out out over the heads of the gathering crowd, she would hurtle through the air to a horrible jolting death, oh my goodness! But it was too late to change her mind — the thing was already moving, faster and faster.

I held on, I held on so tight the chains hurt my hands, and then the seat began to tilt over sideways, I was sitting right out sideways, leaning

320

hard against the side of the chair and the right-side chain, flying along, the wind pulled at my hat and blew my skirts out, Lily down there face turned up, more faces, tops of hats and bonnets, I saw the striped roofs of the stalls and the swing boats to and fro, three distant horses under a tree in the neighbouring field, the tower of St George's, then Lily again still looking up, hello Lily!

Suddenly unafraid, suddenly in an ecstasy of delight, aloft in a chair that had grown wings and set itself free from the earth, Lily waving, striped roofs, swing boats, horses, church tower, Lily, higher and higher, Grace let go of the right-hand chain and waved back from her perfect circular flight; once more round, then she felt the slight drop, the beginning of the end of the ride, as the turning slowed, and the chair began to fall back to its normal perpendicular.

It was wonderful!

Lily was anxious to do something else, though, once Grace was back on the flattened grass beside the roundabout, would hardly stay to hear how wonderful the ride had been. There's a giant, let's go and see him! He was only a penny. So they could both afford him. Grace was still breathless with joy, still full of the glory of bravery. 'Nothing to it,' she said airily to Ted Hall as they passed him on the way to the giant's tent, and she handed over her final penny with hardly a thought. She and Lily passed through a sort of arcade of canvas, smelling sweetly of crushed grass, until they came to a curtain of heavy faded chintz.

Hello, I said, is anybody home? So that Lily laughed, we were both nervous, there was no one else about and there was supposed to be a giant waiting for us on the other side of the curtain. Who's there, said a voice, it was an ordinary voice, not deep, a boy's voice, with a funny accent.

We've come to see the giant.

You paid?

Yes, sir.

You better come on in, then.

So we did. We pulled back the curtain and we both nipped round it. It was dark in the tent. There was a great chair like a throne set up with its back to us. Its wooden back went right up towards the top of the tent far above our heads. We had to walk all the way round it to see if there was anyone sitting in it. First we saw his knees, jutting out from the arm of the chair. They were the biggest knees we had ever seen. We held hands. We went further round and we could see his boots, and they were giant-sized right enough. They were as big as apple boxes. They were laced with rope, and tied in big bows. One end was frayed. The giant's trousers were rough serge, his hands together in his lap. His knees slack against one another. He lay back in the wooden chair, and rested his enormous head against the back of it as if he were exhausted. He had a boy's face,

*but odd-looking, weighed down by his jaw, his
forehead all knobbly brow. I saw his eyes. They
were so deep you could not tell what colour.*

*Afternoon, little lassies, said the giant, and
we did our curtsies, afternoon mister. Lily said
could he get up? The giant said no, he didn't
like to. The tent was too small for him, he
said. He was nearly eight foot high, he said, all
but one inch. But he did not sound proud.*

*And I was not frightened, no, whatever Lily
said afterwards. All of a sudden I could not
stand being in that tent any more not for a
single second I let go of Lily's hand and I said
I had to go and I went, and I started running
as soon as I was outside and I ran all the way
home and lay on the bed and told Mammy
I had a pain in my stomach, which was a lie. I
did not know why I had to leave the giant.
I could not bear to meet his eyes. I did not
know why*

Here Grace stopped in mid-sentence. It had
occurred to her that she was not, as she had first
imagined, writing at random, describing an old
childish memory merely to pass the time.
Somehow she had chosen something important
without even trying. She had chosen something
that still puzzled her; except that, as she wrote, it
puzzled her no longer, as if the act of forming
the letters had been all that was needed.

*I saw that he could not stop being a giant. I
saw that he had no choice. I saw that it was
the first thing everyone always saw about him, the
only thing. He was The Giant. I saw from his*

eyes that he would have liked sometimes to be ordinary, he would have liked to get up and leave his enormous heavy body behind him on the chair in the tent, and go out freely amongst the crowd, and have no one stare or call or ask him anything stupid or mocking or jokey.

She had startled him a little herself, she saw that too.

Grace read over what she had written with pain and exhilaration. The writing itself seemed awkward to her, full of her own clumsy voice. She had seen the picture in her head so clearly, like something at the cinema, and now and then as she wrote seemed to feel the presence of the words that would precisely convey the picture on to the page; as if they were floating around somehow, all ready, waiting for her to catch them. Sometimes she had managed to, but most of the time they drifted out of reach, or vanished like a dream, or turned out when she caught them not to be right after all. She had been forced to try others, and now they looked wrong as well, nothing like the glowing clarity she wanted.

Still, there it was, written down, solid effort, words on a page. On the whole she was pleased with herself, and aware of a strange deep peacefulness inside. She read the several closely scribbled pages over and over again, and saw that what she had written was already somehow separate from her memory. She could change it any way she wanted to, she thought. She could alter things to make them plainer, more pointed.

There was the brown child, there was the

giant, looking at one another.

I ran away in case I saw his eyes say, You too.

'Gracie? What you up to sitting here, you alright?'

'Hello, Ma — oh, I've been busy, I — I'm writing a journal. About my recovery, like Mrs Vowles said.'

'Oh,' said Violet, the opposite of reassured. 'Did you pull us some carrots?'

'I'll go now,' said Grace, but before she went out she carefully hid the leather-covered book, sliding it between her pillow and its case. It was her job to strip the bed, so she felt fairly safe. When the carrots were pulled, though, she had to take the book out again to write something else. She turned to the back; this was not part of the account of the giant, it was the merest stray thought, perhaps connected to what she had written earlier. As yet she did not quite know how, or whether it fitted in at all, but it seemed to have jumped into her mind all by itself as she eased the fork down between the green feathery rows.

No escape from the physical, she wrote, then slipped the book back inside the pillowcase, and went to the kitchen, full of a new satisfaction, to put the dinner on.

* * *

All the next week she wrote further versions of the meeting with the giant. She had as yet no term at all for what she was doing. It was just something she felt like doing, she thought: this week, anyway. She put names in, changed some of the things that were said so that Lily seemed more clearly to be someone else in her mind, hardly Lily at all; she made the other child less herself, and finally not even brown, but a little-girl version of the cripple, Clifford Petty. It had been strangely exciting, being not herself at all, but a version of someone else. She described the boot in some detail, the thick wedged heel of it, the weight, and was vaguely surprised to realize that she had never actually seen Clifford's deformed foot at all, never even heard tell of it. Its hiddenness was part of its horror, she thought.

She knew it was clubbed, but what did that mean?

How could she write about someone with a club foot if she had no idea what a club foot looked like, let alone felt like? I've only ever seen Clifford from the outside, she thought. It was some days before she remembered that she was living with someone who had not only seen poor Clifford's foot, but every other inch of him as well.

'Ma, you know Cliff Petty?'

'What about him?'

'What's his foot like?'

'Gracie — what on earth are you asking that for? What a thing!'

'I'm writing about him, about school and that,' said Grace. 'Is it that bad, his foot, Ma? Go on.'

Violet, most uneasy at being asked, as she saw it, to betray something of a confidence, was at

326

the same time aware that Cliff Petty, maimed as it were in the womb, might well have some new significance for her daughter, so lately maimed by accident. She thought of Dr Summers writing down on the certificate, in his black joined-up difficult scrawl, the one word *equinovarus*, telling her that it was the Latin and medical term for the scrunched-up hoof-like little foot now hidden in the new baby's flannel blanket. She remembered Mrs Petty's wan face.

'It's like — he can't put his foot straight. It wants to stand tippy-toe all the time, it don't bend. The boot just makes him level, see. And his brother had a hole in his heart; died just before Cliff come along, poor little mite. What you writing about him?'

'Nothing really,' said Grace, with some truth. She was calling the story 'The Giant' now. The two little girls went to the fair, one of them rode the roundabout-chairs, and then they went to see the giant, and the giant saw them. It made sense somehow to change herself into the girl-version of Cliff, it felt safer. To be Grace Dimond, the Silkhampton Darkie, writing about being a darkie — no, that would be too much, too much for her, anyway. She would hide behind Clifford Petty's great boot.

⋆   ⋆   ⋆

Presently, without thinking about it a great deal beforehand, she began to go out. At first she could leave the house only after dark and wearing the veil Bea had brought her nearly a

327

whole year before. Her heart pounded, closing the front door behind her after all this time, but soon calmed down again. It was only a street after all, only Silkhampton, where everyone knew her.

And I'm old news now, she thought, as she and Bea made their way to the Picture Palace. She supposed for a while that the streets had always been this busy, that she had forgotten, in her long imprisonment, how packed the High Street could become; but no, said Aunt Bea, it was the war.

'How d'you mean?'

'Well, boys on leave — they want to have a good time, don't they? Pack the pubs out, all the dance halls — they don't hang about at home talking to Mammy, they want a drink and a dance and so on. While they still can, see?'

The crowds were good-humoured, thought Grace, men in uniform jostling past, some of them familiar — wasn't that little Bert Flowerdew? They'd let *him* join? And there, Art Coachman and Tom Winterhouse! Soldiers!

Suppose she met Tommy Dando? What if he were on leave and coming round this very corner right now! Suppose he was in the cinema already!

The thought made her heart speed up again, but she told herself that she was safe behind her veil. He could not see her eyes, her face. She would float right past him, stare all he might, and give not a trace of a start. She would seem not to see him. She would seem never to see him, ever again.

The Palace was full, the atmosphere rather more rowdy than she remembered, the audience more vocal. When Mr Bundy, who usually played in St George's, stepped diffidently up to the piano at the front there was wild applause, so prolonged that Grace eventually realized that there was something teasing in it. When he began playing the whoops of delight drowned him out altogether, and when the lights dimmed several members of the audience appeared almost delirious with excitement, jumping up and down, giving shrill whistles.

'Where's Mr Pyncheon?' Grace shouted into Bea's ear.

Presently, when she had repeated it, Bea shouted back, 'He's joined up — gone to France.'

'Ain't he too old?'

'It's the others too young,' shouted Bea. 'Anyway, he kept showing these here films about the Front and all — gets to thinking he has to go himself. Should a stopped showing 'em, silly beggar.'

On-screen the young men marched and laughed and sang, and practised their drill, and shook hands with visiting bigwigs. The audience, it seemed to Grace, was largely taking no notice whatso-ever; most were talking just as loudly and freely as before poor Mr Bundy had started hammering at the piano. It was just about possible to hear him, over the noise. In front of her big guns jumped, spouted smoke; there were one or two shots of broken trees.

Finally the newsreel ended, and the one-reeler

began, a comedy about a fat man on a beach, chasing after lots of slender pretty young women. It was idiotic, thought Grace, but just then the fat man fell backwards down a flight of stairs, very quickly and as if weightless, his expression resigned, doleful, and she nearly shed tears laughing.

On the way back, after the Charlie Chaplin, trying to explain to Aunt Bea how much better Mr Pyncheon had been at accompanying the films, she realized that she had forgotten to pull the veil back down over her face.

Well, what if he were to pass me in the street right now? I would still not see him. I'd look straight through him; it would just be clearer to him that I *cannot* see him.

If she were ready, how fine it would be, to walk right past him with her nose in the air!

★　★　★

Grace went to see Mrs Ticknell. It was the first time she had left the house alone, but apart from a little surprise at the glaring brightness of the day this hardly registered. The elder Ticknell twin, James, Jim, had died of his wounds a week before, buried by his comrades that same day in France, just behind the front line. The telegram from the War Office had arrived, Violet had told Grace, just before Jim's chatty last letter. It seemed there had been a moment or two of agonized hope, before Mrs Ticknell had understood what the date on the letter must mean.

The wool shop was closed, for the duration.

There was no getting hold of all sorts of fine-sewing essentials, and in any case fine-sewing itself had suddenly become deeply unfashionable, its pleasant uselessness no longer arty but unpatriotic. The shutters facing the street were padlocked, had an unkempt look, and Grace was not surprised, when she went round the back of the shop to the small garden at the rear, to see that the house blinds were still drawn.

It was not the first house she had seen that morning with its windows still shrouded. She took out the leather book, which she carried everywhere now in her handbag, and stopped by the gate to write in it, with some difficulty as she was also carrying a small bouquet of late daisies, and wearing her special gloves; the false fingers were slightly in the way.

The houses eyes kept shut with grief, she wrote, and this was unsatisfying, wrong, not at all what she had felt on seeing them, but it would have to do for now; at least the outline of the thought was recorded. She put everything back in the bag, rearranged the flowers, and opened the gate. The paint was peeling on it, the path untidy with patchy weeds. Mrs Ticknell, poor thing, could have no time for gardening now; she had taken work at Thornby's Department Store in the market square, a humble enough post behind the workaday haberdashery counter, mainly because the smart girls Thornby's usually employed were away coining it in city factories, wearing trousers, it was rumoured, and tying up their hair in turbans, because so many men were at the Front: it was all women's work these days, or no work done at all, or so Aunt Bea had said, and with a certain triumph.

After a long pause the door opened to Grace's knock, and an old woman peered out. She was shrunken and grey-faced and dishevelled, and it was thus several seconds before Grace recognized her, and that was only because the old woman smiled.

'Oh, hello, my lovely, hello, Gracie — why, have you come to see me, ain't that kind, ain't that a kindness!'

Mrs Ticknell began at once to cry; at any rate tears appeared on either side of the unfamiliar nose, though her voice did not change. Her whole face was altered, scoured thin and bony, and the arms she reached out to put round Grace were stringy, the hands ancient, all great knuckles.

'Come in, my own dear, there's a girl,' said Mrs Ticknell, and Grace, her own insides all churned with horror and sadness, followed her old employer into the darkened back kitchen.

There was the green enamel stove, that Grace had set the kettle on so often, her heart as light as the pretty feathers on sale in the shop outside; there was the gas light, dimly burning, though it was near midday. The kitchen smelt stale; maybe a drain was blocked somewhere.

'You heard, then, my dear?' said Mrs Ticknell, and her eyes overflowed again.

'I make you some tea, Mrs Ticknell? Do let me,' said Grace. Mrs Ticknell was starving herself, she thought. She remembered how tight the dress had been across her plump shoulders on the day Gerry had gone to join up. Now, embracing her, Grace had felt Mrs Ticknell's spine start through the cloth. I'll come back tomorrow with a couple of pies, she promised herself.

The kettle on, she understood what Mrs Ticknell had just said; until then, she thought afterwards, the words seemed to have hung in the air, as if waiting for her. Heard? But she had written a letter of condolence at once, and had Mrs Ticknell's anguished little note back. Mrs Ticknell had simply forgotten this, she told herself. Naturally enough. She said, gently: 'Heard what?'

Mrs Ticknell made no answer, but instead opened her left hand, which lay upon the table. There was a folded piece of paper in it. 'Come yesterday,' she said. Grace took it, unfolded a telegram, which regretted to inform that Gerald Ticknell had been killed in action the day before.

'Both my boys,' said Mrs Ticknell. 'I've lost both my boys, Gracie. What am I to do? How am I to bear it?'

Just then a neighbour opened the back door and came in, a woman Mrs Ticknell's age, and presently another. They were mothers, Grace saw, they understood. They had had such telegrams too.

This is just one street, thought Grace, as she made her way back home afterwards. One street in one town. She remembered Mr Vowles, and the white streaks in his beard, how his voice had cracked when he talked of the war and its conduct and its folly.

I have been sitting at home feeling sorry for myself, scribbling stuff; the world has been coming to an end while I have been worrying about grammar. I must work. I must look after Mrs Ticknell, and I must get a job; writing can just fit in somewhere.

The writing will always be there, Grace thought to herself, and began to tremble a little with fresh emotion, for it was the first time she had recognized something important, essential, about herself. That's what I want to do most.

But not only that, not yet. I have to help with the war somehow. I've been fiddling while Rome burnt. No, worse: I've just been tuning up.

She liked that; presently she had to stop, and make a note of it.

* * *

So it felt like fate when Violet came back from her own work at the bakery, full of excitement. 'See here, Gracie, suppose you had a little job to go to, how would that be, eh?'

Grace looked up from the potatoes she was peeling. She had spent the rest of the afternoon making lists, and writing various letters of application in her head. 'Little job' sounded altogether too lightsome for the dutiful hardships she had envisaged.

'What sort of little job?'

'Well, the Redwoods are opening a convalescent hospital, up at Wooton — turning almost the whole place over to it,' said Violet. 'Remember that time you went there, for the Coronation?'

'I remember,' said Grace, after a pause. 'We ran races,' she said lightly.

'That's right, and you won, you was a fast little runner. Anyway, I'm to go there, helping out with the baking, Frank can't be in two place at once, like, and they'll be needing a lot — there's so many away at the war, they're putting a cart on, bring us all out of a morning, take us all home again at night, no need to sleep in, see? I wouldn't want to do that, I says to Frank right off. I got my own place, I says, and I'm too old to leave it. That was when he said about the cart — Gracie, we could both go! What d'you say? You could do just a few days, one or two a week, at first, if you like, see how you get on — you're just as good as what I am, baking and so on, bread and that for the poor lads. Earn a bob or two, and — and it's a hospital, Gracie; they need the help. Maybe in a month or thereabouts, setting up, what d'you say?'

Grace said nothing. She thought about that day at Wooton so long ago, about trying not to laugh with the other top winner, Tommy Dando, Spindleshanks. She remembered Barty Small, the little brown boy beside the painted white-haired lady in silks. How strange, how wonderful it would be, to see Barty Small again!

'Will Mr Billy be there, Billy Redwood?' she asked at last. 'He showed us the ballroom that time.'

Violet's face changed. She hesitated.

'What?' asked Grace.

'I thought you knew, Gracie.'

'Knew what?'

'Well — he's dead. Mr Billy. And his brother, they're both gone. Mr Billy at the Somme, two months ago; Mr Henry at Ypres, last year. I'm sorry, Gracie, I thought you'd a heard, I don't know why, I'm sure. Anyway there ain't no heir; no one but some chap in America, they do say, over to New York.'

Grace thought of Lady Redwood, her face quite hidden at the fete in the shade cast by her vast flower-bedecked hat. She thought of Mr Billy Redwood standing at the side during the races, jumping up and down with excitement, his smooth cheeks flushed.

'What's your name again, little girl?'

He had noticed her, of course, and he had taken her and showed her Barty Small. He had seemed quite a man to her then; though he had probably been the age she was now, she thought, still in his teens. He had been kind and beautiful, and now he was dead.

'I knew about Mr Henry,' she began to say, but found suddenly that she was crying, She had hardly thought of Billy Redwood from that day to this, yet it was unendurable that he was dead. His pink cheeks, his smiling eyes: 'Look here, jolly, don't you think?' And now she must tell Violet that Gerry Ticknell was dead too, her mother's long-ago triumph, the baby she had saved by hanging.

As she wept Grace tried to think. It was hardly nursing or the sort of dirty essential war work she had earlier been considering. But it was still helping, and at a hospital. And if she took it she would not need to leave home, she would not need to find a new place to live. The burden of leaving Silkhampton, of being noticed and stared at and commented on and insulted over and over again, by hosts of unpredictable strangers, all that extra difficulty would be avoided. And she would be able to keep a close loving eye on Mrs Ticknell.

She took the handkerchief Violet was holding out to her and dried her eyes. 'Will they take me on though? Do they . . . know me?'

Violet understood. 'Of course they do — well, the cook there's Joy Berenger, known her all her life. Played with her, when we were children! Course she knows you. They all do.'

'Tell them I say yes, then,' said Grace.

★　★　★

Mrs Berenger knew about Grace, true enough. As a little girl she had played hopscotch in the streets of Silkhampton with those famous minxes the Kitto twins, Violet and Beatrice. All the same, she was one of those people careful to use a special slow voice when speaking to Grace Dimond, so that the poor darkie might more easily follow normal English.

'But they must have put them somewhere, the pictures, I mean,' said Grace, measuring out flour.

'They wrapped 'em all up,' answered Mrs Berenger, demonstrating the wrapping process with her red gnarled hands, 'and put 'em in the attic. They ain't hanging up nowhere.'

A pity; it would have been good to see Barty

337

again, thought Grace. How strange it was, how sad, that the young masters had been so summarily dispatched, while Barty Small had been wrapped up carefully, and kept safe at home. Barty at least would survive the war.

He featured by now in several of her latest writings, leaving the only family he could remember, venturing out on to the dark lane towards manhood. But what on earth did he find on the way? There is so much I don't know about how the world works, thought Grace, adding salt to the flour in the bowl. How much could she learn from books, without ever seeing it?

She visited the Silkhampton library herself now, and read all she could, whenever she was not actually trying to write something herself. Mainly these were attempts to record things that had happened to her long before, though she was finding it more and more difficult to stop herself inventing when memory failed. It was interesting, she thought, how much had happened to her because of her colour. The account of the fair, she saw, had started out being about defiance, foolish courage, and unexpected delight; but it had still ended up being about her otherness, as soon as she saw the giant, as soon as he saw her.

Was that bad, or inevitable? Was there another way for her to remember, another way to write?

'How's your auntie, now, Bea Givens?' said Mrs Berenger, in the same warm cooing tone. 'She still working over at Rosevear?'

If you can call it that when you own the place, Grace thought of smartly saying, though aloud she only said demurely, 'Oh yes.'

Because sooner or later she'll forget to talk like that, Grace reminded herself. They all forget eventually, nearly all of them. For better or worse.

More than once she had been present, at school or at the sewing group or choir practice or some other generally neutral gathering, when someone had said something complaining or angry about dirty lazy natives, or the benefits of Empire for the lesser races; said that sort of thing in front of her, then noticed Grace sitting there too and added, usually without obvious embarrassment, 'Oh, sorry, Gracie — you know I don't mean *you*, don't you!'

Or not even noticing she was there at all, still being black.

★   ★   ★

Once, wondering whether the place still had a library — for Wooton had once been reputed to have the best private collection in Cornwall — she had ventured up the backstairs and out into what she had been told might be the right corridor, carrying a tea towel over one arm as camouflage, and ready to pretend to be lost, should anyone question her.

There were several private rooms, here, for officers, and for their visitors; rooms above them for the medical staff, for the nurses. The Redwoods had spent a fortune turning the house into a hospital, installing all the most modern equipment, from the full operating theatre to the

339

fleet of wheelchairs, and on medical salaries and drugs and bandages, on medical assistants and qualified nurses; no one added, now, that the Redwoods had always had more money than sense.

She did not dare turn any doorknobs, or knock; she was far too afraid of who, what, might open up. There had been plenty of kitchen stories about the wounded men, the ones who had lost their noses or jaws or lips, been burnt or blown up into monstrosity; injuries that made her own wound a trifle.

No, this was hopeless; if there was a library here she would have to ask outright, and first find someone who really knew. Turning a corner to go back Grace almost walked into a soldier. He wore an approximation of uniform, and was standing looking blank at the top of a short flight of stairs. He was the first patient she had actually met face-to-face. Usually she arrived before the men were up, worked all day in the kitchens at the back of the house, where they were forbidden access, and went home on the cart with Violet and the others who lived out while supper was being served. Of course she preferred things that way.

This soldier wore a clean white bandage round his shaven head. His face was round and pale, his build thickset, heavy. His blue eyes stared out at her. It was some time before she realized he simply could not speak, not to her, nor, perhaps, to anyone else.

'Hello,' she said softly. 'You alright?'

For a moment or two more he went on

staring, then swung his head, as if it were too heavy for him, swung his head like a carthorse beset by flies, she thought, turned his head away from her and then with an odd shuffling movement seemed to follow it round with the rest of his body. He stood for a moment with his back to her. Then he put out a shaking hand to the banister, held it, slowly went back down the stairs again, turned a corner, and disappeared.

Grace let out the breath she had not realized she had been holding. Poor thing, how mad he had looked!

She was hardly to know, of course, how great a part Bowen was to play in her life. Certainly Joe Gilder was never going to be fool enough to tell her.

21

They walked together along the clifftop path one fine afternoon in autumn, very slowly, Joe not needing to lean quite so heavily on the stick by then, though the uneven grass bothered him more than he was willing to say.

Beside and beneath them the sea sparkled in a series of pale blues, with deep swathes of clear green towards the shore. Joe thought of the day he had first seen the sea from his bed, and not known where he was. Cornwall, the furthest you could get from where he'd started out. Cornwall, the county the young men left in droves, if they wanted work.

He had noticed the odd bits of building half-fallen down all over the place, the old abandoned mines. You'd be walking along a footpath, middle of nowhere, and all of a sudden you'd see railway lines in the grass, heading off into a bramble bush.

'What's that for?'

'Oh,' Grace had answered, 'they're all disappearing now, getting overgrown, but there were lots when I was a little girl. I remember some went down a hill and straight into the earth. As if they were meant to be like that, and you could catch a train to the underworld, Silkhampton to Hell!'

'Direct line,' said Joe.

They reached the big low rock near the path,

and sat down side by side, with a wide view of the sea. Of course he knew a lot more about her by now. Knew a little what it was like to be her.

'I'm a freak,' Grace had told him. 'I'm the Silkhampton Two-headed Lady.'

'How d'you mean?'

She had looked at him steadily.

' . . . Oh, that,' he had said, at last. 'But haven't they — well, got used to it, then? I mean, it's not the most important thing about you, is it? What? What have I said? What you laughing at?'

'You, of course. It ain't the most important thing — but it's always the *first,* see?'

'Not for me.'

'You think back: you know it was.'

Joe silent, trying to remember. It seemed to him by then that all he saw when first he met Grace was her beauty, her essential heartening smile. Though sometimes when they have been apart for a day or two he finds that he has forgotten quite how dark she is. Some small part of his mind says again, Oh! in surprise at her brownness.

But for him this is only another way in which they are different, and it is these differences, he thinks, that help to make him almost helpless with love and desire.

'And so I'm famous,' said Grace, and this seemed to be true; at any rate, wherever they went in Silkhampton they were noted, sometimes clearly stared at, he'd noticed it straight away. She attracted a certain amount of hard-to-quantify attention, and so did he, for being with her.

''Cause you're a stranger,' said Grace, 'and

I'm me. Famous, see.'

It was unnerving, hard to take at first.

'They ain't got nothing better to do,' said Grace. 'Ignore 'em, that's what I do.'

This was true. She could walk through a crowded pavement, heads turning all about her, and appear to notice nothing, unless, as also frequently happened, she was greeted, 'Morning, Miss', 'Hello there, Gracie!' She didn't even seem to be making an effort. The turning heads baffled Joe, maddened and bored and perplexed him. What were they looking at? They were nearly always locals, women as well as men, who had known her all her life.

'They don't mean nothing by it,' said Grace, 'mostly. It's just idleness. They're clocking me the way they clock the weather. They're thinking, Oh look, there's that Gracie Dimond. It ain't like I'm a surprise. And just now it's, Oh look, there's Gracie Dimond's intended — foreign, ain't he?' and she laughed. 'I had a friend when I was a little girl,' she went on, 'Lily, her name was, left town now. I used to wish I was her, wish I could change places with her for a day or two, just to find out what it was like not to be the one that everyone had to take another look at.'

'Oh, Gracie.'

'No, don't be all sorry for me, I ain't. Later on — well, we grew up, Lily got looked at, you know, in the street and that, because she looked so nice. But it don't matter how nice I think I look. There's always t'other reason, see, the first reason. That's what being a freak is like.'

'You ain't a freak,' says Joe heavily.

'You got to understand what it's going to be like, if you marry me.'

'When. It's when, Gracie.'

'In fact you're very popular in this town, d'you know that?'

'Me? How d'you mean?'

'With one or two young chaps' mothers. Taking me on means no one else can. See?'

And he had noticed that there were occasional visitors, even to a backwater like Silkhampton, whose heads turned with more sharpness, who looked harder. Sometimes that was surely because she was so pretty, thought Joe. Any chap seeing Grace would want another look. If she were this pretty but white, would he resent the stares as much, or less?

No point wondering, Joe decided. She wasn't white. She was Gracie.

But was it the brownness that gave some what they seemed to feel was licence to stare more openly, more crudely? Or Lord, was this what being a pretty girl was like, no matter what colour you were?

Grace laughed, when he suggested this. 'How should I know? I mean, I can't have a go at being a white girl, can I?'

They sat on the broad white rock looking out to sea, making plans. After the wedding they were to spend a whole week in her Aunt Bea's house right beside the sea a few miles away.

'They know me there,' said Grace. 'And 'tis only proper busy high summertime. Then they got ice-cream stalls and donkey rides and all sorts.'

And strangers, thought Joe, whose stares would

not be automatic or idle. Already he understood that *proper busy* meant *best avoided*. Visiting strangers might follow up curious glances with hostile words. It had happened, she said, when he asked. No, not that often. Not always. But it put you off. Made you careful. Surely he could see that?

'So — you'd always want to stay put here then? Not move away, like?'

'Where would I move to? Where would things be different for me, Joe? You tell me that.'

Joe had no idea. Except he wished he hadn't asked her now. The change in her voice went right through his heart.

'I'm sorry, Gracie.'

Grace sat very still. 'You got to understand. Round here's like this: people who really know me don't notice. Everyone else always will. I'm the Two-headed Lady. My friends and all, they talk to my two heads, and they don't notice, they've stopped seeing them. And there's some as think, almost proud-like, look, there she goes, that there's *our* Silkhampton Two-headed Lady! That's what you're letting yourself in for, Joe: I'm the freak. I'm the Silkhampton Darkie.'

She holds his hand with her whole one.

'What about you, then?' he says softly. 'You could have had anybody — no, don't shake your head, it's true. You're beautiful and clever and lovely. What you doing with me? Half a proper bloke, that's me.'

Grace kisses him, leans back to give him a long mock-considering look.

'More like three-quarters,' she says.

Still it's a constant anxiety for him. He's a cripple without a trade, without an education, other than the roughness he has learnt on the streets and in the army. The mud of the bomb crater has gone right into him, he thinks sometimes, gone right in and dirtied him inside, so that he can never be properly cleaned up.

His arse hurts when he walks, and it's all very well talking about weddings and planning honeymoons, but if all that comes to pass he will eventually have to take his trousers off and somehow be a man on his wedding night. And it's all very well too talking about honourable scars and the nobility of a wound gained in battle and that sort of carry-on, but he'd bet what you liked whoever first said all that wasn't thinking about a chap with half his bum shot away.

'What do you see in me?'

I think you will let me be who I want to be, I think you will not interrupt me, is some of the true answer, but Grace is not ready yet to trust him with that.

There is something about you that catches at my heart every time I see you: also true. She can say that, and has. She had liked the look of him straight away, that first day in the kitchen at Wooton. Even before he had stood on the other side of the enamel-topped kitchen table while she kneaded the bun dough, and said what he said.

'What's up with your hand?'

When she looked up, hardly knowing how to respond to this crassness, he had already been blushing, his face and throat a bright deep red with shame. His eyes looked panicky, over-whelmed, as if the painful heat all around was making them water.

She thought piercingly then of Guy Thornby; not Captain Thornby, as of course he had been when the German sniper took him, but the slender boy of fourteen or so, jumping out from behind a stall at the vicarage fete, pointing his fingers and shouting hah! to make two girls laugh; then hauled off by his mother in the taxi that time, not looking at Grace, but flushing as feverishly scarlet as ever a boy could go, his poor ears burning crimson.

The young man on the other side of the table had rather a look of Guy Thornby, she thought. Not just the blush: the delicacy of his mouth, perhaps; his thin wrists.

'Sorry,' he had said, his voice husky, a boy's voice. 'I shouldn't have asked.' She liked his strange accent, so hard to follow, so unclipped. It wasn't a bit posh; no, it was manly, though, she thought. It made him sound tougher than he looked.

'No matter,' she said. ''Twas long ago.' It was pleasant to remember that both sides of this were true. 'What about you?'

And he told her a story that could have come straight out of the *Daily Mail,* derring-do and all-lads-together and gallant soldiery. It was a sort of politeness, she thought. Or did he really believe in that sort of thing? Plenty still seemed to; but something in his eyes seemed to suggest that he did not.

'I'm Joe,' he said after it. 'Joe Gilder. Will you tell me your name, Miss? Please.'

How sweet it sounded in his coaxing accent! She told him, watching his face and wondering how old he was; she guessed twenty. Then he wanted to help her with the kneading, a piece of nonsense, of course, as if he could; but she still felt sorry for him, tender about his helpless regret. When he came closer to wash his hands at the sink beside her, she could see how difficult movement was for him, painful, his knuckles white on the handles of his crutches.

'Is they proper dry?'

'They proper is,' he had said straight away, and his mimicry of her own voice was so accurate, and so unexpected given his earlier awkwardness, that she burst out laughing. But of course, she thought, he thinks the way I speak is just as peculiar as the way I think his; she longed to quickly write this idea down, for it had not occurred to her before, and she knew how maddening it was to go home knowing she had had a possibly-useful-one-day thought, failed to record it, and thus forgotten it for ever.

But her laughter had made him relax, and his answering smile had so altered his face, made him look so playful and aware, that she had at once felt a sudden warm shimmering weakness in her insides, such as that she had not felt for years; hadn't wanted to feel it, had hardly even thought about such things, not since the last night Tommy Dando had come calling.

Then the intentness of his gaze, as she sprinkled the flour over his outspread palms, his curious delight; it was like playing with a child. But his adult look down at her had made her heart flutter.

Very soon after that, of course, he was off, limping away with the other poor boy, the one in the wheelchair. She had stayed where she was beside the table, though the others had clustered about in farewell. He had turned as he went through the doorway, and she had just caught sight of him over Mrs Berenger's shoulder. His eyes had met hers with what felt almost like a click, a touch; and then he was gone.

She was glad of it, she decided. He had been altogether too much, too keen, too eager. Too obvious. The feelings he had somehow inspired were in fact uncomfortable, even unpleasant.

Were Tommy Dando.

She squashed the mess he had made of his dough, worked it back into the rest, then suddenly gathered up the raw shapes she had made herself and pushed all of it back together. She would start the whole process again, she thought. There was calm in bread dough, in the repetitive turn and tuck, turn and tuck, in the clean yeasty smell. You could let yourself think, kneading dough.

There. Now it was as if he had never been.

She paused, one hand on the floury table.

'Alright, Gracie?'

She started, looked up: 'Oh, yes, hello, Ma. Course.'

Her mother's eyes lingered on her for a

350

moment, unreadable. 'They nearly ready? Only it's got so late.'

'Two minutes.'

Violet went away, and Grace bent her head over her work again. Quickly she divided the dough, laid the neat little shapes in place. There was nothing like as much cinnamon as she would have liked; but by now even the vast store cupboards of Wooton were running low. Look out to sea now and all you thought about were the German U-boats hunting the convoys; and everyone had heard about the hospital ship, laden with the wounded, torpedoed and sunk just a few miles off the Cornish coast. It had been in February, the sea at its coldest.

They had thought themselves safe at last, Grace thought, remembering the ship again. They were all so near home.

Sometimes she felt almost sure, for no reason that had much sense to it, apart from the rough approximation of the date, that Tommy Dando had been on board *The Glenart Castle*. All his mother had heard was that he was dead, some three weeks after he had first been reported wounded. The strangest thing was that word had soon got about that Tommy had not only joined up underage, but made use as well of his own dead brother's name. Mrs Bold at the Post Office had at first declared the War Office had made some grisly mistake, reporting the wounding in action of Private Samuel Dando, when everyone knew Sam Dando had died years back, poor little soul, of the diphtheria. But the later telegram confirmed his death: as if Mrs

Dando, it was murmured, had lost the same son twice over.

Once Tommy had loomed huge and terrifying at Grace's every horizon, there had been no direction to turn to that did not finally end with him. But lately, even before his death, he had begun to lose this significance. He isn't coming back, Grace reminded herself, rolling the buns into neat rounds. Sam that was really Tommy, he was never coming home again. There is nowhere on earth I will ever run into him, there is no need to hold myself ready to not-see him. I will always not-see him.

What happens now, surely, is up to me. Am I to go on letting him into my thoughts like this? Is he to stop me smiling at someone else?

Because he has. He just did.

She thought again of the soldier, of his desperate blush, remembering that she had promised him an extra-nice bun. She shaped two into one fine big one. She would label it somehow, she decided, make sure he got it. Joe Gilder.

He had certainly admired her; it had shone from his eyes. That had been very nice to see.

At the same time, and at a level too deep for thought, she felt his handicap as something of an advantage: no chance of someone who could hardly walk turning into Tommy Dando once the door was closed.

I could knock him over with one hand, thought Grace suddenly, in clear playground argot. I could knock him over one-handed, and that's alright, because one good hand is all I've got.

She remembered thinking this much later that

afternoon, as she wrote Joe's name on the paper bag with the special bun inside. But I liked him straight away too, Tommy, she thought, and hearing this tore a page from her latest notebook, and wrote a defiantly forward note on it.

6 May, '18

Dear Corporal Gilding, it was nice to meet you, here is the bun you helped make.
Yours sincerely, Grace Dimond, 7a Market Buildings, Silkhampton

'What do you see in me?' Joe asks, and another true answer would be, You put a final stop to Tommy Dando, but Grace doesn't trust him yet with that one either.

At their first arranged meeting — furtive, barely semi-private — in the kitchen garden at Wooton, they had talked mainly about books, about reading. It had been a shock of delight to discover that Joe Gilder was a reader.

'What else could I do, lying on me front all day? Weeks I had a bloke on one side nattering away nineteen to the dozen, but he's talking to the angels and his mum and dad and he's got a taxi waiting outside, he's off to the Palladium — I mean, sometimes I give up, joined in, it was him and me and the angels — and the bloke on the other side had a jaw wound, couldn't talk at all. So for ages it was read or nowt.'

Like Grace he had struggled at first, reading as haltingly as he had read as a child at school —

'Oh I know, so did I!'

But there had been no choice but to keep going —

'Yes, there's nothing else you can do!'

And one of the nurses had lent him books —

'Don't say H. G. Wells — it was H. G. Wells, wun it!'

'Nay; I do like him, though; but first off, first book I really read, it were Robert Tressell — you read it? *The Ragged-Trousered Philanthropists?*'

'Never heard of it.'

'I'll lend it, it's great. It's all about the working man, letting the bosses crush him. Twelve months in hell, told by one of the damned. It's about socialism.'

'What *is* that?'

Joe was no politician, and his account of the law of surplus and supply confused him almost as much as it mystified Grace. They agreed though that she simply had to read the book for herself; that in return she would lend him her own precious copy of *The History of Mr Polly*.

As first dates go it could hardly have been better.

22

The photograph stood on the chest of drawers for a long time. It was not quite a wedding picture; it had been taken in the small studio at Porthkerris, set up to catch the holiday trade, mysteriously still open, though it was September. They had been lucky with the weather, too — every day was warm and fine enough to walk out with a picnic towards the rocky little beach, or amble slowly up the hill to the woods that lined the clifftop there.

The photograph had been taken on their last full day, and what Grace liked about it most, she said, were the accidental lies it told.

'Look at us, Joe, what d'you see?'

By the time the photograph arrived in its stiffened brown envelope they had moved into the two small rooms above the sweetshop in the square, next door to the bakery where Joe was learning his trade.

This had all been arranged so smoothly, with so little fuss, that it had been months before he had understood how many wheels had been quietly turned within others. How could he have guessed, for example, that his prospective mother-in-law had delivered all three daughters of the baker she now worked for, and that this on the face of it very odd fact was somehow enough in itself, all these years later — the girls long since married, with children of their own — to ensure that any hint or suggestion of Mrs Dimond's as to trial jobs, apprenticeships, payable premiums, the respect due to disability resulting from war wounds, and the length in general of the working day, would fall on astonishingly receptive ears?

There had been money involved, too.

'I got money,' said Grace, sounding perplexed. It was two days before the wedding.

'How d'you mean?'

'My Ma says. She's been sent money every week for years, only she don't know who by.'

'You what?'

'Yes, I know. Ten bob a week, donkey's years. She reckons it's someone done her a bad turn one time, making up for it. Or maybe someone grateful — she used to go to childbeds all the time, see, olden days. Anyway she ain't spent it, the money, or not all of it. She got through some of it right enough when I was ill. And I didn't work for ages, you know, after my accident. She's put it in my name, what's left of it, in the Post Office. Ask me how much it is, go on.'

'It's your money, Grace. Not mine.'

'It'll be ours the day after tomorrow. Close on a hundred pound.'

Joe gaped. 'You pulling my leg?'

'You'd fall over.'

She was joking, but Joe had to sit down anyway. It was wonderful to be freed from a lifetime's anxiety, and at the same time it was dreadful. It was a man's job to support a woman; he knew no proper husband should rely on his wife.

And the worst of it was, he had already been approached, secretly, by his fiancée's aunt. He was still barely used to the idea of Mrs Givens, this keener harder simulacrum of Violet Dimond, the steam-powered version (he thought privately) of what was bad enough just drawn along by holy water. No denying it, he'd been appalled to find that there was two of them, that he was going to be a man with two mothers-in-law.

Bea Givens had hailed him in the street, just after Grace had agreed to marry him. He had left Wooton by then, given his honourable discharge; she took his arm as he was coming away from the doctor's surgery, and insisted on walking with him to Market Buildings. She had been rather smartly dressed, and smiled at him winningly; during the course of their walk home she had never missed a passing acquaintance, waving at several who hailed her, even stopping for a minute or two to chat to someone with a cat mewing in a basket, and the really frightening thing, he thought afterwards, was that she had kept up the talk at him almost the whole time, despite these frequent interruptions and her own polite ladylike tone and expression.

He should understand, she said, that she had money; if he'd suspected that, he was right; if he thought that Grace would inherit he was right again; and there would be more, much more to come in the future, when she, Bea Givens, was pushing up daisies, but he should understand nevertheless that she was going to make sure every last farthing was tied up good and proper, tight as a drum, for Grace and Grace only, so he needn't get any ideas; that she knew what she was talking about when it come to finance, and that never mind the money, if he didn't treat her Gracie right then she, Bea Givens, would skin him alive and fry his balls for breakfast —

— had she really said that? She had!

— but the main thing, she said, nodding pleasantly at Mr Godolphin as he passed, was that she would pay his premium. No, she wouldn't hear another word (and I haven't said one yet, thought Joe, to himself), she was going to set him up in business, make sure he could buy out Frank Lavery when the time came, he could look on it as a loan, if he chose, though she wasn't going to need it back; he could think of it as a reward, if he wanted to, for fighting for his country; as blood money.

Arse money, she added, after a short pause, and at last fell silent; when he had looked into her face he saw that the wicked old thing was actually grinning.

'So — ten bob a week — she really don't know who sent it?' he asked Grace.

'She's got one or two ideas,' said Grace. 'Only, I think she's wrong.'

'Oh?'

He saw her hesitate. Should he say it first? But he felt too new to this game, the mysterious game of Violet and Beatrice, his darling always caught in the middle. Why on earth should Bea Givens send her sister money anonymously, and for years? How could Violet not have noticed so many fairly evident things about Beatrice — had she actually *believed* that the sewing machine

Bea had just given Grace as an engagement present had really been going cheap, as faulty?

She does not want to see that her sister has money, he thought. And so she does not.

'Oh, let's go to the pictures,' said Grace suddenly. 'I'm paying. Go on, Joe, just this once — I've always wanted to try those posh seats at the back.'

★ ★ ★

'Look at us, Joe, what d'you see?'

Grace had made the two rooms over the sweetshop very cosy, with matching curtains and bedspread. They were sitting now at the table beside the window at the front, looking out over the market square. It was late afternoon, a Wednesday, so the stalls outside were just beginning to pack up, and some of them were lit with oil lamps so that the wet cobbles glistened.

They were having tea. Joe took the photograph from her hand. Their last full day at Porthkerris.

'You look beautiful,' he said, and looked up at her across the table, 'but then you always do.'

Sometimes at night when the nightmare glacier of darkness has awoken him, when he has understood with what seems to be finality that he really is, always will be, lying in the shell-hole with the wet earth gritting beneath his fingers, he keeps his eyes on her sleeping face beside him, concentrates on her, until he is able to convince himself, hearing her breath, smelling her particular warm faintly gingery smell, that this is after all reality, the shell-hole part of the past.

Most of the time the shell-hole still feels more likely. How can he explain his luck? Here he is, in secure possession of all the foot soldier's best dearest wishes: alive, back home, fed, dry and warm. On top of these longed-for luxuries, fate has mysteriously piled on the unimaginable, the fabulous treasures, the pots of gold: he loves and is loved, even cosseted; and for the first time in his life he is regularly employed, financially secure, and snugly housed.

All of this is down to her, he thinks, down to Grace. Had he not forgotten his wound for the first time the moment he first saw her face?

'We're complete opposites,' she said once, on their honeymoon week, as they lay in the big double feather bed, the sea turning softly against the harbour outside.

'What d'you mean?'

'Just look at us,' she said, using her caressing hands to point out the differences, 'tall and short; thin and plump; straight and curved; straight and curly, well, frizzy, really; blue and brown; white and black; man and woman. Whatever you are, I'm the opposite.'

This struck Joe as the most erotic speech he had ever heard. He did not have the words to express this idea, though his body immediately expressed it for him. 'You missed one out,' he said.

'Did I? What's that then?'

Her glistening blackberry eyes, as she laughed at him.

'You show me?' she said.

The wound had tormented him at first, not
physically, for it was fully healed by then, but in
his knowledge of it. He could run his fingertips
over the horrible unnatural tucks and folds in the
thin red new skin, touch twisted crevices, rope-
like protuberances. Holding his shaving mirror to
it, the night before the wedding, he had wondered
whether it would not be best all round if he just
did the sort of runner he had done so often as a
homeless near-child, the boy who had left home
and mother behind him. You could always just
disappear in those days, hop on to the nearest
tram and off again before the conductor came
along, jump a goods train, hitch a lift, even keep
going on Shanks's pony until whatever mess that
was worrying you was far behind, gone, forgettable.

But Grace would never be forgettable, he had
the sense to see that. At the thought of really
leaving her his whole stomach seemed to fall
away inside him, with blankness and terror.

She knew of his wound, of course she did. He
would try to make sure she caught full sight of it
as seldom as possible. But she would be frightened and disgusted when she first saw it though,
any normal girl would; and no matter how well
she hid it he would know. That was a nasty
thought. To see that in her eyes! To see horror!

By the time they had gone through the
wedding rigmarole, very quiet, had a wedding
breakfast with Violet and Bea (both of them
looking, Joe thought bleakly, just as he felt, which
was on the lines of someone waiting to be taken

out and shot) and one or two other similarly doleful droopy old females whose names he was unsure of, by the time they had caught the late afternoon train and arrived in Porthkerris just as the chill autumnal dusk was falling, he was in such a state of remorseful misery that he could hardly speak, he could hardly so much as look at his wife. Now that the deed was done he felt all the deep shame of the disfigured. He had committed a vile crime: he had chained Grace to the crippled monster that was himself.

She had opened the door of the place, then stopped, looking up at him, but he could no longer read her expression.

'Can't yer do it?' she said.

Blank. 'Do what?'

'Lift me over!'

'Oh. Sorry — ' Blushing, sweaty, he put down the bag he was carrying, and set his stick against the doorjamb. Nothing wrong with his arms now, or his back, after months of crutches, and lately of hauling sacks of flour about, and sliding loaded trays in and out of the oven. It was just a question of balance; he could do almost anything if he thought about it first. Carefully he picked Grace up and carried her over the threshold. For months the merest thought of her had been enough to transfix him with desire, he had been unable to eat or sleep properly for weeks at the idea of finally being alone with her. Now, her whole plump sweet-smelling liveliness in his arms, he felt only a chill and desperate embarrassment.

He set her gently down beside the low bow window overlooking the harbour, and she said something odd: 'I could still knock you over. Couldn't I!'

He tried to smile. 'D'you want to?'

She seemed to give the question some thought. 'Not at the moment. Look, the fire's lit all ready. Want a cup of tea?'

He looked about him, at the darkening sea beyond the harbour wall, at the clean flags of the floor, the plain whitewashed walls, the hot range, the steep flight of stone stairs turning in one corner up to the single bedroom above. He could hear the sea outside, otherwise nothing. It was all peace here, he thought; all war inside him.

'Shall I — take the bags upstairs?'

'Later. Joe?'

'What?'

'Give me a kiss.'

Suddenly he was trembling as if they had never touched before.

'I'm so glad you're you,' she said, and put up a hand to stroke his cheek.

'Oh, Gracie!' he whispered against her lips.

'What?' she whispered back.

Speech seemed difficult. 'It's just that — I haven't done it — since. Since then. And I've never done it — with you. See?'

'Well, I've never done it with anyone,' she said. 'Good job no one's watching.'

No, he must spell it out: 'Grace — the . . . Huns made a right mess of me.'

'You were a soldier. You fought for your country. How could I ever think the worse of you for that?'

'I mean — the way I look.'

363

'The way your *bum* looks.'

He could not smile. 'It's not a pretty sight.'

Grace held up her right hand. 'Is this?'

'That's — '

'What?'

'That's nothing.' He took the ruined hand, and kissed the palm.

'Yes,' said Grace. 'It's nothing now. I used to think there was no escape from the physical — that you were always what you were lumbered with, what was wrong with you or different, your face, your colour, all that. But there is — escape, I mean. There can be. At home, in private. You and me. D'you see what I mean?'

'I don't know — I think so.'

'Well. Look. Let's take the tea upstairs. Where it's dark. And get into bed. You be scared of me. I'll be scared of you.'

There was a pause. He put his hand on the back of her neck, so slender, and stroked the soft hair at her nape. He put his forehead to hers, and closed his eyes.

'Maybe just the one candle?' she added.

But it turned out they did not need one; the moon soon rose, and lit the room with silver.

★ ★ ★

'You look beautiful,' he said now, across the table set for tea, 'but then you always do.'

She smiled. 'Yes, yes,' she said, 'but keep looking. What d'you see?'

'The two of us,' he said warily. What was she after?

364

The Porthkerris photographer had posed them against a plain white background, with just a bouquet of artificial flowers beside them to add (he said) a further focus. There they stood, side by side in their Sunday best, her arm through his, her gloved hand —

And then he understood. He himself was standing upright in the photograph; he had left his stick in a corner, near enough to hand, but not needed, not when he was just going to stand up straight for a minute or two. He was unwounded, in the picture. And she was wearing a pair of her special gloves, cunningly tricked out, as he knew, on the inside. They looked whole, this young couple. What had she said? Accidental lies?

'I don't mind the odd lie,' he said at last. 'But I want the real thing most of all. I want what I can trust.'

'The truth.'

'Yes, that's it.' He looked out over the square. It was a fine sight, he thought, still busy enough despite the shortages, and full of decent human activity.

The war, so suddenly over, had been a nonsense, he had decided. And if you could let yourself think that, if you could give yourself permission to think like that, like Frank Owen in *The Ragged-Trousered Philanthropists*, you could see how shaky everything else looked: everything, the way the world was running, the things most folk believed in and took for granted, the things that were considered obviously true or obviously wrong — nearly all of it was just talk. Just people scrabbling about for their own, and trying to make sense out of senselessness, and telling themselves something had to be right if it had been as it was for a long enough time.

It's all of it bollocks, thought Joe. It's all of it lies. Some accidental, some that are meant.

The cushion beneath him was real, made for him, to measure, by his wife, so that he could sit at a table like anyone else, without aching too much. The china on the table, the bread and butter. The bread. His wife was real, and lovely, all the love there was in the world.

'You alright, Joe? Joey?'

He passed her back the photograph. 'We'll get it framed, shall we? I'm grand,' he said.

★   ★   ★

Every morning, when she had swept and tidied the two rooms, she sat down at the table before the window and wrote. She had filled the leather-bound book long since; scribbled now in the cheapest of cheap exercise books from the stationer, mainly about her childhood. The more recent past, she felt, was still too close for scrutiny.

'I was sitting there trying to remember how to cast on,' she told Joe, in bed one night. 'I mean, I do know, I can remember. I just wanted to knit a shawl; but soon as I started all I could think of was Ma telling me I wasn't hers. We were knitting, she was teaching me, and the whole thing sort of jumped into my head. So in the end I just sat down and wrote it all down.'

'I read it?'

'Maybe one day.'

She turns away from him and lies on her back, stretching out, full of happiness. For once in her life, she thinks, she is at least partly doing what everyone else does. Every wife who can afford to do so stays at home, industriously housekeeping. It is glorious, this almost unprecedented feeling of doing as others do; playing houses with a real house is a genuinely satisfying game.

At the same time there is her secret pleasure, the pinning down of more and more complicated memories. Last week she threw out poor Clifford Petty, stopped hiding behind that great boot of his, and rewrote 'The Giant' as someone like herself, the brown girl going to the fair. It seemed simple now, plain, from the child's point of view. There seemed nothing left to add to it, nor to take away. She had copied out this finished version on to foolscap, in her best clearest handwriting, signed and dated it, and put it in the lowest drawer of the chest, under the winter blankets, where no one but she would ever see it.

Sometimes she thought about sending a finished story to a magazine. Selling something. But merely picturing herself going to the Post Office and buying the right-sized envelope was enough to make her heart thrill with anxiety. No. She did not dare. Maybe one day, when she had written lots more, when time had passed, and she was more able to judge whether what she had written was any good or not. If you thought something was good you would be able to bear the exposure of yourself that publication must mean. Perhaps.

'It's called 'The Lesson',' she says, but Joe is already asleep.

23

Dr Summers, on the very edge of retirement, had taken on a partner, a big ex-army doctor named Heyward, fresh from field hospitals all over France. He was a forward-looking young man, keen to put the war behind him and practise modern medicine, and it was his particular belief that antenatal care was of paramount importance.

It had long been Dr Summers' habit, on confirming a pregnancy, to end the consultation by rising, shaking his patient's hand, congratulating her if there was the slightest chance that her condition pleased her, and requesting that she be sure to get in touch again once the pains had started. That was if she were a lady, of course, or at any rate in a position to pay his fees; the rest were to call the midwife.

But young Dr Heyward despised such laissez-faire. The fact remained, he said one evening, as they sat with a small brandy each after dinner — for he was lodging with his senior partner while the house he had taken was properly decorated — the fact remained that maternal mortality, despite the recent improvements in antisepsis and surgical technique, remained at distressingly high levels. Indeed there was a case for regarding the whole business of parturition as pathological; as requiring close medical supervision at every stage. A woman today, he told Dr Summers, was no less likely to die in childbirth than her grandmother. Than her great-grandmother. Where was the progress in that?

The solution, said Dr Heyward quickly, in case Dr Summers thought to answer, was in regular antenatal clinics, where trained staff would observe the patient throughout the entire period of gestation, beginning with a thorough examination of the whole person, with notes made of weight, height, general health, obstetrical history, and any physical disorder inimical to normal delivery; later visits would chart the progress of the pregnancy, measuring weight gain, fundal height, blood pressure, testing urine for the albumin traces heralding toxaemia, and for diabetes. He need hardly add, said Dr Heyward, that of course the demobilizing troops would be bringing a host of venereal disorders home with them; the sort of clinic he proposed would certainly play its part in responding to what might well amount to a new national emergency. Had Dr Summers any objection to his setting up such a clinic locally, should the Council approve and at least consider part-funding? He himself would work tirelessly to raise the necessary resources; and of course he would oversee the project himself, and for no added remuneration.

Dr Summers, who had felt quite worn out before his partner began, could only nod in acquiescence. He had had a curious memory, while Dr Heyward was speaking, of going to visit the parish's last handywoman, the untrained midwife Violet Dimond, to tell her what his new partner had more or less just told him: that the good old ways were good enough no longer.

And yet Mrs Dimond had been a clean kindly creature, he thought, who had done much good and little harm, and only charged her patients what they could afford. But of course, he thought, it was already beginning to seem downright wrong, even peculiar, to let an untrained local deliver the children of her neighbours. As wrong and odd as, say, sending little boys up chimneys to sweep them. And yet I remember the sweep arriving to do just that, he thought. Oh, but Mother's face! The sweep grinning as he turned up at the back gate with the two thin little children each carrying a filthy black sack, boys my age, said Mother, and she sent the sweep off with a flea in his ear, and then Father was so . . .

'I beg your pardon,' said Dr Summers aloud. 'Afraid I rather drifted off — forgive me, Heyward, had rather an early start.'

'So — would current staff be available, for purposes of consultation?'

This took a little working out. Does he mean me? Dr Summers asked himself. Then he understood.

'I think you will have to ask Sister Goodrich that. And, of course, Sister Wainwright,' said Dr Summers. The midwives. He had taken some time to get used to Miss Goodrich, whose manner was often so very forthright; but he had grown rather fond of her over the years. She was perhaps a little too ready to scold her patients, to

370

bark commands; but she was absolutely reliable, an expert, kind enough most of the time. Miss Wainwright — younger, more recent, blonde and droopy — he knew less well. He suspected Miss Goodrich of bullying her, partly because, as his own wife had pointed out more than once, the poor woman looked so like a sheep; Miss Goodrich the cross bustling sheepdog.

A thought occurred to him. 'They'd be paid extra, would they?' he asked.

The thought had evidently not occurred to Heyward. 'I expect some small sum might be made available,' he said indifferently, after a moment's surprise. 'Though in fact the clinic would use their time far more efficiently. And to be frank, sir, I shall not want to stop there. In my opinion there is a crying need, in this country, not only for organized antenatal care but — ' here he gave the table a little smack with the flat of his hand — 'for the wholesale improvement of the breeding stock of the nation.'

'Now you really have lost me.'

'Family planning, sir!'

'You mean . . . contraception?' Dr Summers was taken aback; he had always found such talk distasteful.

'One day everyone will — ' began Dr Heyward, but then, perhaps, he noticed his senior partner's expression, and changed tack. 'So — we are in agreement, then, about the antenatal clinic? I may write to the Council informing them of our decision, and speak to Sister Goodrich?'

'Don't forget Sister Wainwright,' said Dr

371

Summers, folding up his napkin and escaping at last.

★ ★ ★

But the Council, it turned out, was most reluctant to commit itself, under the current financial circumstances; and Sister Goodrich, called on one evening and instructed in person, was similarly regressive.

Of course, she said briskly, she approved in principal; but it was simply out of the question for either Sister Wainwright or herself to run Dr Heyward's proposed clinic; they both had more work than they could deal with as it was. No, with regret, she must refuse: there were simply not enough hours in the day.

'Flaming cheek!' cried Miss Goodrich hotly when he had gone. 'If he wants antenatal messing-about with perfectly healthy women he can bloody well pay for it! Improvements indeed.'

For while it was true that the small terraced house shared by the Silkhampton midwifery service was paid for by the Council, with *Light, fire and maidservant* grandly specified in the contract, this translated into town gas, less than half the coal actually needed to keep the place habitable, and a girl called Elsie, not all there, running a dirty mop over the kitchen lino twice a week. Generally in winter the Silkhampton midwifery service dined with its shabby over-coats on. It re-used tea leaves, and could not join the Women's Institute, though collectively it longed to, for the subscriptions were too high;

tonight, now that Dr Heyward had gone, it sat down beside the inadequate fire for dinner: welsh rarebit again. One slice each.

Sister Goodrich, still maddened by Dr Heyward's bland presumption, voiced stirrings of subversion as she ate.

'Seven years' training — I wouldn't mind but that's how long it takes to be a flaming doctor — look at him! And look at us, barely earning enough to live on! Why not? *Why* aren't we earning enough to live on?'

Miss Wainwright looked uncomfortable, for she disliked all talk of money. She reminded Miss Goodrich that nursing was a vocation.

'Oh, Dolly, that's just what they *want* you to think!' cried Miss Goodrich, exasperated, but she knew it was useless to argue.

Nursing was a life of dedication, offered Miss Wainwright, nibbling her rarebit. Especially being part of the everyday miracle of new life. Yes, of course, it was religious — why else were they known as Sisters? We *are* like nuns.

'You speak for yourself,' said Miss Goodrich rudely.

★　★　★

From old habit Dr Summers steeled himself a little before he rang the bell for the next patient; even now there was usually some discomfort in dealing with certain connections. Ready, he asked himself? Ready.

Grace was shown in, and he stood up to greet her.

'My dear Mrs Gilder, how very nice to see you!'

Dr Summers came round the desk, and shook Grace's gloved hand. 'Looking very well!' he added, thinking her indeed a touch more rounded in the face, and more buxom than he remembered. The likeliest reason for her visit was at once clear to him.

'Married life suiting you?'

'Yes, sir, thank you, sir.'

'Mrs Dimond well?'

'And sends you her kind respects, sir.'

'And, ah, Mrs Givens?'

It had generally been noted in the town that Bea Givens was visiting far more than she ever had before. Rumour followed her, as usual: she had lost her place at the Home, for pawning the silverware, or for chucking old bedsteads into the lake, or for letting the children play at skating in the ballroom, with torn-up Rosevear sheets tied round their feet. She was going to open a fish-and-chip shop next to the Picture Palace; no, a tobacconist; she was emigrating to Australia.

'She's very well, sir, thank you.'

'Good, good,' said Dr Summers, retreating behind his desk. The thought of Bea Givens gave him a familiar qualm; he wondered if it was true about Australia. 'Well, now, my dear,' he said. 'What can I do for you?'

'I think I might — ' She hesitated, smiling uncertainly.

He smiled back. 'Might what? Might be with child?'

'Well, sir — '

'What does Mrs Dimond say?'

'She says as I am, sir. Four months along, she says.'

'Does she, indeed. Well, I dare say she is right.' He remembered thinking of her vividly quite recently, when Heyward had been making one of his speeches; Mrs Dimond and the old days, when he himself had been as young as Heyward was now — no, younger. 'When did you last have your . . . monthly, your period, can you remember?'

Embarrassed, of course; they always were. She shook her head. 'Not sure, sir. Might a been . . . Christmas time.'

'Usually regular?'

'No, sir, not really.'

'Any sickness? Needing to pass water more often than usual? Bosom a little tender?'

Presently he got her to lie down on his examination table, the top of her skirt loosened.

'Just going to press down firmly — may feel a trifle uncomfortable — this your bellybutton, here? Good, good. Your mother do this too?'

Halfway between the umbilicus and the edge of the pubic bone: yes, four months at least, he thought.

'She did, sir.'

'When does she think the baby will come?'

'September, thereabouts.' He helped her to sit up, turned his back while she rearranged her dress and took up the patient's chair again.

'She's quite right, of course,' he said. 'You happy about it all?'

She did not at once reply. 'Mostly, sir,' she said

at last. 'Mostly I am. Except sometimes. When I'm afraid.'

'It is rather soon, perhaps. Husband happy about it?'

'Mostly,' she said. 'Except when he's afraid,' and she laughed a little.

He had a sudden memory of a straw hat lying upturned on the grass, full of blackberries. It was so intense, so surprising, it made him catch his breath. 'Oh, there's nothing to be afraid of,' he said, recovering quickly. 'You're a healthy young woman, and you're going to have a fine healthy baby.'

'Thank you, sir.'

'But I want you taking good care of yourself now. Pregnancy is something of a strain, d'you see, on the heart, on the system in general, and yours has been, well, rather severely tried, quite recently, so — no gallivanting about now, Mrs Gilder. No riding, no bicycling, none of your strenuous tennis parties.'

It came to him that she looked extraordinarily like her adoptive mother; apart of course from her colour she was very like the comely Mrs Dimond of long ago. Another strange thought, come from nowhere! 'No Highland flings,' he added, as he usually did, and at her polite smile the likeness vanished, clearly had never been, so now he was imagining things. Or perhaps it had been in her posture, something copied, naturally enough, from Mrs Dimond; or maybe just a trick of the slanting light. But she was speaking:

'See, it's just that — well, me and Joe — my husband, sir — we thought as we wanted you to look after me, when the baby comes. If you're willing, sir, of course.'

'Ah.' He cleared his throat. This was rather a surprise. 'You know my fees, I imagine?' He named them, and she did not seem taken aback. 'And there is a retainer.' He named that too, and she merely nodded. 'So — that's alright, then?'

She smiled. 'Yes, sir, thank you.' Then added in a sudden rush: 'You know, sometimes I can't hardly wait. To see the baby! Be the first time — my own flesh and blood, I mean. The first person I'm related to in the whole wide world.'

'And by chance related to your husband as well,' said Dr Summers lightly, and to his surprise, for she had never dared before, she answered him in the same tone:

'Ain't that a charming coincidence!'

He laughed, and moved on to the list he usually offered those with sufficient income: small but regular and nourishing meals, no constricting undergarments, no lifting, the lightest household duties only. Nothing more energetic than a stroll, plenty of repose, particularly after lunch, when a proper afternoon rest was really essential. Did she drink at all, he meant alcoholic drinks? No, he thought not; good. Here was the name and address of the local midwives, Sister Goodrich, Sister Wainwright, with whom he worked closely; while he would of course be in charge at the cottage hospital, he had every faith in their everyday professional judgement. Well; that was about it; had she any questions? No?

He rose, and so did Grace.

'Congratulations, my dear girl.' Ah, her lovely smile. He took her hand, the right one, so cleverly disguised in its small neat glove, and shook it affectionately, remembering the funny little brown baby of long ago, who had confused her age with her door number. He had privately considered it eccentric of Mrs Dimond, then, to take in so strange a mite; but see, he told himself, how well her kindness has served her!

* * *

'You speak for yourself,' said Miss Goodrich rudely, but of course she was lying. She was far more like a nun than she wanted to be, and was in fact a virgin, since no one had ever come close to trying to seduce her. In a month or two she would be forty years old, and had lately begun telling herself that soon she would think less about such things: she was looking forward to a new lightness and freedom.

All the same she was often conscious of bafflement at the extraordinary unfairness of life in general and of men in particular. Why, for instance, should anyone have married someone as frankly ill-favoured as, say, Agnes Dewey? And yet there she was cheerfully expecting her third, so Mr Dewey was clearly still pleased with his choice. If someone had gone for Agnes Dewey, why not for Eve Goodrich? Had it been mere luck, or had Agnes known or done something essential, that somehow Miss Goodrich had never found out about?

Of course Sister Wainwright was perfectly right in a way: nursing, midwifery, *was* its own reward.

I am lucky in my work, Miss Goodrich often told herself, for it was true that the sense of awe had never left her. Sometimes, after a particularly lovely birth, in some neat clean cottage, a first baby born to a young couple instantly besotted, Miss Goodrich knew herself to be part of something profound, and was altogether transported with shared joy and contentment.

It was curious, regrettable, that the world at large still regarded the work of helping women safely to deliver their children as at once noble and distasteful, important and embarrassing, even slightly comical. In her uniform gabardine and hard round hat Sister Goodrich knew that despite the significant life-and-death of her work she was not so much a figure of authority as of sniggering music-hall fun; this compounded, of course, by her spinsterhood.

There seemed no way round this central puzzle, and no point in complaining about it, or being bitter. However Miss Goodrich often did, and sometimes was. Now and then it occurred to her that of all possible lives and careers, she had managed to choose the two most contrary: a maiden undertaking unmaidenly tasks, an outsider constantly summoned within.

Summoned to take up her special bag and go out in her coat and hat and boots to wherever she was required, sometimes far afield in bitter winds and rain, arriving soaked and chilled, and not always to any degree of household comfort; a trained and experienced and expert professional who nevertheless could not afford a bicycle, while Dr Summers had recently bought himself a bigger, better, more comfortable motor car.

Well, he was a nice old thing, at least.

'What do you think of this Heyward?' she asked now, putting down her empty plate. 'Have you seen him in action yet?'

'Not really,' said Miss Wainwright. Her tone ever so slightly implied rebuke, at Miss Goodrich's disrespectful tone.

Sometimes Miss Goodrich felt quite fed up with Miss Wainwright, especially when she suspected that in her heart Dolly hoped to be thought *ladylike*. Which was pretty bloody hopeless, Miss Goodrich thought, if you came from Ewell and were a railwayman's daughter and sounded like one. More than once she had heard Sister Wainwright chatting to someone posh — Mrs Thornby, for example, or Mrs Grant-Fellowes — and actually trying to talk as they did, *oh yars, how simply ghaastly*, and been dreadfully embarrassed, because poor Dolly had sounded so false; besides, she knew her own accent was pretty cockneyfied.

Still on the whole she was fond of her lieutenant, and sorry for her, poor thing, so much younger than she was herself, barely thirty, but clearly in the same boat, though perhaps not knowing it yet. And surely so much better a person than she was herself, gentle and patient. Feminine, in a word. Whereas I am hardly a proper woman at all, thought Sister Goodrich, on her bad days.

But this was not one of them, and besides she had just seen off that beastly Dr Heyward's attempt to get even more work out of them for

380

no more money, and there was enough milk for cocoa, if it was well-watered. She leant forward, the small fire warming her all down one side.

'Did you know Grace Gilder's expecting?' she said cosily.

'No!' said Miss Wainwright. 'What, the darkie? Oo-er!'

★ ★ ★

When the door had closed behind her Dr Summers sank back in his big chair and leant on his desk with his face hidden in his hands. It was all a nonsense, he told himself; the old nonsense, worse today because he was tired, that was all.

He remembered himself, thirty, no, thirty-five years younger, on horseback one hot still August afternoon in one of the deep lanes above Porthkerris, and taken aback to come across that trusty handywoman, Violet Dimond, miles away from home, idling about all alone in the sunshine. He had had time to wonder a little at himself, that he had never noticed before how handsome her figure was; perhaps because she was dressed so differently, with several buttons undone at the top of the tightly fitting bodice of her dress, and her curly hair coming loose about her face. Her straw hat lay beside her on the soft grass of the verge; as he drew close he saw that it was full of blackberries.

'Good afternoon, Mrs Dimond,' he had said cordially, touching his own hat, 'what brings you here, may I ask?'

But the woman who looked up at him in answer, who had looked right into his eyes and seemed at once to know all there was to know about him, had not been Violet Dimond at all.

'Dr Summers, ain't it?' Bea had said. 'Want a blackberry? They're proper sweet, look.'

Oh Lord, thought Dr Summers now, remembering that long-ago meeting with very mixed feelings. For a long time he had been deeply ashamed of his own subsequent behaviour. It had taken him months to break free of her, of those gross and intemperate desires; years to recover his sense of himself as a moral man, a good father, a decent husband.

But lately, these days, he found himself unable to judge his lapse quite so harshly. After all, no real harm had been done. Her husband, his wife; neither had even suspected. Almost he wondered why he had been so set on quickly ending so passionate an entanglement; it seemed to him now that more than the affair itself he regretted its brevity.

How short life was, after all, and how extraordinary those few blissful and appalling weeks had been! He had never forgotten them, he realized. They had been part of him all these years, never quite disappearing even when he had tried his best to expunge them altogether. And all those years of working with Violet Dimond! How on earth had he managed it, he wondered now, half-smiling to himself. What a strain it had been early on, Mrs Dimond herself all innocence, of course, but even so, a constant unknowing reminder of adultery; more than once in those hectic times, he had dreamt at night of love-making, and woken in shameful longing, unsure which of the two women had come to him in his hot unruly sleep.

It had been strange, painful, to see Bea Givens again after so long, as she waited with her sister outside the operating theatre after Grace's accident. She had seemed as desolate as the adoptive mother; turned up day after day, night after night, just as Mrs Dimond had, while the child lay struggling between life and death.

He came close, then. He almost noticed the thought at the edge of his awareness, that to look like Violet Dimond, matron of unimpeachable virtue, was also to look like her sister Beatrice Givens, of whom he knew a thing or two. But some other part of his mind pushed the thought carefully away, distracted him instead with Bea's grief at the hospital.

Even in sorrow she had not changed a bit, he thought. She was beautiful still. He had wanted to take her in his arms, not with the old lasciviousness, no, but in friendship, to comfort her. It seemed to him now that Bea Givens was simply the dearest of old friends. Whom he had loved, once. Whom he loved still, indeed.

Well, a man may love many times, Dr Summers told himself, and wiped his eyes, for the ready tears of old age had filled them. Then he put his handkerchief back in his waistcoat pocket, and rang for the next patient.

24

He knocked, and opened the door. Her mother was there, or perhaps the other one, he could never be sure at first. Whoever it was signalled to him anyway, *I'm going*, and got up straight away.

They met at the end of the bed.

'How is she?'

'Not so bad,' said whoever it was, and went away quietly. He heard the door close.

'Gracie?' He didn't want to wake her, of course, though the desire to see her look back at him, herself again, was overwhelming. He sat down on the chair beside the bed.

'It's me,' he said. He took her hand, the whole left one, lying limp on the coverlet beside him. He waited a while. It was very quiet. Once he heard someone wheeling a squeaky trolley along the corridor outside, and sometimes there were footsteps. He remembered the trolleys the nurses used to bring to his own bedside in the convales-cent hospital — Wooton, he was beginning to call it himself now, like a local — and how in those days his whole body had flamed all over with fear at the sound of approaching wheels.

'Gracie? Please wake up.'

As if she had heard him she opened her eyes. His own at once filled.

'Hello, Joe.'

He bent towards her, and held as much of her as he could, inhaling her breath, her closeness, the feel of her skin. He had been so sure she would die.

She smiled up at him as he straightened. 'You alright?'

He almost had to laugh at that, though it made his tears spill. He wiped them off with the back of his hand.

'You see him?' she whispered.

He nearly said, 'See who?' but remembered just in time. He nodded. 'He's smashing,' he said, as he knew she would like him to, though in reality he didn't give a damn about the baby, it had just looked like something run over in the street to him, left out in the rain, more than half-dead and anyway part of the horror. The cause of it all. Apart from himself, of course.

He had to say it. 'Thought I'd killed you, Gracie. I thought I had.'

'What? Ain't your fault. Ain't no one's fault.'

'How you feeling now?'

'Not so bad. If I keep still.'

'Doctor says you'll be fine.'

'What him, the new one?'

Grace hadn't cared one way or the other of course, but her mother had been in even more of a taking when they couldn't get her precious Dr Summers after all. But he had been with another patient, an emergency; even someone as clever as he could not be in two places at once. Still, his partner had been ready.

'Good job he was there,' said Joe. He could still hardly think of Heyward without a shudder of loathing. Like the baby, Dr Heyward was all part of the horror, he dimly recognized, part of

385

something he was never going to be able to think about normally. Heyward punching his way down the stairs, full of vigour and bounce, *Hospital case, yes, as soon as possible!*

As if he were pleased, as if he were rubbing his hands at the prospect of

Here Joe had to stop his thought, for the idea of the forceps was still too much for him.

At least they had put Grace into a sort of sleep, so that she would not feel the unspeakable things they were doing to her.

'I seen it done, often enough,' his mother-in-law had said once, as they sat together in the waiting room. It was dimly lit in there, no one about, silent. It was almost midnight by then, on the third day. He had not slept. He had sat on the hard wooden bench as long as he could, then got up and limped about until such time as he could sit down again. The time had gone so slowly. He had got past swearing God promises. Once or twice the glacier of darkness in some way presented itself. It touched his sleeve. He sat very still beside it, the woman who loved his wife on his other side. Warmth on one hand, death on the other. There he sat, very quiet, while vile things were done to his wife's body in order to extract his child.

'I seen it done often enough,' said Violet, but her voice betrayed her. She had not seen it done to her daughter. 'I knew there was something wrong, I said so, straight off, I knew it.'

She had said all this many times already, but he knew she expected no answer anyway. It was true; he had seen her face, when he had run

386

round to tell her. Remembered it afterwards.

'Grace says to tell you her waters broke,' he had said, breathless from trying to hurry. He had called in on the way at Silver Street, where he had spoken to the midwife, the droopy blonde one, who had opened to his excited drumming on the door.

'She got any pains?' Violet had asked.

'None!' he had answered, imagining in his ignorance that this was a good thing. But of course Violet had known better.

It had been hours before the terrible pain had started in Grace's back. It was very bad, she said, her face already drawn, when briefly they let him go in to her, but she could stand it, she said; needs must anyway; of course she could. And she had, without a murmur all day, and then all the following night, but by the late afternoon of the second day she could bear it no longer, and began at last to groan with each return of it. Sitting downstairs with his landlord he had heard her, heard the first one, and the hairs on the nape of his neck had risen with horror. At the end of the second groan old Jim Bullivant had said, Come on you, out of it, and taken him to the pub, but at closing time hours later, with three pints inside him and still stone-cold sober, they had come back along the quiet streets and heard her long thick deep-throated scream.

A No-Man's-Land scream, a mindless invol-untary animal sound, that made him sweat, brought the beer back up. Violet already gone for the doctor, both midwives there, the dog one, the droopy one, darting to and fro, and the doctor not coming and not coming and finally Heyward screeching brakes outside, come in the old one's car, and straight off to the hospital laid out across the back seat, the first time Joe had caught sight of her that day as they carried her down the stairs between them, the rag of half-conscious creature that had been Grace, who was his wife and child.

A nurse coming to find them in the Waiting Room: 'A boy, doing well!'

As if he cared.

I was called to the patient Mrs Grace Gilder, a negress, aged nineteen, primigravida 1+0, at ten o'clock in the evening, at the request of my colleague Sister Wainwright. I found the patient very nervous and fretful. She had for some time been refusing to allow Sister Wainwright to examine her or to carry out other necessary procedures. Dr Summers had already been contacted; messages had been left for him by Mr Gilder as well as by Sister Wainwright and by the patient's adopted mother, Mrs Violet Dimond.

I must state at this early stage that I felt sure that much of the patient's agitation was the direct fault of Mrs Dimond who was already well-known to me as a troublemaker with very inflated notions as to her own medical expertise. It appears she had decided almost with the onset of labour that Mrs Gilder would be unable to bear her child safely and had wasted no time in communicating this idea to her unfortunate daughter.

Her influence on the patient cannot be overestimated. Pregnant women are particularly open to suggestion and never more so than when in labour. I have had cause to cross swords with Mrs Dimond on more than one occasion in the past and I immediately protested in the strongest possible terms about her active and indeed irregular and illegal involvement in the case, though I still had the utmost difficulty in persuading her to leave the room while I examined the patient.

In fact I had to refuse to proceed until such time as she left the flat entirely. My colleague Sister Wainwright accompanied her downstairs to the shop below, where the back room was occupied by Mrs Bullivant. I did not at any time order her to be thrown out on to the street. That is a ridiculous falsehood.

I examined the patient and found her to be febrile (99.3°F, p 92) and exhibiting signs of exhaustion. Fundus at term, lie longitudinal, presentation vertex. Foetal limbs readily palpable, foetal heartbeat heard just above the umbilicus (140 regular). On vaginal examination the vulva appeared normal, cervix fully taken up and fully dilated, sagittal suture palpable in the transverse. I was able to palpate the anterior fontanelle, at the left, at the level of the spines.

Given the length of labour I therefore considered a possible diagnosis of deep transverse arrest and requested that Dr Summers be urgently informed. I also carried out a catheterization of the bladder, though the patient had earlier refused to allow Sister Wainwright to do so. I am unable to offer any explanation for this.

I was not aware at the time that Dr Summers was unwell. Mrs Gilder has a very great regard for him and I was particularly anxious to reassure her that he was on his way. I therefore told her an untruth; Sister Wainwright had not spoken directly to him, as I said she had. I stand by this however. I feel as I felt then that this small lie was in the patient's best interests. Indeed for some considerable time she was less fretful. I do not think the delay had any bearing on the outcome as a whole. Dr Heyward arrived at eleven o'clock and confirmed my diagnosis.

I have nothing more to add in any discussion of this case.

Finding the old boy laid out on the floor of his own consulting room — it was something of a shock, certainly. Though looking back, he had perhaps been even more vague than usual. No telling how long he'd been lying there: twenty minutes? Maybe longer.

Funny looking back, thought Dr Heyward, how instantly he knew he must conceal what had happened as far as he could. You just acted on instinct, in a way, he thought, had quickly made sure Summers was still alive and gone straight out again, closing the door behind him with no appearance, he was sure, of concern. Walked quietly past the full waiting room and nipped upstairs to the sitting room, gentle knock.

'Mrs Summers?'

'Oh, good morning, Dr Heyward — I wasn't expecting you — is everything alright?'

And in a way it had been. By the time they had hurried back downstairs together Summers was sitting up on the carpet, dazed of course, poor old boy, but able to speak again. Luckily there were the backstairs; between them they had got him out of the surgery and helped him up to his room.

After that though — typical — it was simply one thing after another. The place quiet as may be weeks on end and then as soon as you're single-handed all hell breaks loose, waiting room crowded with the usual bellyaches and coughs and fevers, but at the same time the factory incident that took him all afternoon to sort out, and then the motor-car collision, three complex cases there, and the retained placenta in the farmhouse — he'd had to remove it manually there and then, and the noise the woman made had gone right through his head — and then to cap it all the negro — interesting case, of course, and very good experience — had gone off almost before he'd had time to so much as change his shirt.

But he was in his element, and knew it. In charge again, making the decisions, acting on them. Knowing all the time there was nothing else for it anyway. The negro woman was particularly challenging, of course; he had had so little experience with forceps, particularly these new ones. But he had seen others like them used often enough, and knew the theory as well as anyone. And as they had said at medical school: see one, do one, teach one.

And besides there was no real alternative. This way was suffering and possibly life; the other, suffering and certain death, for both parties, as he'd explained to the husband — decent young cove, taking it like the ex-soldier he was.

'The baby's stuck, d'you see? Got his head

facing the wrong way, and he can't turn it. So I come along, use the forceps to turn it round for him. Out he pops — d'you see?'

The soldier looking very sick at this, poor sod, as well he might. And of course there was still no guarantee that the child would deliver alive. But it had all gone pretty well. Thank the Lord for twilight sleep though, after the ear-splitting racket in the farmhouse. Perhaps too it was true about negresses, that they were built more strongly than white women, made of tougher coarser stuff: the good deep cut hadn't bled too much, and each blade of the forceps slipped in as easy as you like.

Locked together.

Hand like a lacemaker's, grip like a sailor's. Medical school stuff again.

Turn.

Turn into full rotation, with your keen sailor's grip. Damage yes obviously to the surrounding parts but no omelette without breaking eggs, and there: the thing was done. Finally, the moulded head in descent at last, a head all caput, like Nefertiti's hat; and then almost at once the whole limp blue body of the child had delivered in a feeble gush of blackened waters, and Wainwright had promptly dived in to make herself useful, taking it away while he was busy with the rest.

So intent he hardly heard the cry at first! But he had to turn round, just to see. Cheerful sight, pink — well, pinkish, as Wainwright pointed out, you could hardly expect a proper colour considering — and screaming like a good 'un. He'd done it. Delivered a live child. Saved a

— yes, saved a life. Saved two.

For a moment then he was almost unmanned. Felt something almost give inside him. But he caught himself at it, and told himself what was what, and got back to work again.

I entered the abode of Mr and Mrs Joseph Gilder with every good intention. Live and let live is my motto. It is true there were regrettable misunderstandings almost from the start. I was not aware that the patient, Mrs Gilder, had arranged for personal care from Dr Summers. It seemed obvious to me that Mr Gilder did not have available means. I therefore did not immediately summon him, though of course as it turns out he would not have been able to attend the patient anyway, due to his indisposition. However I did my best to reassure the patient. It was clear to me that her labour was not going to be a short or easy one, as the baby was posterior and the head not yet fully engaged. I did not tell her this, whatever her 'mother' may claim. It is true that I advised the patient to lie down safely on the bed, and that Mrs Dimond took it upon herself to argue with this elementary nursing care.

It is true I did not stay with the patient throughout her labour. There was never any question of my doing so. I had other patients to deal with and so did my colleague Sister Goodrich. As is normal practice I made several brief visits throughout the first day until labour was sufficiently advanced for the patient to require full attention.

I was not at all happy with the continued presence in the room of Mrs Dimond, and finally was forced to request that she leave. I did so politely, however, especially as the patient herself, poor creature, clearly drew some comfort from her presence, and indeed begged me not to send her 'mother' away. Under these circumstances I departed from my own best practice and allowed Mrs Dimond to re-enter, on condition that she did not make any further attempt to interfere in the case. I made these conditions privately, not in the patient's hearing; and Mrs Dimond agreed to them.

I make no comment on the patient's later refusal to allow me to attend her. She had by then been in strong labour for some considerable time. Also there is the racial difference. I dare say she is unable to account for many of her decisions herself. It is well known that these people are less rational under most circumstances, and in adversity much more prone than the European to complete moral collapse.

He slept all that first day, Sunday, as it turned out, then all the following night, and got to work next day on time still half-asleep, though they'd been very good about it, joshing him a little about fatherhood, and congratulating him, and Mrs Lavery had iced a cake with a little picture of a stork on it, and there was genial talk about wetting the baby's head. Squaring all that with what had happened to Gracie, at home and in the hospital, made as much sense as the old first night on leave from the Front, when you caught a train from deathly chaos, nipped across the Channel, went straight out dancing and heard someone complaining about the band, or that their chicken was a bit stringy.

Everyone at the bakery seemed to think that

things were fine and dandy. But then, surely they were? It had been worse than anything he could possibly have foreseen, but it was over, and Grace would get better, and the baby was alright too, and she was so happy about that.

After work he went to the cottage hospital. It was Monday 15th September, 1919, just on six in the evening, and a beautiful warm evening, the light golden.

Mrs Gilder was in a private room, they said, two doors down, to the right. Visiting time until seven sharp if he pleased; one visitor at a time only.

He went down the corridor pointed out to him and knocked at the right door. Violet opened it, until he saw that it was Bea.

'Alright?'

Bea nodded. For once she seemed to have nothing to say, and took herself off; immediately he forgot all about her. He went round the foot of the bed to the other side. He had flowers with him, a bunch of something Mrs Lavery had put into his hands as he left, little purple things a bit like daisies.

'Hello, my lovely,' he said, and bent to kiss her cheek.

She lay very still in the bed, and hardly opened her eyes, but she smiled at his touch.

'How you feeling?' he whispered.

There was a pause before she said, 'Sleepy,' still with a faint smile.

'You're worn out,' he said.

'See him . . . see . . . the baby . . . ' she murmured.

That made him sit up. He had forgotten the baby again. But there it was on the other side of the bed; he stood up, saw the cradle.

'Oh aye.'

'No . . . get him, pick him up, give him here, they won't let me.'

'Won't let you what?' Joe was uneasy. He didn't want to annoy the nurses, perhaps do something wrong without knowing it.

'Cuddle him. 'Case I fall asleep. Lemme have him, Joe, do.'

Over in the cradle the baby made a very small snuffling noise. Quietly he got up, leaving the flowers on the coverlet near Gracie's hand, and crossed the room to look at it. Only its face was visible, it was so tucked up and wrapped. It looked very small for something that had caused its mother such agony. But then look how small a bullet was, he thought.

He leant over the cradle, peering in closer. It was all forehead, hardly any nose, chin almost non-existent, little bug-eyes tight shut. There was a dark mauve line all across one cheek, a bruise from the steel forcep that had dragged it free.

It was all such a painful mystery.

'Most deliver; but some never will,' Violet had said, in the hospital waiting room. She had feared the worst, but hoped for the best, she said. She had trusted in Him. What else was there? We were all in His hands.

Joe looked at his son, who left to himself would never have delivered. And what exactly was the point, he asked himself, of that? Just the waste of it made him feel — what? Something familiar, he thought. Pointless waste, crazed mismanagement, lousy planning. And then bluff heartlessness pretending to be in charge, telling lies while the dead piled up. Christ. It was familiar alright.

'Joe?'

He straightened, turned.

'Isn't he lovely?' Her smile was heart-breaking, so much her own in her altered face. He looked down at the baby again. So far he had not so much as touched it, let alone pick it up. It looked breakable. Suppose he dropped it!

'I can't!'

'Joe, please!' murmured Grace. So he slid both hands under the wrappings — it was all warm, alive! — and picked the swaddled thing up. It was very light and bendy. He felt it twist in his hands, what was it up to?

'Put your hand under his head!' said Grace, gasping with urgency, he was doing something wrong already, but quickly he cupped his hand beneath the thing's appalling half-made head, took the step towards Gracie, set it down between her arm and her side, and stepped back, breathing again.

Grace almost laughed. 'Your face!' But the tiny movement of her laughter hurt her; he saw her face change, become intent, and then at last relax again. Slowly she worked her other arm free of the sheet, which was tucked in very firmly, and curled it over the bundle of baby. She looked down at it, into the small face. The eyes were very firmly closed, Joe saw, as if the thing were resolutely asleep.

'He likes his kip,' he said finally.

'Oh I hope he wakes up, so you can say hello,' said Grace. 'I want to call him: Barty. Is that alright? It's short for — for . . . ' Her voice trailed away. She was nearly asleep again, he saw. She was worn out! And of course they were giving her stuff.

'Grace?'

There was a pause, then: 'Short for Bartholomew,' said Grace, suddenly rousing. 'D'you like it?'

''S fine. You mean — after the lad in the picture?'

She smiled, her eyes closed again. She whispered, 'Barty Small.'

'Small Barty,' said Joe, and she smiled again.

She slept for a while, the baby unmoving in her arms. Visiting hour ticked slowly by, peacefully. He sat and watched her breathe, in and out, so softly. I had no idea, he thought once more at her quiet face. I had no idea it could be like that, honest. Even though I knew women died sometimes. I didn't know it was like that, before. I didn't know.

Sooner or later, he told himself, he would be able to not think about it. One thing he had learnt: you can leave anything behind you. Or perhaps not behind you, exactly, but beneath you. You could let all sorts of stuff sink slowly to the bottom, lie there deep in the mud, hidden most of the time; all of the time if you were lucky, and took a bit of care how you trod.

★　★　★

So many things she would have liked to say, but she was so deliciously sleepy. The baby snug in the crook of her arm. Sometimes she dreamt that she was awake, and sitting up, and undressing him as she longed to, having a good look at him all over, it seemed essential somehow. Turning him over to see his dear little perfect back, his comical tiny bum, Look, Joe, isn't he sweet, look! and laughing.

She would wake up again sure for a moment that this had really happened, it had seemed so real and vivid. But there he was, dear Joe, white as a sheet still, like the boy in the kitchen at Wooton that time, her mother teasing, 'You reckon they like cake?'

At other times she dreamt of unlikelier things. She stood in the Post Office, stamping the big brown envelope with two of her stories inside, addressed to *The New Age*. Had she really done that, or just thought about it? She would certainly do it soon, just as soon as she was better. What on earth had held her back?

Violet crying. That was unlikely. That had happened. Cups of peculiar tea, they had happened, raspberry leaf tea to ease the pain, except that it hadn't, Mammy, had it? It had been torture for Violet, Grace suddenly understood. Her labour had tortured her mother. She should not have been there at all. But I wouldn't let her leave; I would have died, if she had left me, I would have despaired and died, I know it. Though when I wasn't frightened I was happy all that time, waiting at home for the baby, being like everyone else. Everyone withdraws from the world and lives in secret then. I felt so normal, a normal married woman at home. I felt free. Staying at home sewing baby clothes. Little nightdresses embroidered with flowers. All my life a confinement; but this one set me free.

The baby held out for her to see, his whole body a beautiful colour, so pale, faintly, why, faintly *violet*. Mammy, he is like a violet, not the ordinary purple ones, the violet violets, lovely enough, but no — he is like a white violet, that have the faintest most beautiful hint of lilac to them, so that they match the darker ones, they are all part of the same, the same flower

That woman! I will not let her touch me, get her out, get her out of my house!

Grace waking up, completely wide awake for a while, despite the laudanum, waking up in the dark of the first night after, thinking for a moment that Sister Wainwright was still in the room with her. Staring all round at the strange place, the completely unfamiliar hospital room, until someone spoke to her, and soothed her, and it was Aunt Bea, who stayed there until morning, in case she woke again, but she didn't, she had a lovely long sleep, and no dreams, not when she knew Bea was there to watch over her.

She awoke again, and Joe was there, and the baby, Barty, snuffling a little at her side. The room was bright and warm, and Joe was smiling. All the same Grace knew something was different. Was it the room? No. It was Joe, perhaps. No. The baby moved a little, trying to kick his little legs as he had kicked them inside her for so long, but the swaddling blanket held him fast. Was he different?

'Joe? Can you take him, put him back?' At least, that was what she meant to say, but when she opened her mouth it was strangely difficult to speak. He was leaning over her. She could see the pores of his skin, a blood vessel broken in one eye, threading across the white. She remembered how closely once she had seen Dr Summers, as he stood at the end of the bed promising to keep a close eye on her, the white of his stubble, his lank greying hair, Dr Summers who had broken his promise and never come at all.

She had been asleep again!

The baby not there. Good. Shouldn't be there when she felt so strange. She felt light, very comfortable, as if she lay on a freshly turned feather bed, soft and warm. She was drifting away on it, she thought. But there was something she ought to say to Joe first. Don't let them, she began, but it seemed somehow that the words had not come out at all. She took a deep breath, surprised a little at how it seemed to bubble in her chest, as if there were water down there, very odd, but she took no notice, it wasn't important.

'Joe — '

'Gracie, Gracie!'

What was up with him? Surely he knew there was nothing to be afraid of now?

'Don't let them say — don't let them say he . . . '

★ ★ ★

The room full of people; but there was already nothing anyone could do.

★   ★   ★

Dr Summers had made a fair recovery, but there was no question of his ever working again. His speech was still affected, and he could only walk, slowly, with the help of a stick. He was aware too of a continuing sense of confusion in his own mind, and a tiredness that no amount of sleep seemed able to alleviate. He had already sold the practice: thank heaven he had engaged Heyward when he had!

Not that he had ever quite taken to the man, personally. But he was competent and energetic. Young, in a word.

'Darling?'

Dr Summers looked up from the newspaper that had slid forward on his lap. His wife had her head round the drawing-room door.

'It's Mrs Dimond. Will you see her?'

Immediately he felt something like panic. His heart gave a great painful thump in his chest.

'I'll tell her you're not well enough,' said his wife quickly, clearly seeing some of this in his face. But he called her back before she could close the door.

'W-w-wait. A minute. Please.' He took some breaths, he could hear himself panting. Calm down, he told himself. This was no use. This womanish weakness. 'Let her . . . let her . . . come in,' he said at last.

'Darling, please,' said his wife, coming into the

room and standing over him. 'It will upset you too much. Perhaps another time, yes?'

He shook his head. 'Now,' he managed. 'Now.'

'I'll tell Jane to bring you some tea,' his wife said, clearly disapproving, but she went away, and then the door opened, and he heard Mrs Dimond's quick footsteps, saw her black skirt. He raised his eyes to her face.

Ah.

Bea sat down facing him, on the other side of the fire.

'Didn't want to ask your Missus to let me in,' she said lightly. 'Reckon she always knew.'

'No,' he said. 'Never.' But his heart leapt at her closeness.

'Suit yourself,' said Bea. She drew off her sister's lacy shawl. 'Heard you was off soon,' she said, her tone gentle. 'So I've come to say goodbye. You moving where your lad is?'

'My — daughter,' he said, effortfully.

'Won't hardly know the place without you,' she said.

'I'm so sorry,' he said. 'For your loss.'

'You don't know the half of it,' she said, but then she always was unaccountable, he remembered. Her tone was almost playful, except that her eyes were not.

'And I wanted to ask you — ' she looked straight at him — 'well, what would you have done? If it had been you, not him, that night. Will you tell me? Please.'

What was the point of that, he wondered, wretchedly. What was the good? There was no bringing Grace Gilder back. Surely in any case she knew already; her sister would have told her: he might perhaps have tried the forceps, though the set used by Heyward were of a type unknown to him. But anyone who had worked with him as long as Violet Dimond had would know that with the head so high and labour so hopelessly obstructed he would probably have given the child up for lost, waited until it was dead, and ended the whole sad business with a discreet craniotomy.

Mrs Dimond might not know to call it that. But she would know what it was. And surely not so long ago, he thought, women like her, uneducated, untrained, with no medical man to fall back on, would have undertaken such acts themselves; there was no choice to be made.

That was what he would have done for Grace Gilder, done to her, if all had indeed happened as he had heard. That was what Violet Dimond would already have told her sister. Grace and her husband so young, after all. A second child would almost certainly have fared better. So many women lost the first and went on to manage perfectly well.

He had not been there, though, he had been lying half-senseless in his bed. It had been Heyward's choice, his decision, and heaven knew it might have worked. But in effect, thought Dr Summers, Heyward had saved the child at the expense of the mother. Of Grace.

'What would you have done? Will you tell me?'
'I really . . . cannot say,' he said at last.
'Liar,' she said softly.
'No, I wasn't . . . *there*, Bea. I'm so very sorry.

So . . . sorry.' Tears came into his eyes, in case she chide him for not being brave enough, God knew he had chid himself for it often enough, but she only leant forward, spoke more intently:

'No, just you remember,' she said, 'it was all my fault. Everything. All of it, d'you see?'

What on earth did that mean? Before he could speak again he heard Jane on the landing, shifting the tea tray in her hands before opening the door. Bea heard it too.

'Goodbye, my love,' she said, her tone friendly, and she quickly leant forward again and kissed his cheek. Then she picked up the shawl, and was gone.

The Statue

11 November, 1921

Standing at the drawing-room window upstairs Norah Thornby watched the men outside in the market square dismantle the scaffolding, slide the poles on to a cart, heap and fold the yards of damp canvas. For nearly a month there had been a sort of structured tent out there on the cobbles. It had been a gloomy enough sight on its own account, but she regretted its passing. Now there was so much more to see.

Of course the newly set figure and its plinth were still shrouded. Before the scaffolding came down someone, presumably from the studio, had loosely wrapped it in some thin black material, which was to be ceremonially drawn away that morning. Until then the statue did not officially exist, despite its size. It was taller than Norah remembered. She left the window and walked over to the piano. Yes; she could still see it. Soon there would be no safe room in the whole of the front of the house.

You'll get used to it, Norah told herself. Don't fuss; of course you will. But the implications of getting used to the statue were painful in themselves.

Presently her mother came bustling up the stairs: 'Nearly there, isn't it wonderful!' She stood beside Norah at the far window; the last laden cart was being slowly trundled away. 'There's to be a small cordoned-off area,' she said, 'for the committee, and for Lady Redwood. So we needn't go down much before the time, you know.'

Norah's mother had been a founder member of the committee, had written countless letters, organized and attended meetings and fund-raising events, planned and cajoled and consulted.

'It's been exhausting,' said Mrs Thornby. 'But it had to be done. We all serve our country in our own way; and this has been mine.'

Norah made no answer, though as usual when her mother said something along these lines she felt an instant physical response: her stomach seemed briefly to heave itself over and burn a little, as if it were blushing, and her ears filled with buzzing noises. She was used to these small discomforts though, and had learnt not to make any attempt at actual speech until they had gone away; it seemed that they affected her voice, made her sound hard and unkind, and one simply must not so address poor Mamma. But at least nowadays the difficulty had a name: she had recently come across the phrase in a newspaper, and recognized its truth — Mamma was *Pre-War*. She was better off being Pre-War too; there was no point in trying to argue with her, or explain why other people might feel differently, might be irrevocably *Post*.

The whole statue idea, of course, was essentially Pre-War, even though it was supposed to be about commemoration. Everyone on the Memorial Committee, thought Norah, was Pre-War, to a man, to a woman. The engraving on the plinth was surely Pre-War: officers were to be listed first, then the men. But the sculptor the committee had finally decided upon had, thought Norah, rather surprisingly — or accidentally — turned out to be Post.

Some months before, she had been prevailed upon to accompany her mother to the sculptor's studio in Pimlico, to inspect the work-in-progress. It had been a cold grimy hole of a place too, in some scruffy warehouse-type building down a series of dank alleyways. Norah had felt very seedy in the taxi; hollow, detached. Predictably enough, shown the almost-completed work, Mrs Thornby had burst into tears of . . . well, Norah had wondered, tears of what, exactly? Not happiness, certainly. Not really sorrow. Tears of generalized emotion. Tears of teariness.

While the sculptor, Anthony Something, or Something Else, don't know don't care, thought Norah, dashed about finding her mother a chair, and fussing about glasses of water — and how on earth had he expected her to react, anyway? Norah had become suddenly aware of her own violent trembling and quickly sat down on a packing case nearby. Until that moment she had not realized how much she had been dreading seeing the statue herself. Nor had she understood how much she had feared that her mother, directly or indirectly, on purpose or without meaning to at all, would somehow have caused the sculptor to make the soldier *look like Guy*.

It was strange: the appointment that brought them to the studio had been made weeks before; she had done her best to get out of it; she had been sleeping badly ever since the date was confirmed, and had felt so wretched for the last few days that one of the other secretaries at the office had asked her if she were ill; and yet she had not made any of the connections now so obvious to her. She had been full of nameless dread, when all the time she should have been full of a named variety, she thought, and put a hand to her mouth, to hide the mad shameful snigger.

The statue was beautiful, she thought. He wasn't Guy, thank heaven, nor anyone else she knew, though he was about Guy's age, a slender thing, his head bowed, leaning both hands on his rifle, the uniform just hinted at. He could have been Guy from the back, she thought, rising to walk around him; so slightly built, just a boy. But of course that was true of lots of real living young men anyway, boys who gave your heart a little pang as they jostled past you in the street; she couldn't blame Anthony Something for that.

'Not quite what I was expecting,' Mrs Thornby had said, recovering in the taxi on the way back to the station.

'What were you expecting?'

'Well, I don't know — something a little more, well, commanding, perhaps. You'd think — wouldn't you? you'd almost think, looking at it, that we'd *lost* the War. I'm afraid — ' she was beginning to make up her mind — 'I'm afraid the committee will feel that Mr Broadbent has not fully carried out our commission. It's — it's — ' she struggled for the word — 'it's a little defeatist. Don't you think?'

Norah was silent. The statue was hardly about

the War at all, she thought, but about mourning; he represented loss, but also expressed his own. He looked as if he was thinking about his lost friends. He was Post-War.

But she must not say anything like that to Mamma.

'I'm sorry you don't like it,' she said.

Mrs Thornby was indignant. 'Did I say I didn't like it? I like it very much, as it happens. Don't forget I was one of the ones who insisted on Mr Broadbent in the first place.'

By the time they reached Paddington she had convinced herself that she had suffered not a moment's doubt, and in the intervening weeks talked of almost nothing else. The arrangements, the carriage-costs and insurance, the wording on the plinth, the scaffolding, the trustworthiness of the workmen employed in the final placing, and then, over and over again, about the unveiling ceremony, which was to be a triumph of discreet organization, of civic dignity, and of a sorrow publicly expressed yet fully mindful (said Mrs Thornby) of the true nobility of patriotic death in battle.

Sometimes Norah still tried to feel that nobility herself. All those stories and poems, could they all be lies, all through? Or was it just that this War had been different? When she was a child at the Bishop's Road Council School, the Senior Boys had put on scenes from *Henry V* for the school's summer fete; Norah had never forgotten the awe-inspiring moment when Teddy Hall, until then merely another scruffy footballing wrestling playground-hogging round-faced oafish boy with big front teeth, had suddenly and without any prior warning appeared in full kingly battle-gear of cloak and crown and shining cardboard sword, high above everyone's heads *on the bicycle shed roof*, where to Norah's own knowledge and belief no child had ever set foot before; and while the crowd still gaped Teddy had begun declaiming something she had not then recognized, but which had thrilled her almost as much as his initial appearance there on the forbidden heights.

Follow your spirit, cried Teddy Hall, still waving his sword in Norah's memory; not somehow in the piping treble he would surely then have had no choice about but in a young man's voice, authoritative, compelling, noble. *Follow your spirit; and upon this charge Cry 'God for Harry! England and St George!'*

But the shreds of thinking like this just fell apart, thinnest of soiled rags, when she tried to connect them to Guy. If Guy had really followed his spirit, it would have led him into nightclubs, where his cheerful jazz piano would soon have had everyone dancing. It would have set him organizing more summer picnics by the river, and reminded him to take his banjo. It would surely have indicated further extremes of dandyism, more two-toned shoes, more ethereal boaters. Though of course there was no telling. He hadn't quite turned twenty-one; perhaps he would have become someone else entirely, had he lived.

Most painful to Norah was the knowledge that they had not been real friends for long. All through their childhood they had been enemies, always on the lookout for advantage in their ceaseless nursery warfare, fought, hard to remember now, over the affections, or merely the attention, of their mother. Barely a full year the elder, Norah had stridently insisted on the privileges of seniority, all those she had heard of and many she could imagine; but time and again had been forced against her will to notice evidence that, despite her occasional avowals to the contrary, Mamma consistently favoured Guy. Once when he had jaundice, which Norah against all predictions did not catch herself, she overheard their mother tending to him in his sickbed, using such a special tender voice that Norah's heart yearned inside her with longing and grief. It seemed to her then that Mamma would never have spoken so to her, no matter how yellow and sickly she might be.

The rivalry lost much of its force as they grew older and Guy was sent away to school; but the real change had come when Guy was fourteen. Just before Christmas of that year Norah had tripped on the last turn of the stairs, fallen awkwardly, and smashed the special painted jug that stood on the window sill there.

'Oh no — oh, look what I've done!'

Guy, who had been passing in the hall, joined her on the landing. 'Crumbs,' he said at the mess. 'You alright?'

'Yes, yes,' said Norah, shaking flecks of china from her skirt, 'but I'm for it now.'

'Mm, 'fraid you are.' He pushed some of the larger pieces about with one foot. 'Look, old girl.' He lowered his voice. 'Why don't we just say it was me?'

412

'What? Why — what do you mean?'

'Be less fuss,' he said. He had his hands still in his pockets. 'I wouldn't mind.'

'Well — I would! I can't blame someone else.'

'Why not? I'm volunteering.'

'It wouldn't be right. It's lying, for one thing.'

'So it is. But — go on. Let's just lie. Or you know what she'll do, don't you — she'll stop you going to the Caterhams'.' This was a lavish local party, much anticipated. Refusing Norah permission to attend it was exactly the sort of punishment Mrs Thornby would go in for.

'Well — she'll stop *you* then,' said Norah, but even as she spoke knew that she was wrong. Mamma would never consider such a punishment for Guy.

He had not answered straight away: a thoughtful pause. Then he said, 'She's never going to be fair, is she?' He spoke lightly, as if they had both always acknowledged this. His careful lack of triumph implied too that the unfairness need no longer matter, to either of them; not now, when as far as he was concerned they might so clearly, so usefully, so delightfully, be on the same side. 'Oh, hello, Bella,' he went on in his normal voice to the elderly parlourmaid, who had finally come puffing up the backstairs to see what the crash had been. 'I'm afraid I've gone and fallen all over Mum's poor Ming, or whatever it was. Did she adore it, d'you know?'

Three or four years, then, of deepening friendship, and towards the end a few months of the dearest most painful intimacy; the letters he wrote home bore little resemblance to the things

413

he told her on leave. They had twice met in London, where she was then a VAD, and swopped stories of those matching particular armies, soldiery and nursing — grotesque tales of hierarchical intransigence, demented official-dom, runs of bad luck, incredible escapes, heroism, cowardice and mocking songs. They had talked and talked and laughed so much, even though Guy had looked so ill the second time. Messines awaited him, June 1917, and the noble death his mother clung to.

'I thought I'd get ready really early,' said Mrs Thornby, putting her head round the door. 'So I'm all set. How about you?'

The traffic to all the neighbouring streets was stopped at ten. Norah had forgotten this was to be one of the arrangements. She was standing in the semi-basement kitchen, waiting for the kettle to boil, when she had become aware of the strange heavy silence that seemed to be slowly gathering itself all around her. It felt so like a dizzy spell that for a moment she looked about her for the nearest chair; then remembered. She stood still, listening to the quiet. It didn't feel like an absence, she thought. No, indeed, it was a presence, an invited guest. Guest of honour, perhaps. For already she had noticed how quiet the gathering crowd was, outside in the square. People had begun arriving hours before; now the cars and buses were stopped she could hear the low rumble of many voices. But they were all respectfully lowered, she thought. It was as if the square had for now become the church. It was not so much a crowd outside as a congregation, waiting for the service, in this new religion of death; waiting to garland the idol. No golden calf, of course, but the lost boy himself.

Her mother was having another little lie-down. They were to leave, she said, at ten to; then they wouldn't have to talk to too many people. There were of course places reserved for them in any case, right beside the plinth. They must arrive just before Lady Redwood came out of the private sitting room at the George and Dragon, so that the vicar and all the rest of the Memorial Committee would be lined up to greet her.

From today, thought Norah, the stone soldier would be standing outside in the square for always. He would be out there all night, in sun and rain and snow, for ever and ever amen, and you won't be able to glance out or cross the street or buy so much as a single peach at the market without knowing he is there. She remembered her relief in the Pimlico studio; wondered, now, at her own naivety. It was true that the statue was no portrait, but since the scaffolding had come down she had realized that this was of no account. Once it was uncovered out there in the square it would always say *Guy* to her. It would in some way be him.

From the drawing-room window, hidden behind the curtain, she looked down at the dense crowd gathered there in such quiet around the swathed figure on the plinth. She knew nearly every face; could put a name to most.

There were her Pyncheon cousins, dear Alice, poor darling Freddie, arm in arm, quite close to the platform, so she would be able to speak to them afterwards, she thought. There was Mr Vowles, the headmaster, and Mrs Vowles. Mr Godolphin climbing up already, taking off his hat to Mrs Grant-Fellowes. The doctor, the new one, whose name she kept forgetting. Oh there was Mr Gilder; Norah always kept an eye out for him. Grace's husband. He had the little boy with him, carrying him curled in his arms; she could just see the top of a tartan hat with a tassel. Mrs Dimond next to him, well, probably Mrs Dimond; and the Bullivants, and Mrs Ticknell, and that must be her sister, the Killigrews, and the Barneses, and Sergeant Warburton with most of the other policemen, all in uniform. Heyward, she thought suddenly, going back to where the doctor's handsome head rose high above most of his neighbours. And Sister Wainwright beside him.

Once, not long before, Norah had overheard her telling some story, at the sewing group, about some problematic case, but her tone, at once plaintive and indignant, had made Norah prick up her ears. And who else could she have meant, but Grace Gilder?

'And all I *said* was, 'Good job your husband's so fair.' I only meant — well, you know, the baby'll blend in more. Won't stand out so much. Because it's probably going to look, you know, Spanish or something. Honestly, what was so terrible about that? I was only trying to be kind.'

But not trying hard enough, thought Norah now, looking down at her in the square. All you said was, 'Good job your baby might not look like *you*.' Say that kindly, you silly goose. See if you can.

416

Who was that other woman with her? Ah yes; the new midwife, the one who had replaced Sister Goodrich. Who had so unexpectedly married, and moved away; had caught the eye (it was said) of a recently widowed elderly colonel, and ruthlessly snapped him up before he had a chance to change his mind. Very cheering too — if marriage was possible for Sister Goodrich, thought Norah, moving away from the window, it was clearly possible for anyone, even herself. Though I hope I wouldn't leave it quite that late, she thought, and then realized what she was doing, thinking only about herself again, and today of all days.

Well, it was time to go down now, to get through it. Get it over with.

* * *

After the speeches and the prayers Lady Redwood, poor old thing, tottered forward right on time to carry out her trembling duty: with a jerky movement of her black-gloved hand she pulled on the cord that released the statue's shroud. The flimsy coverings fell away, slipped and rippled noiselessly to the ground, and the crowd at once made the strangest saddest sound, thought Norah afterwards, that she had ever heard or ever would: a long soft sighing murmur that spread and rippled all about the square. It was the sound of recognition, she thought, and of decent people holding back tears. There he stood above them all, his bowed head, his slender shoulders, unreachable, unchanging, the

417

one who wouldn't ever come home again, turned to stone.

Then the church clock began to chime the hour, and the two-minute silence began.

After it Mr Godolphin stepped forward, and said the verses from Binyon, and then moved on to prayer. Norah bowed her head, but kept her eyes open. Beside her on the plinth, listed beneath OUR GLORIOUS DEAD, were the graven names now also revealed for the first time, and she saw that while she had known about all the officers, there were men whose deaths she had missed.

Though she could see only the nearest side, she read several familiar names: young men she had hardly known, never in adulthood met socially, boys who had bidden her a polite good day from behind the counters of various shops, or nodded at her from carts as they passed her in the lanes, or straightened up unsmiling in fields where they were picking strawberries; local young men whose names and faces had still been known to her all her life. Barnes T J, Boscowan T, Coachman A, Crowhurst G, Dando T, not S: the engraver had been a local man.

Some were names she remembered from the Council School: Flowerdew A must be Albert. *Little Bert Flowerdew, fits in your pocket!* So they had called after him sometimes in the playground. No nicknames for the glorious dead, Bert.

Another name she had known about already. Hall E had never been an Edward, despite his crown; Teddy Hall, waving his cardboard sword above them all on the splendid heights of the bicycle shed a Pre-War world ago.

The statue of the soldier was like a fossil, thought Norah: a fine-structured elegance of stone. One day — hard to imagine, of course, but coming all the same — one day no one would be left to miss Guy, or to know that Tommy Dando had had such bright blue eyes. One day, everyone who knew the Glorious Dead would be dead themselves, and no one would ever again look at the statue and think of a real boy they had known. Then he would truly be what he was meant to be, thought Norah, general not personal, all of them and none, the perfect fossil of imperfect grief.

Presently the 'Last Post' sounded. It was Ernie Skewes, cornet player of the old Silkhampton Colliery Band, from the portico of the George and Dragon, playing into more of that terrible stifled silence, playing the 'Last Post', thought Norah, for Guy and for Timmy Boscowan, standoffish, always seemed to think himself a cut above his dad's greengrocery, for Art Coachman who'd scored a century once at school, for beautiful Tommy Dando, for the Ticknell twins, Gerry, Jim, who'd hired a tandem together one day and famously ridden it all the way to Bude, for little Bert Flowerdew, fits in your pocket, and for Teddy Hall, forever eleven years old, crying *God for Harry! England and St George!*

The music fitted the statue, Norah thought. It was very hard to bear. One day, she reminded herself, a whole new Post-War generation will be in charge, a whole generation like me, and we will never again send boys like Guy out to die in foolish wars; and that is the only useful thing this whole mad disaster has achieved.

She looked out over the crowd, saw a small bright face lifted there, chubby, smiling: Barty Gilder, waving a fat little hand at someone he recognized in the crowd. Strange that the silly Wainwright woman had been right all the time; Grace and her husband between them had produced rather a Mediterranean child, yes, quite Spanish-looking, or Greek, something like that, certainly very dark, of course, but nothing like as dark as Grace had been. And that was sad, thought Norah, sad to remember, on this saddest day of remembrance. Grace Dimond had vanished, and for most already it was as if she had never been. For others, death in childbirth had given her memory a certain romance, almost a glamour. Very like the notion of death in battle for men, thought Norah. A sentimental romance. A spurious glamour.

The stone soldier is about loss, Norah told herself. Does he stand for Grace as he stands for all the young men? They say Mankind means women too; but somehow it never quite feels that way.

The 'Last Post' ended, and Ernie was joined by several other band members, shuffling into place beside him, their feet sounding in the quiet; then they played 'God Save the King'. And then it was all over.

★   ★   ★

'Oh, Norah, tell me truly — do you think it went well?'

'Of course it did, really really well. Just right.'

'It *was* beautiful, wasn't it? I so wanted it to be worthy, d'you see, of — of *him*.'

Ah, of Thornby G W. Such a cruel joke, my dearest Guy, that I am at last what I once longed with all my heart to be, God forgive me: her only child. Well. I'm stuck with her now. And she with me.

'It was perfect, honestly. Well done, Mother. Well done, darling,' said Norah.

Acknowledgements

I drew details for this book from many different sources, among them the memoirs of Dr Sara Dunbar Cross, held at the Guildhall Record Office in Bath, the records of the Edinburgh Maternity Hospital at the University of Bristol Medical Library and the transcript of a Wellcome Trust History of Twentieth-Century Medicine Witness Seminar on Maternal Care held in June 2000, edited by D. A. Christie and E. M. Tansey. Useful books included *Distorted Images* by Kenton Bamford (I. B. Tauris, 1999), *George Muller and His Orphans* by Nancy Garton (Churchman Publishing, 1987), *The People in the Playground* by Iona Opie (Oxford University Press, 1993), *Staying Power* by Peter Fryer (Pluto Classics, 1984) and, most importantly, *The Midwife's Tale* (Scarlett Press, 1993), a brilliant piece of oral history by Nicky Leap and Billie Hunter.

We do hope that you have enjoyed reading this large print book.

Did you know that all of our titles are available for purchase?

We publish a wide range of high quality large print books including:
Romances, Mysteries, Classics
General Fiction
Non Fiction and Westerns

Special interest titles available in large print are:
The Little Oxford Dictionary
Music Book
Song Book
Hymn Book
Service Book

Also available from us courtesy of Oxford University Press:
Young Readers' Dictionary
(large print edition)
Young Readers' Thesaurus
(large print edition)

For further information or a free brochure, please contact us at:
Ulverscroft Large Print Books Ltd.,
The Green, Bradgate Road, Anstey,
Leicester, LE7 7FU, England.
Tel: (00 44) 0116 236 4325
Fax: (00 44) 0116 234 0205

Other titles published by
The House of Ulverscroft:

GOLD

Chris Cleave

Kate and Zoe, elite track cyclists, are facing their last and biggest race: the 2012 Olympics. Devoted and self-sacrificing Kate, more naturally gifted but hampered by the demands of her personal life, is training fiercely; whilst her eight-year-old daughter Sophie dreams of the Death Star and of battling alongside the Rebels as evil white blood cells ravage her personal galaxy. Intense, aloof Zoe has always hovered on the periphery of real human companionship, and her compulsive need to win at any cost has more than once threatened her friendship with Kate — and her own sanity. Will she allow her obsession to sever the bond they have shared for more than a decade? Each wants desperately to win gold — and each has more than a medal to lose . . .